U0079110

美國家庭
100 堂閱讀課

親子共讀的
最佳素材

全MP3一次下載

9789864542222.zip

此為ZIP壓縮檔，請先安裝解壓縮程式或APP，iOS系統請升級至iOS 13後再行下載，
為大型檔案（約111M），建議使用WIFI連線下載，以免占用流量，並確認連線狀況，以利下載順暢。

閱讀從美國小學教科書精心挑選的 100 篇學習知識

培養閱讀非小說類文本的自信心！

《美國家庭的 100 篇閱讀課》是嚴選美國小學主要科目必須包含的 100 個主題，並符合台灣小學高年級程度的文章所組成的英文閱讀學習書。這本書以簡單設計為主，即使是不熟悉非小說類文本的學習者，也可以自學。如果學習者持續閱讀各種領域的 100 種學習知識，不僅可以累積學科的背景知識，也能夠將已經知道的學習知識擴展到英文上，就能自然地感受到英文閱讀實力有所提升。

★Features

●兼具閱讀理解和學科知識的美國教科書

透過閱讀 100 篇文章，涵蓋科學、社會、數學、文學等美國小學教課書必修的重要學科主題，為閱讀和學習課程、背景知識奠定良好基礎。

●學習「專注閱讀」，精準、快速地閱讀各式主題的文章

「專注閱讀」的設計讓學習者在閱讀時快速理解主要內容、解決各式各樣的問題，並完整消化新學到的知識，使學習者能夠在短期內增進閱讀理解能力。

●透過各式各樣的學習素材，進行最有效的閱讀訓練

透過總結文章和完成圖表的練習，以提升理解文章組成的閱讀技巧和字彙使用。在組織段落關鍵內容的同時，學習者甚至能夠訓練小學生必須具備的綜合思維能力。

How to Study This Book 如何使用這本書

★第一步★ **聆聽音檔**

讓我們透過聆聽英文母語發音的音檔，來試著理解段落的主要內容，並從標題和圖片猜出文章的內容。

★第二步★ **閱讀文章**

聽著音檔，透過仔細閱讀段落去理解大致掌握的內容。因為不知道意思而在閱讀時遇到困難的部分，請參考 單字下面的中文解釋 專欄的詞彙說明。

Science
03 **Let's Make a Solution** 一起來製作溶液吧

R_03.mp3

A solution is a mixture of substances. It is usually a liquid. In it, one substance breaks down completely in another. Saltwater is a simple solution you can make. Pour some salt in a glass of water. Then stir it. When the salt crystals melt, they do not float or sink. Instead, they make the water salty. The water stays this way. It is like a new substance!

salt

Check True or False 是非題

① One substance breaks down in a solution.　T / F

② Saltwater soon changes back into water and salt.　T / F

一起來製作溶液吧！
溶液是一種物質的混合物，通常是一種液體。在溶液中，其中一種物質會在另一種物質中完全分解。而鹽水就是一種你可以製作出的簡單溶液。只要加一些鹽倒入一杯水裡，然後攪拌一下。當鹽的晶體溶解時，鹽體並不會漂浮或下沉，反而是讓水變鹹。水會一直保持這樣的狀態，就像是極新的物質！

背景知識 Plus!
鹽水（saltwater）只用肉眼看和水沒有區別，如果喝的話，就可以快速地辨別，但如果你不能喝的話，要怎麼分辨呢？因為純淨的水在加熱時會蒸發成水蒸氣，一點也不剩。然而，鹽水在加熱時，水會蒸發掉，並留下這的晶體。

20 美國小學一年級的課程

Comprehension Checkup 理解能力確認

Circle the best answer. 圈選出正確的答案
1. What is an example of a solution?
   ⓐ salt crystal　　ⓑ saltwater　　ⓒ salt and pepper
2. What happens to the salt crystals?
   ⓐ They float.　　ⓑ They sink.　　ⓒ They melt.
3. The salt crystals make the water _____.
   ⓐ sweet　　ⓑ salty　　ⓒ clean
4. The saltwater _____ like a new substance.
   ⓐ stays　　ⓑ stirs　　ⓒ breaks down

Complete the sentence. 完成句子

A solution is a _____ of substances, but it becomes a new substance.

Wrap Up Fill in the blanks. 總複習，將單字填入空格

Making a New ❶ _____

方法　One substance ❷ _____ down in another.　❸ _____

句子　Salt breaks down in ❹ _____　saltwater

breaks	substance	water	solution

一起來製作溶液吧 21

★第三步★ **檢查大致的內容，並延伸背景知識**

透過 Check True or False 以及 Read and Complete 來簡單地確認學習者理解段落的程度，並閱讀中文翻譯來確認學習者是否正確理解段落的意思。背景知識 Plus! 專欄同時也讓學習者增加廣泛的學科知識。

★第四步★ **解決各種類型的問題，並提升閱讀理解力**

Ⓐ 透過解決四題選擇題來再次檢查學習者對段落的理解程度，超越大致理解，並培養將段落內容內化成為自己的能力。

Ⓑ 簡短總結整個段落。總結這一課的段落並改寫，可以讓學習者掌握課文的核心，並簡短文本的長度。

Wrap Up 根據段落的性質總結段落的內容，透過將視覺化和組織單字的填空題來擴展詞彙量。

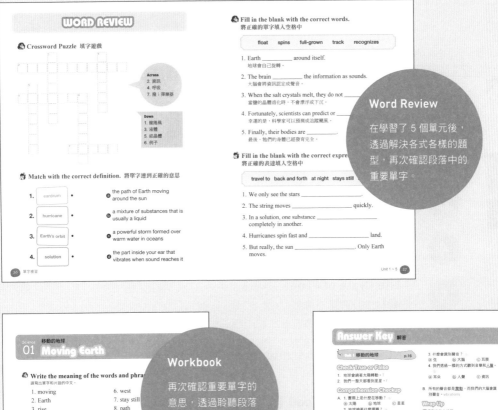

WORD REVIEW

Crossword Puzzle 填字遊戲

Across
2. 資訊
4. 呼吸
7. 撥；彈樂器

Down
1. 龍捲風
3. 液體
5. 結晶體
6. 例子

Match with the correct definition. 將單字連到正確的意思

1. eardrum — the path of Earth moving around the sun

2. hurricane — a mixture of substances that is usually a liquid

3. Earth's orbit — a powerful storm formed over warm water in oceans

4. solution — the part inside your ear that vibrates when sound reaches it

Fill in the blank with the correct words.
將正確的單字填入空格中

float   spins   full-grown   track   recognizes

1. Earth _____ around itself.
地球會自己旋轉。

2. The brain _____ the information as sounds.
大腦會將資訊認定成聲音。

3. When the salt crystals melt, they do not _____
當鹽的晶體溶化時，不會漂浮或下沉。

4. Fortunately, scientists can predict or _____
幸運的是，科學家可以預測或追蹤颶風。

5. Finally, their bodies are _____
最後，牠們的身體已經發育完全。

Fill in the blank with the correct expre___
將正確的表達填入空格中

travel to   back and forth   at night   stays still

1. We only see the stars _____

2. The string moves _____ quickly.

3. In a solution, one substance _____ completely in another.

4. Hurricanes spin fast and _____ land.

5. But really, the sun _____. Only Earth moves.

Word Review

在學習了 5 個單元後，透過解決各式各樣的題型，再次確認段落中的重要單字。

單字複習   Unit 1 ~ 5

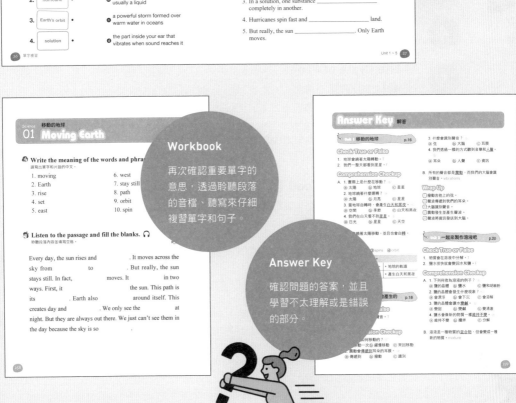

Science
01 Moving Earth
移動的地球

Write the meaning of the words and phra___
請寫出單字和片語的中文。

1. moving
2. Earth
3. rise
4. set
5. east
6. west
7. stay still
8. path
9. orbit
10. spin

Listen to the passage and fill the blanks.
聆聽段落內容並填寫空格。

Every day, the sun rises and _____. It moves across the sky from _____ to _____. But really, the sun stays still. In fact, _____ moves. It _____ in two ways. First, it _____ the sun. This path is its _____. Earth also _____ around itself. This creates day and _____. We only see the _____ at night. But they are always out there. We just can't see them in the day because the sky is so _____.

Workbook

再次確認重要單字的意思，透過聆聽段落的音檔、聽寫來仔細複習單字和句子。

Answer Key

確認問題的答案，並且學習不太理解或是錯誤的部分。

Answer Key 解答

移動的地球 p.16

Check True or False
1. 地球會繞著太陽轉動。
2. 我們一整天都看到星星。

Comprehension Checkup
A. 1. 實際上是什麼在移動？
   ⓐ 太陽   ⓑ 地球   ⓒ 星星
   2. 地球繞著什麼轉動？
   ⓐ 太陽   ⓑ 月亮   ⓒ 星星
   3. 當地球自轉時，會產生白天和黑夜。
   ⓐ 空間   ⓑ 季節   ⓒ 白天和黑夜
   4. 我們白天看不到星星。
   ⓐ 日光   ⓑ 空間   ⓒ 天空

B. _____ 隨著太陽移動，並且也會自轉。
   ⓐ rise   ⓑ spins   ⓒ orbit
   • 地球的軌道
   • 星星會在白天和黑夜

產生的 p.18

on Checkup

3. 什麼會讓我們聽到聲音？
   ⓐ 弦   ⓑ 耳朵   ⓒ 耳膜

   ⓐ 耳朵   ⓑ 大腦   ⓒ 資訊

B. 所有的聲音都是 _____。而我們的大腦會識別這些 _____。

Wrap Up
ⓐ 撥動吉他上的弦。
ⓑ 聲波傳遞到我們的耳朵。
ⓒ 大腦識別聲音。
ⓓ 震動會造成空氣產生。
ⓔ 震動將資訊發送到耳朵。

一起來製作溶液吧 p.20

Check True or False
1. 鹽會在溶液裡分解。
2. 鹽水用快就會變回水和鹽。

Comprehension Checkup
A. 1. 下列何者為溶液的例子？
   ⓐ 鹽的晶體   ⓑ 鹽水   ⓒ 鹽和胡椒粉
   2. 鹽的晶體會發生什麼現象？
   ⓐ 會漂浮   ⓑ 會下沉   ⓒ 會溶解
   3. 鹽的晶體會變成 _____。
   ⓐ 變細   ⓑ 變粗   ⓒ 變得濃
   4. 鹽水會變回的物質一樣還是不一樣。
   ⓐ 維持不變   ⓑ 攪拌   ⓒ 分解

B. 溶液是一種物質的混合物，但會變成一種物質。• mixture

Table of Contents 目錄

Science 科學篇

Language Arts, Art, Music, Math 音樂藝術數學篇

★Daily Reading Plan★

如果學習者根據預定的計畫表學習，你可以在兩個月內學習完
美國教科書核心閱讀 100 篇，並把學習的日期記錄下來。

Day 1	Day 2	Day 3	Day 4	Day 5
Unit 1 Unit 2　　/	Unit 3 Unit 4　　/	Unit 5 Review 1　　/	Unit 6 Unit 7　　/	Unit 8 Unit 9　　/

Day 6	Day 7	Day 8	Day 9	Day 10
Unit 10 Review 2　　/	Unit 11 Unit 12　　/	Unit 13 Unit 14　　/	Unit 15 Review 3　　/	Unit 16 Unit 17　　/

Day 11	Day 12	Day 13	Day 14	Day 15
Unit 18 Unit 19　　/	Unit 20 Review 4　　/	Unit 21 Unit 22　　/	Unit 23 Unit 24　　/	Unit 25 Review 5　　/

Day 16	Day 17	Day 18	Day 19	Day 20
Unit 26 Unit 27　　/	Unit 28 Unit 29　　/	Unit 30 Review 6　　/	Unit 31 Unit 32　　/	Unit 33 Unit 34　　/

Day 21	Day 22	Day 23	Day 24	Day 25
Unit 35 Review 7　　/	Unit 36 Unit 37　　/	Unit 38 Unit 39　　/	Unit 40 Review 8　　/	Unit 41 Unit 42　　/

Day 26	Day 27	Day 28	Day 29	Day 30
Unit 43 Unit 44　　/	Unit 45 Review 9　　/	Unit 46 Unit 47　　/	Unit 48 Unit 49　　/	Unit 50 Review 10　　/

Day 31	Day 32	Day 33	Day 34	Day 35
Unit 51 Unit 52 /	Unit 53 Unit 54 /	Unit 55 Review 11 /	Unit 56 Unit 57 /	Unit 58 Unit 59 /

Day 36	Day 37	Day 38	Day 39	Day 40
Unit 60 Review 12 /	Unit 61 Unit 62 /	Unit 63 Unit 64 /	Unit 65 Review 13 /	Unit 66 Unit 67 /

Day 41	Day 42	Day 43	Day 44	Day 45
Unit 68 Unit 69 /	Unit 70 Review 14 /	Unit 71 Unit 72 /	Unit 73 Unit 74 /	Unit 75 Review 15 /

Day 46	Day 47	Day 48	Day 49	Day 50
Unit 76 Unit 77 /	Unit 78 Unit 79 /	Unit 80 Review 16 /	Unit 81 Unit 82 /	Unit 83 Unit 84 /

Day 51	Day 52	Day 53	Day 54	Day 55
Unit 85 Review 17 /	Unit 86 Unit 87 /	Unit 88 Unit 89 /	Unit 90 Review 18 /	Unit 91 Unit 92 /

Day 56	Day 57	Day 58	Day 59	Day 60
Unit 93 Unit 94 /	Unit 95 Review 19 /	Unit 96 Unit 97 /	Unit 98 Unit 99 /	Unit 100 Review 10 /

R_01.mp3

Every day, the sun <u>rises</u> and <u>sets</u>. It moves across the sky from <u>east</u>
    升起   日落   東方
to <u>west</u>. But really, the sun <u>stays still</u>. In fact, Earth moves. It moves
   西方   靜止不動
in two ways. First, it moves around the sun. This <u>path</u> is its <u>orbit</u>.
                                                 路線，軌道   （天體）運行軌道

Earth also <u>spins</u> around itself.
           旋轉
This <u>creates</u> day and night.
     產生
We only see the stars at
night. But they are always
out there. We just can't see
them in the day <u>because</u> the
                因為～
sky is so <u>bright</u>.
           明亮的

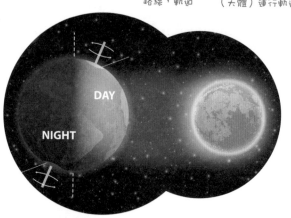

Check True or False 是非題

① Earth moves around the sun.   T / F

② We can see the stars all day long.   T / F

移動的地球

每天，太陽都會升起和落下，在天空中從東邊移
動到西邊。但其實太陽是靜止不動的，事實上是
地球在移動。地球是以兩種方式移動，首先，地
球會環繞著太陽轉動，而這條路線就是它的運行
軌道。另外，地球也會自轉，這產生了白天和黑
夜。我們只有在晚上才能看到星星，但是星星一
直都在天上，只是因為天空太亮了，所以我們在
白天的時候才看不見星星。

背景知識 Plus!

地球（Earth）花了一年的時間
環繞著太陽運轉以及一天的時間自
轉，地球在自轉時會以 1,634 公里／小
時的速度旋轉。我們在這麼快速的旋
轉下，為什麼不會覺得頭暈呢？
那是因為我們也和地球
一起旋轉。

Comprehension Checkup 理解能力確認

Circle the best answer. 圈選出正確的答案

1. What actually moves?
   - ⓐ the sun
   - ⓑ Earth
   - ⓒ stars

2. What does Earth orbit?
   - ⓐ the sun
   - ⓑ the moon
   - ⓒ stars

3. When Earth spins around itself, it creates _____.
   - ⓐ space
   - ⓑ seasons
   - ⓒ day and night

4. We don't see _____ during the day.
   - ⓐ sunlight
   - ⓑ stars
   - ⓒ the sky

Complete the sentence. 完成句子

Earth moves around the sun, and it .... around itself too.

Wrap Up Fill in the blanks. 總複習，將單字填入空格

❶ .... moves in two ways.

• It moves around the ❷	Earth's ❹ ....
• It ❸ .... around itself.	day and night

sun　　Earth　　Spins　　orbit

聲音是由震動產生的
Vibrations Make Sound

R_02.mp3

How can we hear sound? Sound is actually <u>vibrations</u>. Here is an
震動
<u>example</u>. <u>Pluck</u> a <u>string</u> on a guitar. It moves <u>back and forth</u> quickly.
例子　　撥；彈　（樂器的）弦　　　　　　　　來來回回地
This is a vibration, and it makes <u>sound</u>
聲波
<u>waves</u>. The sound waves reach our ears.
They <u>vibrate</u> our <u>eardrums</u> and send
震動　　　　耳膜
the <u>information</u> to the <u>brain</u>. Then the
資訊　　　　　大腦
brain <u>recognizes it as</u> sounds. We hear
將～認成～
all sounds like bells, <u>voices</u>, and music
聲音
the same way.

Check True or False 是非題

❶ Vibrations cause all sounds.　　　　　　　T / F

❷ The eardrums do not vibrate.　　　　　　T / F

聲音是由震動產生的

我們是如何聽到聲音的呢？聲音其實是震動。舉
例來說，撥動吉他上的弦時，弦會快速來回移
動。這就是一種震動，而震動會產生聲波，聲波
又會傳到我們的耳朵，並震動我們的耳膜，再將
資訊傳送到大腦，接著大腦再將它識定為聲音。
我們都是透過一樣的方式聽到所有聲音，像是鐘
聲、人聲和音樂等。

背景知識 Plus!

耳膜（eardrum）是位在從耳朵外
側到內側中細薄、透明的膜，耳膜的
作用是震動從外面傳入的聲波，傳達到
耳蝸。經過耳蝸的聲波透過無數腦細
胞傳達到我們的大腦。

Comprehension Checkup 理解能力確認

Circle the best answer. 圈選出正確的答案

1. How do vibrations move?
   - ⓐ only once
   - ⓑ very slowly
   - ⓒ back and forth

2. Vibrations _____ the eardrums in our ears.
   - ⓐ reach
   - ⓑ pluck
   - ⓒ recognize

3. What recognizes the sound?
   - ⓐ the string
   - ⓑ the brain
   - ⓒ the eardrum

4. We hear sounds like music and _____ the same way.
   - ⓐ ears
   - ⓑ voices
   - ⓒ information

Complete the sentence. 完成句子

All sounds are ...., and our brain recognizes them.

Wrap Up   Number the sentences in order. 寫出句子的順序

1️⃣ We pluck a guitar string.

⬜ The sound waves reach our ears.

⬜ The brain recognizes the sound.

⬜ A vibration <u>occurs</u> and it makes sound waves.
發生

⬜ The sound waves send the information to the brain.

一起來製作溶液吧

Let's Make a Solution

R_03.mp3

A <u>solution</u> is a <u>mixture</u> of <u>substances</u>. It is usually a
溶液　　　　混合物　　　物質
<u>liquid</u>. In it, one substance <u>breaks</u>
液體　　　　　　　　分解
<u>down</u> <u>completely</u> in another. <u>Saltwater</u> is a
完全地　　　　　　　鹽水
simple solution you can make. Pour some
salt in a glass of water. Then <u>stir</u> it. When the
攪拌
salt <u>crystals</u> <u>melt</u>, they do not <u>float</u> or <u>sink</u>.
結晶體　溶化　　　　漂浮　　下沉
Instead, they make the water <u>salty</u>. The water
鹹的
<u>stays</u> this way. It is like a new substance!
保持

Check True or False 是非題

❶ One substance breaks down in a solution.　　T / F

❷ Saltwater soon changes back into water　　T / F
and salt.

一起來製作溶液吧！

溶液是一種物質的混合物，通常是一種液體。在
溶液中，其中一種物質會在另一種物質中完全分
解，而鹽水就是一種你可以製作出的簡單溶液。
只要把一些鹽倒入一杯水裡，然後攪拌一下。當
鹽的晶體溶解時，晶體並不會漂浮或下沉，反而
是讓水變鹹。水會一直保持這樣的狀態，就像是
一種新的物質！

背景知識 Plus!

鹽水（saltwater）只用肉眼看和水
沒有區別，如果嚐的話，就可以快速
地辨別，但如果你不能嚐的話，要怎麼
分辨呢？當你加熱的時候就能看出來
了，因為純淨的水在加熱時會蒸發成
水蒸氣，一點也不剩。然而，鹽
水在加熱時，水會蒸發掉，
並留下鹽的晶體。

Circle the best answer. 圈選出正確的答案

1. What is an example of a solution?
   ⓐ salt crystal ⓑ saltwater ⓒ salt and pepper

2. What happens to the salt crystals?
   ⓐ They float. ⓑ They sink. ⓒ They melt.

3. The salt crystals make the water _____.
   ⓐ sweet ⓑ salty ⓒ clean

4. The saltwater _____ like a new substance.
   ⓐ stays ⓑ stirs ⓒ breaks down

Complete the sentence. 完成句子

A solution is a _____ of substances, but it becomes a new substance.

Wrap Up Fill in the blanks. 總複習，將單字填入空格

Making a New ❶ _____

方法	• One substance ❷ _____ down in another.	▸ ❸ _____
例子	• Salt breaks down in ❹ _____.	▸ saltwater

breaks   substance   water   solution

Powerful <u>storms</u> come every summer. They are <u>hurricanes</u>!
暴風雨   颶風

Hurricanes <u>form</u> over warm water in oceans. And they spin fast
形成

and travel to land. This can be dangerous for people on <u>coasts</u>.
海岸

Hurricanes <u>destroy</u> trees and buildings. They also cause <u>flooding</u>
破壞   （降雨所致的）洪水

and other storms, like <u>tornadoes</u>. These
龍捲風

<u>do</u> the most <u>damage</u>. <u>Fortunately</u>,
造成破壞   幸運地

scientists can <u>predict</u> or <u>track</u> hurricanes.
預報   追蹤

They can <u>issue</u> a hurricane <u>warning</u>. The
發出   警告

warning allows people to <u>prepare</u> for it.
做準備

Check True or False 是非題

❶ Coasts are safe from hurricanes.   T / F

❷ Scientists can give people warnings about   T / F

    hurricanes.

颶風

每年夏天都會出現強大的暴風雨，它們就是颶風！颶風在海洋的暖水上方形成，而它們會快速旋轉，並移動到陸地上，這對在沿海地區的人們來說十分危險。颶風摧毀了樹木和建築物，還會引發洪災和其他風暴，像是龍捲風，這些確實會造成大部分的損害。幸運的是，科學家可以預測或追蹤颶風，他們也可以發佈颶風警報，讓人們能夠為颶風做好準備。

背景知識 Plus!

颶風（hurricane）和龍捲風（tornado）都是由上升的熱空氣引起的旋風，兩者看起來很相似，卻是不同的。龍捲風是一種小型、快速旋轉的漏斗狀強風，移動距離很短，然後很快消散。然而，颶風是具有強風和大降雨量的大型漩渦，可持續長達十天。

Comprehension Checkup 理解能力確認

Circle the best answer. 圈選出正確的答案

1. Where do hurricanes form?
   ⓐ over warm water   ⓑ over hot land   ⓒ over cold water

2. What do hurricanes NOT cause?
   ⓐ flooding   ⓑ tornadoes   ⓒ dry air

3. Scientists can _____ and track hurricanes.
   ⓐ predict   ⓑ destroy   ⓒ spin

4. People can _____ for a coming hurricane.
   ⓐ form   ⓑ prepare   ⓒ travel

Complete the sentence. 完成句子

Hurricanes are strong storms, and they can be ....

Wrap Up Fill in the blanks. 總複習，將單字填入表格

Hurricanes	
形成	• form over warm water in ❶ ....
移動	• spin and travel to ❷ ....
結果	• cause ❸ ....and other storms
預防	• predict and ❹ ....

oceans

flooding

track

land

颶風   23

R_05.mp3

Frogs can live on the land and in the water. They have an interesting
<u>life cycle</u>. First, they <u>hatch</u> as <u>tadpoles</u> from eggs in the water. Like
生命週期   孵化   蝌蚪
fish, tadpoles <u>breathe</u> <u>underwater</u>
呼吸   在水下
and swim with a <u>tail</u>. Later, they
尾巴
grow legs. The tail becomes
shorter and shorter. They also
<u>develop</u> <u>lungs</u> for breathing
生長   肺
above water. Finally, their
bodies are <u>full-grown</u>. Then, they
發育完全的
can live on land.

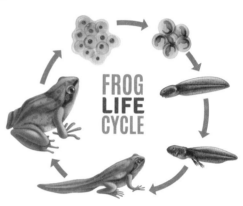

FROG LIFE CYCLE

Check True or False 是非題

❶ Frogs hatch from eggs underwater.   T / F

❷ Tadpoles can breathe above water.   T / F

青蛙的生命週期

青蛙可以在陸地上和在水中生活，牠們有個很有趣的生命週期。首先，牠們會在水中從卵孵化成蝌蚪。蝌蚪就像魚一樣，在水下呼吸並用尾巴游泳。之後，牠們長出了腿，尾巴也變得越來越短。牠們為了在水面上呼吸還發育出肺。最後，牠們的身體已經發育完全，便可以在陸地上生活了。

背景知識 Plus!

和青蛙一樣可以在陸地和水中生活的動物，被稱為兩棲動物（amphibian）。介於魚類和爬蟲類之間，兩棲動物在幼年時用鰓在水下呼吸，但長大後牠們在陸地上會用肺呼吸。除了青蛙，蟾蜍和蠑螈也是兩棲動物家族，然而由於氣候變遷，牠們的數量一直在減少。

Comprehension Checkup 理解能力確認

Circle the best answer. 圈選出正確的答案

1. What are baby frogs called?
   - ⓐ tadpoles
   - ⓑ fish
   - ⓒ life cycles

2. When they are young, how do frogs swim?
   - ⓐ with legs
   - ⓑ with a tail
   - ⓒ with lungs

3. A frog's tail grows _____ as it gets older.
   - ⓐ faster
   - ⓑ longer
   - ⓒ shorter

4. Frogs use lungs for _____ above water.
   - ⓐ swimming
   - ⓑ breathing
   - ⓒ eating

Complete the sentence. 完成句子

> After frogs go through changes, they can live on .... and in water.

Wrap Up Number the sentences in order. 寫出句子的順序

Life Cycle of Frogs

3 They develop lungs for breathing.

⬜ Their bodies are full-grown.

⬜ Their legs grow and their tail becomes shorter.

⬜ They hatch from eggs in the water as tadpoles.

WORD REVIEW

🧑 Crossword Puzzle 填字遊戲

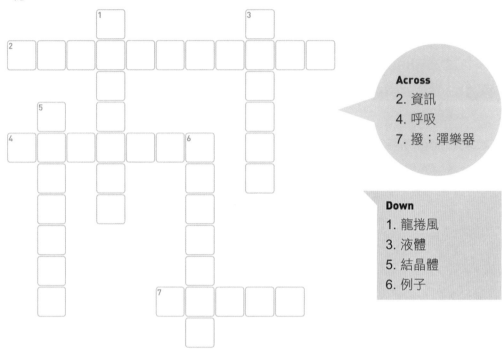

Across

2. 資訊

4. 呼吸

7. 撥；彈樂器

Down

1. 龍捲風

3. 液體

5. 結晶體

6. 例子

🐴 Match with the correct definition. 將單字連到正確的意思

1. eardrum •

2. hurricane •

3. Earth's orbit •

4. solution •

ⓐ the path of Earth moving around the sun

ⓑ a mixture of substances that is usually a liquid

ⓒ a powerful storm formed over warm water in oceans

ⓓ the part inside your ear that vibrates when sound reaches it

Fill in the blank with the correct words.
將正確的單字填入空格中

| float | spins | full-grown | track | recognizes |

1. Earth _____ around itself.
   地球會自己旋轉。

2. The brain _____ the information as sounds.
   大腦會將資訊認定成聲音。

3. When the salt crystals melt, they do not _____ or sink.
   當鹽的晶體溶化時，不會漂浮或下沉。

4. Fortunately, scientists can predict or _____ hurricanes.
   幸運的是，科學家可以預測或追蹤颶風。

5. Finally, their bodies are _____.
   最後，牠們的身體已經發育完全。

Fill in the blank with the correct expressions.
將正確的表達填入空格中

| travel to | back and forth | at night | stays still | breaks down |

1. We only see the stars _____.

2. The string moves _____ quickly.

3. In a solution, one substance _____ completely in another.

4. Hurricanes spin fast and _____ land.

5. But really, the sun _____. Only Earth moves.

You can find some <u>thermometers</u> in your house. Think about
溫度計
your refrigerator, oven, and <u>air conditioner</u>. They simply show
冷氣機
<u>temperatures</u> on the <u>screen</u>. However, old thermometers were glass
溫度　　　螢幕
<u>tubes</u>. There were <u>scales</u> on the tubes.
管子　　　　　刻度

<u>Mercury</u>, a red liquid, was inside. Heat
水銀
<u>expanded</u> the mercury. So on a hot
膨脹
day, it <u>rose</u> higher in the tubes. The
上升
mercury went down when it was
cool. People used the scales to read the
temperature.

Check True or False 是非題

1 Old thermometers were made of glass.　　　T / F

2 Heat made air in the tubes go down.　　　T / F

舊式溫度計是如何運作的？

我們可以在家中找到幾個溫度計，想想家中的冰箱、烤箱和冷氣，僅只是在螢幕上會顯示溫度。然而，舊式溫度計則是玻璃管，在玻璃管上有刻度，裡面裝著一種紅色液體，也就是水銀。水銀遇熱後便會膨脹，所以天氣炎熱的時候，在管子內的水銀就會升得更高；天氣涼爽的時候，水銀則會下降。以前大家就是透過刻度來讀取溫度。

背景知識 Plus!

水銀（mercury）是唯一在室溫下以液體呈現的金屬，在過去水銀被廣泛用在很多地方，在科學設備中包含溫度計、螢光燈、水銀電池以及蛀牙治療用的汞合金等。近年來水銀已經逐漸不被使用，因為它有害健康。

Circle the best answer. 圈選出正確的答案

1. What item in your house has a thermometer?
   ⓐ refrigerator　　　ⓑ TV screen　　　ⓒ glass window

2. What was inside old thermometers?
   ⓐ heat　　　ⓑ glass　　　ⓒ mercury

3. Old thermometers had _____ on the tubes.
   ⓐ screens　　　ⓑ liquid　　　ⓒ scales

4. The red liquid in old thermometers _____ when it was hot.
   ⓐ went down　　　ⓑ rose higher　　　ⓒ turned blue

Complete the sentence. 完成句子

Old thermometers <u>measured</u> .... with mercury.
測量

Wrap Up　Fill in the blanks. 總複習，將單字填入空格

Old Thermometers		scales
溫度顯示方法	• ❶ .... on the ❷ .... tubes	glass
管子中的物質	• ❸	heat
溫度計的原理	• ❹ .... expanded mercury. ▶ The mercury went up.	mercury

How do plants eat? They make their own food. This <u>process</u> is
過程
<u>photosynthesis</u>. A plant needs three things for this. First, it needs
光合作用
<u>carbon dioxide</u>. Its leaves breathe in this <u>gas</u>. Second, its <u>roots</u> get
二氧化碳   氣體   (植物)的根
water from the ground. Finally,
its leaves use sunlight for
energy. The energy <u>combines</u>
結合
carbon dioxide and water.
This creates sugar, or food
for the plant. <u>In turn</u>, the
反過來
plant <u>gives off</u> <u>oxygen</u> for us.
發散~   氧氣

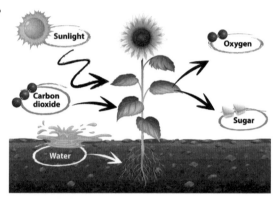

Check True or False 是非題

❶ Plants usually get water through their leaves.   T / F

❷ Plants give off oxygen after photosynthesis.   T / F

植物會自己製造食物

植物都是如何進食的呢？它們會自己製造食物，
這個過程就是光合作用。為此，植物需要三種東
西。首先，植物需要二氧化碳，它的葉子會吸入
這個氣體。第二，植物的根會從土壤取得水分。
最後，植物的葉子會利用太陽光來取得能量。這
種能量結合了二氧化碳和水，為植物製造糖分或
食物。而反過來，植物會為我們發散出氧氣。

背景知識 Plus!

植物的葉子包含稱為葉綠素的微小
綠色分子，當陽光照射在葉子上，這
些分子會利用光，並透過合成水和二氧
化碳的光合作用（photosynthesis）
來製造葡萄糖。葡萄糖對植物來說
就像米飯，它讓植物生長出莖、
葉、花、果實，並成長茁
壯。

Comprehension Checkup 理解能力確認

Circle the best answer. 圈選出正確的答案

1. What does a plant breathe in?
   - ⓐ oxygen
   - ⓑ carbon dioxide
   - ⓒ water

2. What does a plant get water from?
   - ⓐ the ground
   - ⓑ the air
   - ⓒ sugar

3. Plants use _____ as energy for photosynthesis.
   - ⓐ gas
   - ⓑ sunlight
   - ⓒ their leaves

4. Plants combine carbon dioxide and water to make _____.
   - ⓐ fruit
   - ⓑ energy
   - ⓒ sugar

Complete the sentence. 完成句子

Plants make their food through ....

Wrap Up Fill in the blanks. 總複習，將單字填入空格

Photosynthesis

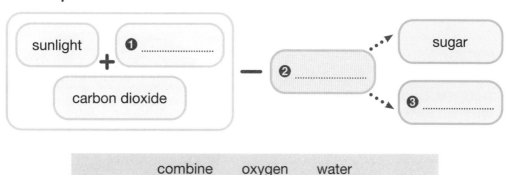

sunlight + ❶ .... — ❷ .... → sugar / ❸ ....

carbon dioxide

combine   oxygen   water

When <u>earthquakes</u> happen, the ground <u>shakes</u>. Most earthquakes
地震　　　　　　　　　　　　　震動
are short and weak. But some can be very dangerous! They destroy
buildings and roads. What <u>causes</u> earthquakes? Well, the earth's
導致
<u>surface</u> is on several <u>plates</u>. These plates
表面　　　　　　　　板塊
float and move around. Sometimes
they <u>rub</u> each other. Then they
摩擦
<u>get stuck</u>. They keep pushing with a
被卡住
huge <u>force</u>. <u>Suddenly</u> they
力量　　　突然地
<u>come loose</u>. This shakes the plates,
鬆開，不穩固
and there is an earthquake.

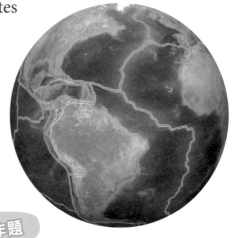

Check True or False 是非題

1 Most earthquakes last a long time. T / F

2 The earth's surface is on the moving plates. T / F

震動的板塊

地震發生時，地面會產生震動。大多數的地震都
很短暫且微弱，但有些地震可能會非常危險！地
震會摧毀建築物和道路。而引發地震的原因是什
麼呢？地球的表面有幾個板塊，這些板塊會漂浮
和移動。有時板塊會互相摩擦，然後就卡住了。
板塊會以一股巨大的力量持續推擠，而突然間，
板塊便鬆動了。這使板塊震動，並引發地震。

背景知識 Plus!

你有聽過「火環帶」這個詞嗎？
這是指在太平洋地震活動最頻繁的地
區，這個名字的由來是因為這些地區聚
在一起形成一個環。這些地區位在板
塊和板塊之間的交界處，受到板塊的
影響最大。

Comprehension Checkup 理解能力確認

Circle the best answer. 圈選出正確的答案

1. Where are the plates?
   a above the surface
   b in the sea
   c under the surface

2. What do the plates do?
   a They sink.   b They float.   c They stay still.

3. Sometimes plates get _____.
   a weak   b stuck   c short

4. When the plates come loose, they _____.
   a shake   b rub   c create

Complete the sentence. 完成句子

When Earth's plates come loose, they shake and cause

....

Wrap Up Number the sentences in order. 寫出句子的順序

What causes earthquakes?

[2] The plates get stuck.

[ ] The plates push with a huge force and suddenly come loose.

[ ] The earth's plates move around and rub each other.

[ ] The sudden change shakes the plates.

Coral reefs are under the sea near Southeast Asia and Australia.
珊瑚礁
They look like marine plants. But they are actually animals called
海生的
polyps. Polyps live on top of the reefs
珊瑚蟲   在～上面
and eat small creatures. They die and
生物
become hard like rocks. Dead polyps
硬的
create coral reefs. Lots of fish live
around the reefs. There are starfish,
海星
clownfish, lionfish, and eels. They all
小丑魚   獅子魚   鰻魚
make the area beautiful.
區域

Check True or False 是非題

❶ Coral reefs are actually marine plants.   T / F

❷ Fish eat polyps and create a coral reef.   T / F

植物還是動物？

珊瑚礁位於東南亞和澳洲附近的海底下，牠們看起來像海洋植物，但珊瑚礁實際上是一種被稱為珊瑚蟲的動物。珊瑚蟲生活在珊瑚礁的上面，並且會吃小生物。它們死亡後會變得像石頭一樣堅硬，而死掉的珊瑚蟲形成了珊瑚礁。有非常多的魚類生活在珊瑚礁的周圍，例如：海星、小丑魚、獅子魚和鰻魚，它們讓這個區域變得非常美麗。

背景知識 Plus!

位在澳洲東北部海岸的大堡礁（Great Barrier Reef），是世界最大的珊瑚礁所在地，這個地區有最多樣的海洋生物。有 1,500 種魚類、360 種珊瑚和 5,000 種軟體動物、175 種以上的藻類。然而，珊瑚礁因為海洋汙染而數量正在縮小。

Circle the best answer. 圈選出正確的答案

1. What are the animals that live on the reefs?
   - ⓐ polyps
   - ⓑ lions
   - ⓒ eels

2. What do polyps eat?
   - ⓐ rocks
   - ⓑ small creatures
   - ⓒ clownfish

3. The bodies of polyps become _____ after they die.
   - ⓐ soft
   - ⓑ big
   - ⓒ hard

4. Coral reefs and lots of _____ around them make the underwater world beautiful.
   - ⓐ stars
   - ⓑ polyps
   - ⓒ fish

Complete the sentence. 完成句子

> Dead Polyps make _____ _____, and lots of fish live around them.

Wrap Up   Choose the right words. 圈選出正確的單字

What are coral reefs?

❶ They are [animals / plants].

❷ Polyps live [under / on] the reefs.

❸ Polyps die and become [hard / soft].

❹ [Dead / Small] polyps form coral reefs.

Earth's Magnetic Field

R_10.mp3

Do you have a <u>compass</u>? Look at it. It always <u>points to</u> the north.
　　　　　　　指南針　　　　　　　　　　　　　　　　指出～
This is because of Earth's <u>magnetic field</u>. The Earth's <u>core</u> has a ball
　　　　　　　　　　　　　磁場　　　　　　　　　　　核心
of <u>iron</u>. This ball spins around and acts
　　鐵
like a <u>magnet</u>. So, Earth has a magnetic
　　　磁鐵
field. Like all magnets, Earth has two

<u>poles</u>. These are north and south,
地極地區
and they <u>attract</u> <u>metal</u>. The poles
　　　　　吸引　　金屬
<u>direct</u> the metal <u>needle</u> of a compass.
給～指方向　　　　針
That's how compasses work.

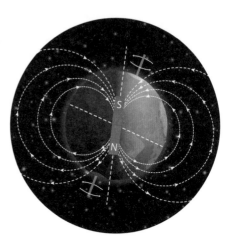

Check True or False 是非題

❶ A compass can attract metal. 　　　　　　　T / F

❷ Earth acts like a magnet with its core. 　　　T / F

地球的磁場

你有指南針嗎？拿出來看看吧。指南針總是指向
北方，而這是因為地球的磁場。地球的核心有一
顆鐵球，這顆球會旋轉，就像磁鐵一樣運作，所
以地球有磁場。如同所有的磁鐵一樣，地球有兩
個磁極，也就是北和南，並且會吸引金屬。兩極
會引導指南針的金屬針，這就是指南針的原理。

背景知識 Plus!

磁場（magnetic field）
是磁鐵的作用範圍，如果你在長條的
磁鐵周圍撒鐵粉，就可以看到鐵粉
在 N 極和 S 極的周圍以圓形的方式
散布到整個磁鐵上。透過這一點，
我們可以確定磁場的存在，而磁
鐵的力量在鐵粉聚集的兩極
部分表現得最強烈。

Comprehension Checkup 理解能力確認

Circle the best answer. 圈選出正確的答案

1. Which <u>direction</u> does a compass always point to?
   ⓐ the east 方向 ⓑ the west ⓒ the north

2. What is in Earth's core?
   ⓐ an iron ball ⓑ a compass ⓒ a pole

3. All magnets have two _____, and they attract metal.
   ⓐ cores ⓑ poles ⓒ needles

4. Earth's poles _____ the needle of a compass.
   ⓐ spin ⓑ point to ⓒ direct

Complete the sentence. 完成句子

A compass shows direction with Earth's .... field.

Wrap Up Fill in the blanks. 總複習，將單字填入空格

How does a compass always point to the north?

- The Earth's core has a(n) ❶ .... ball.

- It spins and makes a(n) ❷ .... field.

- Earth's poles attract ❸ ....

- The poles direct the metal ❹ .... of a compass

magnetic

iron

needle

metal

WORD REVIEW

🧑 Crossword Puzzle 填字遊戲

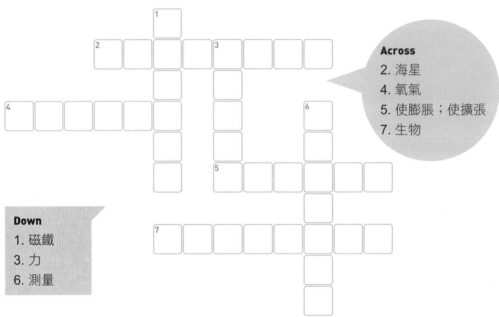

Across

2. 海星
4. 氧氣
5. 使膨脹；使擴張
7. 生物

Down

1. 磁鐵
3. 力
6. 測量

🐱 Match with the correct definition. 將單字連到正確的意思

1. earthquake •

2. mercury •

3. polyp •

4. photosynthesis •

ⓐ the red liquid inside an old thermometer

ⓑ the process where plants make their own food

ⓒ a dangerous situation when the earth's surface shakes

ⓓ an animal that lives on reefs; dead ones make new reefs

Fill in the blank with the correct words.
將正確的單字填入空格中

| core | marine | thermometers | plates | combines |

1. You can find some _____ in your house.
   你可以在家中找到幾個溫度計。

2. The energy _____ carbon dioxide and water.
   能量合成二氧化碳和水。

3. The earth's surface is on several _____.
   地球的表面是在數個板塊上面。

4. Coral reefs look like _____ plants.
   珊瑚礁看起來就像海洋植物。

5. The Earth's _____ has a ball of iron.
   地球的核心有一顆鐵球。

Fill in the blank with the correct expressions.
將正確的表達填入空格中

| get stuck | like rocks | went down | points to | gives off |

1. The mercury _____ when it was cool.

2. In turn, the plant _____ oxygen for us.

3. Sometimes they rub each other. Then they _____ _____.

4. They die and become hard _____.

5. A compass always _____ the north.

Animals Can Use Electricity!

R_11.mp3

Humans make and use <u>electricity</u>. But some animals can too! They
電力
use electricity in many ways. <u>Electric eels</u> live in water, and other
電鰻
fish <u>hunt</u> them. These eels can <u>charge</u> their
追獵　　　　　　　　充電
bodies with electricity. They <u>shock</u>
使電擊
the <u>hunters</u> to protect themselves.
捕獵者
Animals can also find food with
electricity. Sharks can <u>sense</u>
感覺到
electricity in other creatures. They
can find <u>hidden</u> fish this way! They
隱藏的
can even hunt <u>faraway</u> fish.
遙遠的

Check True or False 是非題

❶ Only humans can make and use electricity.　　T / F

❷ Sharks make electricity for faraway fish.　　T / F

動物會使用電力！

人類會製造和使用電力，但有些動物也可以！牠
們以許多方式來使用電力。電鰻生活在水中，而
其他魚類會捕食牠們，這些鰻魚可以幫自己的身
體充電，並電擊獵食者來保護自己。而動物也可
以用電力來尋找食物，鯊魚可以感應到其他生物
的電流，牠們能夠用這種方式找到躲藏的魚！甚
至還可以狩獵在遠處的魚。

背景知識 Plus!

電鰻（electric eel）的電量大約是
650~850 伏特，強大到足以讓像是馬
一樣的大型動物觸電死亡。因此在捕電
鰻時，會用電擊使電鰻受到驚嚇，在
鰻魚放電後，用網子捕鰻魚。而電鰻
電力最強的地方就在尾巴。

Comprehension Checkup 理解能力確認

Circle the best answer. 圈選出正確的答案

1. What do electric eels charge their bodies with?
   - ⓐ electricity
   - ⓑ water
   - ⓒ food

2. What do the eels do with electricity?
   - ⓐ build homes
   - ⓑ shock hunters
   - ⓒ find directions

3. Sharks _____ electricity in other creatures.
   - ⓐ charge
   - ⓑ hunt
   - ⓒ sense

4. With electricity, sharks can find _____ fish.
   - ⓐ caught
   - ⓑ dead
   - ⓒ hidden

Complete the sentence. 完成句子

Some animals use .... for staying safe and finding food.

Wrap Up Fill in the blanks. 總複習，將單字填入空格

Some animals use electricity.

Animals	electric eels	sharks
How	❶ .... their bodies with electricity	❷ .... electricity in other creatures
Result	❸ .... the hunters	❹ .... fish

sense   charge   hunt   shock

Let's throw a ball in the air. Can it fly <u>forever</u>?
永遠

Well, Isaac Newton's First <u>Law</u> of
（科學等的）定律

<u>Motion</u> has the answer. A moving <u>object</u>
（物體的）運動   物體

moves in a <u>straight</u> line with the same <u>speed</u>.
筆直的   速度

Only an outside force can change this.

On Earth, <u>gravity</u> <u>pulls</u> all objects down.
重力   拉

So the ball <u>slows down</u> and falls down.
減低速度

Gravity is the outside force here. Now in

<u>space</u>, there is no gravity. It might fly
宇宙

forever there!

Check True or False 是非題

❶ There is no gravity on Earth.   T / F

❷ A flying ball might not fall down in space.   T / F

球可以永遠飛在空中嗎？

我們把一顆球拋到空中看看吧，球可以永遠都飛在空中嗎？這個嘛，可以從牛頓第一運動定律找到答案。移動中的物體會以相同的速度沿著直線移動，只有外部的力量才能改變這一點。在地球上，重力會將所有物體往下拉，因此球會變慢並落下來，在這裡重力就是外力。如果到了沒有重力的外太空，球就有可能永遠飛在空中！

背景知識 Plus!

地球上所有有重量的物體都有互相吸引的力量，這是萬有引力。重力（gravity）是指萬有引力加上地球自轉的離心力，將物體向下拉。由於地球的重力，我們才能站著而不會漂浮在空中。

Comprehension Checkup 理解能力確認

Circle the best answer. 圈選出正確的答案

1. What is Isaac Newton's law about?
   - **a** a law of force
   - **b** a law of motion
   - **c** gravity in space

2. What stays the same in a moving object with no outside force?
   - **a** wind
   - **b** color
   - **c** speed

3. Only a(n) _____ force can change an object in motion.
   - **a** moving
   - **c** outside
   - **c** slow

4. The _____ of Earth always pulls objects down.
   - **a** gravity
   - **b** space
   - **c** direction

Complete the sentence. 完成句子

On Earth, a ball in the air will always .... to the ground.

Wrap Up Fill in the blanks. 總複習，將單字填入空格

The Law of Motion

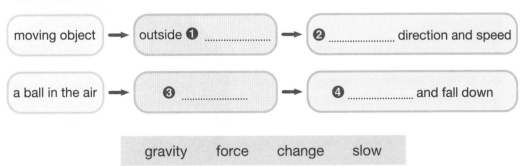

| moving object | → | outside ❶ .... | → | ❷ .... direction and speed |

| a ball in the air | → | ❸ .... | → | ❹ .... and fall down |

gravity　　force　　change　　slow

Deserts are <u>mostly</u> <u>sandy</u> areas with little rain. They are very hot and
沙漠　　大多數地　含沙的

dry. But deserts can be very cold too! In fact,

the sand <u>cools down</u> quickly at night. So,
冷卻

hot deserts become very cold at night.

Sometimes they have a <u>heavy</u> <u>rainfall</u>
大的　　　降雨

too. Some animals and plants can

<u>survive</u> there. For example, <u>cactuses</u>
活下來　　　　　　　　　　仙人掌

store water in their bodies. The <u>spines</u>
貯存　　　　　　　　　　　（動植物的）刺

<u>on the sides</u> help them keep the water.
在側邊

Check True or False 是非題

❶ Deserts become very hot at night.　　　　　　T / F

❷ Some animals can live in the desert.　　　　　T / F

沙漠的天氣
沙漠大部分是少雨的沙地，十分炎熱又乾燥，但沙漠也可能非常寒冷！事實上，沙子在晚上會快速冷卻，因此炎熱的沙漠在晚上會變得非常寒冷。有時沙漠也會下大雨，有些動物和植物能夠在沙漠中生存下來，例如：仙人掌會在體內儲存水分，而側面的刺會幫助它們保存水分。

背景知識 Plus!
植物的水分會從葉子中釋放出來，並蒸發到空氣中。然而，仙人掌（cactus）的葉子是刺（spine），因此水分不會蒸發，而是留在植物體內。而這些刺也會保護仙人掌不被動物吃掉。

Comprehension Checkup 理解能力確認

Circle the best answer. 圈選出正確的答案

1. What do most deserts have?
   - ⓐ sand
   - ⓑ flooding
   - ⓒ waterfalls

2. What is the weather usually like in a desert?
   - ⓐ cold and dry
   - ⓑ hot and dry
   - ⓒ hot and wet

3. Cactuses store _____ to survive in deserts.
   - ⓐ sand
   - ⓑ heat
   - ⓒ water

4. Cactuses have _____ on their sides.
   - ⓐ spines
   - ⓑ leaves
   - ⓒ plants

Complete the sentence. 完成句子

> Deserts have little rain, but some animals and plants
> .... there.

WrapUp Fill in the blanks. 總複習，將單字填入空格

Weather	Day	❶ .... rain, hot, dry
	Night	very cold
	Sometimes	❷ .... rainfall
Plants	Cactuses	❸ .... water ❹ .... help them keep water.

store   heavy   spines   little

Ants and Their Jobs

R_14.mp3

Ants live together in a <u>colony</u>. A colony can have <u>millions of</u> ants!
生物群　　　　　　　　　　　　　　　　　　　　　　數百萬

The ants have different <u>jobs</u>. Most are <u>worker</u> ants. They collect food
工作　　　　　工作者

and build the <u>mound</u>, or home. Some ants are <u>soldiers</u>.
土堆　　　　　　　　　　　　　　　士兵

They <u>defend</u> the colony.
防禦

There are also <u>drones</u>.
雄蟻

These are <u>male</u> ants. They
雄的

<u>mate</u> with the queen and
交配

die shortly after. Finally,

there is the queen ant. She

<u>lays</u> all the eggs.
產卵

Check True or False 是非題

❶ A colony can have more than a million ants.　　　T / F

❷ Drones live longer than the queen.　　　T / F

螞蟻和牠們的工作

螞蟻是集體生活在蟻巢中，一個蟻巢可以容納數百萬隻螞蟻！螞蟻有不同的工作，大部分是工蟻，牠們會收集食物並建造土丘或家園。有些螞蟻則是兵蟻，牠們負責保衛蟻巢。還有雄蟻，這些螞蟻是雄性的，牠們會與蟻后交配，不久之後便會死亡。最後是蟻后，蟻后會產下所有的卵。

背景知識 Plus!

工蟻（worker ant）和兵蟻（soldier）都是雌性，但是不會交配和產卵。反而，牠們在蟻窩內外為蟻后和幼蟲認真工作。而在蟻窩中，只有蟻后（queen ant）可以和雄蟻（drone）交配並繁殖。

Circle the best answer. 圈選出正確的答案

1. What is a group of ants living together called?
   - **ⓐ** an egg
   - **ⓑ** a colony
   - **ⓒ** a mound

2. What do soldier ants do?
   - **ⓐ** collect food
   - **ⓑ** defend the colony
   - **ⓒ** mate with the queen

3. Drones _____ are ants.
   - **ⓐ** male
   - **ⓑ** baby
   - **ⓒ** worker

4. The _____ lays all the eggs.
   - **ⓐ** soldier ant
   - **ⓑ** queen ant
   - **ⓒ** drone

Complete the sentence. 完成句子

Ants have different .... and live together in a colony.

Wrap Up Connect. 總複習，連連看

What do we do?

❶ Queen ant   •   • **ⓐ** lay eggs

❷ Worker ants   •   • **ⓑ** defend

❸ Soldier ants   •   • **ⓒ** collect food

❹ Drones   •   • **ⓓ** mate

The Secret of Fossils

R_15.mp3

You can see <u>dinosaur</u> bones in museums. Are they real bones? They
恐龍
are <u>fossils</u>. Fossils are the old <u>remains</u> of animals and plants. They
化石   遺骨
keep their <u>original</u> <u>shapes</u>. How is this
原先的   外形
<u>possible</u>? After an animal dies, it may
可能的
<u>sink</u> deep into <u>mud</u>. It stays there for
下沉   泥
millions of years. It will not <u>disappear</u>
消失
but become hard like <u>rock</u>. When
岩石
we find a fossil, it gives us lots of
information about the <u>past</u>.
過去

Check True or False 是非題

❶ You can see fossils in some museums.　　　　T / F

❷ Fossils lose their original shapes.　　　　　T / F

化石的祕密

我們可以在博物館裡看到恐龍的骨骸，但那些是
真正的骨骸嗎？它們是化石。化石是動物和植物
的古老遺骸，它們維持著原始的外形。這是怎麼
辦到的呢？在動物死亡後，可能會沉入泥土深
處，並埋在那裡數百萬年。遺骸不會消失，但是
會變得像石頭一樣堅硬。當我們發現化石時，化
石會為我們提供許多關於過去的資訊。

背景知識 Plus!

化石（fossil）字面上是指動物和植
物變成石頭，如果有化石被發現，就
可以知道這個區域的資訊。如果在某個
區域發現很多魚類和貝類的化石，這
個區域可能有很久以前是海洋。另外
分析化石含有的岩石成分，就可
以知道化石的年齡。

Comprehension Checkup 理解能力確認

Circle the best answer. 圈選出正確的答案

1. What can't be a fossil?
   - **a** animals
   - **b** rocks
   - **c** plants

2. Where can an animal sink after it dies?
   - **a** into mud
   - **b** in trees
   - **c** on rocks

3. Fossils can keep the original _____ of the animal remains.
   - **a** years
   - **b** numbers
   - **c** shapes

4. The remains will become _____ like rock.
   - **a** soft
   - **b** hard
   - **c** heavy

Complete the sentence. 完成句子

Fossils form over millions of years and give us ....

Wrap Up Number the sentences in order. 寫出句子的順序

The Formation of Fossils

5 People find it.

☐ It stays there and does not disappear.

☐ It becomes hard like rock.

☐ The dead animal sinks deep into mud.

☐ An animal dies.

WORD REVIEW

🐧 Crossword Puzzle 填字遊戲

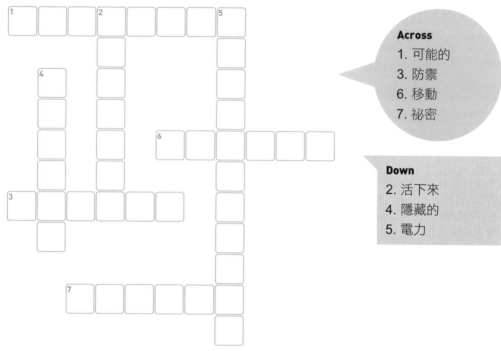

Across
1. 可能的
3. 防禦
6. 移動
7. 祕密

Down
2. 活下來
4. 隱藏的
5. 電力

🐴 Match with the correct definition. 將單字連到正確的意思

1. desert •

   ⓐ the force on Earth that pulls all objects down

2. drone •

   ⓑ a sandy area with little rain

3. fossil •

   ⓒ a male ant that mates with the queen

4. gravity •

   ⓓ old remains of animals and plants with their original shapes

Fill in the blank with the correct words.
將正確的單字填入空格中

colony	charge	past	speed	rainfall

1. Electric eels can _____ their bodies with electricity.
   電鰻可以讓自己的身體充電。

2. A moving object moves in a straight line with the same
   _____.
   移動中的物體會以相同的速度沿著直線移動。

3. Sometimes deserts have a heavy _____ too.
   有時沙漠也會下大雨。

4. Ants live together in a _____.
   螞蟻集體生活在蟻巢中。

5. It gives us lots of information about the _____.
   這為我們提供許多關於過去的資訊。

Fill in the blank with the correct expressions.
將正確的表達填入空格中

cools down	slows down	deep into	millions of	on the sides

1. A colony can have _____ ants!

2. So the ball _____ and falls down.

3. In fact, the sand _____ quickly at night.

4. The spines _____ help them keep the water.

5. After an animal dies, it may sink _____ mud.

Underwater Vents

R_16.mp3

The <u>ocean floor</u> has many holes. These are <u>vents</u>. They <u>shoot out</u> hot
（海底）　　　　　　　　　　　　　　　　　（噴發孔）　　　（像子彈一般衝出）
water and <u>poisonous</u> <u>material</u>. This area is very hot, and the water
　　　　　　（有毒的）　　（物質）
<u>pressure</u> is strong. Also, there is no sunlight.
（壓力）

But strange worms, fish, and shrimp live

here. They can survive the <u>heat</u> and
　　　　　　　　　　　　　（熱度）
pressure. What <u>feeds</u> them? Special
　　　　　　（以～為食物）
<u>bacteria</u> also live near the vents. Some
（細菌）
plants eat these bacteria. And some

animals <u>feed on</u> the plants.
　　　　（靠～為食）

Check True or False 是非題

❶ Water pressure is weak near ocean vents.   T / F

❷ Some animals live near the vents.   T / F

海底熱泉

海底有許多洞，這些都是噴發口，它們會噴出熱水和有毒物質。這個區域非常炎熱，水壓也很強，而且這裡也沒有陽光。但是奇怪的蟲子、魚類和蝦子都在這裡生活，牠們能夠在高溫和高壓下存活。牠們是以什麼為食呢？由於特殊的細菌也生活在熱泉附近，有些植物會吃這些細菌，而有些動物會以這些植物為食。

背景知識 Plus!

海底上的洞被稱為**海底熱泉**（hydrothermal vent），這些洞是火山活動所產生的噴發口。被地熱加熱的熱水和噴發物，從地球的深處像黑煙一樣噴發出來。即使在這種極端的環境，也有各式各樣的生物生存下來，形成海底生態系統的食物鏈基礎。

Comprehension Checkup 理解能力確認

Circle the best answer. 圈選出正確的答案

1. What are underwater vents?
   - ⓐ fish
   - ⓑ holes
   - ⓒ rocks

2. What do the vents shoot out?
   - ⓐ hot water
   - ⓑ sunlight
   - ⓒ worms

3. Life near underwater vents cannot get _____.
   - ⓐ air
   - ⓑ heat
   - ⓒ sunlight

4. Plants near the vents eat special _____.
   - ⓐ bacteria
   - ⓑ shrimp
   - ⓒ poison

Complete the sentence. 完成句子

Underwater .... are homes for strange ocean animals.

Wrap Up Fill in the blanks. 總複習，將單字填入表格

Underwater Vents

環境
- heat
- strong water ❶ ....
- ❷ .... materials

棲息/生物
- strange ❸ .... , fish, shrimp
- plants, special ❹ ....

| pressure | worms | bacteria | poisonous |

Caribou vs. Reindeer

R_17.mp3

Large deer live in the Arctic. These are caribou and reindeer. They
北極地區　　　　　　　　　　　　　　　北美馴鹿　　　馴鹿
belong to the same species. Both have large antlers. But there is
屬於～　　　　　　（生物）種類　　　　　　　　鹿角
one important difference. Caribou are wild. Reindeer are tame.
野生的　　　　　　　馴化的
People use reindeer for their meat or fur. Reindeer can also pull
（獸類的）軟毛
sleds. With good care, reindeer eat
雪橇　　　　照料
more and live better. They

are usually larger than
caribou. However, caribou
must survive in a harsh
嚴酷的
environment.
環境

Check True or False 是非題

❶ Caribou do not have antlers.　　　　　　　T / F

❷ Reindeer can pull sleds.　　　　　　　　　T / F

北美馴鹿和馴鹿

大型的鹿生活在北極地區，牠們是北美馴鹿和馴
鹿，屬於同一個物種，兩者都有很大的鹿角，但
是有一個很重要的區別，那就是北美馴鹿是野生
的，而馴鹿是被馴化的。人們會使用馴鹿的肉或
毛皮，而馴鹿也可以拉雪橇。在良好照顧下，馴
鹿會吃得更多、活得更好。馴鹿通常比北美馴鹿
更大隻，然而北美馴鹿必須在惡劣的環境中存活
下來。

背景知識 Plus!

馴鹿（reindeer）是人類唯一
可以當作家畜飼養的鹿類。
馴鹿對生活在極地的人非常有用，因為
牠們可以生存在寒冷的冬天天氣中。
而在雪地中利用馴鹿雪橇就可以輕鬆
地移動行李和人，另外拉聖誕老
人雪橇的鹿也是馴鹿。

Comprehension Checkup 理解能力確認

Circle the best answer. 圈選出正確的答案

1. What is the same about caribou and reindeer?
   - ⓐ size
   - ⓑ home
   - ⓒ species

2. Which animal is wild?
   - ⓐ a caribou
   - ⓑ a reindeer
   - ⓒ a dog

3. People can get meat or _____ from reindeer.
   - ⓐ sled
   - ⓑ fur
   - ⓒ care

4. Between them, _____ live better and have larger bodies.
   - ⓐ caribou
   - ⓑ reindeer
   - ⓒ humans

Complete the sentence. 完成句子

Reindeer are ...., but caribou live in a harsh environment.

Wrap Up Fill in the blanks. 總複習，將單字填入空格

Caribou	Reindeer
• have large antlers • are ❶ .... • ❷ .... in a harsh environment	• have large antlers • are ❸ .... • eat more, live ❹ .... • are larger than caribou

survive　　wild　　tame　　better

How Muscles Work

R_18.mp3

Do you run and play every day? Then you use your <u>muscles</u> a lot. Muscles make your body 肌肉
<u>move</u>. You need lots of muscles for moving. 移動
<u>Surprisingly</u>, the body has over 600 muscles! 驚人地
They are under the <u>skin</u> and <u>attached to</u> 皮膚　　　　　附屬於～
bones. Muscles <u>stretch</u> and <u>shrink</u>. This 伸長　　　　收縮
moves the <u>skeleton</u> in different ways. When 骨骼
you want to run, you just need to think about it. Then the brain makes your leg muscles work.

Check True or False 是非題

❶ Muscles are under the skin.　　　　　　　　　T / F

❷ Muscles make bones stretch and shrink.　　　T / F

肌肉如何運作

你會每天跑步和玩耍嗎？那麼你就會大量使用到肌肉。肌肉讓你的身體移動，而你需要大量的肌肉才可以移動。令人驚訝的是，我們的身體竟然有超過 600 個肌肉！它們在皮膚底下，並附著在骨頭上。肌肉會伸展和收縮，以不同的方式移動骨骼。當你想要跑步時，只需要想著跑步，接著大腦就會讓腿部的肌肉開始運作。

背景知識 Plus!

最能展現肌肉（muscle）伸展、收縮的是心臟，奇怪的是，不管我們的意志為何，心臟總是一直在活動，心跳是心臟肌肉伸展、收縮的自動運動。

Comprehension Checkup 理解能力確認

Circle the best answer. 圈選出正確的答案

1. What are muscles attached to?
   ⓐ bones   ⓑ hair   ⓒ the brain

2. How do muscles move?
   ⓐ stretch and shrink   ⓑ pull and stretch   ⓒ run and play

3. Muscle movements make the _____ move.
   ⓐ skin   ⓑ skeleton   ⓒ thinking

4. When you run, the _____ makes your muscles work.
   ⓐ face   ⓑ leg   ⓒ brain

Complete the sentence. 完成答案

Muscles help the body .... in different ways.

Wrap Up   Connect. 總複習，連連看

❶ What do muscles do? •

❷ Where are muscles? •

❸ How do muscles move? •

❹ What makes your muscles work? •

ⓐ We think and the brain makes them work.

ⓑ They make your body move.

ⓒ They stretch and shrink.

ⓓ They are under the skin.

The Grand Canyon

R_19.mp3

The Grand <u>Canyon</u> is an <u>amazing</u> place in the
峽谷　　　　　　驚人的
US. It is in Arizona. It is one of Earth's
biggest canyons. Canyons are <u>deep</u>
深的
areas under high mountains. This one
is about 2 km deep! Long ago, the
Colorado River <u>cut into</u> the <u>ground</u>. The
切入～　　　　地面
river made its <u>course</u> through the area.
路線
This slowly formed the canyon and the rock
<u>layers</u> around it. It took over five <u>million</u> years!
層　　　　　　　　　　　　　百萬

Check True or False 是非題

❶ The Grand Canyon is in Colorado.　　　T / F

❷ The canyon was formed five million years ago.　T / F

大峽谷

大峽谷是美國的一個很驚奇的地方，位於亞利桑那州，是地球上其中一個最大的峽谷。峽谷是指高山底下的深處，而美國的大峽谷大約有 2 公里深！在很久以前，科羅拉多河切入地面，河流的路線經過這個區域，便慢慢形成了峽谷以及周圍的岩層。這段過程花了超過五百萬年的時間！

背景知識 Plus!

在大峽谷中可以看到許多不同顏色的岩層（rock layers），因為峽谷形成的時間很長，這些岩層之間的時間差非常顯而易見。由於這些岩層是在不同的年代並以不同的成分形成的，是地質研究的重要資料。

Circle the best answer. 圈選出正確的答案

1. Where are canyons?
   a on rivers
   b under mountains
   c under the ground

2. How deep is the Grand Canyon?
   a 500 m b 2 km c 5 km

3. The Colorado River made its _____ through the area.
   a ground b rocks c course

4. The river formed _____ around the canyon.
   a rock layers b a big rock c oceans

Complete the sentence. 完成句子

A river cut into the .... and formed the Grand Canyon.

Wrap Up Fill in the blanks. 總複習，將單字填入空格

The Grand Canyon

地點	• In Arizona
深度	• 2 km deep
生成過程	• The Colorado River cut into the ❶ .... • The ❷ .... ran through the area. • The ❸ .... and the rock ❹ .... were formed.

river ground layers canyon

大峽谷 59

Everything has <u>countless</u> <u>atoms</u>! They are the <u>basic</u> <u>units</u> of <u>matter</u>.
　　　　　　　　　無數的　　原子　　　　　　　　　　基本的　　單位　　　物質
Atoms are <u>tiny</u>, but they have different sizes. For example, oxygen
　　　　　微小的
atoms are bigger than <u>hydrogen</u>
　　　　　　　　　　　　　　　氫
atoms. Atoms can <u>combine</u> with each
　　　　　　　　　　　結合
other. This makes a <u>molecule</u>. That's
　　　　　　　　　　　　分子
a larger unit. Hydrogen and oxygen

atoms can combine to make water.

A water molecule has two

hydrogen atoms and one oxygen

atom. We call it H_2O.

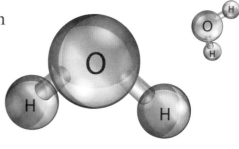

Check True or False 是非題

❶ Atoms are in everything. T / F

❷ Molecules can make a larger atom. T / F

原子和分子

每個物質都有無數個原子！它們是物質的基本單位。原子很微小，但每個原子也具有不同的大小，例如：氧原子比氫原子還大。原子可以互相結合，這就形成了一個分子，是一個更大的單位。氫原子和氧原子可以結合以形成水。一個水分子有兩個氫原子和一個氧原子，我們將其稱之為 H_2O。

背景知識 Plus!

物質最基本的單位是原子（atom），但是原子並不具備我們所知道的物質特性，而物質特性的最小單位是分子（molecule）。如我們所知，「水」是無色無味的液體，然而構成水的氧和氫以原子的形式存在時，是氣體的狀態。

Comprehension Checkup 理解能力確認

Circle the best answer. 圈選出正確的答案

1. What is the basic unit of matter?
   - ⓐ molecule
   - ⓑ atom
   - ⓒ oxygen

2. Which is bigger, a hydrogen atom or an oxygen atom?
   - ⓐ hydrogen
   - ⓑ oxygen
   - ⓒ the same

3. Atoms combine with each other and make a _____.
   - ⓐ size
   - ⓑ smaller unit
   - ⓒ molecule

4. A water molecule has _____ hydrogen atoms.
   - ⓐ two
   - ⓑ three
   - ⓒ countless

Complete the sentence. 完成句子

Atoms and molecules are _____ of matter, and molecules contain atoms.

Wrap Up   Fill in the blanks. 總複習，將單字填入空格

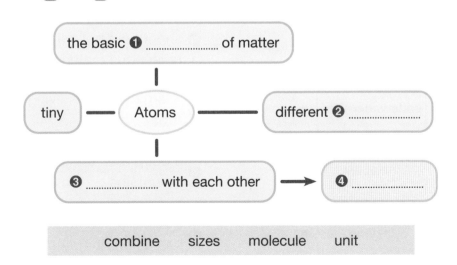

the basic ❶ _____ of matter

tiny — Atoms — different ❷ _____

❸ _____ with each other ⟶ ❹ _____

combine   sizes   molecule   unit

WORD REVIEW

🖊 Crossword Puzzle 填字遊戲

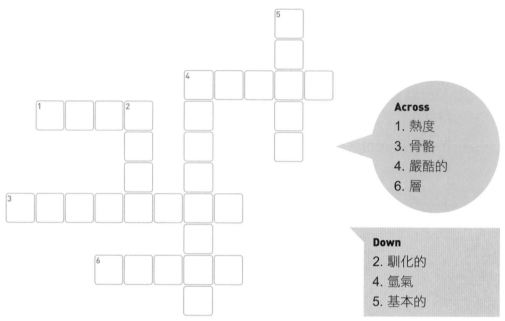

Across
1. 熱度
3. 骨骼
4. 嚴酷的
6. 層

Down
2. 馴化的
4. 氫氣
5. 基本的

🖊 Match with the correct definition. 將單字連到正確的意思

1. canyon •

ⓐ a hole in the ocean floor that shoots out hot water and poisonous materials

2. underwater vent •

ⓑ a large wild deer living in the Arctic

3. molecule •

ⓒ a deep area under high mountains

4. caribou •

ⓓ a larger unit of matter that has different atoms in it

Fill in the blank with the correct words.
將正確的單字填入空格中

| care | course | shrink | countless | pressure |

1. This area is very hot, and the water _____ is strong.
   這個區域非常炎熱，水壓也很強。

2. With good _____, reindeer eat more and live better.
   若是在細心照顧的情況下，馴鹿會吃得更多、活得更好。

3. Muscles stretch and _____.
   肌肉會伸展和收縮。

4. The river made its _____ through the area.
   河流的路線有經過這個區域。

5. Everything has _____ atoms!
   每個物質都有無數個原子。

Fill in the blank with the correct expressions.
將正確的表達填入空格中

| cut into | belong to | feed on | bigger than | attached to |

1. Some plants eat the bacteria. And the animals _____ _____ the plants.

2. Caribou and reindeer _____ the same species.

3. Muscles are under the skin and _____ bones.

4. Long ago, the Colorado River _____ the ground.

5. Oxygen atoms are _____ hydrogen atoms.

Science 21 恆溫動物
Warm-Blooded Animals

R_21.mp3

<u>Mammals</u>, like you and me, are a kind of animal. We are <u>warm-blooded</u>, so our <u>body temperature</u> <u>stays</u> the same. It's the same in a warm or cool <u>environment</u>. Mammals keep their body temperatures the same in different ways. We <u>sweat</u> when we are too warm. Sweat <u>cools down</u> our bodies. Dogs <u>stick out</u> their <u>tongues</u> to cool down. We <u>shiver</u> when we are too cool. That's because it <u>warms up</u> our bodies. Dogs shiver to warm up too. Warming up and cooling down is easy for warm-blooded mammals like us!

哺乳動物 恆溫的 體溫 保持 環境 流汗 使～變涼 伸出～ 舌頭 發抖 變暖

Read and Complete 完成句子

❶ Mammals don't _____ their body temperatures.

❷ People _____ to cool down.

恆溫動物

哺乳動物，就像你和我一樣，是一種動物。我們是恆溫動物，所以我們的體溫會維持一致，無論在溫暖或涼爽的環境中都是一樣的。哺乳動物會以不同的方式來維持體溫一致。當我們太熱時，我們會流汗，汗水會使我們的身體降溫。狗則是會伸出舌頭來降溫。當我們太冷時，我們會發抖，那是因為這樣可以使身體變暖和，狗也會發抖來取暖。對於像我們這樣的恆溫哺乳動物來說，升溫和降溫很容易的！

背景知識 Plus!

狗的平均體溫（body temperature）會因為體型和年齡有差異，據說大約是 38.5°C，比一般人的體溫更高。怕熱的狗會張開嘴吧、伸出舌頭來呼吸，透過蒸發唾液產生的蒸汽來降溫。這時候許多鼻子內的微血管也會交換通過鼻子的空氣和熱量，來降低體溫。

Comprehension Checkup 理解能力確認

Circle the best answer. 圈選出正確的答案

1. What is not an example of a mammal?
   - a fish
   - b dog
   - c human

2. What do humans do when they are cold?
   - a shiver
   - b sleep
   - c sweat

3. What will dogs do in a hot environment?
   - a They will shiver.
   - b They will sweat.
   - c They will stick out their tongues.
   - d They will change their body temperature.

4. What is NOT true about mammals?
   - a They are warm-blooded.
   - b They are a kind of animal.
   - c They keep their body temperatures the same.
   - d They all cool down and warm up the same way.

Complete the sentences. 完成句子

Mammals keep their body temperatures the ❶ ....

People sweat to cool down. Also, they shiver to

❷ .... up.

Wrap Up Fill in the blanks. 總複習，將單字填入空格

How do mammals keep their ❶ .... temperatures?

• to ❷ .... down	▶ They ❸ ....
• to warm up	▶ They ❹ ....

sweat   cool   shiver   body

Communicating with Lights

用燈光溝通

R_22.mp3

How did people <u>communicate</u> before phones and radio? Lights
溝通
helped us communicate over long <u>distances</u>. <u>Flashing</u> a light sent
距離　　　　　　　使閃光
<u>messages</u> as a <u>code</u>. Samuel Morse <u>developed</u> a <u>popular</u> code in the
訊息　　　　密碼　　　　　　　　　發展　　　　受歡迎的
1840s. Morse code uses long and short <u>pulses</u>. A pulse is a flash of
（光波的）脈衝
light or sound. Each letter of the alphabet has its own pulse <u>pattern</u>.
模式
For example, "S" is three short pulses. "O" is three
long pulses. Ships used lights and Morse code to
communicate. <u>Sinking</u> ships would pulse SOS.
沈沒
That means to send help right away!

Read and Complete 完成句子

❶ People communicated over long distances with
_____.

❷ Samuel Morse developed a popular _____ with
pulses.

用燈光溝通

在電話和收音機出現之前，人們是如何溝通的
呢？燈光幫助我們在長距離的情況下溝通，閃爍
的燈光以密碼的形式來傳送訊息。塞繆爾‧摩斯
在 1840 年代開發了一種很受歡迎的的密碼，摩
斯密碼會使用長脈衝和短脈衝，而脈衝指的是燈
光的閃爍或聲音，每個字母都有自己的脈衝模
式。例如，「S」是三個短脈衝，「O」是三個
長脈衝。船隻會使用燈光和摩斯密碼進行溝通，
沉沒的船隻會發出 SOS 的脈衝，意思是立即發
送支援！

背景知識 Plus!

摩斯密碼（Morse code）是一種透
過創造具有長電流和短電流的電報符
號進行通訊的系統，據說韓文的電報代
碼是在 1890 年代創造的。即使在今日
通訊科技的發展，電報碼仍被用作危
急情況下最基本的緊急通訊方式，
而《極限逃生》和《寄生上
流》等電影也有使用電報
密碼的場景。

Comprehension Checkup 理解能力確認

Circle the best answer. 圈選出正確的答案

1. When was Morse code developed?
   - ⓐ recently
   - ⓑ a few years ago
   - ⓒ over 100 years ago

2. What is a pulse?
   - ⓐ a flash of light
   - ⓑ a code with messages
   - ⓒ a pattern of a letter

3. How does a code of each alphabet letter differ?
   (Choose 2 answers.)
   - ⓐ length of pulses
   - ⓑ types of lights
   - ⓒ strength of pulses
   - ⓓ number of pulses

4. Why does the writer mention sinking ships?
   - ⓐ to describe pulses of lights
   - ⓑ to explain how Morse developed codes
   - ⓒ to give an example of using Morse code
   - ⓓ to emphasize some letters of the alphabet

Complete the sentences. 完成句子

> A long time ago, people used lights to ❶ .... over
> long ❷ .... Morse code uses ❸ .... lights
> and we call them pulses. We can send message with pulses.

Wrap Up Fill in the blanks. 總複習，將單字填入空格

Morse Code		long
用途	• to communicate over ❶ .... distances	alphabet
方法	• using a ❷ .... of light as a pulse • making ❸ .... letters with long and short ❹ .... patterns	flash pulse

Designs from Nature

R_23.mp3

Plants and animals are <u>incredible</u>. They have unique <u>features</u> that
難以置信的   特徵
help them <u>survive</u> in their <u>environments</u>. Sometimes scientists use
活下來   環境
natural designs to make useful things. Did you know that <u>Velcro</u> is
魔鬼氈
an <u>invention</u> from nature? In 1941, George de Mestral found <u>burrs</u>
發明   有芒刺的種子殼
in his dog's fur. Burrs are <u>spiky</u> <u>seeds</u> with little <u>hooks</u> at the end.
有尖刺的 種子   鉤
These hooks <u>stick</u> to clothes and hair. George got a great idea from
黏住
the burr's design. He <u>created</u> the first Velcro out of <u>cotton</u>. Velcro
創造   棉花
sticks together and <u>comes apart</u> easily. You've
散開
probably used it on your shoes or bag before!

Read and Complete 完成句子

❶ Natural designs help plants and animals to _____.

❷ Burrs have little spiky _____, so they stick to
   clothes.

來自大自然的設計

植物和動物很不可思議，它們具有獨特的特徵來幫助它們在環境中存活下來。有時候科學家會使用自然的設計來製作出有用的東西。你知道魔鬼氈就是來自大自然的發明嗎？在 1941 年，喬治‧梅斯特拉爾在他的狗的毛中發現了芒刺。芒刺是一種尾端帶有小鉤子的尖刺種子，這些鉤子會黏在衣服和頭髮上。喬治從芒刺的構造中得到很棒的靈感，他用棉花創造出世界上第一個魔鬼氈。魔鬼氈可以輕易地黏在一起和分開。你可能之前在鞋子或包包上就有使用過魔鬼氈了！

背景知識 Plus!

當魔鬼氈（Velcro）剛問世時，據說是由棉花製作而成的，缺點是越常洗滌，鉤子會越延長，黏著力就越差。另外還有一個負面的印象是，人們認為魔鬼氈是用剩下的布料做成的，因此在與拉鍊（zipper）的競爭中落後了。經過研究，魔鬼氈的材料改成尼龍，並用紅外線曬鉤子的部分，就可以達到今日的黏著力。

Comprehension Checkup 理解能力確認

Circle the best answer. 圈選出正確的答案

1. How do scientists use natural designs?
   - ⓐ by creating useful things
   - ⓑ by changing their environment
   - ⓒ by making goods with natural things

2. Where did George de Mestral find burrs?
   - ⓐ on his shoes
   - ⓑ in his clothes
   - ⓒ in his dog's fur

3. What feature of burrs gave Mestral an idea for Velcro?
   - ⓐ It's easy to connect burrs to plastics.
   - ⓑ Burrs' spiky seeds grow fast and easily.
   - ⓒ Burrs' hooks stick and come apart easily.
   - ⓓ Burrs have lots of spiky hooks in the seeds.

4. What is NOT true about Velcro?
   - ⓐ It is in dogs' fur.
   - ⓑ It is a design from nature.
   - ⓒ It sticks and comes apart easily.
   - ⓓ It can be used in shoes and bags.

Complete the sentences. 完成句子

People use natural ❶ .... to make useful things.

❷ .... comes from the ❸ ....'s design.

WrapUp Fill in the blanks. 總複習，將單字填入空格

Burr	Velcro	
• ❶ .... seeds with little hooks	• invented from burr's design	stick
	• ❸ .... together and come apart easily	shoes
• the little hooks stick to clothes and ❷	• used on ❹ .... or bag	spiky
		hair

R_24.mp3

Mena and his father were in the forest outside their <u>village</u> in India.
村莊

They saw <u>hundreds of</u> foxes <u>hanging</u> in the trees. These foxes had
數以百計的～   懸掛

<u>strange</u>, <u>leathery</u> arms. "Father, I'm scared," Mena said. His father
奇怪的   皮質的

smiled and answered, "Those are Indian flying foxes, my son. They

are actually a kind of <u>bat</u>. They are <u>a bit</u> scary because they often
蝙蝠   有點

carry <u>diseases</u>. But they eat only fruit, flowers, and insects. Flying
疾病

foxes also help <u>pollinate</u> flowers by drinking
給～傳播花粉

<u>nectar</u>. So, they are an important
花蜜

part of the environment."

Read and Complete 完成句子

❶ Indian flying foxes live in forests in _____.

❷ Indian flying foxes have strange, _____ arms.

印度狐蝠

梅納和他的父親在印度村莊外的森林裡，他們看到數百隻狐蝠掛在樹上。這些狐蝠有奇怪的皮質雙臂。梅納說：「爸爸，我好害怕。」。梅納的爸爸微笑著回答：「孩子，那些是印度狐蝠，牠們其實是蝙蝠的一種。因為牠們經常傳染疾病，所以有點可怕，但是牠們只吃水果、花和昆蟲。狐蝠也會透過吸取花蜜來幫花朵授粉，因此牠們是環境中很重要的一部分。」

背景知識 Plus!

印度狐蝠（Indian flying fox）也被稱為「大印度果蝠」，因為牠們以香蕉、芒果等水果為主食。主要分佈於印度、孟加拉和西藏。印度狐蝠在吃水果或花蜜的過程中，會負責傳遞和分配花粉和種子。

Circle the best answer. 圈選出正確的答案

1. Where did Mena find Indian flying foxes?
   ⓐ in the trees　　　ⓑ in his village　　　ⓒ near flowers

2. What kind of animal are Indian flying foxes?
   ⓐ a fox　　　ⓑ a bat　　　ⓒ an insect

3. Why are Indian flying foxes dangerous?
   ⓐ They can carry diseases.
   ⓑ They eat helpful insects.
   ⓒ They fly around villages.
   ⓓ They have strange leathery arms.

4. What is NOT true about Indian flying foxes?
   ⓐ They help pollinate flowers.
   ⓑ They eat fruits and drink nectar.
   ⓒ They are bats, but look like foxes.
   ⓓ They scare people to get food.

Complete the sentences. 完成句子

Indian flying foxes are found in India. They may be ❶ .... because they can carry ❷ .... But Indian flying foxes help their environment by ❸ .... flowers.

WrapUp Fill in the blanks. 總複習，將單字填入空格

Indian Flying Foxes		pollinate
身體特徵	have strange, ❶ .... arms	leathery
風險	carry ❷	environment
優點	help ❸ .... flowers ▶ good for the ❹	diseases

I'm a <u>materials</u> <u>engineer</u>. I <u>especially</u> study materials, like wood and
材料　　　工程師　　　　專門
<u>metal</u>. I check to see how well they <u>absorb</u> sound. Sound travels in
金屬　　　　　　　　　　　　　吸收
<u>waves</u>. Sound waves can get absorbed by a material or <u>go through</u>
波　　　　　　　　　　　　　　　　　　　　　　　　　　　　　　通過
it. Soft materials, like <u>fabric</u>, sponge, or <u>cardboard</u>, absorb sounds
布料　　　　　　硬紙板
well. Builders put these materials inside walls to <u>stop sound from</u>
阻止～做～
<u>traveling</u>. Hard materials, like wood or
glass, don't absorb sound well. The sound
waves usually <u>bounce off</u> these materials.
彈出
Builders also use these hard materials to
<u>block sound from entering</u> an area.
阻止～做～

Read and Complete 完成句子

❶ Soft materials _____ sound from traveling.

❷ _____ materials don't absorb sounds well.

聲音的傳播

我是一名材料工程師，我專門研究材料，像是木
頭和金屬。我會檢查這些材料吸收聲音的能力。
聲音是以波的形式傳播，聲波能夠被材料吸收或
穿透過去。柔軟的材料，像是布料、海綿或紙
板，可以充分吸收聲音。建築工人會將這些材料
放在牆壁內，來阻止聲音傳播。硬質材料，像是
木頭或玻璃，不能充分吸收聲音，聲波通常會在
這些材料中反彈，因此建築工人也會用這些硬質
材料來阻止聲音進入某個區域。

背景知識 Plus!

據說柔軟的材料和有小孔的材料在
建築中最常用於吸音，這個原理是在
孔內空氣因為聲波而震動，產生摩擦，
聲音能量轉化成熱能，被材料吸收。
現在你就知道，為什麼在電影院的地
板和牆壁上有地毯材料的原因了
吧？

Comprehension Checkup 理解能力確認

Circle the best answer. 圈選出正確的答案

1. Which material absorbs sound well?
   - ⓐ wood
   - ⓑ glass
   - ⓒ sponge

2. How does sound travel?
   - ⓐ in waves
   - ⓑ in materials
   - ⓒ by bouncing

3. How do builders make walls to be <u>soundproof</u>? 隔音的
   - ⓐ They make walls with soft materials.
   - ⓑ They put soft materials inside walls.
   - ⓒ They make thicker and higher walls.
   - ⓓ They cover walls with fabric or cardboard.

4. What is NOT true about sound waves?
   - ⓐ They bounce off hard materials.
   - ⓑ They can get absorbed by fabrics.
   - ⓒ They go through soft materials.
   - ⓓ Sometimes they are stopped from traveling.

Complete the sentences. 完成句子

Sound travels in ❶ .... Soft materials ❷ .... sound well.
On the other hand, sound waves ❸ .... off hard materials.

Wrap Up Fill in the blanks. 總複習，將單字填入空格

Sound Travels

分類	種類	聲音的移動
• ❶ .... materials	▸ fabric, sponge, cardboard	▸ ❸ .... sounds well
• ❷ .... materials	▸ wood, metal, glass	▸ sound waves ❹ .... off these materials

absorb   hard   bounce   soft

WORD REVIEW

Crossword Puzzle 填字遊戲

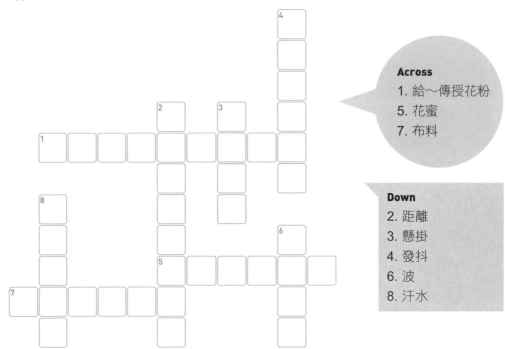

Across
1. 給～傳授花粉
5. 花蜜
7. 布料

Down
2. 距離
3. 懸掛
4. 發抖
6. 波
8. 汗水

Match with the correct definition. 將單字連到正確的意思

1. absorb •

2. burr •

3. pulse •

4. warm-blooded •

ⓐ a flash of light or sound

ⓑ having a warm body temperature that is not changing

ⓒ a spiky seed with little hooks at the end

ⓓ to take in sound and not allow it to bounce off

Fill in the blank with the correct words.
將正確的單字填入空格中

> diseases   environment   materials   sinking   survive

1. Mammals' body temperatures are the same in a warm or cool
   _____.　恆溫動物的體溫在溫暖或涼爽的環境都保持不變。

2. _____ ships would pulse SOS to say "Send help right
   away!"　沉沒的船隻會發出 SOS 的脈衝，意思是「立即發送支援！」

3. Natural designs help plants and animals _____ in their
   environments.　自然的設計幫助植物和動物在環境中生存。

4. Indian flying foxes are a bit scary because they often carry
   _____.　印度狐蝠有點可怕，因為牠們經常帶有疾病。

5. I especially study _____, like wood and metal.
   我專門研究材料，像是木頭和金屬。

Fill in the blank with the correct expressions.
將正確的表達填入空格中

> cool down   go through   hundreds of   stick to   stop ~ from

1. Dogs stick out their tongues to _____.

2. Burrs' hooks easily _____ clothes and hair.

3. Mena saw _____ foxes hanging in the
   trees in the forest.

4. Sound waves can get absorbed by a material or _____
   _____ it.

5. Builders put soft materials inside walls to _____
   sound _____ traveling.

Bees are <u>disappearing</u>. Their <u>colonies</u> are <u>collapsing</u>. Scientists
消失　　　　　生物群　　　瓦解
think that <u>pesticides</u> are killing <u>millions of</u> bees each year. Farmers
殺蟲劑　　　　數百萬～
use pesticides on food crops to <u>keep insects away</u>. Pesticides are
避免～靠近
<u>poisonous</u>, and bees are <u>contacting</u> them. They <u>weaken</u> the bees so
有毒的　　　　　接觸　　　　　使～虛弱
diseases <u>harm</u> them. Also, pesticides <u>affect</u> the brains of the bees.
傷害　　　　　　影響
This causes them to <u>get lost</u> while looking for nectar. When bees
迷路
travel for nectar, they help pollinate crops. Bees cannot
survive alone, and humans wouldn't have very
much to eat without bees. We should change
how we farm or bees might disappear.

Read and Complete 完成句子

❶ Bee ＿＿＿＿＿＿ are disappearing.

❷ Pesticides are ＿＿＿＿＿＿ millions of bees.

以後沒有蜜蜂了嗎？

蜜蜂正在消失，蜂群正在瓦解。科學家認為，殺蟲劑每年都會殺死數百萬隻蜜蜂。農夫在農作物上使用殺蟲劑來驅蟲，但殺蟲劑有毒，而蜜蜂會接觸到殺蟲劑。殺蟲劑使蜜蜂變虛弱，讓蜜蜂生病。此外，殺蟲劑會影響蜜蜂的大腦，這導致蜜蜂在尋找花蜜時會迷路。當蜜蜂去尋找花蜜時，就是在幫助農作物授粉。蜜蜂無法獨自生存，而沒有蜜蜂的話，人類就沒有很多食物可以吃。我們應該要改變我們耕作的方式，否則蜜蜂可能會消失。

背景知識 Plus!

當一隻蜜蜂找到有蜂蜜的地方，牠要怎麼回去告訴其他同伴呢？蜜蜂會透過舞蹈來溝通。如果蜂蜜在離蜂巢10 公尺的範圍內，蜜蜂會繞一圈；如果超過 100 公尺，蜜蜂則會跳八字舞。而舞蹈的速度和持續時間也會顯示出蜂蜜的豐富程度。

Comprehension Checkup 理解能力確認

Circle the best answer. 圈選出正確的答案

1. What do farmers use to protect their crops?
   ⓐ colonies   ⓑ insects   ⓒ pesticides

2. What harms bees?
   ⓐ crops   ⓑ nectar   ⓒ diseases

3. How do pesticides affect bees?
   ⓐ Pesticides remove their food crops.
   ⓑ Pesticides make them stop eating.
   ⓒ Pesticides weaken them and get sick.
   ⓓ Pesticides cause them to contact dangerous crops.

4. What can be inferred from the passage?
   ⓐ Humans should raise more bees.
   ⓑ Bees play important roles in producing crops.
   ⓒ Bees are stealing lots of nectar from humans.
   ⓓ Humans have no choice but to use pesticides.

Complete the sentences. 完成句子

Pesticides are ❶ .... and make bees get sick. They ❷ .... brains of bees. Then, bees have a hard time to look for ❸ .... Humans must change how they farm.

WrapUp Fill in the blanks. 總複習，將單字填入空格

Disappearing Bees	brains
Farmers use ❶ .... pesticides.	contact
▶ Bees ❷ .... them and become sick.	
▶ The pesticides affect their ❸	poisonous
▶ It's hard for them to find ❹ ...., and they cannot survive.	nectar

We live on the Earth's <u>crust</u>, but it is really hot <u>underneath</u>. Under
　　　　　　　　　　　地殼　　　　　　　　　　　　在～下面
the crust is the <u>mantle</u>. The mantle <u>is made up of</u> hot, red rocks.
　　　　　　　　地函　　　　　　　　　由～組成
We <u>call it magma</u>. This <u>magma</u> sometimes comes to the <u>surface</u>.
　　將～稱呼為～　　　　岩漿　　　　　　　　　　　　表面
Magma can <u>erupt</u> from <u>volcanoes</u>! We call it <u>lava</u>. Lava can only
　　　　　噴發　　　　火山　　　　　　　　熔岩
erupt from <u>active volcanoes</u>. There are over
　　　　　活火山
1,900 active volcanoes on Earth! There are

also volcanoes that are not active. They

won't erupt for a long time. The other

volcanoes are <u>extinct volcanoes</u>, and
　　　　　死火山
they will never erupt again.

Read and Complete 完成句子

❶ It's very hot underneath the Earth's _____.

❷ Magma comes to the surface, and we call it _____.

爆炸性的事實！

我們生活在地球的地殼上，但地殼的下面非常炎
熱。地殼下面是地函，而地函是由熾熱的紅色岩
石所組成的，我們將它稱為岩漿。這種岩漿有時
會噴出地表，岩漿也有可能從火山中噴發出來！
我們將它稱為熔岩，而熔岩只能從活火山噴發。
地球上有超過 1,900 座活火山！也有不活躍的火
山，它們在很長一段時間內都不會噴發。其他的
火山則是死火山，永遠都不會再噴發。

背景知識 Plus!

有可能爆發，但在一定期間內維持
休眠狀態的火山，稱為休火山。那麼
韓國的白頭山和漢拏山是被劃分為活火
山、死火山還是休火山？令人驚訝的
是，白頭山和漢拏山都是休火山，這
是因為它們的地殼下仍然存在著
岩漿。

🐧 Circle the best answer. 圈選出正確的答案

1. What is under the Earth's surface called?
   - ⓐ crust
   - ⓑ mantle
   - ⓒ volcanoes

2. What is magma made of?
   - ⓐ lava
   - ⓑ crust
   - ⓒ hot rocks

3. What happens when a volcano erupts?
   - ⓐ It becomes extinct.
   - ⓑ Lava erupts to the surface.
   - ⓒ The mantle becomes cold.
   - ⓓ The Earth's surface becomes two pieces.

4. What is NOT true about volcanoes?
   - ⓐ Active volcanoes produce lava.
   - ⓑ Extinct volcanoes are unable to erupt again.
   - ⓒ Some volcanoes won't erupt for a long time.
   - ⓓ Over 1,900 volcanoes will be extinct soon.

🐴 Complete the sentences. 完成句子

❶ .... erupt when magma under the crust comes out.
We call magma on the surface ❷ .... It only comes
out of ❸ .... volcanoes.

Wrap Up Fill in the blanks. 總複習，將單字填入空格

Volcanoes

active volcanoes	❷ .... volcanoes	volcanoes not
magma erupts and becomes ❶	never erupt ❸	❹ .... for a long time

| lava | active | extinct | again |

奇蹟的洞穴！
Cave of Wonders!

R_28.mp3

Caves are dark and mysterious. They are large, natural holes leading
　　洞穴　　　　　　神秘的　　　　　　　自然的　洞
into Earth's surface. They are big enough for people and animals to
　　　　　　　　　　　　　足夠的
enter and live. How were these large caves made? Most were formed
　　　　　　　　　　　　　　　　　　　　　　　　　　　形成
by erosion. Erosion happens when the acid in water wears away
　　侵蝕　　　　　　　　　　　　酸的　　　　磨損
rock. It can take millions of years for rock to

erode. Son Doong in Vietnam is the largest
侵蝕　　　　　　越南
cave in the world. It's over 2 million years

old. It is much bigger than scientists first

thought. It's about 9 kilometers long!

Read and Complete 完成句子

❶ Caves are large _____ leading into Earth's

surface.

❷ Caves are formed by _____.

奇蹟的洞穴！

洞穴既陰暗又神祕，它們是通向地球表面的大型
天然孔洞，並且大到足以讓人類和動物進入並在
裡面生活。這些大洞穴是如何形成的呢？大多數
是透過侵蝕作用所形成的。水中的酸性物質磨損
岩石時，就會發生侵蝕，岩石的侵蝕可能會花數
百萬年的時間。越南的山水洞是世界上最大的洞
穴，有超過兩百萬年的歷史。山水洞比科學家們
一開始想的還要大很多，總長約 9 公里！

背景知識 Plus!

世界上最深的洞穴是黑海附近的庫
魯柏亞拉洞穴（Krubera），有 2,197
公尺深。世界上最大的冰洞是奧地利的
冰洞（Eisriesenwelt），原本是一個
天然的石灰岩洞穴，但它位於海拔
1,500 公尺的區域，因此洞穴裡
的水結凍，形成一個冰洞。

Circle the best answer. 圈選出正確的答案

1. What caused erosion?
   ⓐ acid in water   ⓑ rocks in water   ⓒ animals in caves

2. How long is the largest cave in the world?
   ⓐ about 2 kilometers long   ⓑ about 9 kilometers long
   ⓒ about 10 kilometers long

3. Why does the writer mention people and animals?
   ⓐ to explain how caves are formed
   ⓑ to emphasize how big some caves are
   ⓒ to give an example of a famous cave
   ⓓ to complain some caves were damaged

4. What is NOT true about Son Doong?
   ⓐ We can find it in Vietnam.
   ⓑ It's over 2 million years old.
   ⓒ It's the largest cave in the world.
   ⓓ It's much older than scientists first thought.

Complete the sentences. 完成句子

> Caves are large holes in Earth's ❶ .... Erosion
> causes them. ❷ .... in water ❸ .... away
> rock over millions of years.

Wrap Up Fill in the blanks. 總複習，將單字填入空格

Caves		acid
定義	❶ ...., natural ❷ .... leading into Earth's surface	erosion
如何形成	The ❸ .... in water wears away rocks. ▶ ❹ .... happens over millions of years.	holes
最大的洞穴	Son Doong in Vietnam	large

From Birth to Death

R_29.mp3

All <u>living things</u> on Earth have a <u>life cycle</u>. This cycle always <u>includes</u>
生物   生命週期   包括
<u>birth</u> and death. Each living thing has a <u>unique</u> cycle between being
出生   獨特的
born and dying. For example, butterflies start as an egg. Then, the
egg <u>hatches</u> and a <u>larva</u> is born. It eats and grows into a <u>caterpillar</u>.
     （蛋）孵化   幼蟲   毛蟲
But it's still in the larva <u>stage</u>. Next, it builds a hard <u>protective</u>
                          階段   保護的
<u>shell</u> around itself. It's a <u>pupa</u>. After 10 to 14 days, an
殼   蛹
adult butterfly hatches from the shell. The
butterfly then <u>lays</u> eggs before it dies,
              產卵
and the cycle begins again!

Read and Complete 完成句子

❶ A butterfly starts its life cycle as an _____.

❷ A caterpillar builds a protective _____ and
becomes a pupa.

從出生到死亡

地球上的所有生物都有一個生命週期，這個週期
包括出生和死亡。而每個生物從出生到死亡之
間，都有獨特的週期。例如，蝴蝶一開始是一顆
卵，接著在卵孵化後，幼蟲出生。幼蟲會進食，
並成長為毛毛蟲，但牠仍處於幼蟲階段。接下
來，牠會在自己的周圍建立一個堅硬的保護殼，
也就是蛹。在 10 到 14 天後，一隻成年的蝴蝶
就會從殼中孵化。接著蝴蝶在死亡前會產卵，而
週期會再度開始了！

背景知識 Plus!

蟬是具有獨特生命週期
（life cycle）的代表性生物。雌蟬會
在樹皮上產卵，一年後孵化，孵化出來
的幼蟲進入地底下，吃樹根的汁液，
牠們在地底下生活了大約 5 年。之
後，爬到地上、脫皮、曬乾身
體，然後靠在樹上，大聲蟬
叫尋找配偶。

Comprehension Checkup 理解能力確認

Circle the best answer. 圈選出正確的答案

1. What is the next step after an egg of a butterfly?
   - ⓐ a pupa
   - ⓑ a larva
   - ⓒ an adult butterfly

2. What hatches from the protective shell?
   - ⓐ an egg
   - ⓑ a caterpillar
   - ⓒ an adult butterfly

3. How does the life cycle of butterflies start again?
   - ⓐ A butterfly eats as much food as it can.
   - ⓑ A butterfly teaches its babies to get food.
   - ⓒ A butterfly lays eggs before it dies.
   - ⓓ A butterfly becomes a caterpillar again after it dies.

4. What is NOT true about the life cycle of butterflies?
   - ⓐ A pupa has a hard protective shell.
   - ⓑ A caterpillar is in the larva stage.
   - ⓒ It starts with being born and ends with dying.
   - ⓓ A caterpillar looks almost the same as an adult butterfly.

Complete the sentences. 完成句子

A life cycle begins with ❶ .... and ends with
❷ .... Different living things have ❸ ....
life cycles between beginning and end.

Wrap Up Fill in the blanks. 總複習，將單字填入空格

The Life Cycle of Butterflies

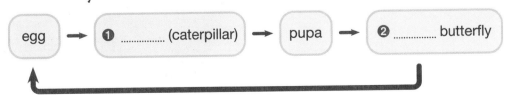

egg → ❶ .... (caterpillar) → pupa → ❷ .... butterfly

We use <u>electricity</u> for our computers and lights. That electricity is
電
<u>generated</u> in <u>power plants</u>. Often, power plants use and burn
產生   發電廠
<u>non-renewable</u> <u>sources</u> like <u>coal</u>, oil, or gas for energy. That's
不可再生的   來源   煤
because they're easy to get and use. But most non-renewable sources
generate air and water <u>pollution</u>. Also, they will <u>run out</u> someday.
汙染   耗盡
These days, scientists are <u>improving</u> <u>renewable</u> energy sources. <u>Solar</u>
改進   可再生的   太陽的
energy comes from the sun, so it's renewable.

<u>Wind power</u> and <u>hydrogen</u> energy are also
風力發電   氫
renewable energy sources. They <u>produce</u>
製造
almost no pollution and will never run out.

Read and Complete 完成句子

❶ Power plants generate _____.

❷ Wind power is a _____ energy source.

能源的來源

我們的電腦和電燈都要用電，而電力是由發電廠
所產生的。通常，發電廠使用和燃燒像是煤炭、
石油或天然氣等非再生資源當作能源，那是因為
這些資源很容易取得及使用。但大多數非再生資
源會造成空氣汙染和水污染，而且它們將來有一
天會耗盡。當今，科學家們正在改進可再生能
源。太陽能來自於太陽，所以它是可再生能源。
風力發電和氫能源也是可再生能源。這些資源幾
乎不會有污染，而且也永遠不會耗盡。

背景知識 Plus!

我們丟棄的垃圾可以變成可再生能
源，能夠將廢料轉化成能源。從商業
場所和家庭產生的可燃垃圾中，將能量
高的廢棄物透過多種加工處理方法製
成固體燃料、液體燃料和氣體燃料。

Comprehension Checkup 理解能力確認

Circle the best answer. 圈選出正確的答案

1. What is an example of a non-renewable source?
   ⓐ sun ⓑ coal ⓒ wind

2. Which energy source doesn't generate pollution?
   ⓐ oil ⓑ gas ⓒ hydrogen

3. Why do power plants often use non-renewable energy sources?
   ⓐ Because they are easy to use.
   ⓑ Because they will run out soon.
   ⓒ Because they generate air pollution.
   ⓓ Because they generate water pollution.

4. What is NOT true about renewable energy sources?
   ⓐ They will not run out. ⓑ They are made in plants.
   ⓒ They generate electricity. ⓓ They don't produce pollution.

Complete the sentences. 完成句子

Coal, oil, and gas are ❶ .... energy sources. They are easy to use but generate ❷ .... Renewable energy from the sun, wind, or ❸ .... are improving.

Wrap Up Fill in the blanks. 總複習，將單字填入空格

	non-renewable sources	renewable sources
例子	• coal, oil, and gas	• ❸ .... and hydrogen energy, wind power
汙染	• generate air and water ❶	• no pollution
特性	• easy to get and ❷ .... • run out someday	• ❹ .... run out

use   never   solar   pollution

能源的來源 85

WORD REVIEW

Crossword Puzzle 填字遊戲

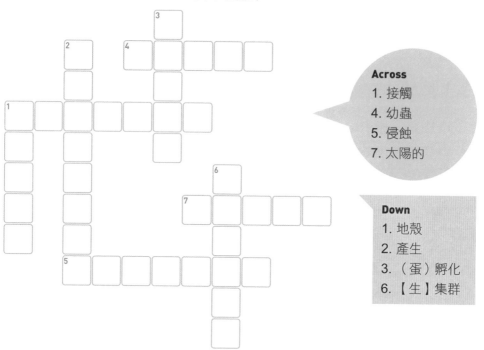

Across
1. 接觸
4. 幼蟲
5. 侵蝕
7. 太陽的

Down
1. 地殼
2. 產生
3. （蛋）孵化
6. 【生】集群

Match with the correct definition. 將單字連到正確的意思

1. cave •

       (a) Farmers use it on food crops to keep insects away.

2. lava •

       (b) When magma comes to the surface, magma turns into it.

3. pesticide •

       (c) a large, natural hole leading into Earth's surface

4. pupa •

       (d) a butterfly in the stage between larva and adult

Fill in the blank with the correct words.
將正確的單字填入空格中

| erode | erupt | life cycle | non-renewable | pollution |

1. Lava can only _____ from active volcanoes.
   岩漿只能從活火山噴發。

2. It can take millions of years for rock to _____.
   岩石的侵蝕作用可能需要花費數百萬年的時間。

3. The butterfly lays eggs before it dies, and the _____ begins again.
   蝴蝶在死亡之前會產下卵，然後生命週期又會重新開始。

4. Often, power plants burn _____ sources like coal or gas for energy.
   通常，發電廠會燃燒非再生資源作為能源。

5. Wind power and hydrogen energy produce almost no _____.   風力發電和氫能幾乎不會造成汙染。

Fill in the blank with the correct expressions.
將正確的表達填入空格中

| hatches from | is made up of | get lost | run out | wears away |

1. Pesticides cause bees to _____ while looking for nectar.

2. The mantle _____ hot, red rocks.

3. Erosion happens when the acid in water _____ rock.

4. After 10 to 14 days, an adult butterfly _____ the shell.

5. Renewable energy sources will never _____.

Welcome to the Jungle

R_31.mp3

We <u>breathe</u> in <u>oxygen</u> and breathe out <u>carbon dioxide</u>. Around 40%
呼吸　　　氧氣　　　　　　　　　　二氧化碳
of Earth's oxygen comes from <u>rainforests</u>. You can find rainforests
熱帶雨林
near the <u>equator</u>. The equator is a line. It goes around <u>the middle of</u>
赤道　　　　　　　　　　　　　　　　　　　　　　～的中間
the Earth. Rainforests have a warm and <u>wet</u> <u>environment</u>. Plants
潮濕的　　環境
grow well there. In rainforests, <u>billions of</u> plants produce oxygen
數十億的～
and <u>consume</u> carbon dioxide. This helps keep
消耗
oxygen and carbon dioxide in balance.

This <u>balance</u> is important for plant and
平衡
animal life on Earth. We can't breathe
with too much or too little oxygen.

Read and Complete 完成句子

❶ Rainforests produce a lot of _____.

❷ The _____ goes around the middle of the Earth.

歡迎來到叢林

我們吸入氧氣，呼出二氧化碳。地球上大約有
40% 的氧氣來自熱帶雨林，你可以在赤道附近
找到熱帶雨林。赤道是一條線，環繞著地球的中
間，熱帶雨林的環境溫暖又潮濕，植物在那裡生
長得很好。在熱帶雨林中，數十億株的植物製造
氧氣並消耗二氧化碳，這有助於保持氧氣和二氧
化碳的平衡，這種平衡對地球上動植物的生命很
重要。氧氣若過多或過少，我們就不能呼吸。

背景知識 Plus!

亞馬遜熱帶雨林（rainforest）占
世界雨林的 40%，產生四分之一地球
所需的氧氣。自從 1960 年代以來，巴
西不斷通過開發政策，破壞了亞馬遜
的森林，據說每年約有韓國面積五分
之四的雨林正在消失，亞馬遜雨
林正面臨氣候變遷和森林砍
伐的危機。

Comprehension Checkup 理解能力確認

Circle the best answer. 圈選出正確的答案

1. Where are most rainforests located?
   - ⓐ under the equator
   - ⓑ around the equator
   - ⓒ in the middle of the equator

2. What do plants consume?
   - ⓐ carbon dioxide
   - ⓑ oxygen
   - ⓒ oxygen and carbon dioxide

3. Why is the balance of oxygen and carbon dioxide important?
   - ⓐ Because plants can't grow with too much oxygen.
   - ⓑ Because people can't mix oxygen and carbon dioxide.
   - ⓒ Because people can't grow with too little carbon dioxide.
   - ⓓ Because people can't breathe if the balance is lost.

4. What is NOT true about rainforests?
   - ⓐ They have lots of plants.
   - ⓑ They are in warm and wet places.
   - ⓒ They produce 40% of Earth's carbon dioxide.
   - ⓓ They are important for life on Earth.

Complete the sentences. 完成句子

❶ .... are near the equator. They help the ❷ .... of carbon dioxide and oxygen in the air. This balance is important for life on ❸ ....

Wrap Up Fill in the blanks. 總複習，將單字填入空格中

Rainforests		balance
地點	near the ❶	
氣候	Warm and ❷ .... environment makes ❸ .... grow well.	plants
環境作用	They keep oxygen and carbon dioxide in ❹	equator
		wet

Coyotes are very adaptive to their environment. In North America,
郊狼   適應的   北美洲

wolves and coyotes competed for food and territory. Wolves often
                    競爭   領土

killed people and farm animals. So, they were hunted to near

extinction. This caused the coyote population to grow and expand
絕種   動物的總數   擴展

in the last 200 years. They even expanded into northern Canada and

Alaska. The harsh, cold environment forced the coyotes
阿拉斯加   嚴酷的   迫使～

to adapt. Their fur color slowly changed to white. It let
適應

them hide better in the snow. Their fur also became

thicker to protect them from the harsh cold.

Read and Complete 完成句子

❶ The coyote _____ began
   to grow as wolves disappeared.

❷ Coyotes were forced to _____ in the cold environment.

北極的郊狼

郊狼很能適應環境。在北美洲，狼和郊狼會競爭
食物和領地，狼經常殺害人類和農場的動物，因
此牠們被獵殺到瀕臨絕種的程度，這也造成郊狼
的總數在過去兩百年裡不斷成長並擴大，牠們甚
至擴展到加拿大北部和阿拉斯加。郊狼被迫要去
適應嚴酷、寒冷的環境，而牠們的毛色慢慢改變
成白色，這讓牠們可以在雪地裡隱藏得更好。而
牠們的皮毛也變得更厚，以保護牠們免受嚴寒。

背景知識 Plus!

在美洲原住民之間，郊狼
（coyote）和獾之間的特殊友誼非常
知名，據說郊狼和獾會一起捕食。一般
而言，獾會挖嚙齒動物等小型哺乳動
物的地下洞穴，當獵物出現在地面上
時，郊狼會配合獾捕捉牠。和單
獨狩獵相比，這種狩獵方式
節省了時間和體力消
耗。

Circle the best answer. 圈選出正確的答案

1. What did wolves and coyotes fight for?
   a areas to live   **b** places with snow   **c** people to live with

2. Where did the coyotes expand into?
   a Alaska   **b** Europe   **c** North America

3. Why did people hunt wolves?
   a Because wolves killed coyotes.
   b Because wolves killed farm animals.
   c Because wolves stole food from people.
   d Because people wanted to get their fur.

4. How did coyotes adapt to the harsh environment?
   (Choose 2 answers.)
   a Their fur got thicker to keep them warm.
   b They began to attack farms to find food.
   c They went north to expand their territory.
   d Their fur changed to a different color.

Complete the sentences. 完成句子

Coyotes and wolves competed, but people hunted ❶ ....
.... So, the coyote population grew quickly. Coyotes even
❷ .... into the Alaska. They were able to ❸ ....
.... to their new environment.

Wrap Up   Number the sentences in order. 寫出句子的順序

3️⃣ The coyote population expanded into northern Canada and Alaska.

⬜ Wolves and coyotes competed for food and territory.

⬜ Coyotes adapted to the cold environment.

⬜ Wolves were hunted to near extinction.

Powerful Flash Floods

R_33.mp3

<u>Natural disasters</u> (自然災害) can happen suddenly and <u>unexpectedly</u> (意外地).
<u>Flash floods</u> (暴洪) are one type of disaster. A flash flood is when <u>water levels</u> (水平面) <u>rise</u> (上升) within six hours of <u>rainfall</u>. <u>Heavy rains</u> (降雨) (暴雨) or a broken dam <u>raise</u> (提升) the water level of rivers or <u>streams</u> (溪流). The rising water moves powerfully and quickly over land. It causes <u>damage</u> (損害) to <u>property</u> (財產). And it can be <u>deadly</u> (致命的) to people. In 2013, a flood in Kedarnath, India killed around 5,000 people!

Local <u>weather warnings</u> (天氣警報) can help you avoid these disasters. They can also tell you when to get to higher ground.

Read and Complete 完成句子

1 Flash floods are a natural _____.

2 During a flash flood, water levels _____ suddenly.

強大的山洪暴發

自然災害可能會在突然和出乎意料的情況下發生，而山洪暴發是一種災害。山洪暴發指的是，在降雨後，水位在六小時內上升，暴雨或損壞的水壩提高河流或溪流的水平面。上漲的水在陸地上強大、快速地移動，不只會造成財產損失，也可能會使人致命。在 2013 年，印度凱達爾納特的一場山洪暴發造成大約五千人喪生！當地的天氣警報可以幫助人們避免這些災害，也可以告訴人們什麼時候該往更高處的地面去。

背景知識 Plus!

在 2020 年 1 月，破紀錄的大雨造成印尼雅加達附近發生洪災。40% 的地區被淹沒，大約四十萬人被迫被疏散。印尼當局表示，該地區非法開鑿水井造成地基變弱，容易受到洪水侵襲。自然災害會因為人類的貪婪而變得更嚴重嗎？

Circle the best answer. 圈選出正確的答案

1. What is a sign of a flash flood?
   - ⓐ any rainfall
   - ⓑ high water levels
   - ⓒ property damage

2. What can be helpful for people to avoid natural disasters?
   - ⓐ closing dams
   - ⓑ making long streams
   - ⓒ watching weather reports

3. What is NOT true about flash floods?
   - ⓐ They destroy people's property.
   - ⓑ Broken dams or heavy rain can cause floods.
   - ⓒ We can prevent them in advance.
   - ⓓ People should find higher ground when it happens.

4. Why does the writer mention a flood in Kedarnath?
   - ⓐ to explain where flash floods happen often
   - ⓑ to describe an example of a deadly flash flood
   - ⓒ to emphasize the importance of weather warnings
   - ⓓ to give an example of the most sudden flash flood

Complete the sentences. 完成句子

> Natural disasters like ❶ .... floods can be deadly.
> During a flash flood, ❷ .... levels rise unexpectedly.
> People should watch weather ❸ .... when floods happen.

Wrap Up Fill in the blanks. 總複習，將單字填入空格

Flash Floods		six
發生條件	• water ❶ .... rise within ❷ .... hours of rainfall	dam
造成水平面上升	• heavy rains or a broken ❸	levels
結果	• cause ❹ .... to property • can be deadly to people	damage

Iron is a strong metal. People can shape it into useful things such as
鐵   塑造   有用的
weapons and tools. People have used it for thousands of years. But,
武器   工具
iron has a serious weakness. It can rust and decay, or break apart.
        嚴重的 弱點   生鏽   腐朽   裂開
Water and air cause a chemical reaction
                  化學的   反應
with iron. This reaction creates rust.

Rust can make an iron tool useless. An
                              無用的
iron tool outside in the rain will rust in
a few days. To protect iron from rust,
          保護
you can cover it with paint or oil.

Read and Complete 完成句子

❶ People make lots of useful things with _____.

❷ Iron tools can be useless when they _____ and
  decay.

水和鐵

鐵是一種堅固的金屬，人們可以將它塑造成有用的東西，像是武器和工具。人們已經使用鐵幾千年了，但是鐵有一項嚴重的缺點，就是鐵可能會生鏽、腐朽或斷裂。水和空氣會與鐵產生化學反應，這種反應使鐵生鏽，而生鏽會讓鐵製工具失去作用。把一個鐵製工具放在室外淋雨，過幾天就會生鏽。為了防止鐵生鏽，可以用油漆或油覆蓋在鐵的表面上。

背景知識 Plus!

當鐵製的（iron）物品生鏽時，有幾種簡單的方法可以去除生鏽。最簡單的方法是將生鏽的物體浸泡在醋裡，或者用浸泡過醋的布擦拭生鏽的地方。在生鏽的地方撒上大量的鹽，然後用萊姆或檸檬皮擦拭也是一個好方法。或者在生鏽的地方撒上大量的小蘇打，然後倒入水、並放置一段時間後，再擦拭乾淨。

Circle the best answer. 圈選出正確的答案

1. What is the weakness of iron?
   ⓐ rusting　　　　ⓑ melting　　　　ⓒ bending

2. A chemical reaction between what things makes rust?
   ⓐ oil and iron　　　ⓑ water and air　　　ⓒ water and iron

3. How can you prevent iron from decaying?
   ⓐ by painting it with oil　　　ⓑ by leaving it in the rain
   ⓒ by placing it in a box　　　ⓓ by covering it with cardboard

4. What is NOT a feature of iron?
   ⓐ It is a strong metal.
   ⓑ It rusts as soon as it meets rain.
   ⓒ It is a good material for weapons.
   ⓓ It can be shaped into useful tools.

Complete the sentences. 完成句子

Iron is a strong metal and people ❶ .... it into weapons and tools. Water and ❷ .... can cause it to rust. In order to ❸ .... iron from decay, it's good to cover it with paint or oil.

Wrap Up　Fill in the blanks. 總複習，將單字填入空格

Iron has a serious weakness.

原因	a chemical ❶ .... with ❷ .... and air
結果	It can ❸ .... and decay, or break apart.
保護方法	You can ❹ .... it with paint or oil.

rust　　cover　　reaction　　water

瀕臨絕種的北極熊

Endangered Polar Bears

R_35.mp3

Humans are changing the environment. As our population grows and expands, we are <u>destroying</u> the <u>habitats</u> of several animals. Some
破壞　　　　　棲息地
animals fail to adapt to their changed habitats. Then, they become <u>endangered</u>. <u>Polar bears</u> are adapted to live in <u>the Arctic</u>. Their
瀕臨絕種的　　北極熊　　　　　　　　　　　　　　　　北極地區
white fur keeps them warm and <u>hidden</u>. They <u>are good at</u> hunting
隱藏的　　　　　擅長～
<u>seals</u> and <u>whales</u> in Arctic waters. However,
海豹　　鯨魚
<u>global warming</u> is <u>melting</u> the Arctic ice.
全球暖化　　　融化
Polar bears' habitats are <u>shrinking</u> and
縮小
disappearing. They cannot survive south of
the Arctic. Soon, they may only live in zoos.

Read and Complete 完成句子

❶ Humans are destroying animals' _____.

❷ Polar bears are one of the _____ animals.

瀕臨絕種的北極熊

人類正在改變環境，隨著人口的增加和擴大，我們正在破壞一些動物的棲息地。有些動物無法適應牠們被改變的棲息地，接著牠們就成了瀕臨絕種的動物。北極熊適應生活於北極地區，牠們的白色皮毛使它們保持溫暖並隱藏起來。牠們擅長在北極海域獵捕海豹和鯨魚，然而全球暖化正在融化北極的冰層，北極熊的棲息地正在縮小和消失，牠們無法在北極以南的地區存活。在不久之後，牠們很有可能只能生活在動物園裡。

背景知識 Plus!

北極（the Arctic）的冰是由凍結海水所形成的「海冰」，據說它的融化速度是普通冰的兩倍。由於最近氣溫升高，北極的冰層正在消失。也因為如此，隨著海獅從一個棲息地遷徙到另一個棲息地，北極熊失去食物來源，使得在北極地區生存變得越來越困難。

Circle the best answer. 圈選出正確的答案

1. What makes the Arctic ice melt?
   a building zoos   **b** global warming   **c** endangered seals

2. What is happening to the polar bears' habitats?
   a They're decreasing.   **b** They're getting cold.
   c Seals and whales are dying.

3. What is NOT an example of polar bears adapting to the Arctic?
   a They can be in cold waters.
   b They hunt seals and whales.
   c They can move to the south.
   d Their white fur helps them hide.

4. What can be inferred from the passage?
   a Humans are the main factor of global warming.
   b Humans are hunting polar bears to keep in zoos.
   c South of the Arctic is too narrow for polar bears to live.
   d Many people are visiting the Arctic to see polar bears.

Complete the sentences. 完成句子

Animal habitats are changing because of ❶ .... Polar bears live in the Arctic. But global warming is ❷ .... the Arctic ice. Polar bears' habitats are shrinking and ❸ ....

Wrap Up   Fill in the blanks. 總複習，將單字填入空格

原因	• Humans change the ❶ .... • We are destroying the habitats of ❷	animals habitats
結果	• Global ❸ .... is melting the Arctic ice. • Polar bears' ❹ .... are disappearing.	warning environment

WORD REVIEW

🧑 Crossword Puzzle 填字遊戲

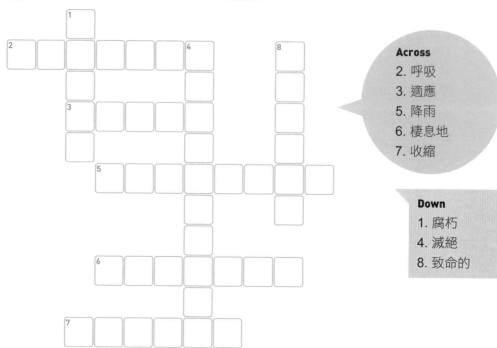

Across
2. 呼吸
3. 適應
5. 降雨
6. 棲息地
7. 收縮

Down
1. 腐朽
4. 滅絕
8. 致命的

🧑 Match with the correct definition. 將單字連到正確的意思

1. endangered •

ⓐ imaginary line around the middle of Earth

2. equator •

ⓑ Floods and earthquakes are examples.

3. iron •

ⓒ a strong metal

4. natural disaster •

ⓓ When animals fail to adapt to their changed habitats, they become it.

Fill in the blank with the correct words.
將正確的單字填入空格中

avoid	competed	consume	global warming	useless

1. Plants produce oxygen and _____ carbon dioxide.
   植物產生氧氣並消耗二氧化碳。

2. Wolves and coyotes _____ for food and territory.
   狼和郊狼會競爭食物和領地。

3. Local weather warnings can help you _____ these
   disasters.　　當地的天氣警報可以幫助人們避免這些災害。

4. Rust can make an iron tool _____.
   生鏽會讓鐵製工具失去作用。

5. _____ is melting the Arctic ice.
   全球暖化正在融化北極的冰層。

Fill in the blank with the correct expressions.
將正確的表達填入空格中

are good at	break apart	cause ~ to	forced ~ to	in balance

1. Rainforests keep oxygen and carbon dioxide _____.

2. The harsh environment _____ the coyotes _____
   adapt.

3. Flash floods _____ damage _____ property.

4. Iron can rust and decay, or _____.

5. Polar bears _____ hunting seals and whales in Arctic
   waters.

How can sunlight <u>travel</u> through space to Earth? It's because light
（光、聲音）行進

is a type of <u>electromagnetic</u> <u>wave</u>(EW). EWs are energy, and they
電磁（體）的　　　　波

can travel through a <u>vacuum</u>. A vacuum is a place with no <u>matter</u> in
真空　　　　　　　　　　　物質

it, like <u>outer space</u>. <u>Radio waves</u> are another type of EW. The waves
外太空　　　無線電波

can travel from your phone to a <u>satellite</u> in space. The satellite can
衛星

then send those waves to someone on the other

side of the world! <u>Microwaves</u> are also
微波

electromagnetic. They travel very

fast, and they can cook food

<u>in minutes</u>!
在幾分鐘內

Read and Complete 完成句子

① A _____ is a place with no matter in it.

② Electromagnetic waves _____ through space.

能量波

陽光是如何穿過太空傳導到地球的？這是因為光是一種電磁波（EW）。電磁波是一種能量，可以在真空中傳導。真空是指一個沒有任何物質的地方，就像外太空一樣。而無線電波則是另一種類型的電磁波，這種波可以從我們的手機傳導到太空中的衛星，接著衛星可以將這些電波發送給世界另一端的人！微波也是一種電磁波，它們的傳導速度非常快，而且可以在幾分鐘內烹煮食物！

背景知識 Plus!

利用微波（microwaves）做料理的產品就是微波爐，微波爐的英文是 **microwave oven**，它的原理是微波被物質所吸收，並震動分子來產生熱能，被含水量多的部分所吸收，就會更容易變熱。

Circle the best answer. 圈選出正確的答案

1. What is an example of a vacuum?
   a a satellite　　b outer space　　c electromagnetic waves

2. What is an example of an electromagnetic wave?
   a sound　　　　b electricity　　c sunlight

3. How do people use microwaves?
   a They use them to find their way.
   b They use them to cook food.
   c They use them to brighten the dark.
   d They use them to move around.

4. What does a satellite do with radio waves?
   a It helps radio waves to travel fast.
   b It makes radio waves much stronger.
   c It gathers various radio waves in the world.
   d It receives and sends radio waves from phones.

Complete the sentences. 完成句子

Electromagnetic waves like sunlight, ❶ .... waves, and
❷ .... can travel through a ❸ .... People use these
for many things, like talking to each other and cooking food.

Wrap Up Fill in the blanks. 總複習，將單字填入空格

EW: ❶ .... wave		energy
特性	• waves of ❷ .... • travel through a ❸	electromagnetic microwaves
種類	• sunlight, radio waves, ❹	vacuum

Every night, the moon looks <u>a little</u> different. That's because each
一點

night it is at a different stage of its <u>journey</u>. The moon travels
行程

around the Earth in 29.53 days. Each month, the moon

<u>goes through</u> 8 <u>phases</u>. The first phase is the
經歷　　　　階段

<u>new moon</u>. New moons <u>appear</u> very small
新月　　　　　　　看起來好像

because they <u>reflect</u> <u>little</u> of the sun's light.
反射　不多的

It <u>eventually</u> grows into a <u>full moon</u>. It
最終　　　　　　　　滿月

reflects the sun's light like a circle. Over the

next phases, the moon appears smaller and

smaller. Then, it <u>returns</u> to a new moon.
返回

Read and Complete 完成句子

❶ The moon moves around the _____.

❷ The moon has 8 phases according to its _____.

月亮的週期

每天晚上，月亮看起來會有一點不一樣，這是因
為月亮每天晚上都處於週期的不同階段。月亮繞
地球一周的時間為 29.53 天。每個月，月亮會經
歷 8 個階段。第一個階段是新月，新月看起來
非常小，因為它們反射少許的太陽光。而月亮最
終會漸漸成為一個滿月，它像一個圓圈一樣反射
太陽光。在接下來的階段裡，月亮看起來會越來越
小，然後回到了新月。

背景知識 Plus!

月球環繞地球運行的 29.53 天
中，月球形狀的變化稱為月相變化
（phase）。月相變化的順序如下：
「朔→新月→眉月→上弦月→滿月→
虧凸月→下弦月→殘月→新月」。月
亮本身不發光，只能接受陽光來
反射光線，因而看起來很明
亮。

Comprehension Checkup 理解能力確認

Circle the best answer. 圈選出正確的答案

1. How long does it take for the moon to travel around the Earth?
   - ⓐ 8 days
   - ⓑ 29.53 days
   - ⓒ 8 months

2. What makes the moon appear bigger and smaller?
   - ⓐ the sunlight it reflects
   - ⓑ its speed when traveling
   - ⓒ its distance from the Earth

3. Why does the moon look different every night?
   - ⓐ Because it regularly appears and disappears.
   - ⓑ Because sometimes it fails to reflect sun's light.
   - ⓒ Because it shows us a different phase as it travels.
   - ⓓ Because the weather is different from night to night.

4. What is NOT true about the moon?
   - ⓐ People call the first phase the new moon.
   - ⓑ A new moon becomes smaller to a full moon.
   - ⓒ A full moon reflects the sun's light like a circle.
   - ⓓ A new moon doesn't reflect much of the sun's light.

Complete the sentences. 完成句子

The moon goes through 8 ❶ .... as it travels. At each phase, it ❷ .... more or less sunlight. This makes the moon look bigger or ❸ ....

Wrap Up Fill in the blanks. 總複習，將單字填入空格

The moon ❶ .... around the Earth.		circle
a ❷ .... moon	small, reflect little of the sun's ❸	travels
a full moon	reflect the sun's light like a ❹	light
		new

月亮的週期 103

Roles in the Food Chain

R_38.mp3

Plants and animals live in a habitat. All habitats have a <u>food chain</u>.
（生態）食物鏈

Food chains <u>are made up of</u> <u>producers</u>, <u>consumers</u>, and <u>decomposers</u>.
由～組成　　生產者　　消費者　　分解者

Let's <u>take a look at</u> an example in a habitat like the African <u>plains</u>.
看一看～　　　　　　　　　　　　　　　平原

Plants and grass <u>produce</u> energy from the sun and the <u>ground</u>.
生產　　　　　　　　　　　　地面

These producers are then eaten by a consumer, such as a zebra. The zebra uses the plant's energy to grow. When the zebra dies, it falls to the ground. Decomposers, such as <u>worms</u> and
蟲

<u>bacteria</u>, turn the zebra's energy into the <u>soil</u>.
細菌　　　　　　　　　　　　　　　　土壤

Producers then use that energy to make food!

Read and Complete 完成句子

❶ Producers, consumers, and _____ live together in a habitat.

❷ Consumers eat _____.

食物鏈中的角色

植物和動物生活在一個棲息地，所有的棲息地都有一條食物鏈。食物鏈是由生產者、消費者和分解者所組成的，讓我們來看一下棲息地的例子，例如非洲平原。植物和草從太陽和土地中生產能量，然後這些生產者被像是斑馬等消費者吃掉，而斑馬利用植物的能量成長。斑馬死亡時會倒在地上，而像是蟲子和細菌的分解者則會將斑馬的能量轉移到土壤中，生產者接著會使用這些能量來製造食物！

背景知識 Plus!

食物鏈（food chain）由生產者、消費者、分解者組成，但實際的情況更複雜。在鹿吃草、老虎獵食鹿的情境中，鹿是第一消費者，而老虎是第二消費者。在現實的生態系統中，各個食物鏈錯綜複雜地交織在一起，並被稱為「食物網」。

Circle the best answer. 圈選出正確的答案

1. How do plants get energy?
   - ⓐ from the consumers
   - ⓑ from the animals
   - ⓒ from the sun and soil

2. What is an example of a decomposer?
   - ⓐ grass
   - ⓑ worm
   - ⓒ zebra

3. What do decomposers do?
   - ⓐ They eat producers.
   - ⓑ They kill consumers, such as zebras.
   - ⓒ They produce energy from plants.
   - ⓓ They return energy to the ground.

4. What is NOT true about food chains?
   - ⓐ They are found in habitats.
   - ⓑ Producers are eaten by consumers.
   - ⓒ Consumers are the most important.
   - ⓓ Decomposers break down consumers.

Complete the sentences. 完成句子

Each ❶ _____ has a food chain. Food chains are made up of producers, consumers, and decomposers. ❷ _____ get energy from producers. They return it to the ❸ _____ by decomposers.

WrapUp Connect. 總複習，連連看

Food Chain

❶ Producers •

❷ Consumers •

❸ Decomposers •

• ⓐ turn the consumers' energy into the soil.

• ⓑ produce energy from the sun and ground.

• ⓒ eat producers.

Four Important Spheres

R_39.mp3

The Earth <u>consists of</u> four <u>systems</u>. We call them <u>spheres</u>. The
由～構成　　　　系統　　　　　　　　　圈層
first system is the <u>biosphere</u>. It <u>includes</u> all living things on Earth.
生物圈　　　　包含
Next, the <u>geosphere</u> system is all of the rocks and <u>minerals</u> on
岩石圈　　　　　　　　　　　礦物
Earth. All of the water on Earth is part of the <u>hydrosphere</u>. Finally,
水圈
the <u>atmosphere</u> is the gases or air, and it <u>surrounds</u> Earth. These
大氣圈　　　　　　　　　　　　圍繞
4 systems are all <u>closely</u> <u>connected</u>. For
緊密地　　連結
example, wind from the atmosphere causes
erosion in the geosphere. All the plants and
animals of the biosphere need water from
the hydrosphere.

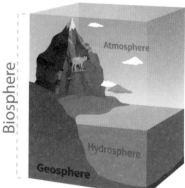

Read and Complete 完成句子

❶ The Earth has four systems called _____.

❷ The four systems are _____ closely.

四個重要的圈層

地球由四個系統所組成的，我們將它們稱為圈層。第一個系統是生物圈，包括地球上所有的生物。接著，岩石圈是指地球上所有的岩石和礦物。而在地球上所有的水都是水圈的一部分。最後，大氣圈是指氣體或空氣，而它包圍著地球。這四個系統全都緊密連結著，例如：來自大氣層的風會在岩石圈造成侵蝕，而生物圈中所有的動植物都需要來自水圈的水。

背景知識 Plus!

在地球的四個圈層（sphere）中，各種生物和物理過程正在緊密相互作用中發生。讓我們輕鬆分析的圈層名稱。我們來看 sphere（意思是「領域」）前面的字母吧！Bio- 在希臘語的意思是「生命」，geo- 的意思是「地球」，hydro- 的意思是「水」，atmo- 的意思是「空氣」。看起來很難記住的名詞，變得更容易記住了吧？

Comprehension Checkup 理解能力確認

Circle the best answer. 圈選出正確的答案

1. Which system are humans in?
   ⓐ biosphere　　ⓑ hydrosphere　　ⓒ atmosphere

2. What is a part of the geosphere?
   ⓐ rain　　ⓑ minerals　　ⓒ plants

3. How does the atmosphere affect the geosphere?
   ⓐ Animals eat plants.
   ⓑ Heavy rain causes floods.
   ⓒ Plants need water to grow.
   ⓓ Wind slowly causes erosion of rocks and soil.

4. What can be an example of the connection between the biosphere and the atmosphere?
   ⓐ People pollute the air.　　ⓑ People eat other animals.
   ⓒ People live on the ground.　　ⓓ People dig valuable minerals.

Complete the sentences. 完成句子

The Earth's four systems include the ❶ ...., atmosphere, geosphere, and ❷ .... These spheres are all ❸ .... connected.

Wrap Up　Fill in the blanks. 總複習，將單字填入空格

Earth's Systems

biosphere	geosphere	hydrosphere	atmosphere
all ❶ .... things	rocks and ❷	❸	gases or air surrounding ❹ ....

minerals　　living　　water　　Earth

一閃一閃亮晶晶
Twinkle, Twinkle, Little Star

R_40.mp3

Why do some stars in the sky look brighter than others? The
<u>apparent magnitude</u> of a star is how bright it looks to us. We
視星等
<u>measure</u> it with the <u>brightness</u> of the star and its <u>distance</u> from
測量　　　　　　　亮度　　　　　　　　　距離
Earth. The sun appears really bright. That's because it's very large
and close to Earth. However, the <u>absolute magnitude</u> is how bright a
絕對星等
star really is. Many stars <u>far away</u> in space
離～很遠
are bigger and brighter than the sun. But

they appear less bright than the sun. They
have a greater absolute magnitude than
their apparent magnitude.

Read and Complete 完成句子

1 The _____ magnitude tells us how bright a star looks.

2 The _____ magnitude is how bright a star really is.

一閃一閃亮晶晶

為什麼天上的幾顆星星看起來比其他星星還亮？
恆星的視星等是指它在我們肉眼中看到的亮度，
我們用恆星的亮度和它與地球的距離來測量視星
等。太陽看起來真的很亮，那是因為太陽非常
大，而且離地球很近。然而，絕對星等指的是一
顆恆星真正的亮度。許多遠在太空中的恆星比太
陽更大、更亮，但它們看起來沒有太陽來得明
亮，這是因為它們的絕對星等大於視星等。

背景知識 Plus!

絕對星等（absolute magnitude）
比太陽還高的星大約有 83 顆。到
目前為止所觀測到的星星中，最亮的
是太陽絕對等級的 870 萬倍。視星等
（apparent magnitude）稱為「視
覺等級」，用肉眼看的話，最暗
的 6 級星比最亮的 1 級星要
高出 100 倍。

Comprehension Checkup 理解能力確認

Circle the best answer. 圈選出正確的答案

1. What do people NOT use to measure apparent magnitude?
   - ⓐ the brightness of the star
   - ⓑ the number of nearby stars
   - ⓒ the distance of the star from Earth

2. What do people consider to measure absolute magnitude?
   - ⓐ the brightness of the star itself
   - ⓑ the distance of the star from Earth
   - ⓒ the distance of the star from the sun

3. Why does the sun appear really bright?
   - ⓐ Because it's far away from Earth.
   - ⓑ Because it's the brightest star in space.
   - ⓒ Because it's very big and close to Earth.
   - ⓓ Because it doesn't have any stars around it.

4. Why do some big and bright stars look less bright to us?
   - ⓐ Because they're far away from Earth.
   - ⓑ Because they often cover each other.
   - ⓒ Because their temperatures are too high.
   - ⓓ Because they're too close to the sun.

Complete the sentences. 完成句子

> Apparent magnitude is how bright a star appears from
> ❶ .... The absolute magnitude tells us how bright a
> star ❷ .... is.

Wrap Up Fill in the blanks. 總複習，將單字填入空格

apparent magnitude	❶ .... magnitude	absolute
• how bright a star looks from Earth	• how bright a star ❹ .... is	brightness
• the ❷ .... of a star		really
• a star's ❸ .... from Earth		distance

WORD REVIEW

Crossword Puzzle 填字遊戲

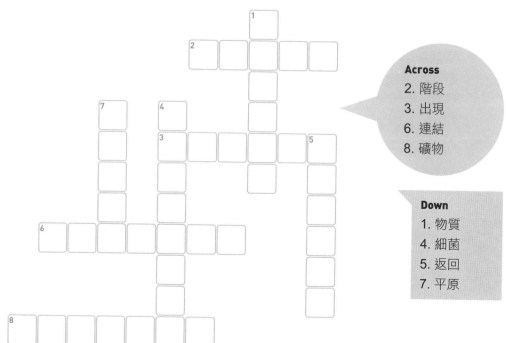

Across
2. 階段
3. 出現
6. 連結
8. 礦物

Down
1. 物質
4. 細菌
5. 返回
7. 平原

Match with the correct definition. 將單字連到正確的意思

1. decomposer •

2. new moon •

3. soil •

4. vacuum •

ⓐ a place with no matter in it

ⓑ a first phase of the moon's journey

ⓒ part of the food chain that breaks down consumers

ⓓ the substance on the surface of the earth in which plants grow

Fill in the blank with the correct words.
將正確的單字填入空格中

| includes | measure | reflects | satellite | surrounds |

1. Radio waves can travel from your phone to a _____ in space.　無線電波可以從手機傳播到太空中的衛星。

2. A full moon _____ the sun's light like a circle.
   滿月像一個圓圈一樣反射太陽光。

3. The atmosphere is the gases or air, and it _____ Earth.
   大氣圈是氣體或空氣，它包圍著地球。

4. The biosphere _____ all living things on Earth.
   生物圈包括地球上所有的生物。

5. We _____ the apparent magnitude with the brightness of the star and its distance from Earth.
   我們用恆星的亮度和它與地球的距離來測量視星等。

Fill in the blank with the correct expressions.
將正確的表達填入空格中

| consists of | far away | in minutes | goes through | take a look at |

1. Microwaves travel so fast, and they can cook food _____.

2. Each month, the moon _____ 8 phases.

3. Let's _____ an example in a habitat like the African plains.

4. The Earth _____ four systems, and we call them spheres.

5. Many stars _____ in space are bigger and brighter than the sun.

大家庭 The Extended Family

R_41.mp3

Parents and their children make up most families. This is a
<u>nuclear family</u>. But there are larger types of families too. For example,
核心家庭

Brady has a mother, a father, and an <u>elder</u> sister. But his <u>grandparents</u>
年齡較大的   祖父母

live with them too. Also, his
<u>unmarried</u> aunt lives with the
未婚的

family. This is an <u>extended family</u>.
大家庭

In this family, all the <u>adults</u> are
成年人

<u>related</u> to <u>each other</u>. And they all
有關的   彼此

<u>work</u> together for the family.
工作

Check True or False 是非題

① Nuclear families are larger than extended families.　　T / F

② An extended family can include grandparents.　　T / F

大家庭

大多數的家庭是由父母和孩子組成，這是核心家庭，但也有更大的家庭類型。例如，布雷迪有一個母親、一個父親和一個姐姐，但他的祖父母也和他們住在一起。另外，布雷迪未婚的姑姑也和這家人住在一起，這就是大家庭。在這個家庭中，所有成年人都是有親緣關係的，而且他們都會為了這個家庭共同努力。

背景知識 Plus!

在過去的農業社會是以**大家庭**（extended family）為主，並未家庭提供農業所需的勞動力。然而逐漸發展成工業社會時，由於人口遷移到城市，發展出新型態的**核心家庭**（nuclear family），而核心家庭也變成今日最普遍的家庭型態。

Comprehension Checkup 理解能力確認

Circle the best answer. 圈選出正確的答案

1. Which family type has only parents and their children?
   - ⓐ a nuclear family
   - ⓑ an extended family
   - ⓒ a large family

2. How many members are in Brady's family?
   - ⓐ 4
   - ⓑ 6
   - ⓒ 7

3. Brady's _____ lives with Brady's family.
   - ⓐ brother
   - ⓑ aunt
   - ⓒ uncle

4. In an extended family, _____ work for the family.
   - ⓐ all the adults
   - ⓑ the grandparents
   - ⓒ only the mother

Complete the sentence. 完成句子

A(n) .... family includes adults related to the parents.

Wrap Up — Fill in the blanks. 總複習，將單字填入空格

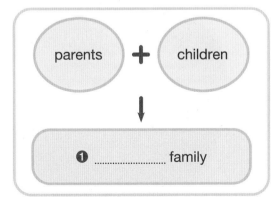

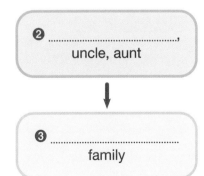

North America on the Globe

R_42.mp3

North America is a large <u>continent</u> in the north part of the <u>globe</u>.
北美洲　　　　　　　　　　　　　　大陸　　　　　　　　　　　　　　地球

Three countries <u>cover</u> most of it. Canada is the <u>farthest</u> north. It
　　　　　　　　包含　　　　　　　　　　　　　　最遠的

has the largest area. Just below that is the United States. It has the

largest <u>population</u>. Below that is Mexico,
　　　　人口

and there are 20 more countries. Two

<u>oceans</u> <u>surround</u> the continent.
海洋　　圍繞

The Pacific Ocean <u>lies</u> to the west.
太平洋　　　　　　位於

The Atlantic Ocean lies to the east.
大西洋

Check True or False 是非題

❶ Mexico has the largest area in North America.　T / F

❷ The Pacific Ocean lies west of North America.　T / F

地球上的北美洲

北美洲是北半球的一個大陸，有三個國家涵蓋了大部分的面積。加拿大在最北方的區域，佔了最大的區域。在加拿大下面的是美國，有最多的人口。在美國下面是墨西哥，還有 20 多個國家。在北美大陸的周圍有兩大洋，西邊是太平洋、東邊是大西洋。

背景知識 Plus!

美國（the United States）
是由美國領土和包含阿拉斯加、夏威夷的五十個州與首都（D.C.）所組成的聯邦國家。在 15 世紀發現美洲大陸後，美國由英國殖民統治，然而在 1775 年的獨立戰爭勝利後，成為獨立的國家。

Circle the best answer. 圈選出正確的答案

1. Which country is farthest north in North America?
   - ⓐ Canada
   - ⓑ Mexico
   - ⓒ the United States

2. Which country in North America has the most people?
   - ⓐ Canada
   - ⓑ Mexico
   - ⓒ the United States

3. North America has a total _____ countries on it.
   - ⓐ 3　　　　　　　ⓑ 20　　　　　　　ⓒ 23

4. The Atlantic Ocean is to the _____ of North America.
   - ⓐ east　　　　　　ⓑ north　　　　　　ⓒ west

Complete the sentence. 完成句子

North America is a large .... in the north part of the globe.

Wrap Up Fill in the blanks. 總複習，將單字填入空格

North America

Countries	Surrounding Oceans
• Canada • ❶ .... • Mexico and others	• the ❷ .... Ocean • the ❸ .... Ocean

Culture <u>refers to</u> people's <u>shared</u> ideas or <u>lifestyles</u>. This can be
提到～　　共同的　　　生活方式
the foods, arts, and <u>languages</u> of a country. But culture is always
語言
changing. Why? First, young people change it. They do things
<u>differently</u> from <u>older</u> people. And they create a new culture.
不同地　　　年長的
They may listen to different music.

<u>Rock</u> and <u>hip-hop</u> became <u>popular</u>
搖滾樂　　嘻哈音樂　　　流行的
this way. Also, <u>media</u> and <u>technology</u>
媒體　　　　科技
can change culture. TVs and
smartphones <u>continue</u> to do so today.
持續

Check True or False 是非題

1. Culture include a country's food.　　　　　T / F

2. Young people don't like to change older　　T / F
   people's way.

文化正在改變

文化是指人們共同的觀念或生活方式，這可以是一個國家的食物、藝術和語言，但文化總是在改變。為什麼呢？首先，是年輕人在改變文化，他們會做與年長者不同的事，並且創造了新的文化。而且他們也有可能會聽不同風格的音樂，搖滾樂和嘻哈樂就是這樣流行起來的。此外，媒體和科技也能夠改變文化，電視和智慧型手機現在也持續在改變文化。

背景知識 Plus!

嘻哈（hip-hop）是結合 "hip"（意思是「臀部」）和 "hop"（意思是「跳舞」），這與從 1980 年代的紐約青少年開始的整個文化有關。不只是饒舌音樂代表嘻哈，地板舞、DJ 與塗鴉藝術等各式各樣的活動，也確立了今日所流行的嘻哈文化。

Comprehension Checkup 理解能力確認

Circle the best answer. 圈選正確的答案

1. What are shared ideas and lifestyles among people?
   ⓐ culture　　　ⓑ music　　　ⓒ media

2. What is a characteristic of young people?
   ⓐ do not change　　　ⓑ become popular
   ⓒ do things differently

3. Young people listen to different music like rock and
   _____.
   ⓐ hip-hop　　　ⓑ classics　　　ⓒ country songs

4. Technology like _____ change people's lifestyle.
   ⓐ arts　　　ⓑ food　　　ⓒ smartphones

Complete the sentence. 完成句子

Young people, media, and technology always ....
culture.

Wrap Up Fill in the blanks. 總複習，將單字填入空格

Culture		language
意義	• people's ❶ .... ideas or lifestyles	
包含	• food, arts, and ❷	media
特性	• It always ❸	changes
改變的原因	• young people • ❹ .... and technology	shared

We get many <u>resources</u> from <u>nature</u>. These include <u>oil</u> and <u>coal</u> for
資源　　　　　　自然　　　　　　　　石油　　　煤
energy. We also use trees for paper and <u>wood</u>. <u>Unfortunately</u>, we
能源　　　　　　　　　　　　　　　　木頭　　　不幸地
<u>waste</u> many resources. Sometimes people waste energy. Also, they
浪費
build new buildings all the time. This
wastes land, trees, and other <u>natural</u>
自然的
resources. Because of this, our
resources are quickly disappearing!
We may <u>run out of</u> them
耗盡～
<u>in the near future</u>.
在不久的將來

Check True or False 是非題

❶ People sometimes use too much energy. T / F

❷ We have enough natural resources for the T / F
future.

消失的資源

我們從大自然中取得許多資源，這包括用於能源
上的石油和煤炭，我們也會使用樹木當作紙張和
木材。不幸的是，我們浪費了許多資源，有時人
們會浪費能源。此外，他們總是在建造新的建築
物，這浪費土地、樹木和其他自然資源。因為如
此，我們的資源正在快速消失！在不久的將來，
我們可能會耗盡這些資源。

背景知識 Plus!

自然資源（natural resource）包含
用完就會消失的「不可再生能源」和可
以保存並持續使用的「可再生能源」。
像是石油、煤炭的能源屬於不可再生能
源；但是像是樹木、水、森林屬於可
再生能源，然而這些可再生能源
由於濫開發和汙染，也面臨
逐漸消失的情況。

Comprehension Checkup 理解能力確認

Circle the best answer. 圈選出正確的答案

1. Where do people get energy resources?
   ⓐ nature   ⓑ paper   ⓒ buildings

2. What do we use for paper?
   ⓐ coal   ⓑ trees   ⓒ oil

3. New buildings can _____ land and other resources.
   ⓐ get   ⓑ build   ⓒ waste

4. We may _____ natural resources in the future.
   ⓐ reuse   ⓑ throw away   ⓒ run out of

Complete the sentence. 完成句子

People waste many natural ...., so they are disappearing.

Wrap Up Fill in the blanks. 總複習，將單字填入空格

Disappearing Resource	
Resources we get from nature	• oil and coal for ❶ .... • trees for ❷ .... and wood
Problem	• People ❸ .... them.
Result	• We may ❹ .... out of them.

energy   waste   run   paper

Social Studies
45
做個好公民！
Be a Good Citizen!

R_45.mp3

Are you a <u>citizen</u>? Yes, you are! You are a <u>member</u> of your country
公民　　　　　　　　　　　　　　　　　　　（團體的）成員
and <u>community</u>. Citizens have <u>responsibilities</u> to their communities.
社區　　　　　　　　　　　　　　　責任
It <u>means</u> they must <u>take care of</u> their
表示～的意思　　　　　照顧～
communities. Usually, adults <u>vote</u> and
投票
<u>pay</u> <u>taxes</u>. Some may <u>serve in the army</u>.
付費　　稅　　　　　　　服兵役
As a young citizen, you can help in
other ways. You can clean up trash or
help <u>needy</u> people. This way, you can
貧窮的
be a good citizen!

Check True or False 是非題

❶ Citizens are members of a community.　　　　　T / F

❷ You can clean up trash in your neighborhood.　　T / F

做個好公民！

你是公民嗎？是的，你是！你是國家和社區的一
份子。公民對他們的社區負有責任，這表示他們
必須照顧他們的社區。通常，成年人可以投票並
且要繳稅，有些人可能會到軍隊服役。身為一個
年輕的公民，你可以透過其他方式來提供幫助，
可以幫忙清理垃圾，或是幫助貧困的人。這樣一
來，你就可以成為一個好公民了！

背景知識 Plus!

公民（citizen）在古代社會中也存
在過，然而以前的概念和現代有很大
的差別。在古希臘，只有成年男性會被
當作公民。另一方面，女性、奴隸和
外國人則會被排除在公民之外，還會
遭到歧視。

Circle the best answer. 圈選出正確的答案

1. What do citizens have toward their communities?
   ⓐ members   ⓑ money   ⓒ responsibilities

2. What do citizens NOT do to take care of their communities?
   ⓐ vote   ⓑ pay taxes   ⓒ break rules

3. Some citizens serve in _____ for their country.
   ⓐ the army   ⓑ prison   ⓒ a company

4. As a young citizen, you can help _____ people.
   ⓐ rich   ⓑ needy   ⓒ clean

Complete the sentence. 完成句子

Citizens have responsibilities and take care of their
....

Wrap Up Fill in the blanks. 總複習，將單字填入空格

Citizens have responsibilities.

Adults should	Young citizens can
• ❶	• clean up ❸ ....
• pay ❷	• help ❹ .... people
• serve in the army	

taxes   vote   needy   trash

WORD REVIEW

Crossword Puzzle 填字遊戲

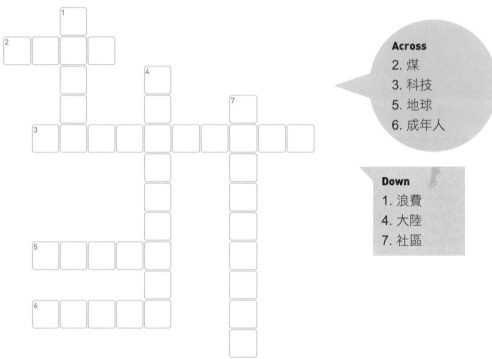

Across
2. 煤
3. 科技
5. 地球
6. 成年人

Down
1. 浪費
4. 大陸
7. 社區

Match with the correct definition. 將單字連到正確的意思

1. culture •

2. nuclear family •

3. citizen •

4. North America •

ⓐ a family type that has only parents and their children

ⓑ a continent in the north part of the globe that includes Canada, the United States, and Mexico

ⓒ shared ideas or lifestyles among people

ⓓ a member of a country or a community

Fill in the blank with the correct words.
將正確的單字填入空格中

> nature   oceans   vote   grandparents   popular

1. But his _____ live with them too.
   但是他的祖父母也和他們住在一起。

2. Two _____ surround the continent.
   兩大海洋環繞著大陸。

3. Rock and hip-hop became _____ this way.
   搖滾和嘻哈就是這樣變流行的。

4. We get many resources from _____.
   我們從大自然中取得許多資源。

5. Usually, adults _____ and pay taxes.
   通常，成年人可以投票並且要繳稅。

Fill in the blank with the correct expressions.
將正確的表達填入空格中

> run out of lies to each other take care of differently from

1. In an extended family, all the adults are related to
   _____.

2. The Pacific Ocean _____ the west.

3. They do things _____ older people.

4. We may _____ our resources in the near future.

5. It means citizens must _____ their communities.

St. Patrick's Day is a popular <u>holiday</u>. It <u>honors</u> <u>Ireland</u>'s Saint
聖徒　　　　　　　　　　　節日　　　　向～致敬　　愛爾蘭
Patrick on March 17. He <u>spread</u> <u>Christianity</u> <u>throughout</u> Ireland.
　　　　　　　　　　　擴散　　　基督教　　　遍及
At first, only <u>Irish</u> people celebrated it. Today,
　　　　　愛爾蘭的
people all around the world do. On
this day, people have many parties and
<u>parades</u>. And they wear green and even
遊行
eat green food! Why green? Green is
the color of a <u>shamrock</u>. It's
　　　　　　酢醬草
a small green Irish plant. It
is a <u>symbol</u> of the saint.
　　　象徵

Check True or False 是非題

❶ St. Patrick spread a religion in America.　　T / F

❷ People have parades on St. Patrick's Day.　　T / F

慶祝聖派翠克節

聖派翠克節是一個受歡迎的節日，人們在 3 月
17 日這一天紀念愛爾蘭的聖派翠克，他將基督
教擴散到整個愛爾蘭。一開始，只有愛爾蘭人會
慶祝這個節日，到現在，世界各地的人也會慶
祝。在當天人們會舉辦許多聚會和遊行，而大家
會穿綠色的衣服，甚至還會吃綠色的食物！為什
麼是綠色呢？綠色是酢漿草的顏色，而酢漿草是
一種小型的綠色愛爾蘭植物，也是聖人的象徵。

背景知識 Plus!

聖派翠克節（St. Patrick's Day）
最大的特點是穿著綠色的領結和帽
子，這是為了紀念聖派翠克。據說，他
會用三葉的酢漿草（shamrock）向人
們解釋基督教的三位一體，從此之
後，綠色變成了象徵他的顏色。

Circle the best answer. 圈選出正確的答案

1. What is St. Patrick's Day for?
   - ⓐ a festival
   - ⓑ honoring a saint
   - ⓒ the environment

2. What did St. Patrick spread throughout Ireland?
   - ⓐ Christianity
   - ⓑ parades
   - ⓒ a holiday

3. People usually wear _____ on St. Patrick's Day.
   - ⓐ green
   - ⓑ red
   - ⓒ white

4. The shamrock is a _____ of St. Patrick.
   - ⓐ country
   - ⓑ food
   - ⓒ symbol

Complete the sentence. 完成句子

People celebrate St. Patrick's Day with .... clothes and food.

WrapUp Fill in the blanks. 總複習，將單字填入空格

St. Patrick's Day

日期	• March 17
意義	• Ireland's ❶ .... • to ❷ .... Saint Patrick
活動	• celebrate it with parties and ❸ .... • wear green and eat green food
象徵	• the shamrock, a small green Irish ❹ ....

plant   parades   honor   holiday

什麼是運河？
What Are Canals?

R_47.mp3

<u>Canals</u> are <u>man-made</u> <u>waterways</u>. People <u>dig</u> <u>channels</u> and
運河　　　　人造的　　　航道　　　　　　　挖掘　　水道
<u>fill them with water</u>. Canals have many <u>uses</u>.
用～填裝～　　　　　　　　　　　　　　用途
Small canals bring water to farms. This helps

<u>crops</u> grow well. Big canals <u>connect</u> lakes
作物　　　　　　　　　連接
and oceans. Look at the Panama

Canal. It is 77 km. It connects the

Atlantic and Pacific Oceans. Ships

use this as a <u>shortcut</u>. <u>Without</u> it,
　　　　　　捷徑　　　沒有～
they would have to travel around

South America. That's almost 13,000 km!

Check True or False 是非題

❶ People must dig channels for canals.　　　　T / F

❷ People can use small canals for farming.　　T / F

什麼是運河？

運河是人造的航道，人們會開挖渠道，並用水填滿。運河有許多用途，小的運河可供水給農場，幫助農作物成長良好。大的運河連接湖泊和海洋，看看巴拿馬運河，有 77 公里長，連接大西洋和太平洋。船隻將這條運河當作捷徑，如果沒有這條運河，就必須繞過南美洲，那樣將近是一萬三千公里！

背景知識 Plus!

如果美洲有巴拿馬運河，中東地區則是擁有世界最大的蘇伊士運河（Suez Canal），蘇伊士運河是一條重要的航道，連接了亞洲和歐洲，並且不需繞到非洲。船隻不用經過印度洋和大西洋，而是透過蘇伊士運河穿過紅海和地中海，將航行距離縮短了一半。

Comprehension Checkup 理解能力確認

Circle the best answer. 圈選出正確的答案

1. How do canals help farmers?
   - ⓐ build farms
   - ⓑ clean soil
   - ⓒ bring water

2. How long is the Panama Canal?
   - ⓐ 107 km
   - ⓑ 77 km
   - ⓒ 13,000 km

3. The Panama Canal connects two _____.
   - ⓐ oceans
   - ⓑ continents
   - ⓒ ships

4. Without the Panama Canal, ships must travel around _____.
   - ⓐ the Indian Ocean
   - ⓑ North America
   - ⓒ South America

Complete the sentence. 完成句子

Canals are man-made _____ with many uses.

Wrap Up Fill in the blanks. 總複習，將單字填入空格

Canal	
字義	• man-made ❶ ....
製作方法	• dig ❷ .... and fill them with water
用途	• They bring water to ❸ .... • They connect ❹ .... and oceans.
例子	• Panama Canal

farms　　waterways　　lakes　　channels

Abraham Lincoln became the 16th US president in 1861. That year,
總統
the Civil War also began. America's North and South fought over
南北戰爭   為～爭吵
slavery. Black slaves were not free in the
奴隸制   奴隸
US. The North wanted to end this.

The South didn't. In 1863, Lincoln

ordered an end to Southern
命令   終止   （美國）南方
slavery. And the North finally won

the war in 1865. After this, Lincoln

passed many laws. These ended
通過
slavery and united the country.
統一

Check True or False 是非題

1 Abraham Lincoln was the 6th US president.   T / F

2 The North and South fought in the Civil War.   T / F

林肯與南北戰爭

亞伯拉罕・林肯在 1861 年成為美國第 16 任總
統。那一年，南北戰爭也開始了。美國的北方和
南方為了奴隸制度而戰。黑人奴隸在美國並不自
由，北方想要終止這種制度，南方則不願意。
1863 年，林肯下令終止南方的奴隸制度，而北
方終於在 1865 年贏了這場戰爭。在這之後，林
肯通過了多項法案，這些法案終結了奴隸制度，
並統一美國。

背景知識 Plus!

亞伯拉罕・林肯（Abraham
Lincoln）是出生於美國肯塔基州的貧
窮農家，具有黑人和白人血統的混血
兒，林肯幾乎沒有受過學校教育。但
是他透過自學當上律師、進入政治
圈，最後成為反奴隸制的總統，
他的名言「民有、民治、民
享」至今仍非常有
名。

Circle the best answer. 圈選出正確的答案

1. When did Abraham Lincoln become president?
   ⓐ in 1861　　　　　ⓑ in 1863　　　　　ⓒ in 1865

2. Who wanted to end slavery in the US?
   ⓐ the North　　　　ⓑ the South　　　　ⓒ both

3. During the war, Lincoln ordered an end to _____ slavery.
   ⓐ Northern　　　　ⓑ Southern　　　　ⓒ civil

4. The North _____ the war, and slavery ended in the country.
   ⓐ united　　　　　ⓑ passed　　　　　ⓒ won

Complete the sentence. 完成句子

Abraham Lincoln ended .... and united the country.

WrapUp Number the sentences in order. 寫出句子的順序

4 The North won the war.

☐ The Civil War began.

☐ Abraham Lincoln became the 16th US president.

☐ Lincoln passed many laws and ended slavery.

☐ Lincoln ordered an end to Southern slavery.

Don't <u>throw away</u> your paper or plastic. You can use it again in
扔掉
new products. This is <u>recycling</u>, and it has many <u>benefits</u>.
回收   好處
First, it <u>saves</u> <u>resources</u>. People <u>cut down</u> trees
節省   資源   砍倒
for new paper. So recycling paper can
save trees. Also, recycling <u>reduces</u>
減少
<u>pollution</u>. When you <u>recycle</u>
汙染   回收利用
plastic, it won't <u>pollute</u> water or
汙染
land. Also, factories will make
less new plastic. This also reduces
<u>smoke</u> in the air!
煙

Check True or False 是非題

❶ You can recycle and save resources.　　　　T / F

❷ Recycling plastic will pollute the air.　　　　T / F

回收的好處

不要丟掉紙張或塑膠，因為你可以在新的產品中
再次使用。這就是回收，而它有許多好處。首
先，回收可以節省資源，人們為了取得新的紙張
而砍伐樹木，所以回收紙張可以拯救樹木。此
外，回收還可以減少污染。回收塑膠時，並不會
對水或土地造成汙染，而且工廠也會製造更少的
新塑膠，這也會減少空氣中的煙霧！

背景知識 Plus!

節約資源有兩種方式：**重複
利用（reusing）**和**回收利用
（recycling）**。重複利用是指將要丟棄
的物品按照原本的用途重新使用，像是
重新使用電視、冰箱、電腦等。回收利
用是指以不同的方式重新使用已經使
用過並被丟棄的物品，例如：用
廢紙製作成一個新的紙箱，
這就是回收利用。

Circle the best answer. 圈選出正確的答案

1. What is recycling?
   ⓐ cutting down trees
   ⓑ using materials again
   ⓒ making plastic

2. How can we save trees?
   ⓐ recycle paper
   ⓑ make less plastic
   ⓒ throw away trash

3. Recycling does not _____ water or land.
   ⓐ save   ⓑ clean   ⓒ pollute

4. If factories make less new plastic, they create less _____ in the air.
   ⓐ resources   ⓑ smoke   ⓒ forest

Complete the sentence. 完成句子

Recycling can save resources and .... pollution.

WrapUp Connect. 總複習，連連看

Benefits of Recycling

Recycling paper •   • save trees •   • reduce smoke

Recycling plastic •   • make less new plastic •   • save resources

People live in different areas. Many people live in <u>urban</u> areas. These
城市的
are large cities with big buildings. They have good <u>transportation</u>.
交通車輛
There are many <u>businesses</u> and museums
企業
too. Streets are <u>crowded</u>, but they are
擁擠的
<u>lively</u>. People also live in <u>suburban</u>
生氣勃勃的   郊區的
areas. These are outside cities, but

they are close to cities. They are

smaller than urban areas. They <u>mainly</u>
主要地
have houses, schools, and green areas. People

here enjoy a <u>peaceful</u> life.
寧靜的

Check True or False 是非題

❶ Urban areas don't have big buildings.　　　　　　T / F

❷ Suburban areas are close to urban areas.　　　　T / F

都市與郊區

人們生活在不同的地區。許多人居住在都市地區，這些是有高聳建築物的大城市，這些城市有良好的交通，也有許多企業和博物館，街道很擁擠，但非常熱鬧。有些人也住在郊區，郊區位於都市地區之外，但是離城市很近。郊區比都市地區更小，主要有房屋、學校和綠地。住在這裡的人們享受著平靜的生活。

背景知識 Plus!

隨著工業化的發展，人們湧入大城市，城市地區出現嚴重的人口過多和住房短缺等問題。為了解決這些問題，城市的郊區會建造住宅和生活設施，讓人們可以住在這裡並通勤到城市上下班，而這樣的郊區現在也因為很多人居住在這裡，而變得越來越複雜。

Comprehension Checkup 理解能力確認

🙎 Circle the best answer. 圈選出正確的答案

1. What are urban areas?
   ⓐ small towns　　　ⓑ large cities　　　ⓒ areas with forest

2. Which one is NOT usually in urban areas?
   ⓐ good transportation　　　ⓑ businesses
   ⓒ many houses

3. Suburban areas are _____ urban areas.
   ⓐ smaller than　　　ⓑ bigger than　　　ⓒ the same as

4. Suburban areas have mainly houses, schools, and
   _____.
   ⓐ big buildings　　　ⓑ green areas　　　ⓒ museums

🐴 Complete the sentence. 完成句子

People live in urban areas or .... areas, and they are different.

Wrap Up　Write the numbers in the chart. 在表格中填數字

Urban	Suburban

❶ large cities with big buildings

❷ crowded and lively

❸ houses, green areas

❹ businesses and museums

❺ outside cities

❻ smaller and peaceful

WORD REVIEW

Crossword Puzzle 填字遊戲

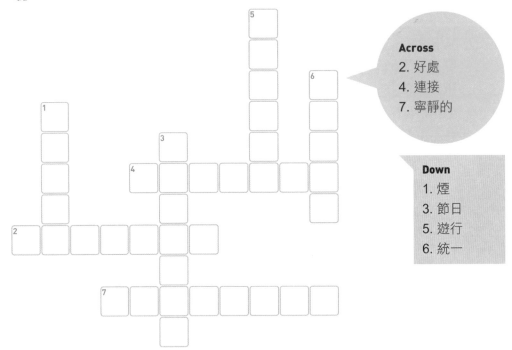

Across
2. 好處
4. 連接
7. 寧靜的

Down
1. 煙
3. 節日
5. 遊行
6. 統一

Match with the correct definition. 將單字連到正確的意思

1. recycling •

2. urban area •

3. canal •

4. the Civil War •

ⓐ a man-made waterway

ⓑ the war between America's North and South over slavery

ⓒ using paper or plastic again in new products

ⓓ a large city with big buildings and good transportation

Fill in the blank with the correct words.
將正確的單字填入空格中

| dig | crowded | spread | pollute | president |

1. He _____ Christianity throughout Ireland.

   他將基督教擴散到整個愛爾蘭。

2. People _____ channels and fill them with water.

   人們挖掘渠道，並用水填滿渠道。

3. Abraham Lincoln became the 16th US _____ in 1861.

   亞伯拉罕・林肯於 1861 年成為美國第 16 任總統。

4. When you recycle plastic, it won't _____ water or land.

   當你回收塑膠，就不會汙染水或土地。

5. Streets are _____, but they are lively.

   街上十分擁擠，但非常熱鬧。

Fill in the blank with the correct expressions.
將正確的表達填入空格中

| as a shortcut | smaller than | wear green | an end to | cut down |

1. On that day, people _____ and even eat green food!

2. Ships use the Panama Canal _____.

3. Lincoln ordered _____ Southern slavery.

4. People _____ trees for new paper.

5. Suburban areas are _____ urban areas.

Maps show places on the globe. They use lines of longitude and
地圖　　　　　　　　　　　　　　　　　　　線條　　　　經度
lines of latitude. Lines of longitude run from north to south. They
緯度
measure degrees east or west of the
測量　　度數
prime meridian. Lines of latitude
本初子午線
run from east to west. They

measure degrees north or

south of the equator. Lines
赤道
of longitude cross lines of
相交
latitude. The points where they

meet show exact locations.
確切的　　位置

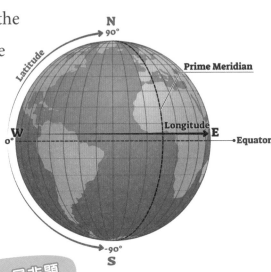

Check True or False 是非題

❶ Maps have four types of lines.　　　　　　　　　　T / F

❷ Latitude measures north or south of the equator.　T / F

地圖上的線條

地圖可以顯示地球上的地點，會使用經線和緯線。經線從北向南延伸，用來測量本初子午線以東或以西的度數。緯線從東向西延伸，用來測量赤道以北或以南的度數。經線會與緯線相交，它們的交會點會顯示出確切的位置。

背景知識 Plus!

緯度（橫線）和經度（直線）是為了準確表達一個地區的位置而在地球上劃定的假想線。緯度以赤道為基準，為北緯（N）、南緯（S）0°～90°，經度以格林威治皇家天文台所訂定的本初子午線為基準，為東經（E）、西經（W）0°～180°。

Circle the best answer. 圈選出正確的答案

1. What do the lines on the map show us?
   - ⓐ locations
   - ⓑ time
   - ⓒ spaces

2. Which direction do lines of longitude run from north?
   - ⓐ east
   - ⓑ west
   - ⓒ south

3. Longitude lines measure degrees east or west of the _____.
   - ⓐ location
   - ⓑ prime meridian
   - ⓒ equator

4. Lines of latitude and longitude _____ each other.
   - ⓐ miss
   - ⓑ run
   - ⓒ cross

Complete the sentence. 完成句子

Lines of longitude and latitude show exact .... on the map.

Wrap Up Fill in the blanks. 總複習，將單字填入空格

Lines of ❶	Lines of ❷ ....
• run from north to south	• run from east to west
• measure degrees east or west of the prime meridian	• measure degrees north or south of the ❸ ....

They cross each other. ▶ They show exact ❹ ....

locations   equator   longitude   latitude

52 華盛頓的紀念碑 The Washington Monument

R_52.mp3

What is the world's tallest <u>stone</u> building? It's the Washington

<u>Monument</u>! It <u>is located in</u> Washington, D.C. That's the US <u>capital</u>.

石材   紀念碑   位於～   首都

This white tower is almost 170 meters tall. It honors George

Washington, the first US president. Its <u>construction</u> began in 1848.

建造

However, construction stopped

several times because of the Civil

War. It was finally finished in

1884. Today, the <u>elevator</u> takes

【美】電梯

people to the top. They can see

the <u>whole</u> city from there.

整個的

Check True or False 是非題

1 The monument is made of stone.　　　　T / F

2 The monument doesn't have an elevator.　　　　T / F

華盛頓的紀念碑

世界上最高的石製建築是什麼？是華盛頓紀念碑！位於華盛頓特區，也就是美國的首都。這座白色的塔將近有 170 公尺高，是為了紀念美國第一任總統喬治・華盛頓。在 1848 年開始建造，然而由於南北戰爭的緣故，建設工程曾經中斷好幾次，最後在 1884 年完工。現今，有電梯可以將人們載至最高處，人們可以在那裡欣賞整個城市的風景。

背景知識 Plus!

喬治・華盛頓

（George Washington）是美國的第一任總統，被稱為「美國開國元勳」，在成功領導美國獨立運動後當選總統。從那時起，他透過制定憲法和建立財政和外交政策，奠定了美國成為獨立國家的基礎。

Comprehension Checkup 理解能力確認

Circle the best answer. 圈選出正確的答案

1. Where is the Washington Monument?
   - ⓐ in New York
   - ⓑ in Washington State
   - ⓒ in the US capital

2. Whom does the monument honor?
   - ⓐ the first US president
   - ⓑ Civil War heroes
   - ⓒ its designer

3. The Civil War _____ the monument's construction several times.
   - ⓐ started
   - ⓑ stopped
   - ⓒ located

4. The monument's construction took _____.
   - ⓐ 48 months
   - ⓑ 24 years
   - ⓒ 36 years

Complete the sentence. 完成句子

The Washington Monument is the world's .... stone building.

Wrap Up Fill in the blanks. 總複習，將單字填入空格

The Washington Monument

特別之處	the world's tallest ❶ .... building (almost 170 meters)
建築緣由	to ❷ .... George Washington, the first US ❸ ....
建造期間	from 1848 to 1884

president　　stone　　honor

The <u>steam engine</u> changed history forever. It <u>brought</u> the Industrial
蒸汽機　　　　　　　　　　　　　　　　　（原形：bring）引起　　工業革命
<u>Revolution</u> in the 1700s. England was first to build <u>factories</u>. The
　　　　　　　　　　　　　　　　　　　　　　　　　　　　工廠
factories quickly <u>produced</u> <u>goods</u> like clothes and tools. This made
　　　　　　　　生產　　商品
goods cheaper. More people could buy

them. People had new jobs in cities

too. So many people moved to cities.

This created new ways of <u>travel</u>.
　　　　　　　　　　　　旅行
The <u>railroad</u> and <u>steamship</u> allowed
　　　鐵路　　　　　汽船
<u>long-distance</u> travel.
長距離的

Check True or False 是非題

❶ The Industrial Revolution started in the 1700s.　T / F

❷ The revolution brought the steam engine.　T / F

工業革命

蒸汽機永遠改變了歷史，它在 1700 年代引起了
工業革命。英國是第一個建立工廠的國家。這些
工廠迅速生產像是衣服和工具等商品，也讓商品
變得更便宜，就有更多人能夠購買這些商品。人
們在城市裡也有了新的工作，所以有很多人搬到
城市。而這也創造了新的旅行方式，鐵路和蒸汽
船也讓人們能夠長途旅行。

背景知識 Plus!

蒸汽機（steam engine）發明之
前，工廠會使用像是水車的水力來運
作，許多工廠因為必須蓋在水邊，因此
無法建造。然而由於蒸汽機使用煤碳
產生的蒸汽，讓許多工廠得以建造。
但是當工廠燃燒太多煤碳時，歐
洲的天空就被煙囪排出的煙
霧給覆蓋了。

Comprehension Checkup 理解能力確認

Circle the best answer. 圈選出正確的答案

1. What did England first build during this revolution?
   ⓐ cities　　　　ⓑ factories　　　　ⓒ tools

2. What did the steam engine do to goods?
   ⓐ made them rare　　　　　ⓑ made them worse
   ⓒ made them cheaper

3. More people moved to _____ for new jobs.
   ⓐ cities　　　　ⓑ farms　　　　ⓒ England

4. New ways of travel like _____ and steamships appeared.
   ⓐ long-distance　　　ⓑ railroads　　　ⓒ new jobs

Complete the sentence. 完成句子

The <u>birth</u> of the .... engine began the Industrial
出生
Revolution.

Wrap Up　Number the sentences in order 寫出句子的順序

1 The steam engine was invented.

☐ New jobs were created in cites.

☐ The railroad and steamship carried people to the cities.

☐ Factories quickly produced many goods.

☐ England built factories.

Every society has a culture. But some have more than one. These are <u>multicultural</u> societies. America is an example. Most <u>Americans</u> 美國人 have <u>European</u> <u>ancestors</u>. They brought their culture to America. 歐洲人 祖先 Later, people came from all over the world. Some came from South America. Others came from Africa and Asia. They all brought their cultures too. They have different foods, <u>languages</u>, 語言 and <u>religions</u>. But they must <u>respect</u> 宗教 尊重 each other. That way, they can live together <u>peacefully</u>. 和平地

多元文化的

Check True or False 是非題

1. Some Americans came from South America.　　T / F

2. There are different foods and religions in America.　T / F

多元文化

每個社會都有文化,但有些社會不只有一種文化,這就叫做多元文化的社會。美國就是一個例子,大多數美國人都有歐洲人的祖先,他們將自己的文化帶到了美國。後來,人們從世界各地來到這裡。有些人來自南美洲,其他人來自非洲和亞洲,大家也都帶來了他們的文化,他們有不同的食物、語言和宗教,但是大家必須互相尊重,這樣才能和平共處。

背景知識 Plus!

在多元文化(multicultural society)中,各種文化互相交集、影響、共同發展,而食物就是其中一個例子,融合(fusion)食物是以其他國家的食材和烹煮方式混合而成,這種食物第一次在美國加州被製作出來。如果你在吃融合食物,能夠體驗各式各樣的新文化。

Circle the best answer. 圈選出正確的答案

1. Where did most early Americans come from?
   - ⓐ Europe
   - ⓑ Asia
   - ⓒ Africa

2. How many cultures does America have?
   - ⓐ none
   - ⓑ one
   - ⓒ many

3. Different people all brought their _____ to America.
   - ⓐ societies
   - ⓑ cultures
   - ⓒ ancestors

4. People from different cultures must _____ each other.
   - ⓐ bring
   - ⓑ know
   - ⓒ respect

Complete the sentence. 完成句子

A .... society has many different cultures.

WrapUp Fill in the blanks. 總複習，將單字填入空格

Multicultural Society

特性	• It has more than one ❶ .... • People must ❷ .... each other.
例子	• Most early ❸ .... have European ancestors. • People from South America, ❹ ...., and Asia brought their cultures.

Americans   Africa   culture   respect

55 What Is a Civilization?

R_55.mp3

People living together is part of <u>human</u> history. There, a <u>civilization</u>
人類的
文明
starts. And different <u>systems</u> help it. First, people have a system for
系統
food. This was usually through <u>farming</u> in the past. They also have
農業
a <u>government</u> system. This makes laws
政府
and <u>protects</u> the people. These
保護
people also create a culture and
<u>share</u> it. They share a language,
分享
a religion, and <u>customs</u>. This
（社會）習俗
is how a civilization unites
people.

Check True or False 是非題

1. Farming was not a system for food in the past.　　T / F

2. People share a language in a civilization.　　T / F

什麼是文明？

人們共同生活是人類歷史的一部分，在那裡是一
個文明的起源，而不同的系統可以幫助建立文
明。首先，人們有食物的系統，在過去通常是透
過農業來取得的。人們也有政府的系統，會制定
法律並保護人民。這些人也創造一種文化並與他
人共享。大家共享語言、宗教和習俗，這就是文
明如何使人們團結的方式。

背景知識 Plus!

在古代，所有文明（civilization）
最早出現的地方都是在河流沿岸，人
們需要水來維持農業來獲得食物。而人
類四大文明分別是美索不達米亞、印
度河、埃及和黃河。

Comprehension Checkup 理解能力確認

Circle the best answer. 圈選出正確的答案

1. What starts where people live together?
   ⓐ a civilization　　ⓑ nature　　ⓒ the past

2. What was a system for food in the past?
   ⓐ a law　　ⓑ culture　　ⓒ farming

3. A _____ system makes laws for people.
   ⓐ custom　　ⓑ government　　ⓒ language

4. People create a culture and share a language, a religion, and
   _____.
   ⓐ customs　　ⓑ systems　　ⓒ people

Complete the sentence. 完成句子

A civilization has different _____ to unite its people.

Wrap Up　Fill in the blanks. 總複習，將單字填入空格

Systems for a Civilization

• food system	▶ ❶ .... in the past
• ❷ .... system	▶ make laws, protect people
• ❸	▶ language, religion, ❹ ....

government　　culture　　farming　　customs

WORD REVIEW

Crossword Puzzle 填字遊戲

Across
1. 人類
2. 地點
4. （國家）首都
5. 尊重

Down
1. 歷史
3. 語言
6. 分享

Match with the correct definition. 將單字連到正確的意思

1. multicultural •

    a lines running from north to south on the globe

2. lines of longitude •

    b the thing which brought the Industrial Revolution

3. government •

    c having more than one culture

4. steam engine •

    d a system in a society that makes laws and protects people

Fill in the blank with the correct words.
將正確的單字填入空格中

> ancestors　　exact　　farming　　goods　　construction

1. This point where they meet show _____ locations.
   它們交會的點顯示了確切的位置。

2. Its _____ began in 1848.　它的建造工程始於 1848 年。

3. The factories quickly produced _____ like clothes and tools.
   工廠快速生產衣服和工具等商品。

4. Most Americans have European _____.
   大多數美國人的祖先是歐洲人。

5. This was usually through _____ in the past.
   過去通常是透過耕作取得。

Fill in the blank with the correct expressions.
將正確的表達填入空格中

> to the top　　moved to　　is located
>
> came from　　long-distance travel

1. The Washington Monument _____ in Washington, D.C.

2. Today, the elevator takes people _____.

3. The railroad and steamship allowed _____.

4. People _____ all over the world.

5. People _____ cities. This created new ways of travel.

美洲原住民的土地
Land for Native Americans

R_56.mp3

Before Europeans came to America, people lived there. These were Native Americans. Europeans called them "Indians." Disease and
美洲原住民   疾病
war made their lives hard. Over time, their population grew smaller.
戰爭   艱難的   隨著時間
Today, some of them live on reservations. These are special areas
保留區域
for the native tribes. Reservations have their own
原住民 部落
government and laws. The Native
Americans want to protect their own
culture there. This includes their
包含
languages, stories, arts, and religions.

Check True or False 是非題

① Europeans called Native Americans "Indians."　　T / F

② Reservations do not protect Native American　　T / F
culture.

美洲原住民的土地

在歐洲人來到美洲之前，就有人們在那裡生活，他們是美洲原住民，歐洲人將他們稱為「印第安人」。疾病和戰爭使他們過著艱困的生活，他們的人口隨著時間變得越來越少。現在，其中有些原住民住在保留地，這些是專門為原住民部落設立的特別區域。保留區有他們自己的政府和法律，美洲原住民希望在那裡保護自己的文化，這包括了他們的語言、故事、藝術和宗教。

背景知識 Plus!

哥倫布在 1492 年抵達美洲大陸，當時美洲大約有 150 萬個原住民。然而哥倫布以為自己登陸印度，因此稱這些原住民是**印第安人（Indians）**。自此此後，隨著歐洲人湧入美洲大陸，原住民因領土紛爭和疾病而飽受痛苦。

Comprehension Checkup 理解能力確認

Circle the best answer. 圈選出正確的答案

1. Who lived in America first?
   - ⓐ Europeans
   - ⓑ English people
   - ⓒ Native Americans

2. What made life hard for Native Americans?
   - ⓐ religion
   - ⓑ disease and war
   - ⓒ small population

3. Reservations have their own _____ and laws.
   - ⓐ disease
   - ⓑ government
   - ⓒ hard lives

4. Native Americans want to protect their _____.
   - ⓐ culture
   - ⓑ war
   - ⓒ time

Complete the sentence. 完成句子

In America, some native tribes live on ....

Wrap Up Fill in the blanks. 總複習，將單字填入空格

Reservations for Native Americans		culture
人口減少的原因	• ❶ .... and war	government
居住地	• ❷	disease
原住民法律	• their own ❸ .... and laws	reservations
他們想要什麼	• to protect their ❹	

Governments <u>provide</u> many <u>services</u> for people. These include
提供　　　　　　服務
<u>health care</u> and <u>education</u>. And people must pay taxes for these
健康照護　　　教育
services. But there are many ways of paying taxes. First, everyone
can pay the same <u>amount</u>. Let's say everyone pays $100
數量
in taxes. For a person with $1,000, that's only
ten percent. But a person with $200
pays <u>half</u> of their money! Many
一半
people think this is <u>unfair</u>. So most
不公平的
countries have different ways to
<u>collect</u> taxes.
收款

Check True or False 是非題

❶ Taxes pay for education.　　　　　　　　　　　　T / F

❷ It's fair if everyone pays the same amount of tax.　T / F

一樣的稅金？

政府為人們提供許多服務，其中包括健康照護和
教育，而人們必須為這些服務繳稅。但是有很多
繳稅的方式，首先每個人可以繳納相同金額的稅
金，假如每個人都要繳 100 美元的稅金，對於
一個有 1,000 美元的人來說，這只是百分之十而
已。但對於只有 200 美元的人來說，卻要繳出身
上一半的錢！許多人認為這樣是不公平的事，因
此大多數國家都有不同的收稅方式。

背景知識 Plus!

稅（tax）的種類有分很多種，
比較具代表性的是所得稅，根據收入
的多少繳納特定的比例。如果規定要繳
納 10% 的稅，所得 100 萬元的人必須
繳 10 萬元的稅金，所得 200 萬的人
則必須繳 20 萬的稅金。而收入超
過一定金額的人則要繳納更
高的所得稅。

Comprehension Checkup 理解能力確認

Circle the best answer. 圈選出正確的答案

1. What do people pay taxes for?
   - ⓐ businesses
   - ⓑ religion
   - ⓒ government services

2. What do people think about the same amount of tax?
   - ⓐ unfair
   - ⓑ fair
   - ⓒ no opinion

3. In the example, people with $1,000 pay _____.
   - ⓐ five percent
   - ⓑ ten percent
   - ⓒ twenty percent

4. Most countries have _____ ways of collecting taxes.
   - ⓐ the same
   - ⓑ different
   - ⓒ no other

Complete the sentence. 完成句子

People must pay ...., but it is unfair for everyone to pay the same amount.

Wrap Up Fill in the blanks. 總複習，將單字填入空格

Paying Taxes	
• where taxes go	▶ the ❶ ....
• what taxes are for	▶ health care and ❷ ....
• ❸ .... of paying taxes	▶ the same ❹ .... for everybody ▶ different ways

> ways   education   amount   government

全球化
Globalization

R_58.mp3

Nations are getting closer every day. How? Through globalization.
靠得更近　　　　　　　　　通過～　　全球化
Companies from different countries always trade. A Russian company
公司　　　　　　　　　　　　　　　貿易　　俄羅斯的
provides oil. A Canadian company provides wood. And Chinese
加拿大的
factories make products. They all trade money, goods, and resources.
產品
Also, many people often travel
to foreign countries. They watch
外國的
foreign TV programs and movies
too. This spreads cultures. Someone
in Italy can watch a Hollywood
movie and eat tacos.
墨西哥煎玉米捲

Check True or False 是非題

❶ Companies from different countries do not trade. T / F

❷ Globalization spreads cultures across the world. T / F

全球化

國家之間的關係一天比一天更緊密。這是怎麼辦到的呢？這是透過全球化。來自不同國家的公司一直在進行貿易。俄羅斯公司提供石油，加拿大公司提供木材，而中國的工廠製造產品，他們都在交易金錢、貨物和資源。此外，許多人經常到國外旅行，他們也會收看外國的電視節目和電影，這也讓文化擴散出去。在義大利的人，可以收看好萊塢電影和享用墨西哥玉米捲。

背景知識 Plus!

交通和通訊在拉近世界的距離中扮演重要的角色，我們可以在一天之內從一個國家飛到地球另一端的國家，也可以和在國外的朋友在現實中聊天。然而全球化（globalization）也有副作用，只是單方面接受部分國家的文化，每個國家獨一無二的文化也會逐漸消失。

Circle the best answer. 圈選出正確的答案

1. What make(s) nations closer?
   - ⓐ globalization
   - ⓑ wood and oil
   - ⓒ a Russian company

2. What do different countries trade with each other?
   - ⓐ laws
   - ⓑ factories
   - ⓒ money and resources

3. Many people travel to foreign countries and spread _____.
   - ⓐ religions
   - ⓑ cultures
   - ⓒ nations

4. People can enjoy food and movies from other _____.
   - ⓐ countries
   - ⓑ foreigners
   - ⓒ TV programs

Complete the sentence. 完成句子

Through globalization, people from different countries get
....

WrapUp Fill in the blanks. 總複習，將單字填入空格

Globalization

- ❶ ....
- ▶ money, goods, and resources
- ❷ .... to foreign countries
- ❸ .... foreign TV programs and movies
- ▶ ❹ .... cultures

spread　　trade　　travel　　watch

In the 1800s and 1900s, many Europeans came to America. They
歐洲人
had difficult lives in their countries. They wanted a better life in
更好的　生活（可數）
America. Most arrived first on Ellis Island near
到達
New York. This small island was an

immigration station.
移民站
Government officers worked
政府公務員
there. The station was very busy.
（機構）站
Ships arrived with thousands of
成千上萬～
immigrants every day. And these
移民
people settled all over the US.
定居

Check True or False 是非題

❶ Ellis Island was not in America.　　　T / F

❷ Government officers worked on the island.　　T / F

移民站

在 1800 年代和 1900 年代，許多歐洲人來到美國。由於他們在自己的國家過得很困苦，想在美國過上更好的生活。大多數人首先會抵達紐約附近的埃利斯島，這個小島是一個移民站，政府公務員在那裡工作。移民站非常繁忙，每天都有船隻載著數千名的移民到那裡，而這些人會在美國各地定居下來。

背景知識 Plus!

艾利斯島（Ellis Island）位於可以俯瞰自由女神像的位置。在當時，有很多移民經過這裡，因此被稱為「通往新世界的入口」。這裡曾是美國大型移民站，但是在 1924 年關閉，現在已經成為世界知名的旅遊勝地。

Comprehension Checkup 理解能力確認

Circle the best answer. 圈選出正確的答案

1. What did many immigrants want in America?
   a difficult lives   **b** a better life   **c** an island

2. Where was Ellis Island located?
   a near New York   **b** in Europe   **c** all over the US

3. Ships came to the island with lots of _____.
   a money
   b government officers
   c immigrants

4. These people left the island and _____ all over the US.
   a settled   **b** helped   **c** came from

Complete the sentence. 完成句子

Many immigrants came to Ellis Island and began new
.... in America.

Wrap Up Fill in the blanks. 總複習，將單字填入空格

Ellis Island

位置	• near New York
當時的角色	• an ❶ .... station
抵達的人們	• ❷ ....
移民的原因	• They ❸ .... a better life.
抵達後的生活	• People ❹ .... all over the US.

wanted

immigration

Europeans

settled

In the 1960s, black people had few <u>legal</u> rights in America. Schools
合法的
did not <u>allow</u> black students. Stores and restaurants did not <u>serve</u>
准~進入   服務
black <u>customers</u>. It was especially bad in the
顧客
South. So they decided to fight this. Lots
of black people <u>marched</u> in the streets.
遊行抗議
Martin Luther King was the <u>leader</u> of
領導人
this peaceful <u>movement</u>. This <u>Civil</u>
（有特定目標的）運動   公民權
<u>Rights</u> Movement changed America a
lot. Black Americans <u>won</u> their <u>rights</u>.
（原形：win）贏得   權力

Check True or False 是非題

❶ Many black Americans couldn't go to school   T / F
in the 1960s.

❷ Black Americans had more rights in the South.   T / F

美國黑人的權利

在 1960 年代，黑人在美國幾乎沒有合法權利。學校不准黑人學生入學，商店和餐廳也不服務黑人顧客。這種情況在南方特別嚴重，因此他們決定為此抗爭。許多黑人上街遊行抗議，而馬丁‧路德‧金恩是這場和平運動的領導者。這場民權運動使美國做了很多改變，而美國黑人也爭取到他們的權利。

背景知識 Plus!

馬丁‧路德‧金恩（**Martin Luther King**）是美國牧師，也是黑人人權運動的領導人。一名黑人婦女因為在公車上沒有讓座給一名白人乘客而被逮捕，這使金恩發起了「抵制公車運動」，而很多人持續上街遊行抗議超過一年的時間，以廢除不平等的法律。

Comprehension Checkup 理解能力確認

Circle the best answer. 圈選出正確的答案

1. When did the Civil Rights Movement start?
   - ⓐ 1940s
   - ⓑ 1960s
   - ⓒ 1980s

2. How did black Americans fight the bad <u>treatment</u>?
   對待
   - ⓐ left America
   - ⓑ moved to the South
   - ⓒ marched in the streets

3. Martin Luther King led the _____ movement.
   - ⓐ unfair
   - ⓑ better
   - ⓒ peaceful

4. After the movement, black Americans won more _____.
   - ⓐ money
   - ⓑ rights
   - ⓒ leaders

Complete the sentence. 完成句子

The Civil .... Movement helped many black people in America.

Wrap Up Fill in the blanks. 總複習，將單字填入空格

The Civil Rights Movement

背景
- Black people had few ❶ .... rights in America.
- no ❷ .... for them
- no stores or restaurants for them

執行內容
- Black people ❸ .... in the streets.
- They changed America and Black Americans ❹ .... their rights.

marched   won   legal   schools

WORD REVIEW

🙂 Crossword Puzzle 填字遊戲

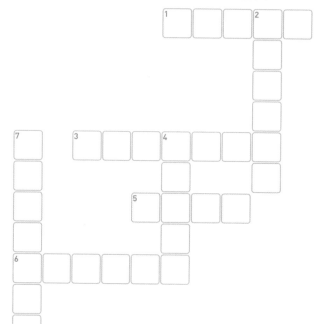

Across
1. 合法的
3. （機構）站
5. 生活
6. 抵達

Down
2. 數量
4. 部落
7. 公司

🐴 Match with the correct definition. 將單字連到正確的意思

1. tax •

2. Native Americans •

3. immigrants •

4. The Civil Rights Movement •

ⓐ people who lived in America before Europeans came

ⓑ the money that people pay for government services

ⓒ people who go to another country to live there

ⓓ the movement that black Americans started in the 1960s for their rights

Fill in the blank with the correct words.
將正確的單字填入空格中

> unfair　　settled　　disease　　marched　　foreign

1. _____ and war made their lives hard.
   疾病和戰爭使他們過著艱困的生活。

2. Many people think this is _____.
   許多人認為這樣是不公平的事。

3. They watch _____ TV programs and movies too.
   他們也可以收看外國的電視節目和電影。

4. And these people _____ all over the US.
   而這些人在美國各地定居下來。

5. Lots of black people _____ in the streets.
   許多黑人上街遊行抗議。

Fill in the blank with the correct expressions.
將正確的表達填入空格中

> half of　　thousands of　　the leader of　　over time　　getting closer

1. _____, their population grew smaller.

2. For a person with $200, $100 is _____ their money!

3. Nations are _____ every day.

4. Ships arrived with _____ immigrants every day.

5. Martin Luther King was _____ this peaceful movement.

鄰里與社群
Neighborhoods vs. Communities

R_61.mp3

When the teacher was explaining something, I was <u>confused</u>. So I
迷惑的
<u>put up</u> my hand. "What's the <u>difference</u> between a <u>neighborhood</u>
升起   差別   近鄰
and a <u>community</u>? I don't get it." He answered, "A neighborhood is
群體
where you and your <u>neighbors</u> live. It's a <u>physical</u> place, and you can
鄰居   實物的
find it on a map. My neighborhood is in South Chicago.

<u>On the other hand</u>, a community is a group of people, and they
在另一方面
<u>have something in common</u> such as <u>race</u>, <u>occupation</u>, or interests.
有～的共同點   種族   職業
In my neighborhood, for example, we

have a large <u>Asian</u> community and a
亞洲人
community of <u>volunteers</u>."
志工

Read and Complete 完成句子

① The teacher explains a _____ and a community.

② The people in a community have something in _____.

鄰里與社群

老師在解釋的時候，我一頭霧水，於是舉手發問：「鄰里和社群的差別是什麼？我不太懂。」老師回答：「鄰里是指你和鄰居居住的地方，它是一個實際的地方，可以在地圖上找到，像我的鄰里就在南芝加哥。而另一方面，社群指的是一群人，他們有一些共同點，像是種族、職業或興趣。舉例來說，在我的鄰里，我們有一個很大的亞裔社群，和一個志工社群。」

背景知識 Plus!

社群（community）的特點是不受地區和空間的限制，以共同的價值觀所創造出來的，尤其是現在，像是 SNS（社群網路服務）、網站、部落格、論壇等網路社群都是以網路科技為基礎來積極組織和運營。網路社群已經進化成線下社群，並發揮了新的作用。

Comprehension Checkup 理解能力確認

Circle the best answer. 圈選出正確的答案

1. Where is the teacher's neighborhood?
   - **ⓐ** Asia
   - **ⓑ** community
   - **ⓒ** South Chicago

2. What is NOT a community?
   - **ⓐ** an area of New York
   - **ⓑ** a group of Koreans in LA.
   - **ⓒ** a group of lawyers in New York

3. What is a neighborhood?
   - **ⓐ** It's a map of a city or a town.
   - **ⓑ** It's a place where people live.
   - **ⓒ** It's a special place for the same race.
   - **ⓓ** It has something in common with jobs.

4. Why does the teacher mention a community of volunteers?
   - **ⓐ** to give an example of a neighborhood
   - **ⓑ** to indicate his neighborhood on the map
   - **ⓒ** to say that he is interested in volunteering
   - **ⓓ** to compare a neighborhood and a community

Complete the sentence. 完成句子

A neighborhood is where your ❶ .... live. You can find it on a ❷ .... A ❸ .... is a group of people. They have something in common such as jobs and hobbies.

Wrap Up Fill in the blanks. 總複習，將單字填入空格

neighborhood	community	
• ❶ .... places • where neighbors ❷	• a group of ❸ .... with things in common • ❹ ...., occupation, interest	race live physical people

寬扎節快樂！
Merry Kwanzaa!

R_62.mp3

Most <u>African Americans</u> wake up early on December 26. It's the
非裔美國人

first day of Kwanzaa. Kwanzaa is an African American <u>holiday</u>. It
節日

<u>connects African Americans to</u> their <u>traditional</u> African culture.
連結～到～ 傳統的

They <u>celebrate</u> their African <u>identity</u>. African families in America
慶祝 身分

put up African <u>flags</u>. And they <u>prepare</u> a large <u>feast</u>. They have the
旗 準備 盛宴

feast together with family and friends. Then, they play traditional

African drums. Everyone dances to the

<u>rhythm</u>. January 1 is the last day of Kwanzaa.
節奏

Time to open the Kwanzaa presents!

Read and Complete 完成句子

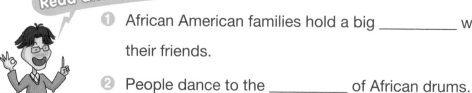

❶ African American families hold a big _____ with
their friends.

❷ People dance to the _____ of African drums.

寬扎節快樂！

大多數的非裔美國人在 12 月 26 日會早起，因為這是寬扎節的第一天。寬扎節是非裔美國人的節日，它將非裔美國人連結到他們的傳統非洲文化。他們會慶祝自己的非裔身份。在美國的非裔家庭會掛起非洲的旗幟，他們還會準備了一場盛大的宴會，並與家人和朋友一起享用這場盛宴。接著他們會演奏傳統的非洲鼓，每個人都隨著節奏起舞。而 1 月 1 日是寬扎節的最後一天，那時就可以打開寬扎節的禮物了！

背景知識 Plus!

寬扎（Kwanzaa）意為「初熟的果實」，這對非裔美國人來說是一個重要的節慶。最近有很多家庭都喜歡在聖誕節慶祝寬扎節，除了聖誕節的裝飾，還有象徵寬扎節的 7 支燭臺裝飾 "Kinara"，每支蠟燭代表著「團結、自我決定、集體工作和責任、合作經濟學、目的、創造力、信仰」。

Comprehension Checkup 理解能力確認

Circle the best answer. 圈選出正確的答案

1. Who celebrates Kwanzaa?
   ⓐ Africans   ⓑ Americans in Africa   ⓒ African Americans

2. When do they open the presents?
   ⓐ after Kwanzaa is finished   ⓑ on the last day of Kwanzaa
   ⓒ on the first day of Kwanzaa

3. Why is Kwanzaa meaningful to African Americans?
   ⓐ Because it allows them to go back to Africa.
   ⓑ Because it shows the power of African music.
   ⓒ Because it introduces African culture to Americans.
   ⓓ Because it links them to their traditional African culture.

4. What is NOT true about Kwanzaa?
   ⓐ People hang African flags.
   ⓑ People enjoy it for 3 or 4 days.
   ⓒ People prepare a gift for each other.
   ⓓ People eat and dance at the parties.

Complete the sentence. 完成句子

Kwanzaa is a big holiday for African ❶ ....
Kwanzaa lets them enjoy their ❷ .... culture. They
celebrate their African ❸ ....

Wrap Up Fill in the blanks. 總複習，將單字填入空格

期間、意義	from December 26 to January 1, ❶ .... American holiday
紀念	African Americans ❷ .... their traditional culture.
緣由	They are proud of their African ❸ ....
會做的事情	They have a large ❹ .... together.

celebrate   African   feast   identity

寬扎節快樂！ 163

你可以買什麼

What You Can Buy

R_63.mp3

What do you usually buy with your money? Money can be used to buy <u>goods</u> or <u>services</u>. Goods are <u>physical</u> things, so you can see or
商品　　　服務　　　　　　　有形的
touch them. A <u>meal</u> from a restaurant is a good. It takes money to
一餐
make goods, so it <u>costs</u> money to buy them. Services are what people
花費～
do to <u>earn</u> money. Servers in a restaurant
賺得
<u>provide</u> a service by bringing the meals
提供
to <u>customers</u>. Their time, <u>skill</u>, and
顧客　　　　　　　　技能
<u>effort</u> cost money. Customers <u>pay</u> for
努力　　　　　　　　支付
both goods and services at places like
stores and restaurants.

Read and Complete 完成句子

❶ People use money to buy _____ and services.

❷ _____ at restaurants pay for services.

你可以買什麼

你通常會用你的錢來買什麼呢？錢可以用來購買商品或服務。商品是有形的東西，所以你可以看得到也摸得到商品，由餐廳做出的餐點就是一種商品。製造商品需要錢，所以購買商品也需要花錢。服務則是人們為了賺錢而做的事情，在餐廳的服務生透過送餐給顧客來提供服務。他們的時間、技能和努力都要花錢，顧客在像是商店和餐廳的場所支付商品和服務的費用。

背景知識 Plus!

商品（goods）和服務（service）之間有什麼差別？評估產品的品質很簡單，但評估服務品質卻相對複雜的。人們可以儲存商品，但不能儲存服務。此外，商品從生產到被消費需要時間，然而服務則是在提供的同時也在被消費。

Circle the best answer. 圈選出正確的答案

1. What is an example of goods?
   ⓐ concerts ⓑ hamburgers ⓒ bus rides

2. What is an example of a service?
   ⓐ a book ⓑ a phone ⓒ a piano lesson

3. What is true about goods?
   ⓐ You can't see or touch goods.
   ⓑ People like customers can be goods.
   ⓒ Money is needed to make goods.
   ⓓ Goods are time and skill for you.

4. Why should customers pay for services?
   ⓐ Because effort to provide services costs money.
   ⓑ Because services are actions to make food.
   ⓒ Because services are free for the customers.
   ⓓ Because services are provided by customers.

Complete the sentence. 完成句子

Customers use ❶ .... for goods and services. Goods
are ❷ .... things. Services are what people do to
❸ .... money.

Wrap Up Fill in the blanks. 總複習，將單字填入空格

Customers pay ❶ .... for...		goods
❷	❸	time
• physical things	• people's actions	services
• You can see or touch them.	• ❹ ...., skill, effort	money

Remembering Heroes

R_64.mp3

<u>Soldiers</u> keep their countries safe. Sometimes, they <u>take part in</u> a
　　軍人　　　　　　　　　　　　　　　　　　　　　　　　　　　　參加～
war, and even give their lives to protect their countries.

<u>Memorial Day</u> in America is a holiday <u>dedicated</u> to <u>fallen</u> soldiers. It
（美國）陣亡將士紀念日　　　　　　　　　　　　　　專注的　　　死去的
was started in 1868 after the American <u>Civil War</u>. American <u>citizens</u>
　　　　　　　　　　　　　　　　　　　　　美國南北戰爭　　　　　　　公民
remember their soldiers' <u>sacrifice</u> on Memorial Day. They visit
　　　　　　　　　　　　犧牲
<u>cemeteries</u> and bring flowers. Many volunteers place American flags
墓地
on soldiers' <u>graves</u>. Memorial Day is on the last
　　　　　墳墓
Monday of May. Most workers and students
have the <u>day off</u>. It is important not to forget
　　　休息日
the <u>noble</u> sacrifice soldiers made.
高尚的

Read and Complete 完成句子

❶ Some soldiers died to _____ their countries.

❷ Sometimes, soldiers fight in a _____.

銘記英雄

軍人要持續守護他們的國家安全，有時他們要上戰場打仗，甚至為了保護國家而犧牲自己的性命。美國的陣亡將士紀念日是一個專門紀念殉職軍人的節日，始於美國南北戰爭後的 1868 年。美國公民在陣亡將士紀念日緬懷軍人的犧牲，他們來到墓地並獻上鮮花。許多志工會將美國國旗放在軍人的墳墓上。陣亡將士紀念日是在五月的最後一個星期一。大多數的上班族和學生會在這一天放假，重要的是不要忘記軍人崇高的犧牲。

背景知識 Plus!

每個國家都有紀念為國家犧牲生命的軍人紀念日。韓國有顯忠日（6 月 6 日），為了紀念 625 戰爭（韓戰）參戰先烈的亡魂紀念日，並在 1956 年首次被訂定。英國則是名為 Remembrance Day 的節日（又稱為國殤星期日），訂在第一次世界大戰停戰紀念日 11 月 11 日的前一個星期天。

Comprehension Checkup 理解能力確認

Circle the best answer. 圈選出正確的答案

1. What does Memorial Day celebrate?
   ⓐ hard workers   ⓑ brave citizens   ⓒ fallen soldiers

2. When was Memorial Day started?
   ⓐ after the American Civil War
   ⓑ after the last Monday of May
   ⓒ after many volunteers' day off

3. Why is Memorial Day important?
   ⓐ Because it keeps America safe.
   ⓑ Because it gives volunteers more work to do.
   ⓒ Because it lets people remember soldiers' sacrifice.
   ⓓ Because it is one of the biggest American holidays.

4. What do American citizens NOT do on Memorial Day?
   ⓐ They remember fallen soldiers.   ⓑ They experience a war.
   ⓒ They put flags on graves.   ⓓ They bring flowers to cemeteries.

Complete the sentence. 完成句子

> Memorial Day is dedicated to fallen soldiers. American citizens
> ❶ .... the soldiers' sacrifice to protect their country.
> They bring ❷ .... and flags to the soldiers' ❸ ....

Wrap Up Fill in the blanks. 總複習，將單字填入空格

Memorial Day		cemeteries
日期	• the last ❶ .... of May	remember
意義	• a holiday to ❷ .... fallen soldiers	sacrifice
會做的事	• remember soldiers' ❸ .... • visit ❹ .... with flowers and flags	Monday

Julius Caesar is in many history museums and books. He lived over 2,000 years ago. He was a <u>Roman</u> <u>politician</u>. We know about his life 羅馬的 政治家 from <u>primary sources</u>. Primary sources are letters and pictures from (primary 最初的) 第一手資料 the <u>past</u>. Caesar kept a <u>journal</u>, and it survived until <u>modern times</u>. 過去的 日記 現代 <u>Historians</u> learned a lot about his life from his journal. We can also 歷史學家 see Caesar's <u>appearance</u> on <u>ancient</u> Roman <u>coins</u>. These primary 外表 古代的 硬幣 sources help us understand people from the past. Without them, much of their past would be a <u>mystery</u>. 神秘的事物

Read and Complete 完成句子

❶ Julius Caesar was a _____ of Rome.

❷ Historians studied _____ sources to know Caesar's life.

Comprehension Checkup 理解能力確認

Circle the best answer. 圈選出正確的答案

1. Which primary source did Caesar make?
   - ⓐ a journal
   - ⓑ a museum
   - ⓒ a historian

2. How do we know what Caesar looked like?
   - ⓐ from coins
   - ⓑ from letters
   - ⓒ from books

3. What is NOT a primary source?
   - ⓐ coins
   - ⓑ letters
   - ⓒ museums
   - ⓓ journals

4. Why are primary sources important?
   - ⓐ Because they lived over 2,000 years.
   - ⓑ Because they make the past mysterious.
   - ⓒ Because they make historians study Rome.
   - ⓓ Because they help us know historical people.

Complete the sentence. 完成句子

❶ .... use primary sources to understand the past. Roman coins showed us what Julius Caesar ❷ .... like. His ❸ .... told us about his life.

Wrap Up Fill in the blanks. 總複習，將單字填入空格

Primary Sources		understand
種類	letters and pictures from the ❶	journal
意義	help us ❷ .... people from the past	historians
例子	Julius Caesar's ❸ ....: ❹ .... learned a lot about his life.	past

WORD REVIEW

Crossword Puzzle 填字遊戲

Across
2. 賺得
3. 高尚的
5. 有形的
7. 種族

Down
1. 古代的
4. 身分
6. 日記
8. 努力

Match with the correct definition. 將單字連到正確的意思

1. community •

     ⓐ where you and your neighbors live

2. goods •

     ⓑ a group of people with something in common

3. neighborhood •

     ⓒ physical things that you can see or touch

4. primary source •

     ⓓ letters and pictures from the past

Fill in the blank with the correct words.
將正確的單字填入空格中

> dedicated   mystery   prepare   provide   sacrifice

1. African Americans _____ a large feast to celebrate Kwanzaa.   非裔美國人會為了慶祝寬扎節，而準備一場盛大的宴會。

2. Servers _____ a service by bringing the meals to customers.   服務生透過為顧客送餐來提供服務。

3. Memorial Day is a holiday _____ to fallen soldiers.   陣亡將士紀念日是專門紀念逝世軍人的節日。

4. It is important not to forget the noble _____ soldiers made.   重要的是，我們不可以忘記軍人做出的崇高犧牲。

5. Without primary sources, much of the past would be a _____.   如果沒有第一手資料，許多過去都會是個謎團。

Fill in the blank with the correct expressions.
將正確的表達填入空格中

> connects ~ to   pay for   for example   put up   take part in

1. When the teacher was explaining something, I was confused and _____ my hand.

2. Kwanzaa _____ African Americans _____ their traditional African culture.

3. In my neighborhood, _____, we have a large Asian community.

4. Customers _____ both goods and services at places like restaurants.

5. Sometimes, soldiers _____ a war.

Where do you keep your money? Most kids have a <u>piggy bank</u> or
（豬形）撲滿
another safe place to keep their money. Most <u>adults</u> use <u>regular</u>
成年人   正規的
banks. Banks <u>keep peoples' money safe</u> and pay <u>interest</u> for it.
保持～安全   利息
Interest is the cost of money. So, you can make money by saving it
in a bank. <u>Meanwhile</u>, banks use customers'
同時
saved money. They <u>lend</u> it to other people.
貸款
The <u>borrowers</u> must pay back the money
借方
<u>on time</u> and pay interest for it to the
準時
bank. In this way, interest lets both
people and banks <u>earn</u> some money.
賺得

Read and Complete 完成句子

① People keep their _____ in a bank.

② Banks pay _____ for customers' money.

金錢與利息

你的錢會放在哪裡？大多數的小朋友都有一個小
豬撲滿，或是找其他安全的地方來存放他們的
錢。而大多數的成年人會使用正規的銀行，銀行
將人們的錢安全地保存起來，並支付錢的利息。
利息是金錢的成本，因此我們可以透過把錢存在
銀行來賺錢。同時，銀行會使用客戶的存款，並
把錢借貸給其他人。借款人必須準時還錢，並向
銀行支付利息。透過這種方式，利息讓人們和銀
行都賺到了一些錢。

背景知識 Plus!

你知道「定期存款」和「零存整
付」的差別嗎？定期存款是指在一定
期間內在銀行存放大量金額，到期時會
收到本金和利息（interest）。零存整
付是指每個月儲蓄一定的金額，存
款的利率通常高於活期存款的利
率，因為銀行很容易透過管理
客戶存入的大量資金來
增加收入。

Comprehension Checkup 理解能力確認

Circle the best answer. 圈選出正確的答案

1. Where do people NOT keep their money?
   - **ⓐ** safe places
   - **ⓑ** piggy banks
   - **ⓒ** regular places

2. What is the cost of money?
   - **ⓐ** safety
   - **ⓑ** interest
   - **ⓒ** borrower

3. How can you make money by using a bank?
   - **ⓐ** Banks keep your money and give you interest.
   - **ⓑ** You can keep your money safe with no interest.
   - **ⓒ** You can lend your money to banks with interest.
   - **ⓓ** You can get interest by introducing banks to your friends.

4. How do banks make money?
   - **ⓐ** Borrowers pay interest to banks.
   - **ⓑ** Banks connect lenders and borrowers.
   - **ⓒ** Banks keep the customers' saved money.
   - **ⓓ** Customers pay interest to banks for saving their money.

Complete the sentence. 完成句子

People ❶ .... their money in banks. Banks give them some interest. Banks use customers' saved money to ❷ .... it to other people. Borrowers should ❸ .... back the money with some interest.

Wrap Up Fill in the blanks. 總複習，將單字填入空格

Who	What They Do	About Interest
customer	❶ .... their money safe in banks	❷ .... interest
bank	They ❸ .... customers' money to other people.	Borrowers ❹ .... back with interest.

pay   lend   keep   get

法律與規定
Laws and Rules

R_67.mp3

Parents and teachers make <u>rules</u> to keep children safe. The
　　　　　　　　　　　　　規定
<u>government</u> also makes rules to keep citizens safe. It's one of the
政府
many <u>functions</u> of a government. <u>Politicians</u> make <u>laws</u> for citizens
　　　功能　　　　　　　　　　　　政治家　　　　法律
to follow. They can make laws <u>against</u> killing and <u>stealing</u>, for
　　　　　　　　　　　　　　　預防～　　　　　偷竊
example. Those are <u>universal</u> laws. Every country has these laws.
　　　　　　　　普遍的
However, governments often make <u>local</u> laws.
　　　　　　　　　　　　　　　當地的
These laws are important to the <u>residents</u>
　　　　　　　　　　　　　　　居民
in that area. In <u>Singapore</u>, for example, it's
　　　　新加坡
against the law to feed <u>pigeons</u>. But in most
　　　　　　　　　　　鴿子
other countries, you can!

Read and Complete 完成句子

❶ Laws help keep _____ safe.

❷ Governments make both _____ and local laws.

法律與規定

家長和老師制定規定以保護孩子的安全，政府也
會制定規定以維持公民的安全，這也是政府許多
功能中的其中一項。政客制定法律讓公民遵守。
例如，他們能夠立法預防殺人和偷竊，那些是普
遍法律，而每個國家都有這些法律。然而，政府
通常也會制定當地法律，這些法律對該地區的居
民很重要。例如，餵鴿子在新加坡是違法的，但
在大多數的其他國家則可以餵鴿子！

背景知識 Plus!

讓我們來了解美國獨特的當地法
律，冰淇淋車在印第安納州是違法
的，這是為了防止城市中的食品卡車式
的商店數量過多；以及在維農山莊採
花是違法的；此外在晚上 10 點 30
分之後，壘球場內的燈光必須關
閉，這是因為法律禁止在超
過的時間打壘球。

🐧 Circle the best answer. 圈選出正確的答案

1. What is one thing that universal laws want to prevent?
   - ⓐ smoking
   - ⓑ raising pigeons
   - ⓒ stealing something

2. What is one thing that local laws want to prevent?
   - ⓐ following rules
   - ⓑ feeding pigeons
   - ⓒ killing someone

3. What is NOT true about laws?
   - ⓐ Politicians make laws.
   - ⓑ Citizens should follow laws.
   - ⓒ Local laws are the same everywhere.
   - ⓓ Laws against killing people are universal.

4. What can be inferred about politicians from the passage?
   - ⓐ They don't have to follow laws.
   - ⓑ They can make local laws only.
   - ⓒ They have to live in a certain area.
   - ⓓ They work for governments and citizens.

🐴 Complete the sentence. 完成句子

Politicians in a government make ❶ .... to keep its citizens safe. ❷ .... laws must be followed everywhere, but ❸ .... laws are only for certain places.

WrapUp Fill in the blanks. 總複習，將單字填入空格

Making Laws		country
目標	• to keep citizens ❶	safe
種類	• ❷ .... laws: for every ❸ .... • local laws: for residents in that ❹	universal area

Some Help From Pocahontas

來自寶嘉康蒂的幫助

R_68.mp3

Life was difficult in Jamestown, Virginia. In 1607, English <u>settlers</u>
殖民者
built a town there. But, they couldn't grow or find enough food.
The <u>Native Americans</u> often <u>attacked</u> their town. One day,
美洲原住民　　　　　　襲擊
they <u>captured</u> John Smith, the <u>captain</u> of the settlers. The
俘虜　　　　　　　　　上尉
<u>chief</u> of the <u>tribe</u> wanted to kill Smith. His daughter felt
酋長　　　部落
<u>mercy</u> and saved Smith. Soon, Smith became friends
憐憫
with the tribe. Pocahontas showed the English the
way to grow and find food. She became a <u>symbol</u> of
象徵
<u>peace</u> between the two groups. Today, we can even see
和平
Pocahontas' story in a Disney movie!

Read and Complete 完成句子

❶ English ＿＿＿＿＿＿ built a town in Jamestown.

❷ Pocahontas was a daughter of the ＿＿＿＿＿ of the tribe.

來自寶嘉康蒂的幫助

在維吉尼亞州詹姆士敦的生活很困苦。1607
年，英國的殖民者在當地建立了城鎮，但是他們
無法種植或找到足夠的食物。美洲原住民經常襲
擊他們的城鎮，有一天他們俘虜了殖民者的上尉
約翰・史密斯，部落的首長想要殺了史密斯，但
是他的女兒寶嘉康蒂心生憐憫，並救了史密斯。
不久之後，史密斯就與這個部落變成朋友。寶嘉
康蒂向英國人展示種植和尋找食物的方法，她成
為兩個群體之間的和平象徵。今日，我們甚至可
以在迪士尼的電影中看到寶嘉康蒂的故事。

背景知識 Plus!

迪士尼動畫《風中奇緣》中，原
住民女孩寶嘉康蒂（Pocahontas）
愛上了白人青年約翰・史密斯（John
Smith），透過阻止白人與原住民之間的
戰爭來維護和平。然而真實故事卻是，
寶嘉康蒂在 1613 年被英國人綁架為
人質，英國人與原住民的關係並不
順利，寶嘉康蒂因為感染天花
病逝，年僅 21 歲。

Circle the best answer. 圈選出正確的答案

1. What difficulty did the English settlers have?
   - ⓐ growing food
   - ⓑ building towns
   - ⓒ finding friends

2. Who tried to kill John Smith?
   - ⓐ the settlers
   - ⓑ Pocahontas
   - ⓒ the chief of the tribe

3. What is NOT true about the Native Americans?
   - ⓐ They consisted of tribes.
   - ⓑ They often attacked the settlers.
   - ⓒ They wanted to be friends with the settlers.
   - ⓓ They caught the captain of the English settlers.

4. How did Pocahontas help the English settlers?
   (Choose 2 answers.)
   - ⓐ She saved the captain of the settlers.
   - ⓑ She taught them how to find food.
   - ⓒ She captured the chief of the tribe.
   - ⓓ She built a town in Virginia for them

Complete the sentence. 完成句子

Captain John Smith was an English ❶ .... in Virginia.
Pocahontas ❷ .... his life, and helped the settlers. She
also helped bring peace between the ❸ .... Americans
and the settlers.

Wrap Up Number the sentences in order. 寫出句子的順序

[3] Pocahontas helped an English man.

☐ The Native Americans attacked English settlers.

☐ English settlers built a town in Jamestown, Virginia.

☐ Pocahontas became a symbol of peace.

Why is gold more <u>expensive</u> than water? It's because of <u>supply</u> and
昂貴的　　　　　　　　　　　　　　供應
<u>demand</u>. If many people want to buy a <u>good</u>, then there is high
需求　　　　　　　　　　　　　商品
demand. High demand makes something more <u>valuable</u>. Supply
有價值的
is <u>the amount of</u> a good in markets. Low supply of a good makes
～的數量
it more valuable. Many people want to
buy gold or water, so both have high
demand. Water is <u>everywhere</u>, but
到處
there isn't much gold in the world. So,
high demand and low supply makes
gold more expensive than water.

Read and Complete 完成句子

❶ Some people want to buy a good, and it is _____.

❷ Gold is _____ because there isn't much of it in the world.

黃金的價值

為什麼黃金會比水還貴？這是因為供應和需求的
關係。如果很多人想購買商品，那樣就會有很高
的需求，高需求使某些東西更有價值。供應是指
市場上商品的數量，商品的供應量低會使它更有
價值。許多人想購買黃金或水，所以兩者都有很
高的需求。水到處都有，但世界上沒有很多黃
金。因此，需求量高和供應量低使得黃金比水更
昂貴。

背景知識 Plus!

假設有一家公司以三千元的價格賣
一個鉛筆盒，而鉛筆盒的價格已降至
五百元，公司會減少供應（supply），
因為他們不想虧本販售。相反的是，當
鉛筆盒的價格上漲到六千元時，由於
他們想賣更多的物品，供應量就會
增加。物品的價格上漲時，供應
量就會增加；價格下降時，
供應量就會減少。

Comprehension Checkup 理解能力確認

Circle the best answer. 圈選出正確的答案

1. What is the amount of a good in the market?
   - **ⓐ** value
   - **ⓑ** demand
   - **ⓒ** supply

2. What can make something more valuable?
   - **ⓐ** low demand
   - **ⓑ** low supply
   - **ⓒ** high supply

3. What does high demand for a good mean?
   - **ⓐ** That good is easy to buy.
   - **ⓑ** No one wants that good.
   - **ⓒ** Some people want that good.
   - **ⓓ** Lots of people want that good.

4. What is NOT true about gold?
   - **ⓐ** It has low supply.
   - **ⓑ** Few people want it.
   - **ⓒ** It has high demand.
   - **ⓓ** It has more value than water.

Complete the sentence. 完成句子

Gold is more expensive than water because of low
❶ .... Both goods have ❷ .... demand, but
gold isn't easy to get. So it's more ❸ ....

Wrap Up Fill in the blanks. 總複習，將單字填入空格

The Value of Goods

high ❶ ....
: Many people want to buy.

+

low ❷ ....

→

expensive,
❸ ....
like ❹ ....

gold   demand   valuable   supply

民俗中的民間故事
Folktales in Folklores

R_70.mp3

Folklore is the stories and traditions of a culture. They are passed
（民俗）   （傳下來）
down from generation to generation. This helps preserve and continue
      （世代）   （保存）   （繼續）
the culture over time. Folktales are an important part of folklore. Every
          （隨著時間）（民間故事）
culture has its own tradition of folktales. In Europe, these stories often

begin with, "Once upon a time…" Parents teach their

children through these stories. Folktales often teach

children lessons about honesty, kindness, or bravery.
        （教訓）   （誠實）   （仁慈）   （勇敢）
Some famous folktales include *The Little Red Hen*
                                （小紅母雞）
and *Cinderella*. What folktales have your parents
   （灰姑娘）
passed down to you?

Read and Complete 完成句子

❶ _____ is the traditions of a culture.

❷ Folktales contain _____ for children.

民俗中的民間故事

民俗是一種文化的故事和傳統，它們代代相傳，這有助於隨著時間保存並延續文化。民間故事是民俗中很重要的部分。每個文化都有自己民間故事的傳統。在歐洲，這些故事通常會以「很久很久以前……」來開頭，父母透過這些故事來教導孩子。民間故事經常教導孩子關於誠實、善良或勇敢的教訓，有些著名的民間故事包含《小紅母雞》和《灰姑娘》等。你的父母傳承了哪些民間故事給你呢？

背景知識 Plus!

在美國的傳統民間故事（folktale）《The Little Red Hen》中，狗、貓、老鼠只喜歡睡午覺，家事由小紅母雞負責。小紅母雞用辛勤勞動收成的小麥烤了蛋糕，狗、貓、老鼠卻說蛋糕要分給大家吃，但是小紅母雞是說那些小麥自己種的，她決定要自己享用。從那以後，朋友們也開始認真做家務了。

Comprehension Checkup 理解能力確認

Circle the best answer. 圈選出正確的答案

1. Who usually tells children folktales?
   - **a** parents
   - **b** teachers
   - **c** lecturers

2. What lessons do folktales often teach children?
   - **a** how to make money
   - **b** how to be smarter
   - **c** how to behave well

3. What is NOT true about folklore?
   - **a** It preserves traditions.
   - **b** It mostly comes from Europe.
   - **c** It is an important part of culture.
   - **d** It is passed down from generation to generation.

4. What can be inferred about folktales from the passage?
   - **a** Folktales have a set format.
   - **b** Europeans especially loved folktales.
   - **c** Each culture has its own famous folktales.
   - **d** *Cinderella* is the most famous folktale in the world.

Complete the sentence. 完成句子

Folklore helps ❶ .... the traditions of a culture. Parents teach their children lessons about honesty and bravery with ❷ .... This passes down a culture to the next ❸ ....

WrapUp Fill in the blanks. 總複習，將單字填入空格

Folklore	Folktale
• ❶ .... of a culture • pass down from generation to generation • preserve and continue the ❷	• an important part of ❸ .... • teach children lessons like honesty, kindness, or ❹ ....

bravery   traditions   folklore   culture

WORD REVIEW

Crossword Puzzle 填字遊戲

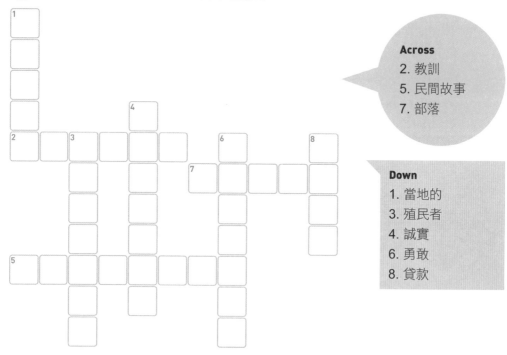

Across
2. 教訓
5. 民間故事
7. 部落

Down
1. 當地的
3. 殖民者
4. 誠實
6. 勇敢
8. 貸款

Match with the correct definition. 將單字連到正確的意思

1. demand •

2. folklore •

3. interest •

4. supply •

ⓐ the costs of money / Banks gives you it for your saved money.

ⓑ the need to buy a good or service

ⓒ the amount of a good in markets

ⓓ the stories and traditions of a culture

Fill in the blank with the correct words.
將正確的單字填入空格中

| earn | functions | peace | regular | residents |

1. Most adults use _____ banks to keep their money.
   大多數的成年人使用正規的銀行來存錢。

2. Interest makes both people and banks _____ some
   money.　利息讓人們和銀行都賺了一些錢。

3. Making rules is one of the many _____ of a
   government.　制定規定是政府的眾多功能之一。

4. Local laws are important to the _____ in a certain area.
   當地的法律對特定地區的居民很重要。

5. Pocahontas became a symbol of _____ between the
   two groups.　寶嘉康蒂成為兩個群體之間和平的象徵。

Fill in the blank with the correct expressions.
將正確的表達填入空格中

| begin with | more ~ than | passed down |
| pay back | showed ~ the way |

1. The borrowers must _____ the money on time and pay
   interest for it to the bank.

2. Pocahontas _____ the English _____ to grow
   and find food.

3. High demand and low supply makes gold _____
   expensive _____ water.

4. In Europe, folktales often _____, "Once upon a time..."

5. What folktales have your parents _____ to you?

Slavery in America
美國的奴隸制度

R_71.mp3

Slavery was common in Colonial America. In the 18th century,
奴隸制度　　常見的　　殖民的
plantation owners used African slaves for farmwork. These slaves
農園　　物主　　　　　奴隸
lived on the plantation and were owned like property. After working
擁有　　　資產
all day in the hot sun, they returned to their huts. The whole family
返回　　　　（簡陋的）小屋
lived and slept on the floors of their small huts.
Dinner was often rice, beans, or other plants.
Meat was usually only for the plantation
owners. Slaves owned few possessions and
所有物
no money. They just had some blankets for
毛毯
sleeping and dishes for cooking.

Read and Complete 完成句子

1 Colonial Americans had many _____.

2 Most of these slaves came from _____.

美國的奴隸制度

奴隸制度在殖民時期的美國十分普遍。在 18 世紀，農園園主會雇用非洲奴隸從事農務。這些奴隸住在農園裡，並被當作財產來擁有。他們在烈日下工作了一整天後，會回到自己的小屋，全家人都住在簡陋的小屋裡，並睡在地板上。晚餐通常是米飯、豆類或其他蔬菜，通常只有農園園主可以吃到肉類。奴隸擁有少許的財產，也沒有錢，他們只有一些睡覺用的毯子和煮飯用的餐具。

背景知識 Plus!

在美國殖民時期，會種植棉花和菸草，並出口到歐洲。有很多大型農場，然而因為沒有足夠的機器和技術，就需要大量的勞動力。農園會將黑人奴隸（slave）作為勞動力。奴隸可以在奴隸市場買賣，而且不需支付他們工資。

Comprehension Checkup 理解能力確認

Circle the best answer. 圈選出正確的答案

1. Where did most slaves work?
   - ⓐ on a plantation
   - ⓑ at the owners' huts
   - ⓒ on the farms in Africa

2. What did slaves receive for their work?
   - ⓐ nothing
   - ⓑ small property
   - ⓒ small amount of money

3. What is NOT true about slaves' living conditions?
   - ⓐ They didn't have enough basic items.
   - ⓑ They couldn't eat food of good quality.
   - ⓒ They slept on the floors of their small huts.
   - ⓓ They were never allowed to have a family.

4. What is true about the plantation owners?
   - ⓐ They treated slaves poorly.
   - ⓑ They raised farm animals for meat.
   - ⓒ They worked during the day with slaves.
   - ⓓ They paid some money to support slaves.

Complete the sentence. 完成句子

Many slaves lived in ❶ .... America in the 18th century. They were owned like ❷ .... so the owners didn't pay them. They lived and worked on their owners' ❸ ....

Wrap Up Fill in the blanks. 總複習，

Slavery in America		
身份狀態	生活	owned
• ❶ .... in Colonial America in 18th century	• working all day	huts
	• living in their ❸	
• being ❷ .... like property	• eating rice, beans	possessions
	• few ❹	common

美國的奴隸制度 185

加州的掏金熱
Gold Rush in California

R_72.mp3

John Marshal helped build <u>the State of</u> California. In 1848, he
~州
<u>discovered</u> gold in California. The news soon <u>spread</u> around the
發現   （原形：spread）散布
world. Anyone could find free gold there! At the time, only about
1,000 Americans lived in California. The rush to find gold <u>brought</u>
（原形：bring）帶來
over 300,000 people from around the world there. Most could not
find any gold. But many <u>businesses</u> made a lot of money. They sold
企業
food, clothes, and <u>equipment</u> to the <u>miners</u>. The
設備   礦工
miners and <u>businessmen</u> needed roads, churches,
商人
and schools. So the <u>government</u> <u>built</u> them.
政府   （原形：build）建造

Read and Complete 完成句子

❶ John Marshal was the first man to

discover _____ in California.

❷ Thousands of people rushed to _____ to find gold.

加州的掏金熱

約翰・馬歇爾幫助建設了加州。1848年，他在加州發現了黃金，這個消息很快就散布到全世界，任何人都可以在那裡找到免費的黃金！當時，只有大約一千名美國人住在加州。尋找黃金的熱潮把來自世界各地超過 30 萬人都帶到那裡。大多數人都沒有找到任何黃金，但是許多企業賺了很多錢，他們向礦工販售食物、衣服和設備。而礦工和商人需要道路、教堂和學校，所以政府建造了這些設施。

背景知識 Plus!

由於淘金熱（Gold Rush），牛仔褲也被製造出來。當時到加州開採金礦的人搭起帳篷當作臨時住所。李維・史特勞斯（Levi Strauss）當時從事製造帳篷布料的生意，他用帳篷布料製作褲子，靈感源自礦工的褲子容易穿脫的概念，而礦工也喜歡穿這種耐穿的褲子，這就是牛仔褲的起源。

Circle the best answer. 圈選出正確的答案

1. Before the Gold Rush, how many people lived in California?
   - ⓐ about 1,000
   - ⓑ 1,848
   - ⓒ about 300,000

2. Who made a lot of money during the Gold Rush?
   - ⓐ teachers
   - ⓑ businessmen
   - ⓒ the government

3. Why was the news of John Marshal interesting to many people?
   - ⓐ Because it made them dream of being rich.
   - ⓑ Because he was looking for people to find gold.
   - ⓒ Because it helped them become miners.
   - ⓓ Because it advertised new jobs in California.

4. What is NOT true about the Gold Rush?
   - ⓐ Many people failed to find gold.
   - ⓑ It helped build the State of California.
   - ⓒ The government hired miners to find gold.
   - ⓓ People from around the world came to California.

Complete the sentence. 完成句子

John Marshal ❶ .... gold in California in 1848. People from around the world came to find gold. During the Gold Rush, ❷ .... that sold food and clothes made lots of ❸ ....

Wrap Up Write the numbers in order. 寫出句子的順序

[3] Many businesses made a lot of money.

◯ John Marshal discovered gold in California.

◯ The government built roads, churches, and schools.

◯ The rush to find gold brought over 300,000 people.

These days, <u>millions of</u> people enjoy <u>animated</u> shows and movies.
數百萬~   動畫的

Walt Disney was the first to create one, and it became popular.

He was an <u>entrepreneur</u> with a great idea. He wanted to turn his
企業家

drawings and characters into a business. TV shows at the time only

had real actors in them. His idea was to make TV

shows and movies with his animated drawings.

But, he was <u>fired</u> and <u>rejected</u> over 300 times
解雇   拒絕

before becoming <u>successful</u>! Entrepreneurs like
成功的

Disney <u>face</u> <u>risks</u> and <u>failure</u>. But they also have
面對   風險   失敗

<u>opportunities</u> for great <u>success</u>!
機會   成功

Read and Complete 完成句子

① Walt Disney was an _____ with great ideas.

② People still enjoy Walt Disney's _____ movies.

動畫產業的企業家

現在，有數百萬人喜歡看動畫節目和電影。華特·迪士尼是第一個創作動畫作品的人，而動畫也變得廣受歡迎。他是一位有偉大想法的企業家，他想把他的畫作和角色變成一門生意。當時的電視節目中只有真人演員，而他的想法是用他的動畫畫作來製作電視節目和電影。但是他在成功前，他被解僱過以及被拒絕超過三百次！像迪士尼這樣的企業家也會面對風險和失敗，但他們也有大獲成功的機會！

背景知識 Plus!

華特·迪士尼（**Walt Disney**）從小就展現出繪畫天賦，**7**歲在賣報紙時，偶然接觸到漫畫，並萌生了繪畫和漫畫的夢想，因此他從高中就開始畫商業漫畫。從藝術學校畢業後，他製作了商業動畫。之後，歷經多次的挫折和挑戰，在**1937**年他的第一部動畫電影《白雪公主》上映，並獲得了廣大的迴響。

🧑 Circle the best answer. 圈選出正確的答案

1. What did Walt Disney create first?
   - ⓐ movies
   - ⓑ TV shows
   - ⓒ animated shows

2. What did people see in TV shows before Walt Disney's idea?
   - ⓐ voice actors
   - ⓑ only real actors
   - ⓒ animated drawings

3. What is true about entrepreneurs like Walt Disney?
   - ⓐ They never face risk or failure.
   - ⓑ They sometimes copy old ideas.
   - ⓒ They have opportunities for success.
   - ⓓ They hate watching TV shows and movies.

4. What can you infer about Walt Disney from the passage?
   - ⓐ He wanted to be an actor in a TV show.
   - ⓑ He was interested in drawing characters.
   - ⓒ He was sick and tired of watching TV shows.
   - ⓓ He was rich enough to make his dreams come true.

🦔 Complete the sentence. 完成句子

> Walt Disney was a famous entrepreneur. His new ❶ .... was to use animated ❷ .... for TV shows and movies. He succeeded at last after facing ❸ .... and failure.

Wrap Up Fill in the blanks. 總複習，將單字填入空格

Entrepreneurs	Walt Disney
• people with great ideas • ❶ .... risks and failure • ❷ .... something first	• animated TV shows and movies • was ❸ .... and rejected • turned his ❹ .... into a business

face	fired	drawings	create

Just 100 years ago in America, women had few <u>legal</u> <u>rights</u>. They
合法的　權利
couldn't <u>vote</u>, own homes, or do most jobs. The women's rights
投票
<u>movement</u> began in the 1800s. They <u>fought</u> for <u>equal</u> rights. The
運動　　　　　　　　　　　　　（原形：fight）為～而戰　平等的
right to vote, Women's <u>Suffrage</u>, was their <u>main</u> <u>goal</u>. But, the laws
選舉權　　　　　　　　　主要的　目標
of the United States did not allow them to vote. They
<u>formed</u> <u>political</u> groups to change the law. Susan
組織　政治的
B. Anthony was an important <u>leader</u> of these
領袖
groups. Because of their <u>efforts</u>, the law was
努力
changed. Women now have equal legal rights.

Read and Complete 完成句子

❶ Until about 100 years ago, women in America could
not _____.

❷ Women worked hard to change the _____.

女性的投票權

只是在一百年前的美國，女性擁有很少的合法權
利。她們不能投票，不能擁有房產，也不能從
事大部分的工作。女權運動始於 1800 年代。她
們爭取平等權利。投票權，也就是女性投票的權
利是她們的主要目標，但是美國的法律不允許她
們投票，於是她們組成政治團體以改變法律。蘇
珊・安東尼是這些團體的重要領導人。因為她們
的努力，法律被修改了。婦女現在有平等的合法
權利。

背景知識 Plus!

曾是教師的蘇珊・安東尼（Susan
B. Anthony）在美國南北戰爭時代主
張廢除奴隸制度、禁酒運動等，並投身
於社會活動。另外，她以爭取女性權
利為目標，發行週刊、展開了運動。
她在 1872 年以女性的身分參加美
國總統選舉，被處以 100 美
元的罰鍰。

Comprehension Checkup 理解能力確認

Circle the best answer. 圈選出正確的答案。

1. What was the purpose of the women's movement in the 1800s?
   - ⓐ to have equal rights
   - ⓑ to fight against men
   - ⓒ to change the president

2. What does Women's Suffrage mean?
   - ⓐ the right to vote
   - ⓑ efforts to own homes
   - ⓒ the right to have jobs

3. What did women do to change the law?
   - ⓐ They left their jobs.
   - ⓑ They made political groups.
   - ⓒ They voted for women.
   - ⓓ They asked men to help them.

4. What is NOT true about the women's movement?
   - ⓐ It helped change the unfair law.
   - ⓑ It gave equal legal rights to women.
   - ⓒ Its main goal was to get the right to have property.
   - ⓓ Susan B. Anthony was the leader of women's groups.

Complete the sentence. 完成句子。

In the 1800s, the women's rights ❶ .... started to fight for the equal right to ❷ .... Women formed political groups to ❸ .... the law. Thanks to their efforts, women now have equal legal rights.

Wrap Up Fill in the blanks. 總複習，將單字填入空格

100 years ago in America	• ❶ .... rights.	political
What Woman Wanted	• suffrage: the right to ❷	vote
What Women Did	• formed ❸ .... groups and changed the law • have ❹ .... legal rights now	equal legal

權力的平衡
Balance of Power

R_75.mp3

Three <u>branches</u> of the American government <u>balance</u> each other's
部門   平衡
power. The first branch is <u>Congress</u>. <u>Congressmen</u> can create new
立法機關   美國國會議員
laws. The next branch is the <u>President</u>. He is the <u>leader</u> of the country.
總統   領導人
The <u>final</u> branch is the <u>judges</u>. Judges can change or <u>remove</u> laws.
最後的   法官   除去
Each branch can <u>check</u> the power of the other branches. This <u>makes</u>
檢查   確定
<u>sure</u> that all three branches follow the law. They even have the power

to cancel the actions of other branches. For example,

the President can <u>reject</u> new laws of Congress.
駁回
Congress can even vote to remove judges or

the President.

Read and Complete 完成句子

① The American government is made up of three _____.

② The _____ of the three branches is balanced.

權力的平衡
美國政府的三個部門平衡彼此的權力。第一個部門是立法機關，國會議員可以制定新的法律。另一個部門是總統，總統是國家的領導人。最後一個部門是法官，法官可以修改或廢除法律。每個部門都可以檢查其他部門的權力，這確保了三個部門全都遵守法律，他們甚至有權撤回其他部門的行動。例如，總統可以否決立法機關的新法律，而立法機關甚至可以投票罷免法官或總統。

背景知識 Plus!
如果國家只有一個部門，並像國王一樣統治會怎麼樣呢？如果一個部門制定並執行法律，就不會有時間和精力去達到很高的效率。但是，在民主國家，三權分立由制定法律的立法部、執行法律的行政部和執行法律的司法部所組成，這是為了分散權力來保障人民的權利和自由，並增加效率。

Comprehension Checkup 理解能力確認

Circle the best answer. 圈選出正確的答案

1. What do Congressmen do?
   - ⓐ make new laws
   - ⓑ remove laws
   - ⓒ lead the country

2. How can Congress make sure judges follow the law?
   - ⓐ by voting to remove them
   - ⓑ by rejecting laws for judges
   - ⓒ by asking the President to remove them

3. What is true about the President?
   - ⓐ He has the right to break new laws.
   - ⓑ He has the power to reject new laws.
   - ⓒ His main task is finding problems of laws.
   - ⓓ He checks the judges by removing them.

4. Why do the three branches check each other?
   - ⓐ Because they try not to influence each other.
   - ⓑ Because they have to make sure all of them follow the law.
   - ⓒ Because they want to have as much power as possible.
   - ⓓ Because they have to discuss new laws.

Complete the sentence. 完成句子

The American government has three branches: the
❶ ...., Congress, and the judges. They
❷ .... and ❸ .... each other's power.

Wrap Up Fill in the blanks. 總複習，將單字填入句子

The American Government

❶	❷	❸ ....
• create new laws • vote to remove judges and presidents	• the leader of the country • can reject new laws	can change or remove laws

WORD REVIEW

🐧 Crossword Puzzle

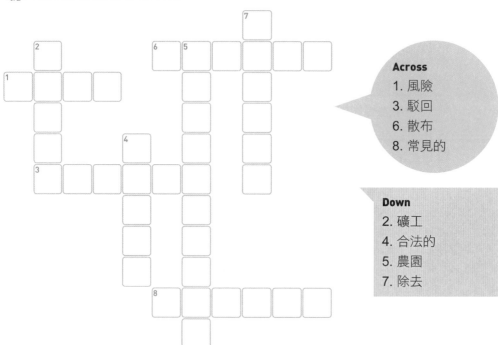

Across
1. 風險
3. 駁回
6. 散布
8. 常見的

Down
2. 礦工
4. 合法的
5. 農園
7. 除去

🐴 Match with the correct definition. 將單字連到正確的意思

1. entrepreneur •

2. gold rush •

3. president •

4. slave •

ⓐ someone who is owned like property

ⓑ when people around the world went to California to find gold

ⓒ a person who starts or runs a business to make money

ⓓ the leader of the country

Fill in the blank with the correct words.
將正確的單字填入空格中

> businessmen Colonial congressmen political opportunities

1. Slavery was common in _____ America in the 18th.
   奴隸制度在 18 世紀殖民時期的美國很普遍。

2. _____ sold food, clothes, and equipment to the miners.
   商人向礦工販售食物、衣服和設備。

3. Entrepreneurs have _____ for great success.
   企業家有大獲成功的機會。

4. Women formed _____ groups to change the law.
   女性組成政治團體來修改法律。

5. _____ can create new laws.
   國會議員可以制定新的法律。

Fill in the blank with the correct expressions.
將正確的表達填入空格中

> allow ~ to   fought for   lived on   make sure   turn ~ into

1. African slaves _____ the plantation.

2. Walt Disney wanted to _____ his drawings and
   characters _____ a business.

3. Women _____ equal rights in the 1800s.

4. The laws of the United States did not _____ women
   _____ vote.

5. Checks and balances _____ all three
   branches follow the law.

Before 1830, Native Americans lived free in the <u>Southern</u> USA.
南方的
But, the American <u>population</u> was growing quickly. They wanted
人口
to <u>expand</u> into Native American lands. The government <u>passed</u>
擴展　　　　　　　　　　　　　　　　　　　　　　　通過
the Indian <u>Removal</u> <u>Act</u>. This law created the Indian <u>Territory</u>
捆邊　　（大寫）法案　　　　　　　　　　　　　領土
in Oklahoma. This territory was very far away from the Native
Americans' <u>homeland</u>. Government <u>soldiers</u> <u>marched</u> the Native
宗鄉　　　　　　軍人　　迫使～前進
Americans thousands of kilometers to their new home. There wasn't
much food, and the <u>journey</u> took months. Thousands of
旅程
Native Americans became sick and died. That's why it's
remembered as the <u>Trail</u> of Tears.
小道

Read and Complete 完成句子

1 The Indian _____ Act removed Native Americans from their homes.

2 Native Americans _____ thousands of kilometers to their new home.

眼淚之路

在 1830 年以前，美洲原住民在美國南方自由地生活，然而美國的人口快速增長，他們想擴大到美洲原住民的土地。政府通過了《印第安人遷移法案》，這條法律在奧克拉荷馬州建立了印第安領地，但是這片領地距離美洲原住民的家園非常遙遠。政府的軍隊迫使美洲原住民行走數千公里來到他們的新家。那裡沒有很多食物，而且旅程要花費幾個月的時間。數千名美洲原住民生病和過世，這就是為什麼人們將它記憶為「眼淚之路」的原因。

背景知識 Plus!

《印第安人遷移法》（Indian Removal Act）用條件將密西西比河西邊土地跟美洲原住民交換東部土地，但大多數的原住民都不同意。然而，總統傑克遜（Andrew Jackson）強制執行這項法案，並在 1830 年至 1850 年間強迫遷移原住民部落。據說，一萬七千名原住民中約有五千人在途中喪生。

Comprehension Checkup 理解能力確認

🐧 Circle the best answer. 圈選出正確的答案

1. Where did the Native Americans move to?
   ⓐ Oklahoma　　　ⓑ Southern USA　　　ⓒ American's territory

2. Who led Native Americans to their new home?
   ⓐ Indians　　　　　　　　　ⓑ government soldiers
   ⓒ the leader of the government

3. Why did the government pass the Indian Removal Act?
   ⓐ Because Native Americans often attacked them.
   ⓑ Because they wanted to take Native American lands.
   ⓒ Because they wanted to live with Native Americans.
   ⓓ Because they tried to make Native Americans' lives better.

4. What is NOT true about the Trail of Tears?
   ⓐ It was difficult to find enough food.
   ⓑ It was thousands of kilometers long.
   ⓒ Lots of Native Americans got sick and died.
   ⓓ It took years to get Native Americans' new home.

🐴 Complete the sentence. 完成句子

In 1830, the Indian Removal Act made the ❶ ....
Americans move to new territory. They marched thousands
of kilometers. Many people became sick and ❷ ....
So we call it the Trail of ❸ ....

Wrap Up Number the sentences in order. 寫出句子的順序

[3] Native Americans were forced to a new home.

◯ The government passed the Indian Removal Act.

◯ Many Native Americans became sick and died during the journey.

◯ The American population grew quickly.

Choices Have Costs

R_77.mp3

In <u>economics</u>, <u>opportunity cost</u> is the <u>value</u> you lose when you make
　經濟學　　　　機會成本　　　　　　價值

a <u>choice</u>. Every choice has a value and a cost. Sometimes we have
　選擇

to <u>decide</u> between two <u>valuable</u> choices. But value and costs are
　決定　　　　　　有價值的

not just <u>measured</u> in money. For example, friendship, <u>education</u>,
　　　衡量　　　　　　　　　　　　　　　　教育

and <u>happiness</u> all have value. <u>Imagine</u> you should <u>choose</u> to play or
　　幸福　　　　　　　　　　設想　　　　　　選擇

study. Both <u>activities</u> are valuable. When you choose to play,
　　　　活動

you are happy. But the opportunity cost is <u>knowledge</u>.
　　　　　　　　　　　　　　　　　　知識

Choosing to study can allow you to <u>gain</u>
　　　　　　　　　　　　　　　　獲得

knowledge, but losing fun is the

opportunity cost.

Read and Complete 完成句子

❶ Choices often have _____ costs.

❷ Opportunity cost happens when both choices have
_____.

選擇是有成本的

在經濟學中，機會成本是指你做出選擇時失去的
價值。每一個選擇都有其價值和成本，有時我們
必須在兩個有價值的選擇之間做決定，但是價值
和成本不只是用金錢來衡量的。例如，友誼、教
育和幸福全都是有價值的。假設你應該要選擇去
玩耍或學習，這兩種活動皆是有價值的。當你選
擇玩耍時，你很快樂，但機會成本則是知識。選
擇去學習會讓你獲得知識，但是其機會成本就是
失去樂趣。

背景知識 Plus!

機會成本（opportunity cost）是
指在選擇時，放棄其中最有價值的東
西。這包含了所有選擇都有背後代價的
人生原則，人魚公主沒有得到腿，而
是失去了他美妙的聲音。孝女沈清沒
有讓父親睜開眼睛，而是選擇犧
牲生命。大家可以思考在生
活中會發生的機會成
本。

Circle the best answer. 圈選出正確的答案

1. Where did the idea of opportunity cost come from?
   - ⓐ science
   - ⓑ economics
   - ⓒ mathematics

2. How do we measure opportunity cost?
   - ⓐ in time
   - ⓑ in money
   - ⓒ in lost value

3. What is the opportunity cost of NOT studying?
   - ⓐ losing fun
   - ⓑ losing time
   - ⓒ being happy
   - ⓓ getting knowledge

4. Which choice does NOT have an opportunity cost?
   - ⓐ sleeping or having a meal
   - ⓑ studying or meeting friends
   - ⓒ reducing stress or getting stressed
   - ⓓ having a job or going to university

Complete the sentence. 完成句子

Opportunity ❶ .... can happen when we make a
❷ .... between two ❸ .... activities. The
lost value of our choice is the opportunity cost.

Wrap Up Fill in the blanks. 總複習，將單字填入句子

Opportunity Cost

意義	the value you lose when you make a ❶ ....
發生情況	when you ❷ .... between two valuable choices
特性	Some ❸ .... and costs are not ❹ .... in money.

measured   decide   choice   values

兩種類型的民主

Two Kinds of Democracy

R_78.mp3

Democratic governments are ruled by their citizens. There are two
民主的　　　　　　　　　　　　　　統治　　　　　　公民

different kinds of democracy. In a direct democracy, citizens meet
民主　　　　　　　直接的

and vote for every decision of the government. Most countries are
選舉　　　　　　決定

too large and their citizens are too busy for a direct democracy.

Instead, in a representative democracy, citizens choose government
代表的

leaders. Citizens vote for leaders in free and fair elections. It's
公正的　選舉

important all citizens have the equal right to vote in a representative
平等的　權利

democracy. These leaders represent the citizens and
代表

make decisions for them. America, France, and

India are examples of representative democracies.
印度

Read and Complete 完成句子

❶ _____ have power in a democracy.

❷ In elections, citizens can _____ for their leaders.

兩種類型的民主

民主政府是由他們的公民統治，並且有兩種不同
類型的民主。在直接民主中，公民集會並投票表
決政府的每項決定。但是大多數的國家都太過龐
大，而且公民也太過忙碌，無法實行直接民主。
相反地，在代議民主中，公民會選出政府領袖。
公民在自由和公平的選舉中投票選出領袖，所有
公民在代議民主中擁有平等的選舉權是非常重要
的，這些領袖代表公民，並為他們做出決定。美
國、法國和印度就是代議民主國家的例子。

背景知識 Plus!

在古希臘和羅馬實行的是直接民主
（direct democracy）。雅典有「公
民議會」的制度，公民在這裡可以不受
限制提出並通過法律。然而隨著人口
增加和城市擴展，議會很難聚會，並
難以保障多數人參與政治。

Comprehension Checkup 理解能力確認

Circle the best answer. 圈選出正確的答案

1. How do citizens have power over the government decisions in a direct democracy?
   ⓐ by meeting and voting
   ⓑ by making other decisions
   ⓒ by choosing the government leaders

2. What do the leaders do for citizens in a representative democracy?
   ⓐ control citizens' rights
   ⓑ make decisions for them
   ⓒ gather citizens to vote

3. Why do some countries have a representative democracy?
   ⓐ Because most governments don't trust citizens.
   ⓑ Because citizens are too busy in most countries.
   ⓒ Because citizens hate to make important decisions.
   ⓓ Because a good leader can be smarter than citizens.

4. Why does the writer mention America, France, and India?
   ⓐ to disagree with direct democracies
   ⓑ to explain why elections should be fair
   ⓒ to give examples of representative democracies
   ⓓ to compare direct and representative democracies

Complete the sentence. 完成句子

In a ❶ .... democracy, citizens meet and vote for decisions made by the government. On the other hand, citizens ❷ .... for their leaders in a ❸ .... democracy.

WrapUp Fill in the blanks. 總複習，將單字填入句子

direct democracy	• Citizens ❶ .... and vote for every ❷ .... of the government.	elections
		decision
representative democracy	• Citizens ❸ .... government leaders. • Citizens vote for leaders in free and fair ❹	meet
		choose

The US Constitution was written in 1787. Its authors included George
憲法   作者   包含
Washington, Ben Franklin, and other early founders of America. The
                                        創立者
Constitution is a set of laws. It says how the American government
          一套～
works. The founders imagined a new kind of free society. At that
                    想像   社會
time, some governments in Europe had a powerful king and queen.
Unlike them, the founders believed that governments should have
                          相信
limited power. They designed the Constitution to give citizens control
有限的   設計   控制
of the government. A limited government and
free citizens helped America grow and become
powerful.

Read and Complete 完成句子

❶ The early founders of America wrote the US _____.

❷ The founders hoped to make a society with free

_____.

為了共同的利益：美國憲法

美國憲法起草於 1787 年，其作者包括喬治·華盛頓、班傑明·富蘭克林和其他早期的美國開國元勛。憲法是一套法律，說明了美國政府的運作方式。開國元勛想像了一種新的自由社會。在當時，歐洲有些政府擁有權力強大的國王和女王。與它們不同的是，開國元勛認為政府應該擁有有限的權力。他們設計憲法是為了讓公民能夠控制政府。有限的政府和自由的公民，幫助美國成長並變得強大。

背景知識 Plus!

1776 年，由殖民地代表組成的大陸會議宣佈美國獨立，很快成立了 13 個州，並同意國民擁有主權。1781 年，在與英國的獨立戰爭中獲勝的美國各州代表，為了強化雙邊關係而通過了《邦聯條例》。1787 年他們決定修改邦聯條例，之後直接制定新的憲法（constitution）。

Comprehension Checkup 理解能力確認

🎤 Circle the best answer. 圈選出正確的答案

1. What does the US Constitution tell us?
   - ⓐ the way the government functions
   - ⓑ how the early founders built the government
   - ⓒ how to control the power of a king and a queen

2. What was important for the founders to make a society?
   - ⓐ laws
   - ⓑ citizens' freedom
   - ⓒ a strong government

3. What is true about the American government?
   - ⓐ It had limited power.
   - ⓑ It was led by citizens from Europe.
   - ⓒ A king and a queen controlled it.
   - ⓓ Its power was controlled by the early founders.

4. How did the US Constitution help America grow?
   - ⓐ by making citizens less powerful
   - ⓑ by removing the government system
   - ⓒ by giving citizens freedom and power
   - ⓓ by designing the powerful government system

🧑 Complete the sentence. 完成句子

In 1787, the early ❶ .... of America wrote the US Constitution. They ❷ .... the Constitution to give more ❸ .... to the citizens.

WrapUp Fill in the blanks. 總複習，將單字填入句子

The US Constitution		limited
意義	• a set of ❶ .... saying how the American government works	laws
制定理由	• for a new ❷ .... with freedom	control
制定方向	• to give citizens ❸ .... of the government • a ❹ .... government and free citizens	society

The Bill of Rights allows American citizens to live freely and safely.
權利法案　　　　　允許～去做～　　　　　　自由地　　安全地

James Madison created it in 1789. The basic human rights from it
人權

are now common in democracies everywhere. One important right

is freedom of speech. With this right, citizens cannot be arrested
自由　　演說　　　　　　　　　　　　　　逮捕

for giving their opinions. They can even protest government
意見　　　　　　　　抗議

decisions. Other human rights make laws fair for

citizens. For example, citizens are innocent until
無罪的

judges prove them guilty in modern democracies.
證明　　　有罪的　　現代的

Another basic right is freedom of religion. Citizens
宗教

are free to choose and follow any religion.

Read and Complete 完成句子

❶ The Bill of Rights protects American citizens' basic
_____.

❷ Human rights are important in _____.

人人享有人權

《權利法案》讓美國公民能夠自由和安全地生活。詹姆斯·麥迪遜在 1789 年創造了《權利法案》，法案中基本人權的觀念，現在在世界各地的民主國家都很普遍。而一項重要的權利是言論自由，有了這項權利，公民不能因為提出意見而被逮捕，他們甚至能夠抗議政府的決定，其他人權使法律公平對待公民。例如，在現代的民主國家中，直到公民在法官證明他們有罪之前都是無罪的。另一項基本權利是宗教自由，公民可以自由選擇和信奉任何宗教。

背景知識 Plus!

權利法案（Bill of Rights）包含以下內容，以保護個人的權利不受政府侵害：1. 宗教、新聞和新聞自由 2. 擁有武器的權利 3. 軍事職責 4. 禁止無理搜查和逮捕 5. 刑事訴訟中的權利 6. 公平和公開審判的權利 7. 民事案件中由陪審團審判的保障 8. 禁止過度懲罰 9. 人民的一般權利 10. 國家和人民的權力。

Comprehension Checkup 理解能力確認

Circle the best answer. 圈選出正確的答案

1. What is the purpose of the Bill of Rights?
   - ⓐ to create laws
   - ⓑ to be free from arrest
   - ⓒ to live safely with freedom

2. What was James Madison's achievement?
   - ⓐ making the Bill of Rights
   - ⓑ making laws of religion
   - ⓒ making a process how to prove a person's guilt

3. What is freedom of speech? (Choose 2 answers.)
   - ⓐ Citizens can do newspaper work.
   - ⓑ Citizens are free to follow any religion.
   - ⓒ Citizens can express their opinions freely.
   - ⓓ Citizens can protest government decisions.

4. Which is the example of ignoring human rights?
   - ⓐ changing one's religion often
   - ⓑ gathering to express disagreement
   - ⓒ arresting a person before he or she is proved guilty
   - ⓓ moving to a new place without anyone's agreement

Complete the sentence. 完成句子

The Bill of ❶ .... protects the rights of American citizens. Human rights such as freedom of ❷ .... and ❸ .... are important.

Wrap Up Fill in the blanks. 總複習，將單字填入空格

the Bill of Rights	
制定時間	James Madison ❶ .... it in 1789.
制定原因	to allow American citizens to live freely and ❷ ....
主要內容	freedom of speech, ❸ .... laws for citizens, ❹ .... of religion

fair

safely

created

freedom

WORD REVIEW

Crossword Puzzle 填字遊戲

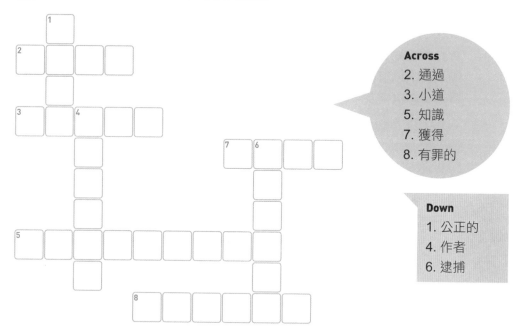

Across
2. 通過
3. 小道
5. 知識
7. 獲得
8. 有罪的

Down
1. 公正的
4. 作者
6. 逮捕

Match with the correct definition. 將單字連到正確的意思

1. election •

ⓐ the value you lose when you make a choice

2. innocent •

ⓑ a fair way for citizens to choose government leaders

3. opportunity cost •

ⓒ a set of laws

4. constitution •

ⓓ not guilty

Fill in the blank with the correct words.
將正確的單字填入空格中

| imagined | marched | measured | protest | represent |

1. Government soldiers _____ the Native Americans thousands of kilometers to their new home.
   政府的軍隊迫使美洲原住民行走數千公里到達新家。

2. Value and costs are not just _____ in money.
   價值和成本不僅是用金錢來衡量的。

3. The leaders _____ the citizens and make decisions for them.　這些領導人代表公民，並為他們做出決定。

4. The founders _____ a new kind of free society.
   開國元勳們想像了一種新的自由社會。

5. Citizens can even _____ government decisions.
   公民甚至可以抗議政府的決定。

Fill in the blank with the correct expressions.
將正確的表達填入空格中

| are free to | expand into | give ~ control | have to | vote for |

1. Americans wanted to _____ Native American lands.

2. Sometimes we _____ decide between two valuable choices.

3. Citizens _____ leaders in free and fair elections.

4. They designed the Constitution to _____ citizens _____ of the government.

5. Citizens _____ choose and follow any religion.

Hit or <u>shake</u> some <u>instruments</u>, and they make sound. These
搖動　　　　　樂器
are <u>percussion</u> instruments. Some create a <u>beat</u>. <u>Drums</u> do this.
打擊樂器　　　　　　　　　　　　　拍子　　鼓
Musicians hit drums and make a beat. But you shake <u>maracas</u> and
沙鈴
<u>tambourines</u>. They <u>rattle</u> and make <u>rhythm</u>.
鈴鼓　　　　乒乓響　　　　　節奏
Other percussion instruments create

notes. <u>Xylophones</u> and bells do this.
木琴
There are different sizes of bells

and xylophone <u>keys</u>. They produce
琴鍵
different <u>notes</u>. Together, the notes
音符
make <u>melody</u>, like in songs.
旋律

Check True or False 是非題

❶ Some percussion instruments create rhythm.　　　T / F

❷ Maracas can create different notes.　　　　　　　T / F

打擊樂器

打擊或搖動一些樂器，它們就會發出聲音，這些
就是打擊樂器。有些樂器會產生節拍，鼓就是這
樣演奏的，音樂家會打鼓、產生節拍。然而搖動
沙鈴或鈴鼓時，它們會發出聲響、產生節奏。其
他的打擊樂器會產生音符，像木琴和鈴鐺就是這
樣演奏的。有不同大小的鈴鐺和木琴琴鍵，它們
產生不同的音符，而這些音符一起構成旋律，就
像歌曲中一樣。

背景知識 Plus!

沙鈴（maracas）在拉丁音樂中是
不可或缺的打擊樂器，它看起來像是
嬰兒在玩的搖鈴，在搖動時，裡面的小
顆粒會彼此碰撞並發出獨特的聲音。而
沙鈴的名字源自南美洲原住民語言的
maraca，是「拉」的意思。因為演
奏時都會用到兩個沙鈴，所以
會加上「複數 -s」，寫成
maracas。

Circle the best answer. 圈選出正確的答案

1. How do musicians make sounds on drums?
   - ⓐ shake them
   - ⓑ rattle them
   - ⓒ hit them

2. How do tambourines make rhythm?
   - ⓐ ring
   - ⓑ make notes
   - ⓒ rattle

3. Xylophones and _____ can make different notes.
   - ⓐ drums
   - ⓑ bells
   - ⓒ beats

4. Xylophone keys have different _____.
   - ⓐ sizes
   - ⓑ musicians
   - ⓒ melody

Complete the sentence. 完成句子

You can make sound by hitting or shaking .... instruments.

Wrap Up Fill in the blanks. 總複習，將單字填寫到空格中

Percussion Instruments

發聲方法	音樂元素 1	音樂元素 2
• hit or ❶	• beat or ❷	• ❹ ....
	▸ ❸ ...., maracas, tambourines	▸ xylophones and bells

rhythm   drums   notes   shake

In a <u>barn</u>, a dog <u>fell asleep</u> on <u>hay</u>. Later, a hungry <u>ox</u> came in. He
穀倉　　　　　　　　睡著　　　　乾草　　　　　　　　　　公牛
wanted to eat the hay. However, the dog <u>woke up</u> and <u>growled</u> at the
　　　　　　　　　　　　　　　　　　　　醒來　　　　咆哮
ox. The farmer saw this. He <u>waved</u> a <u>stick</u>
　　　　　　　　　　　　　　揮動　　木棍
and <u>chased the dog away</u>. "You <u>greedy</u>
　　　驅逐～　　　　　　　　　貪婪的
dog!" he yelled. "You don't eat hay.
But the ox can only eat hay! Sleep
somewhere else!" The dog must not
<u>take hay from</u> the ox.
從～拿走～

Check True or False 是非題

❶ The dog can only eat hay.　　　　　T / F

❷ The farmer got angry at the dog.　　T / F

狗與乾草
在一個穀倉裡，有隻狗在乾草上睡著了。後來，一頭饑餓的公牛走了進來，牠想吃這些乾草。然而狗醒了過來，並對著公牛吠叫。農夫看見了這個情況，便揮舞著棍子、把狗趕走了。農夫喊道：「你這隻貪心的狗！你不吃乾草，但公牛只能吃乾草！去別的地方睡覺！」所以狗絕對不行從公牛那邊把乾草帶走。

背景知識 Plus!
伊索（Aesop）是生活在古希臘的說書人，他留下的 725 則故事被稱為伊索寓言（Aesop's Fables），直到今日仍教給我們許多教訓。在他的故事中出現了各式各樣的動物，但是狗通常會被描述成貪婪、愚蠢的角色，就如同這則故事一樣。

Comprehension Checkup 理解能力確認

Circle the best answer. 圈選出正確的答案

1. Who fell asleep in the barn?
   - **a** the ox
   - **b** the farmer
   - **c** the dog

2. Who wanted to eat the hay?
   - **a** the ox
   - **b** the dog
   - **c** a horse

3. The dog _____ at the ox.
   - **a** yelled
   - **b** growled
   - **c** smiled

4. The farmer chased the dog away with _____.
   - **a** hay
   - **b** a stick
   - **c** food

Complete the sentence. 完成句子

The .... dog must not take hay from the hungry ox.

Wrap Up Number the sentences in order. 寫出句子的順序

[4] The dog woke up and growled at the ox.

☐ A dog was sleeping on hay.

☐ The ox wanted to eat the hay.

☐ The farmer chased the dog away.

☐ A hungry ox came in.

<u>Ancient</u> Egypt had many <u>giant</u> <u>stone</u> <u>statues</u>. Some were statues of
古代的　　　　　　　　　　巨大的　石材　雕像
<u>pharaohs</u>. They were the <u>rulers</u> of ancient Egypt. Many thought the
法老　　　　　　　　　　統治者
pharaohs were <u>gods</u>. So people made their statues for <u>temples</u>. The
神　　　　　　　　　　　　　　　　　神殿
statues are in pharaohs' <u>tombs</u> too because
墳墓
<u>Egyptians</u> believed in an <u>afterlife</u>. They
埃及人　　　　　　　來世
thought that pharaohs lived there

forever. Ramses II is a famous pharaoh.

The number of his statues is the

highest! <u>That's why</u> many people
這就是為甚麼～
<u>remember</u> him.
記得

Check True or False 是非題

❶ There were many statues of pharaohs in Egypt.　T / F

❷ Egyptians did not believe in an afterlife.　　　　T / F

法老的雕像

古埃及有許多巨大的石像，有些是法老的雕像，他們是古埃及的統治者。許多人認為法老是神，所以人們為神廟製作他們的雕像。這些雕像也在法老的墳墓裡，因為埃及人相信有來世，他們相信法老永遠會在那裡生活。拉美西斯二世是一位知名的法老，而他的雕像數量也是最多的！這也是很多人會記得他的原因。

背景知識 Plus!

提到法老，人們都會想到拉美西斯二世（Ramses II），他是帶領古埃及進入全盛期的統治者。他在青少年時開始統治埃及，並在六十多年的期間完成許多成就。因此，為了讓人民記住自己，甚至以自己的形象重建了許多古代法老的雕像。

Comprehension Checkup 理解能力確認

Circle the best answer. 圈選出正確的答案

1. Who were pharaohs in ancient Egypt?
   ⓐ rulers   ⓑ artists   ⓒ soldiers

2. What did many people think pharaohs were?
   ⓐ statues   ⓑ temples   ⓒ gods

3. Statues of pharaohs are in temples and _____.
   ⓐ afterlife   ⓑ tombs   ⓒ mountains

4. Ramses II is a famous pharaoh with the most _____.
   ⓐ statues   ⓑ people   ⓒ numbers

Complete the sentence. 完成句子

Ancient Egyptians made statues of .... for their afterlife.

Wrap Up   Fill in the blanks. 總複習，將單字填入空格

Statues of Pharaohs

誰是法老？
- the ❶ .... of ancient Egypt
- People thought they were
  ❷ ....

法老石像的位置
- temples and pharaohs'
  ❸ ....
- Egyptians believed in a(n)
  ❹ ....

tombs   gods   rulers   afterlife

With a set of numbers, you can study their
一組～
range. Say you have five numbers:
範圍 假設～
2, 4, 10, 2, and 7. First, add these
加
numbers. Then divide the sum by
除   總和
5. The answer 5 is the mean. Next,
平均數
order the numbers from lowest to
給～排序
highest. The middle number, or 4, is
the median. Finally, there is the mode.
中位數   眾數
That number appears the most. Here, it is 2.
出現

Check True or False 是非題

❶ You can study the range of numbers in   T / F

three ways.

❷ The median is the highest number.   T / F

平均數、中位數和眾數

如果有一組數字，你就可以來研究它們的範圍。
假設有五個數字：2、4、10、2 和 7。首先，將
這些數字相加，然後再將總和除以 5，答案 5 就
是平均數。接下來，將這些數字從最低排列到最
高，中間的數字 4，就是中位數。最後是眾數，
也是指出現最多次的數字，而這裡的眾數是 2。

背景知識 Plus!

為了更了解特定數字的範圍
（range），我們通常會找出平均數
（mean）。當三個數字的平均數是 3，
這些數字可能是 3、3、3，但也可能是
1、1、7 或 1、3、5。因此為了更準
確理解這些數字的分布，我們也
需要找出中數（median）和
眾數（mode）。

Comprehension Checkup 理解能力確認

Circle the best answer. 圈選出正確的答案

1. With five numbers, how do you find the mean?
   - a add the numbers
   - b divide the sum by 5
   - c find the middle number

2. In the example, what is the median?
   - a 2
   - b 4
   - c 10

3. The _____ appears the most.
   - a sum
   - b median
   - c mode

4. In the example, the mode is _____.
   - a 2
   - b 4
   - c 7

Complete the sentence. 完成句子

For a .... of numbers, you can find the mean, median, and mode.

Wrap Up Fill in the blanks. 總複習，將單字填入空格

Study the Range

mean	median	mode
Add all the numbers and divide the ❶ .... by the number of numbers.	Find the ❷ .... number in order.	Find the number that appears the ❸ ....

顏色產生其他顏色
Colors Make Other Colors

R_85.mp3

Colors come in three types. <u>Primary colors</u> are basic. These are
原色
red, blue, and yellow. Now let's <u>mix</u> different colors. Red and
混合
blue <u>form</u> <u>purple</u>. Red and yellow form orange.
形成　　紫色
Blue and yellow form green. These are

<u>secondary colors</u>. Last, there are
二次色
<u>complementary colors</u>. These are
互補色
<u>pairs</u> of one primary and one
一對
secondary color. These pairs make

each other <u>brighter</u>. So red letters on
（顏色）鮮明的
green paper will <u>stand out</u>.
顯著

❶ Green and yellow mix and make orange.　　　　T / F

❷ Primary colors make secondary colors.　　　　T / F

顏色產生其他顏色

顏色有三種類型，原色是基本色，有紅色、藍色
和黃色。現在讓我們把不同的顏色混在一起。紅
色加藍色會形成紫色，紅色加黃色會形成橘色，
藍色加黃色會形成綠色，這些是二次色。最後還
有互補色，是指一個原色以及一個二次色形成的
顏色組合，這個組合會讓兩種顏色彼此都變得
更鮮明，因此紅色的字母在綠色的紙上會非常顯
著。

背景知識 Plus!

顏料的三原色（primary colors）
是紅色、黃色、藍色，但光的三原色
則是紅色、綠色、藍色。而光的三原色
也是各個光的顏色結合來形成二次色
（secondary colors），這時紅光
和綠光會結合並產生黃光。

Circle the best answer. 圈選出正確的答案

1. Which is a primary color?
   ⓐ green   ⓑ red   ⓒ orange

2. Which is NOT a secondary color?
   ⓐ blue   ⓑ orange   ⓒ purple

3. _____ colors make each other brighter.
   ⓐ Primary   ⓑ Secondary   ⓒ Complementary

4. Red and _____ stand out together.
   ⓐ yellow   ⓑ blue   ⓒ green

Complete the sentence. 完成句子

The three types of colors can _____ or make pairs with each other.

Wrap Up   Fill in the blanks. 總複習，將單字填入空格

primary colors	secondary colors	❶ _____ colors
• red, yellow, ❷ _____	• mix two ❸ _____ colors ▶ purple, orange, ❹ _____	• pairs of one primary and one secondary color

primary   complementary   green   blue

WORD REVIEW

👩 Crossword Puzzle 填字遊戲

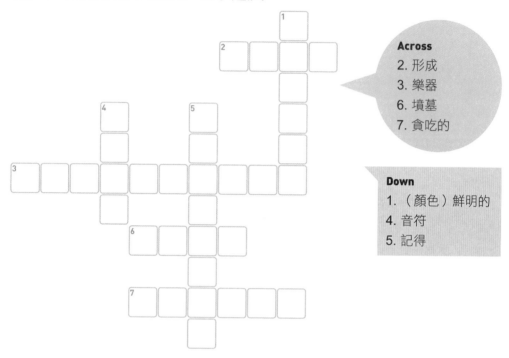

Across
2. 形成
3. 樂器
6. 墳墓
7. 貪吃的

Down
1. （顏色）鮮明的
4. 音符
5. 記得

🦓 Match with the correct definition. 將單字連到正確的意思

1. mode •

2. pharaoh •

3. primary colors •

4. percussion instrument •

ⓐ a musical instrument that you hit or shake to make sound

ⓑ a ruler of ancient Egypt

ⓒ the number that appears the most in a set of numbers

ⓓ the three basic colors: red, blue, and yellow

Fill in the blank with the correct words.
將正確的單字填入空格中

> divide　giant　pairs　beat　growled

1. Musicians hit drums and make a _____.
   音樂家會打鼓，並產生節奏。

2. However, the dog woke up and _____ at the ox.
   結果狗醒了過來，對著公牛吠叫。

3. Ancient Egypt had many _____ stone statues.
   古埃及有許多巨大的石像。

4. First, add these numbers. Then _____ the sum by 5.
   首先將這些數字相加，然後再將總和除以 5。

5. These are _____ of one primary and one secondary color.
   這些就是由一個原色加上一個二次色混合而成的一組顏色。

Fill in the blank with the correct expressions.
將正確的表達填入空格中

> fell asleep　to highest　there are　that's why　stand out

1. _____ different sizes of bells and xylophone keys.

2. In a barn, a dog _____ on hay.

3. The number of his statues is the highest! _____ many people remember him.

4. Order the numbers from lowest _____.

5. Red letters on green paper will _____.

《狼婆婆》的故事
The Tale of Lon Po Po

R_86.mp3

Some cultures have <u>common</u> stories.
共同的
For example, *Lon Po Po* is a <u>Chinese</u>
中國的
<u>tale</u>. This story is like a European one,
故事
Little Red Riding Hood. In *Lon Po Po*, a
<u>wolf</u> visits three sisters. It <u>acts</u> like their
狼   扮演
grandmother. But the girls know this
and <u>trick</u> the wolf. They talk about <u>tasty</u>
哄騙   美味可口的
<u>nuts</u> in a tree. When the wolf <u>climbs</u>
堅果   爬
the tree, the girls shake it. The wolf falls and dies.

Check True or False 是非題

① Some cultures have the same tales.   T / F

② *Lon Po Po* is like an American story.   T / F

《狼婆婆》的故事

有些文化有著共同的故事。舉例來說，《狼婆婆》是一則中國的故事，這則故事就像是歐洲的故事《小紅帽》。在《狼婆婆》中，有一頭大野狼去拜訪三姊妹，牠假扮成她們的奶奶，但是被女孩們識破了，並欺騙那隻大野狼。她們說到樹上有美味的堅果，當大野狼爬到樹上時，這些女孩就去搖晃那棵樹，最後大野狼墜地而亡。

背景知識 Plus!

"Lon Po Po" 是以《小紅帽》的架構為基礎的故事，但是加上了東方色彩。"Po Po" 在中文的意思是「婆婆」，而故事的堅果也是我們所熟悉的情節，狼被「吃銀杏可以長命百歲」這句話給騙了，作者改編這個知名的古老故事，以符合中國文化。

Comprehension Checkup 理解能力確認

Circle the best answer. 圈選出正確的答案

1. Whom does the wolf visit?
   ⓐ his grandparents　　ⓑ three sisters　　ⓒ close friends

2. Whom does the wolf act like?
   ⓐ a mother　　　　ⓑ a girl　　　　ⓒ a grandmother

3. The girls talk about tasty _____ in a tree.
   ⓐ nuts　　　　　　ⓑ apples　　　　ⓒ birds

4. The wolf climbs the tree, and the girls _____ it.
   ⓐ trick　　　　　　ⓑ shake　　　　ⓒ cut down

Complete the sentence. 完成句子

Lon Po Po is a Chinese tale, but it is like a .... one.

Wrap Up Fill in the blanks. 總複習，將單字填入空格

Lon Po Po

國家	❶ ....
相似的故事	*Little Red Riding Hood*
登場角色	wolf: acts like a ❷ ....
	three sisters: They ❸ .... the wolf and the wolf ❹ ....

grandmother　　trick　　China　　dies

Jazz is popular nowadays. It is a mix of various types of music.
爵士樂　　　　當今　　　　　　　混合

But it is unique. Why? Most musicians play only written music.
獨特的　　　　　　音樂家　　　　　　寫下的

Jazz players change parts as they play. They often
演奏者

play different notes. So, a song sounds

different each time. Also, jazz has

complex beats. These are
複雜的

not steady. The beat may
穩定的

become faster or slower

throughout the song. But it
遍及

goes well with the song.
在～進展順利

Check True or False 是非題

❶ Jazz musicians only play written music.　　　T / F

❷ A jazz song has simple steady beats.　　　T / F

爵士樂：一種獨特的音樂風格

爵士樂在當今很流行，它是各種類型音樂的混合，但它是獨特的，為什麼呢？大多數的音樂家只演奏寫好的音樂，但爵士樂手在演奏時會改變內容，他們通常會演奏不同的音符，所以一首歌每次聽起來都不一樣。此外，爵士樂的節拍很複雜，並且不穩定，節拍在整首歌曲當中可能會變快或變慢，但是卻與歌曲搭配得很好。

背景知識 Plus!

爵士樂（Jazz）在 20 世紀初期在美國紐奧良的黑人之間開始流行演奏，而在今天已經是流行於全世界的音樂風格。是由薩克斯風、低音提琴、小號和鼓等各種樂器一起創造出美妙的音樂。由於有很多即興演出的地方，表演者的風格和表現功力非常重要。

Comprehension Checkup 理解能力確認

Circle the best answer. 圈選出正確的答案

1. What is jazz made of?
   - ⓐ various types of music
   - ⓑ new music
   - ⓒ simple beats

2. What do jazz players do as they play?
   - ⓐ write music
   - ⓑ change notes
   - ⓒ make mistakes

3. A jazz song can sound _____ every time.
   - ⓐ simple
   - ⓑ steady
   - ⓒ different

4. Jazz _____ become faster or slower in a song.
   - ⓐ players
   - ⓑ beats
   - ⓒ instruments

Complete the sentence. 完成句子

Unlike most music, jazz musicians .... parts of songs in unique ways.

Wrap Up Fill in the blanks. 總複習，將單字填入空格

Jazz is unique.

- Jazz musicians change parts and play different ❶ ....
- ▶ A song sounds ❷ .... each time.

- Jazz has ❸ .... beats.
- ▶ The ❹ .... becomes faster or slower.

complex   notes   different   beat

非常有才華的人

R_88.mp3

Leonardo da Vinci <u>was born</u> in 1452 in Italy. He had many <u>talents</u>.
出生   天賦

As a <u>painter</u>, Leonardo painted two great
畫家
<u>paintings</u>. The first is *Mona Lisa*, a
畫
<u>smiling</u> woman. The other is *The Last*
微笑的
<u>Supper</u>, from <u>the Bible</u>. Leonardo was
晚餐   聖經
also a great <u>inventor</u> and <u>designer</u>.
發明家   設計師
He <u>designed</u> many buildings and
設計
<u>machines</u>. You know what? He even
機器
designed an airplane over 500
years ago!

Mona Lisa

Check True or False 是非題

❶ Leonardo was born in France.   T / F

❷ Leonardo didn't paint a woman.   T / F

非常有才華的人

李奧納多‧達文西在 1452 年出生於義大利，他非常有才華。身為畫家，達文西畫了兩幅偉大的畫作。第一幅是《蒙娜麗莎》，一名微笑的女子，而另一幅是源自《聖經》的《最後的晚餐》。達文西也是一位偉大的發明家和設計師，他設計了許多建築物和機器。你知道嗎？他甚至早在五百多年前就設計出一架飛機了！

背景知識 Plus!

李奧納多‧達文西（Leonardo da Vinci）既是音樂家、建築師、發明家、化學家、作家，也是一名傑出的畫家。他具備觀察力和探索力，持續研究和記錄自然現象和原理。他到去世前都保持作筆記的習慣，留下了超過一萬三千頁的手稿。不幸的是，只有一半的手稿被保留下來。

Comprehension Checkup 理解能力確認

Circle the best answer. 圈選出正確的答案

1. What is the painting *Mona Lisa* of?
   ⓐ a smiling woman   **ⓑ** a talented man   **ⓒ** a machine

2. What is *The Last Supper* from?
   ⓐ a design   **ⓑ** a Bible story   **ⓒ** a building

3. Leonardo designed buildings and _____.
   ⓐ paintings   **ⓑ** inventors   **ⓒ** machines

4. Leonardo designed _____ over 500 years ago.
   ⓐ Italy   **ⓑ** an airplane   **ⓒ** a supper

Complete the sentence. 完成句子

Leonardo was a talented painter, designer, and ....

Wrap Up   Fill in the blanks. 總複習，將單字填入空格

Leonardo da Vinci

As a(n) ❶	As a designer and a(n) ❷ ....
• *Mona Lisa* • *The Last Supper*	• designed many buildings and machines • designed a(n) ❸ ....

airplane   inventor   painter

Zero is important in mathematics. It means "no amount." Also,
零   (= math) 數學

it creates new amounts. Put one or more zeros

after a number. This creates tens, hundreds,
一百

and thousands. So who created zero? Some
一千

ancient people did. But their zeros had

different shapes or meanings. Today's
意思

version comes from India. It appeared about
版本   印度

1,500 years ago! People there developed

it for math. And this modern zero
現代的

spread all over the world.
傳播   世界各地

0	1	2	3	4	5	6	7	8	9
०	१	२	३	४	५	६	७	८	९

Check True or False 是非題

1. Ancient zeros had different shapes.　　　　　T / F

2. The modern zero first appeared 150 years ago.　T / F

誰創造了零？

零在數學中很重要，它的意思是「沒有數量」。
此外，它也創造了新的數量。只要在一個數字後
面放一個或更多個零，就創造出了幾十、幾百和
幾千的數值。所以是誰創造了零的呢？零是由古
代人所創造出來的，但是他們的零有不同的形狀
或含義。現在的版本來自於印度，它出現在大約
一千五百年以前！當時的人們為了數學而發展出
零，而這個現代的零也傳播到世界各地。

背景知識 Plus!

古代的數字與我們今天使用的數
字有很大的差別，古代馬雅人用點
（‧）來代表 1，用橫線（－）來代表
5。例如，17 是在 ≡ 上面放兩個點
表示。而 0（zero）據說是以貝殼的
形狀來呈現。

Circle the best answer. 圈選出正確的答案

1. What does zero mean in mathematics?
   ⓐ version   ⓑ no amount   ⓒ no limit

2. How many zeros do you need for one hundred?
   ⓐ 2   ⓑ 3   ⓒ 4

3. _____ people created different forms of zero.
   ⓐ Modern   ⓑ Ancient   ⓒ Indian

4. People in India _____ zero for math.
   ⓐ found   ⓑ removed   ⓒ developed

Complete the sentence. 完成句子

The modern zero first appeared in India and .... over the world.

WrapUp Fill in the blanks. 總複習，將單字填入空格

Zero

○ 的意義	○ 的創造與進化
• It means "❶ .... amount."	• Ancient people ❸ .... it.
• It creates ❷ .... amounts.	• Indian people developed it for ❹ .... ▸ today's version

math   new   created   no

90 A Boy and the Television

R_90.mp3

Philo Farnsworth was born in Utah in 1906. He was a <u>genius</u> with
天才

<u>electric</u> <u>devices</u>. As a <u>teenager</u>, he read many science <u>magazines</u>.
用電的　裝置　　　　青少年　　　　　　　　雜誌

And he <u>was interested in</u> TV. At that time,
對～感興趣

TVs didn't send <u>images</u> quickly, like
影像

today. So he designed a special device.

This could show electric images

quickly. He was still a teenager then!

He <u>continued</u> his work. In 1929, he
持續

developed the first electric television.

Check True or False 是非題

1 Philo Farnsworth was born in 1929.　　　　　T / F

2 He designed a device when he was a teenager.　T / F

男孩與電視

費羅・法恩斯沃斯在 1906 年出生於猶他州，他
是電子裝置方面的天才。在青少年時期，他閱讀
了許多科學雜誌，而且對電視很感興趣。在那個
時候，電視並不能像現在這樣快速發送影像，因
此他設計了一個特殊的裝置，這能夠快速顯示電
子影像，當時他還只是個青少年！而他後來也持
續從事這項工作，在 1929 年，他開發了世界上
第一台電子電視。

背景知識 Plus!

費羅（Philo）發明了電子電視，
之後卻被捲入了專利糾紛，這是因為
似乎在費羅之前就已經有人發明電子電
視。然而，費羅的高中老師提供了他
在學生時期所畫的電視素描，費羅因
而得到專利局的支持。

Comprehension Checkup 理解能力確認

Circle the best answer. 圈選出正確的答案

1. What was Philo a genius with?
   - ⓐ TV programs
   - ⓑ electric devices
   - ⓒ photography

2. What did Philo read when he was a teenager?
   - ⓐ newspapers
   - ⓑ science magazines
   - ⓒ comic books

3. At that time, _____ didn't send images quickly.
   - ⓐ TVs
   - ⓑ electricity
   - ⓒ science

4. Philo's device showed _____ images quickly.
   - ⓐ photo
   - ⓑ interesting
   - ⓒ electric

Complete the sentence. 完成句子

Philo Farnsworth made the first electric ....

Wrap Up Fill in the blanks. 總複習，將單字填入空格

Philo Farnsworth: a ❶ .... with electric devices

As a teenager	In 1929
• interested in TV	• developed the first
• designed a device to ❷ .... electric images ❸	❹ .... television

quickly   electric   genius   show

WORD REVIEW

Crossword Puzzle 填字遊戲

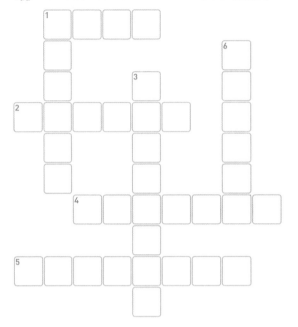

Across
1. 故事
2. 天才
4. 機器
5. 青少年

Down
1. 天賦
3. 音樂家
6. 現代的

Match with the correct definition. 將單字連到正確的意思

1. zero •

ⓐ a type of music with complex beats in which players change notes as they play

2. inventor •

ⓑ the number that has no amount and creates new amounts

3. the Bible •

ⓒ someone who made a useful thing for the first time

4. jazz •

ⓓ the book that has holy stories for Christians

Fill in the blank with the correct words.
將正確的單字填入空格

| meanings | designed | electric | trick | unique |

1. But the girls know this and _____ the wolf.
   但是女孩們識破了，並欺騙那隻大野狼。

2. Jazz is a mix of various types of music. But it is _____.
   爵士樂是各種類型的音樂的混合，但是它是獨特的。

3. He _____ many buildings and machines.
   他設計出許多建築物和機器。

4. But their zeros had different shapes or _____.
   但是他們的零有不同的形狀或含義。

5. In 1929, he developed the first _____ television.
   1929 年，他開發出世界上第一台電子電視。

Fill in the blank with the correct expressions.
將正確的表達填入空格

| goes well | acts like | was born | interested in | all over the world |

1. A wolf visits three sisters. It _____ their grandmother.

2. The beat may become faster or slower. But it _____ _____ with the song.

3. Leonardo da Vinci _____ in 1452 in Italy.

4. This modern zero spread _____.

5. Philo Farnsworth was _____ TV.

Can you play the <u>banjo</u>? How about the guitar? Both are
班卓琴
<u>string instruments</u>. Sounds are made by <u>plucking</u> their strings.
弦樂器　　　　　　　　　　　　　　　　　撥
Thicker or longer strings make lower sounds. Thinner or shorter
strings make higher sounds. Banjos and guitars sound different
<u>though</u>. That's because banjos have a different body than guitars.
然而
The body of a banjo is round and <u>looks like</u> a drum.
看起來像～
This <u>produces</u> a <u>unique</u> sound. It is <u>popular</u> in
產生　　　　　獨特的　　　　　　受歡迎的
<u>traditional</u> American music. You can hear that
傳統的
sound in a song like "Oh! Suzanna."

Read and Complete 完成句子

❶ Banjos and guitars are _____ instruments.

❷ Banjos' sound is popular in traditional American
_____.

所有美國的聲音
你會彈班卓琴嗎？那麼吉他呢？這兩者都是弦樂器。聲音是透過撥動琴弦來產生的，較粗或較長的琴弦會發出較低沉的聲音，較細或較短的琴弦則會發出較高亢的聲音。然而班卓琴和吉他的聲音是不同的，那是因為班卓琴的琴身與吉他不同。班卓琴的琴身是圓的，又看起來像鼓，這產生了一種獨特的音色。班卓琴在傳統的美國音樂中很受歡迎，可以在《哦，蘇珊娜》這樣的歌曲中聽到這種音色。

背景知識 Plus!
班卓琴（banjo）是爵士樂或民謠音樂中使用的一種吉他，而根據推測，阿拉伯或歐洲的吉他已經流傳到非洲並被改造。據說在西非被稱為巴尼亞（bania），由非洲人帶到美國，並變成班卓琴。外觀有長的琴頸，以及像手鼓一樣以皮革包覆的圓形琴身，而琴弦有 4 條到 9 條。

Comprehension Checkup 理解能力確認

🐧 **Circle the best answer. 圈選出正確的答案**

1. What kind of strings makes higher sounds?
   - ⓐ long strings
   - ⓑ short strings
   - ⓒ thick strings

2. What causes the different sound between banjos and guitars?
   - ⓐ body shapes
   - ⓑ how to play
   - ⓒ how popular it is

3. What is true about a banjo?
   - ⓐ It looks like a guitar.
   - ⓑ It sounds like a drum.
   - ⓒ American people love its unique sound.
   - ⓓ Its thinner strings make lower sounds.

4. Why does the writer mention "Oh! Suzanna"?
   - ⓐ to compare banjos and guitars
   - ⓑ to explain the history of American music
   - ⓒ to show the great performance with banjos
     表演
   - ⓓ to give an example of music with banjos

🦔 **Complete the sentence. 完成句子**

Guitars and banjos are both string ❶ .... They look different, so they ❷ .... different sounds. Banjos are ❸ .... in traditional American music.

WrapUp Fill in the blanks. 總複習，將單字填入空格

Banjo		
發聲方式	• by plucking their ❶	
音域	• thin and short strings: high sound • thick and long strings: ❷ .... sound	
特別之處	• produce a ❸ .... sound • popular in ❹ .... American music	

unique

low

strings

traditional

Are You in 2D or 3D Shape?

R_92.mp3

You and I have three <u>dimensions</u> (3D). <u>In other words</u>, we have
維　　　　　　　　　　　　　　換句話說
<u>height</u>, <u>length</u>, and <u>width</u>. But a picture or drawing of you only has
高度　 長度　　　　寬度
two dimensions (2D). It only has height and length. The same is
true for some shapes, and they can be <u>either 3D or 2D</u>. Sometimes,
不是～就是～
you can take a 2D shape and
<u>add</u> width to make a 3D shape.
增加
If you give a square width, it
becomes a <u>cube</u>. A 2D circle
立方體
becomes a 3D <u>sphere</u>. What
球體
are some other 3D shapes?

Read and Complete 完成句子

❶ 3D shapes have ＿＿＿＿＿＿, length, and width.

❷ Shapes can be 2 or 3 ＿＿＿＿＿.

你是 2D 還是 3D 的形狀？

你和我都具有三個維度（3D）。換句話說，我們
具有高度、長度和寬度。但是你的照片或圖畫只
有兩個維度（2D），它只有高度和長度。對於
某些形狀也是一樣的，它們不是 3D 就是 2D。
有時可以將一個 2D 的形狀加上寬度，並做成一
個 3D 的形狀。如果你幫正方形加上寬度，它就
會變成立方體。2D 的圓形也可以變成 3D 的球
體。還有哪些 3D 的形狀呢？

背景知識 Plus!

像普通的 2D 印表機可以列印
出字母或圖片，而 3D（three
dimensions）印表機是一種根據輸入
的圖像來創造出 3D 形狀的機器。2D
印表機只能前後移動（x 軸）和左右
移動（y 軸），但是 3D 印表機會
以此基礎增加上下移動（z
軸）來創造三維的形
狀。

Circle the best answer. 圈選出正確的答案

1. What is an example of a 2D shape?
   - ⓐ a cube
   - ⓑ a sphere
   - ⓒ a square

2. How can you change a 2D shape into a 3D shape?
   - ⓐ by adding length
   - ⓑ by adding width
   - ⓒ by adding height

3. Why does the writer mention "a picture of you"?
   - ⓐ to explain the meaning of 3D
   - ⓑ to give an example of 2 dimensions
   - ⓒ to describe how to make 3D shapes
   - ⓓ to prove 2D shapes are more natural than 3D shapes

4. What is NOT true about 2D and 3D?
   - ⓐ Drawings of something have two dimensions.
   - ⓑ If you give a circle width, it becomes a sphere.
   - ⓒ Shapes in 2 dimensions have height and length.
   - ⓓ If you take width away from a square, it becomes a cube.

Complete the sentence. 完成句子

❶ .... in 2 dimensions have height and
❷ .... If we add ❸ .... to a 2D shape, it
can be a shape in 3 dimensions.

Wrap Up Fill in the blanks. 總複習，將單字填入空格

| 2 dimensions | — | height, ❶ .... | — | ❸ ...., circle |

| 3 dimensions | — | height, length, ❸ .... | — | cube, ❹ .... |

width   length   sphere   square

We can <u>count</u> <u>whole numbers</u>. Whole numbers greater than 1 can
(計算)(整數)
either be prime or <u>composite numbers</u>. How do we <u>distinguish</u>
(合數)(區分)
between <u>prime numbers</u> and composite numbers? It's easy! Prime
(質數)
numbers can only be <u>divided</u> without <u>remainder</u> by 1 or the prime
(除)(餘數)
number itself. Is 3 a prime number? Yes, because 3 can only be

divided without remainder by 1 or 3.
How about 4? Is it a prime number? No,
because 4 can also be divided by 2 without
remainder. It is a composite number. Is 5 a
prime or composite number?

Prime Numbers				
2	3	5	7	11
13	17	19	23	29
31	37	41	43	47
53	59	61	67	71
73	79	83	89	97

Read and Complete 完成句子

❶ We are able to _____ whole numbers.

❷ Whole numbers are either _____ or composite.

那個數字是質數還是合數？

我們可以計算整數。大於 1 的整數可以是質數
或是合數。我們要如何區分質數和合數呢？很簡
單！質數只能被 1 或質數本身的數字除、沒有
餘數。3 是質數嗎？是的，因為 3 只能被 1 或 3
除、沒有餘數。那麼 4 呢？它是質數嗎？不是，
因為 4 也可以被 2 除、沒有餘數，它是合數。那
麼 5 是質數還是合數呢？

背景知識 Plus!

0、1、2、3…等用在計算或排
列的數字稱為「自然數」。自然數
分成質數（prime number）和合數
（composite number）。質數是只能
被 1 和自己整除的數，而能被 2 或更
多數字整除的數字是合數。比自然數
更廣泛的概念是「整數」，包括
了「負數（-1、-2、-3…）」
和「正數（1、2、
3…）」。

Circle the best answer. 圈選出正確的答案

1. What is an example of a prime number?
   a 0   b 7   c 8

2. What is an example of a composite number?
   a 3   b 5   c 6

3. What can prime numbers be divided without remainder by?
   a They can be divided by any number.
   b They can be divided by any prime number.
   c They can be divided by any composite number.
   d They can be divided by the prime number itself.

4. What is NOT true about composite numbers?
   a They are whole numbers.
   b They include numbers like 9.
   c They can only be divided by 1 without remainder.
   d They can be divided by more than 2 numbers.

Complete the sentence. 完成句子

> Prime and ❶ .... numbers are ❷ ....
> numbers. Prime numbers can only be ❸ .... by 2
> numbers without remainder. Composite numbers can be
> divided by more than 2 numbers without remainder.

Wrap Up Fill in the blanks. 總複習，將單字填入空格

❶ .... **Numbers**

prime numbers	composite ❸ ....
can be divided by only 1 or the prime number ❷	can be divided by ❹ .... than 2 numbers without remainder

more   whole   numbers   itself

The <u>Ancient</u> <u>Greeks</u> had a story about how <u>Demeter</u> changed the
seasons. There was only one season before this story. Demeter was
<u>goddess</u> of the <u>harvest</u>. Long ago, the god <u>Hades</u> <u>fell in love with</u>
Demeter's daughter, <u>Persephone</u>. But she didn't love him back.
He took Persephone to the <u>underworld</u>. Demeter was upset so she
didn't allow any plants to grow. Hades <u>agreed</u> to let Persephone
<u>return</u> for six months every year. During those six months, Demeter
was happy and everything grew. People call this
season summer. People call the season when
nothing grows winter.

Read and Complete 完成句子

1 Hades loved Persephone, Demeter's _____.

2 Demeter was _____ because Hades took
Persephone away.

關於季節的故事

古希臘人有個關於狄蜜特如何改變季節的故事。
在這個故事出現之前，世界上只有一個季節。狄
蜜特是豐饒女神。很久以前，冥王黑帝斯愛上了
狄蜜特的女兒珀耳塞福涅，但珀耳塞福涅並不愛
他，於是黑帝斯就把她帶到了冥界。狄蜜特很生
氣，所以她不讓任何植物生長。黑帝斯同意讓珀
耳塞福涅每年回去六個月。在那六個月期間，狄
蜜特很高興，所以萬物都在生長。人們將這個季
節稱為夏天，沒有東西生長的季節則稱為冬天。

背景知識 Plus!

珀耳塞福涅的父親宙斯要求黑帝斯
（Hades）讓他的女兒回來。在將珀
爾塞福涅送到人間之前，黑帝用石榴籽
餵了珀爾塞福涅。為了換取冥界的食
物，珀耳塞福涅沒辦法完全回到人
間。一年中有一半的時間與冥界的
黑帝斯一起度過，而另一半的
時間則是與人間的狄蜜特
一起度過。

Circle the best answer. 圈選出正確的答案

1. What is this Greek story mainly about?
   ⓐ mother and daughter   ⓑ seasons   ⓒ underworld

2. Where did Hades take Persephone?
   ⓐ to Greece   ⓑ to Demeter   ⓒ to the underworld

3. What is NOT true about Demeter?
   ⓐ She fell in love with Hades.
   ⓑ She was goddess of the harvest.
   ⓒ She stopped plants from growing.
   ⓓ She was happy when her daughter returned.

4. Why do plants only grow during summer?
   ⓐ Because Demeter was upset during the summer.
   ⓑ Because Hades allowed plants to grow only for six months.
   ⓒ Because Demeter let plants grow while Persephone came back.
   ⓓ Because Persephone was in the underworld during the summer.

Complete the sentence. 完成句子

> Hades took Persephone to the underworld. Angry Demeter made nothing ❶ .... This season is ❷ .... Hades let Persephone return for six months a year. Then, Demeter allowed everything to grow. This season is ❸ ....

Wrap Up Write the numbers in order. 寫出句子的順序

[5] Demeter was happy and everything grew during those six months.

☐ Hades fell in love with Persephone.

☐ Demeter was upset and didn't let any plants grow.

☐ Hades took Persephone to the underworld.

☐ Hades agreed to let Persephone return for six months every year.

歡樂的亡靈節
A Joyful Day of the Dead

R_95.mp3

In Mexico, the Day of <u>the Dead</u> is an important holiday. Families
<u>gather</u> together to remember their <u>ancestors</u>. On this day, they
亡者
聚集   祖先
believe the <u>spirits</u> of the dead can join their families again. It may
靈魂
sound sad and a bit scary, but it's a <u>joyful</u> <u>celebration</u>. Families
高興的   慶祝
make <u>altars</u> in their homes. Then, they put
祭壇
their ancestors' favorite food and drinks
there. After that, they bring gifts to their
ancestors' <u>graves</u>. Often, they wear <u>ghost</u>
墳墓   幽靈
or <u>skeleton</u> <u>costumes</u>. On the Day of the
骨架   服裝
Dead, the <u>cemeteries</u> are full of celebration!
墓地

Read and Complete 完成句子

❶ The Day of the Dead is a holiday in _____.

❷ Families get together to remember their _____.

歡樂的亡靈節

在墨西哥，亡靈節是一個重要的節日，家人會聚
集在一起來紀念他們的祖先。在這一天，他們相
信逝者的靈魂可以再次與家人相聚。這聽起來可
能很悲傷又有一點恐怖，但這是一個歡樂的慶祝
活動。家家戶戶都會在家裡設一個祭壇，接著他
們在那裡放上祖先最喜歡的食物和飲料放在那
裡。在那之後，他們帶著禮物到祖先的墳墓，大
家通常會穿上幽靈或骷髏的服裝。在亡靈節這
天，墓地裡充滿了慶祝的氛圍！

背景知識 Plus!

墨西哥人相信亡者會在亡靈節
（Day of the Dead）來到人間探望
家人和朋友。他們會在十月底設立祭
壇，並在 11 月 1 日為去世的孩子祈
禱，以及在 11 月 2 日為去世的成年
人祈禱。骷髏雕像和骨頭形狀的
糖果是用糖或巧克力製作而
成的，並會放在祭壇
上。

Comprehension Checkup 理解能力確認

Circle the best answer. 圈選出正確的答案

1. Where do some families make altars?
   - ⓐ on graves
   - ⓑ in their homes
   - ⓒ in cemeteries

2. On the Day of the Dead, what joins their families again?
   - ⓐ elderly people
   - ⓑ scary ghosts
   - ⓒ the spirits of the dead

3. What is NOT true about the Day of the Dead?
   - ⓐ It is a sad day for Mexican families.
   - ⓑ People often wear special costumes.
   - ⓒ People bring gifts to their ancestors' cemeteries.
   - ⓓ Food and drinks for ancestors are put on altars.

4. What can be inferred from the passage?
   - ⓐ Mexicans hate to feel sadness.
   - ⓑ Mexicans believe in the life after death.
   - ⓒ The symbols of ghosts are popular in Mexico.
   - ⓓ Graves in Mexico are bigger than graves in other countries'.

Complete the sentence. 完成句子

In Mexico, many families celebrate the Day of the ❶ .... It is an important ❷ .... because families ❸ .... to remember their ancestors with joy.

Wrap Up Fill in the blanks. 總複習，將單字填入空格

The Day of the Dead		
意義	Families gather and remember ancestors.	costumes
特別之處	The ❶ .... of the dead join again. ▶ a ❷ .... celebration	joyful spirits
會做的事	make ❸ ...., bring gifts to graves, wear ❹	altars

歡樂的亡靈節 241

WORD REVIEW

🐧 Crossword Puzzle 填字遊戲

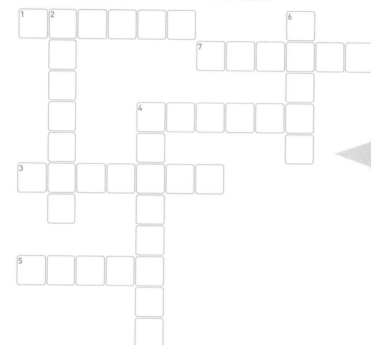

Across
1. 球體
3. 收成
4. 靈魂
5. 計算
7. 【數】除

Down
2. 受歡迎的
4. 骨架
6. 寬度

🦔 Match with the correct definition. 將單字連到正確的意思

1. composite number •

    ⓐ an instrument that makes a sound when its strings are vibrated

2. prime number •

    ⓑ height, length, and width

3. string instrument •

    ⓒ a number that can only be divided by 1 or itself

4. three dimensions •

    ⓓ a number that can be divided by more than 2 numbers without remainder

Fill in the blank with the correct words.
將正確的單字填入空格中

> add　　agreed　　altars　　gather　　underworld

1. You can take a 2D shape and _____ width to make a 3D shape.　你可以拿一個 2D 形狀，並加上寬度，來作成 3D 形狀。

2. Hades took Persephone to the _____.
黑帝斯把珀耳塞福涅帶到了冥界。

3. Hades _____ to let Persephone return for six months every year.　黑帝斯同意每年六個月讓珀耳塞福涅回到人間。

4. Families _____ together to remember their ancestors.
家人會聚集在一起，來紀念他們的祖先。

5. Families make _____ in their homes.
家家戶戶都會在家裡設立祭壇。

Fill in the blank with the correct expressions.
將正確的表達填入空格中

> are full of　　between ~ and　　either ~ or
>
> fell in love with　　looks like

1. The body of a banjo is round and _____ a drum.

2. The same is true for some shapes, they can be _____ 3D _____ 2D.

3. How do we distinguish _____ prime numbers _____ composite numbers?

4. The god Hades _____ Demeter's daughter, Persephone.

5. On the Day of the Dead, the cemeteries _____ celebration.

Millions of Americans love <u>country music</u>. It's a popular <u>genre</u> of
鄉村音樂　　　　　　　　　　　　　（藝術的）風格
music. It first <u>appeared</u> around 100 years ago with traditional
出現
<u>folk music</u> from <u>Ireland</u> and <u>Scotland</u>. And then, it changed and
民俗音樂　　　　　愛爾蘭　　　蘇格蘭
mixed with other cultures when <u>Europeans</u> moved into North
歐洲人
America. Folk music usually uses guitars and banjos. Modern
country music still uses these instruments. The songs
tell stories about life outside of big cities. The
<u>lyrics</u> are about <u>romance</u>, <u>struggles</u>, <u>pride</u>, and
歌詞　　　　　浪漫　　　奮鬥　　自豪
traditions. In America, country music continues
to grow and change, and it is still popular today!

Read and Complete 完成句子

❶ Country is a popular _____ of music.

❷ Modern country music is still growing and _____.

鄉村音樂仍然活躍著

數百萬的美國人喜歡鄉村音樂，這是一種流行的音樂類型，最早出現在大約一百年前、來自愛爾蘭和蘇格蘭的傳統民俗音樂中。而之後在歐洲人移居到北美洲時，音樂改變並與其他文化混合在一起。民間音樂通常會使用吉他和班卓琴，而現代鄉村音樂仍然會使用這些樂器。這些歌曲在講述關於大城市外生活的故事，歌詞是關於浪漫、努力、驕傲和傳統。在美國，鄉村音樂持續在成長和變化，而且今日仍然很受歡迎！

背景知識 Plus!

1920 年代從歐洲到北美洲的移民帶來了歐洲的樂器和音樂。透過與北美洲多元文化的交流和回應，獨特的音樂：鄉村音樂（country music）就此誕生。在 1950 年代，鄉村音樂大受歡迎，也創造出融合其他音樂風格的「鄉村靈魂」和「鄉村搖滾」等新曲風。

Comprehension Checkup 理解能力確認

🧑 Circle the best answer. 圈選出正確的答案

1. Where did country music first appear?
   ⓐ Ireland   ⓑ North America   ⓒ big cities in America

2. Which instrument does folk music usually NOT use?
   ⓐ banjo   ⓑ violin   ⓒ guitar

3. What is country music NOT about?
   ⓐ missing Africa   ⓑ pride and traditions
   ⓒ romance and struggles   ⓓ life outside of big cities

4. What is true about country music?
   ⓐ It means folk songs from Ireland.
   ⓑ It's still very popular in North America.
   ⓒ It is almost the same as traditional folk music.
   ⓓ It failed to interest the new generations.

🐴 Complete the sentence. 完成句子

> ❶ .... music is popular in ❷ .... America.
> Country music grew and ❸ .... over time.

Wrap Up Fill in the blanks. 總複習，將單字填入空格

Country Music	
起源	• traditional ❶ .... music from Ireland and Scotland
主要樂器	• guitars, ❷ ....
討論的主題	• ❸ .... outside of big cities • romance, struggles, pride, and ❹ ....

traditions   life   banjos   folk

奇妙的華茲塔
Wonderful Towers of Watts

R_97.mp3

Simon Rodia created <u>impressive</u> art by finding <u>objects</u> himself and
令人印象深刻的　　　　　　　　物體
using only them. In Watts, California, he created <u>sculptures</u> and
雕刻品
<u>structures</u> from <u>garbage</u>. He <u>collected</u> it because he didn't have
建築物　　　　垃圾　　　　收集
much money. Rodia did all of this work alone, and with simple
<u>tools</u>. He was <u>passionate</u> about his <u>artwork</u>. He spent
工具　　　　　熱情的　　　　　　藝術品
34 years working on it! His work <u>eventually</u> covered
最後
an 800-meter-long area of Watts. He made many tall

structures in this area. The tallest was over 30 meters
high! Today, the Watts Towers is a popular <u>outdoor</u>
戶外的
museum.

Read and Complete 完成句子

❶ Simon Rodia made the Watts Towers from _____.

❷ These days, people enjoy his work as an outdoor
_____.

奇妙的華茲塔

西蒙・盧地亞透過自己找到物品，並只使用這些物品，來創造出了令人印象深刻的藝術作品。在加州的華茲，盧地亞用垃圾創造了雕刻品和建築物，他收集垃圾是因為他沒有很多錢。盧地亞獨自完成了所有的工作，並只使用簡單的工具。他對自己的藝術作品充滿熱忱，花了 34 年在作品上！他的作品最後在華茲涵蓋了八百公尺長的區域。他在這個區域建造許多高聳的建築，最高的超過 30 公尺！現在，華茲塔是很受歡迎的戶外博物館。

背景知識 Plus!

西蒙・盧地亞（Simon Rodia）與家人分離並過著孤獨的生活，他開始在貧民居住的華茲建造一座塔樓。他使用自己取得的材料：鋼筋、陶瓷、瓷磚、玻璃碎片和貝殼。1956 年洛杉磯試圖以醜陋為由要拆除這座塔樓，但由於世界各地的人們努力保護華茲塔，至今仍然是著名的旅遊勝地。

Comprehension Checkup 理解能力確認

Circle the best answer. 圈選出正確的答案

1. How did Rodia get objects to make artworks?
   - ⓐ by collecting them himself
   - ⓑ by buying them from neighbors
   - ⓒ by borrowing them from museums

2. How long did Rodia work on his art?
   - ⓐ 800 days
   - ⓑ 30 months
   - ⓒ 34 years

3. How did Rodia work? (Choose 2 answers.)
   - ⓐ He worked very slowly.
   - ⓑ He used only garbage.
   - ⓒ He worked by himself.
   - ⓓ He spent money for objects.

4. What is NOT true about Rodia's artworks in Watts?
   - ⓐ They are still popular today.
   - ⓑ There are many structures in Watts.
   - ⓒ The tallest tower is over 30 meters high.
   - ⓓ They covered an 800-meter-long area of the museum.

Complete the sentence. 完成句子

Simon Rodia used garbage and simple ❶ _____ to create tall towers. It is the Watts ❷ _____ in California. It took 34 ❸ _____ for him to finish them.

WrapUp Fill in the blanks. 總複習，將單字填入空格

Towers of Watts			
材料	❶ _____ and use garbage		
建造方法	work ❷ _____, use ❸ _____ tools		
建造時間	34 years		
成品	the Watts Towers: a popular ❹ _____ museum		

outdoor
alone
simple
collect

<u>Idioms</u> are <u>creative</u> and common ways to <u>express</u> <u>language</u> in a
慣用語　　　有創意的　　　　　　　　　表達　　語言
certain culture. You cannot understand idioms simply by knowing

<u>grammar</u> or the words in the idiom. You can only understand them
文法
by their popular <u>use</u>. What does it mean when someone kicked the
使用
<u>bucket</u>? It usually doesn't mean <u>literally</u> that a person really kicked a
水桶　　　　　　　　　　　　照字面地
bucket. It means that someone died. Here's another idiom: I hit the

books! The <u>literal</u> meaning is that I <u>punched</u> the
照字面的　　　　　　　用拳猛擊
books. It really means that I studied. What do

you think "<u>spill</u> the <u>beans</u>" means? It means to
灑出　　豆子
<u>reveal</u> a <u>secret</u>!
揭露　　秘密

Read and Complete 完成句子

❶ _____ are commonly understood in a certain culture.

❷ "Don't spill the beans" means, "Don't reveal a _____."

認識慣用語

慣用語是在某個文化中，有創意和常見的表達語言的方式。我們沒辦法只透過慣用語中的文法或單字就理解它的含義，而是只能透過它們流行的用法來理解慣用語。「有人踢到水桶」是什麼意思呢？這通常不是指字面上「真的踢到水桶」的意思這種字面上的意思，而是指「某個人過世了」。這裡還有另一個慣用語：I hit the books! 字面上的意思是「我拳擊了書本」，而真正的意思是「我念書了」。你認為「打翻豆子」是什麼意思呢？意思是「洩漏祕密」！

背景知識 Plus!

英文中有很多與身體部位相關的慣用語（idiom）。Don't pull Steve's leg. 是「不要取笑 Steve」的意思。Mary has a big mouth. 是「Mary 很會講出別人的祕密」的意思。I have butterflies in my stomach. 和 I'm so nervous. 的意思相同。是不是覺得慣用語能夠更生動地表達情境或情緒？

Circle the best answer. 圈選出正確的答案

1. What does "He kicked the bucket" mean?
   (a) He died.   (b) He is angry.   (c) He kicked the trash can.

2. When you're studying, which idiom can express your situation?
   (a) I'm spilling the beans.   (b) I'm punching the books.
   (c) I'm hitting the books.

3. What is NOT true about idioms?
   (a) They are not used literally.
   (b) They are creative and popular.
   (c) They are common in language.
   (d) They often use wrong grammar.

4. You want to make sure your friends keep a secret. Which idiom can you use?
   (a) Don't spill the beans.   (b) Don't kick the bucket.
   (c) I hope you spill the beans.   (d) I want you to kick the bucket.

Complete the sentence. 完成句子

Idioms are ❶ .... and common expressions. They are different from their ❷ .... meaning. You can understand idioms by their popular ❸ ....

Wrap Up Fill in the blanks. 總複習，將單字填入空格

Idioms		
特色	• ❶ .... and common ways to express language in a certain ❷.......................... • understand them by their popular ❸ .... • not a literal ❹	culture meaning creative
例子	• kick the bucket, hit the books, spill the beans	use

用點點作畫
Painting with Points

R_99.mp3

Pointillism is a creative way to paint pictures. It uses dots or points
點描法（用小點表達的繪畫方式）　　　　　　　　　　　　　　　點
of color to create images. If you look closely, you can see many
　　　　　　　　圖像　　　　　　　　仔細地
individual points. If you look from far away, it looks like a regular
個別的　　一小點　　　　　　　遠處
painting. That's because the points of color
畫作
appear to blend together. Georges Seurat was
　　　混合
a French artist, and he created Pointillism in
the 1800s. He made some famous paintings,
such as *The Circus*. It describes the circus
　　　　馬戲團　　　描繪
performers and people watching them. And, it
表演者
is made up of countless colored dots!
　　　　　　無數的

The Circus

Read and Complete 完成句子

❶ _____ of color can create images in Pointillism.

❷ Many individual points appear to _____ together.

用點點作畫

點描法是一種很有創意的的繪圖方式，它使用彩色的點來創作圖像。如果你仔細觀察，可以看到許多單獨的點。但是如果從遠處看，它看起來就像一幅正常的畫。那是因為這些彩色的點似乎融合在一起。喬治‧秀拉是一位法國藝術家，他在 1800 年代創造了點描法。他創作了許多著名的畫作，例如《馬戲團》。這幅畫描繪了馬戲團的表演者和觀看表演者的人，而且它是由無數個彩色的點所組成的！

背景知識 Plus!

喬治‧秀拉（George Seurat）在 1880 年代開始受到關注，當時他與畫家同伴保羅‧希涅克（Paul Signac）一起發展點描法。他的代表作《大碗島上的星期天下午》花了將近兩年的時間才完成，用點描法繪畫需要花很長的時間，並且還要有十足的耐心。

👧 **Circle the best answer.** 圈選出正確的答案

1. What do artists use in Pointillism?
   ⓐ dots of colors　　ⓑ blended images　ⓒ creative pictures

2. What is the painting *The Circus* about?
   ⓐ countless colors　　　　ⓑ a music performance
   ⓒ performers of a circus

3. What is the creative feature of Pointillism?
   ⓐ Artists can express anything with one color.
   ⓑ It looks different based on how far away it is.
   ⓒ Paintings of Pointillism should be looked at closely.
   ⓓ Points of color look different when they're upside down.

4. What is NOT true about Georges Seurat?
   ⓐ He was from France.
   ⓑ He was the first artist of Pointillism.
   ⓒ He used only one color in his paintings.
   ⓓ One of his famous paintings is *The Circus*.

👨 **Complete the sentence.** 完成句子

❶ .... was created in the 1800s by Georges Seurat.
Artists can express anything with dots of ❷ .... *The
Circus* is one of the most famous ❸ .... in Pointillism.

Wrap Up Fill in the blanks. 總複習，將單字填入空格

Pointillism				far away
使用方法	• ❶ .... or points of color			individual
效果	• look ❷ .... ▶ many ❸ .... points			closely
	• look from ❹ .... ▶ a regular painting			
代表畫家	• Georges Seurat ▶ created Pointillism			dots

100 The Declaration of Independence

R_100.mp3

Long ago, America was a <u>British</u> <u>colony</u>. But the American <u>colonists</u>
英國的　殖民地　　　　　　　　　　　殖民地居民
were angry at the British government. That's because they never

<u>respected</u> Americans. So on July 4, 1776, Thomas Jefferson wrote
尊重
<u>The Declaration of Independence</u>. Let's take a look at part of it. "All
獨立宣言
men are equal and certain basic rights <u>support</u> them. These are life,
支持
<u>liberty</u>, and the <u>pursuit</u> of happiness." Also, the Declaration <u>stated</u>
自由　　　　　追求　　　　　　　　　　　　　　　　　說明
why Americans should be <u>independent</u>. It said that <u>Britain</u> had no
獨立的　　　　　　　　英國
right to <u>govern</u> Americans. Following the
統治
Declaration of Independence, America
started its fight for freedom.

Read and Complete 完成句子

① Britain made America its _____.

② The Americans wanted _____ from Britain.

獨立宣言

很久以前，美國是英國的殖民地，但是美國的殖
民地居民對英國政府感到憤怒，這是因為他們不
曾尊重美國人。因此在 1776 年 7 月 4 日，湯馬
斯‧傑弗遜寫出了《獨立宣言》。讓我們來看看
《獨立宣言》的部分內容吧！「人人生而平等，
並有某些權利支持著他們，包括生命權、自由權
和追求幸福的權利。」此外，《獨立宣言》闡明
了美國人應該獨立的原因。文中指出，英國無權
統治美國人。在發表《獨立宣言》之後，美國開
始了他們的自由之戰。

背景知識 Plus!
促使美國渴望脫離英國並獨立
（independence）的背景是什麼？首
先，這是因為英國對美洲殖民地徵收過
高稅金的政策。再者，英國人選擇俄
亥俄河周遭地區作為印第安人保護
區，這與想要前進該地肥沃區域
的居民期望相反。

Circle the best answer. 圈選出正確的答案

1. What is NOT included in the Declaration of Independence?
   ⓐ the right to protest　　　ⓑ the right to be free
   ⓒ the right to be happy

2. What did Americans let Britain know through the Declaration?
   ⓐ the rights all people should have　　ⓑ Americans' excellence
   ⓒ their right to govern the British

3. Why were the colonists upset at the British government?
   ⓐ Because they didn't value Americans.
   ⓑ Because they arrested Thomas Jefferson.
   ⓒ Because they kept expanding their colony.
   ⓓ Because they couldn't speak American English.

4. What happened right after The Declaration of Independence?
   ⓐ America made a new country.
   ⓑ Britain destroyed America.
   ⓒ America became the biggest colony of Britain.
   ⓓ Americans began to protest against the British.

Complete the sentence. 完成句子

In 1776, American ❶ .... declared independence from Britain. According to their declaration, all men are ❷ .... and have basic rights. Also, they didn't want the British to ❸ .... America anymore.

Wrap Up　Fill in the blanks. 總複習，將單字填入空格

The Declaration of Independence		equal
日期	• written on July 4, 1776	liberty
目的	• to state American's independence from ❶	
內容	• All men are ❷ .... • They have basic rights like life, ❸ .... , and the ❹ .... of happiness.	pursuit Britain

WORD REVIEW

Crossword Puzzle 填字遊戲

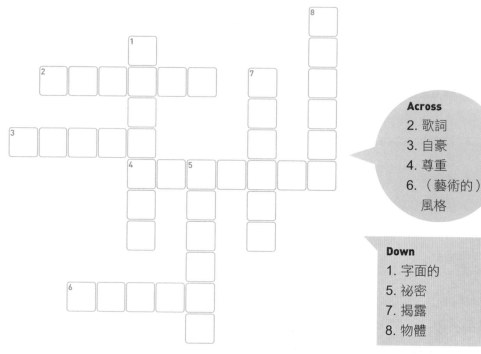

Across
2. 歌詞
3. 自豪
4. 尊重
6. （藝術的）
　 風格

Down
1. 字面的
5. 祕密
7. 揭露
8. 物體

Match with the correct definition. 將單字連到正確的意思

1. country music •

　　ⓐ a popular genre of music played on guitars and banjos.

2. idiom •

　　ⓑ a creative and common way to express language in a certain culture

3. independent •

　　ⓒ a creative way to paint pictures using points of color

4. Pointillism •

　　ⓓ not being governed by others

Fill in the blank with the correct words.
將正確的單字填入空格中

countless	govern	grammar	passionate	outside

1. The songs tell stories about life _____ of big cities.
   這些歌曲講述著關於大城市外面生活的故事。

2. Simon Rodia was _____ about his artwork.
   西蒙・盧地亞對自己的藝術作品充滿熱情。

3. People cannot understand idioms by _____ or words.
   人們沒辦法只透過文法或單字就能理解慣用語。

4. *The Circus* is made up of _____ colored dots.
   《馬戲團》是由無數個彩色的點組成的。

5. The Declaration of Independence said that Britain had no right to _____ Americans.
   《獨立宣言》闡明了英國人無權統治美國人。

Fill in the blank with the correct expressions.
將正確的表達填入空格中

appear to	continues to	the pursuit of	working on	such as

1. In America, country music _____ grow and change.

2. Simon Rodia spent 34 years _____ his artwork.

3. That's because the points of color _____ blend together.

4. Georges Seurat made some famous paintings, _____ *The Circus*.

5. Basic rights are life, liberty, and _____ happiness.

Practice

練習題

Write the meaning of the words and phrases in Chinese.

請寫出單字和片語的中文。

1. moving
2. Earth
3. rise
4. set
5. east

6. west
7. stay still
8. path
9. orbit
10. spin

Listen to the passage and fill the blanks. 🎧

聆聽段落內容並填寫空格。

R_01.mp3

Every day, the sun rises and _____. It moves across the sky from _____ to _____. But really, the sun stays still. In fact, _____ moves. It _____ in two ways. First, it _____ the sun. This path is its _____. Earth also _____ around itself. This creates day and _____. We only see the _____ at night. But they are always out there. We just can't see them in the day because the sky is so _____.

聲音是由震動產生的

Vibrations Make Sound

 Write the meaning of the words and phrases in Chinese.

請寫出單字和片語的中文。

1. vibration
2. example
3. pluck
4. string
5. back and forth

6. sound wave
7. vibrate
8. eardrum
9. information
10. brain

Listen to the passage and fill the blanks.

聆聽段落內容並填寫空格。

R_02.mp3

How can we hear _____? Sound is actually _____.
Here is an example. Pluck a _____ on a guitar. It moves
_____ and _____ quickly. This is a vibration,
and it makes _____. The sound waves
reach our ears. They vibrate our _____ and send the
information to the _____. Then the brain recognizes it
as _____. We hear all sounds like _____, voices
and music the same way.

Write the meaning of the words and phrases in Chinese.
請寫出單字和片語的中文。

1. solution
2. mixture
3. substance
4. break down
5. completely

6. stir
7. crystal
8. melt
9. float
10. sink

Listen to the passage and fill the blanks. 🎧
聆聽段落內容並填寫空格。

R_03.mp3

A solution is a _____ of substances. It is usually a _____. In it, one substance _____ down completely in another. Saltwater is a simple _____ you can make. Pour some salt in a glass of water. Then _____ it. When the salt crystals melt, they do not _____ or _____. Instead, they make the water _____. The water _____ this way. It is like a new _____!

✏️ Write the meaning of the words and phrases in Chinese.

請寫出單字和片語的中文。

1. hurricane
2. storm
3. form
4. coast
5. destroy

6. flooding
7. do damage
8. fortunately
9. predict
10. track

🐴 Listen to the passage and fill the blanks. 🎧

聆聽段落內容並填寫空格。

R_04.mp3

Powerful storms come every summer. They are   !

Hurricanes form over warm water in   . And

they spin fast and   to land. This can be

                         for people on coasts. Hurricanes

trees and buildings. They also cause   and other

                         , like tornadoes. These do the most damage.

Fortunately, scientists can predict or   hurricanes.

They can issue a hurricane warning. The   allows

people to prepare for it.

Write the meaning of the words and phrases in Chinese.

請寫出單字和片語的中文。

1. life cycle
2. hatch
3. tadpole
4. breathe
5. underwater

6. tail
7. develop
8. lung
9. full-grown

Listen to the passage and fill the blanks.

聆聽段落內容並填寫空格。

R_05.mp3

Frogs can live on the land and in the water. They have an interesting _____ . First, they hatch as _____ from eggs in the water. Like _____ , tadpoles _____ underwater and swim with a _____ . Later, they grow legs. The tail _____ shorter and shorter. They also develop lungs for breathing _____ water. Finally, their bodies are _____ . Then, they can live on _____ .

舊式溫度計是如何運作的？

How Did Old Thermometers Work?

Write the meaning of the words and phrases in Chinese.

請寫出單字和片語的中文。

1. thermometer
2. work
3. measure
4. air conditioner
5. temperature

6. screen
7. scale
8. tube
9. mercury
10. expand

Listen to the passage and fill the blanks.

聆聽段落內容並填寫空格。

R_06.mp3

You can find some _____ in your house. Think about your _____, oven, and air conditioner. They simply show temperatures on the _____. However, old thermometers were _____ tubes. There were _____ on the tubes. Mercury, a red liquid, was inside. Heat expanded the _____. So on a hot day, it rose _____ in the tubes. The mercury went down when it was cool. People used the _____ to read the temperature.

植物會自己製造食物

Plants Make Food Themselves

 Write the meaning of the words and phrases in Chinese.
請寫出單字和片語的中文。

1. process   6. combine

2. photosynthesis   7. in turn

3. carbon dioxide   8. give off

4. gas   9. oxygen

5. root

 Listen to the passage and fill the blanks. 🎧
聆聽段落內容並填寫空格。

R_07.mp3

How do plants eat? They make their own _____ . This
_____ is photosynthesis. A plant needs _____
things for this. First, it needs carbon dioxide. Its leaves
_____ in this gas. Second, its roots get _____
from the ground. Finally, its leaves use _____ for
energy. The energy _____ carbon dioxide and water.
This creates _____ , or food for the plant. In turn, the
plant _____ oxygen for us.

Write the meaning of the words and phrases in Chinese.

請寫出單字和片語的中文。

1. shake
2. plate
3. earthquake
4. cause
5. surface

6. rub
7. get stuck
8. force
9. come loose
10. suddenly

Listen to the passage and fill the blanks. 🎧

聆聽段落內容並填寫空格。

R_08.mp3

When earthquakes happen, the _____ shakes. Most earthquakes are short and weak. But some can be very _____! They destroy buildings and _____. What causes _____? Well, the earth's surface is on several _____. These plates float and _____ around. Sometimes they _____ each other. Then they _____. They keep pushing with a huge _____. Suddenly they come loose. This shakes the _____, and there is an _____.

Write the meaning of the words and phrases in Chinese.
請寫出單字和片語的中文。

1. coral reef
2. marine
3. polyp
4. on top of
5. area

6. creature
7. hard
8. starfish
9. clownfish
10. eel

 Listen to the passage and fill the blanks. 🎧
聆聽段落內容並填寫空格。

R_09.mp3

Coral reefs are _____ the sea near Southeast Asia and Australia. They look like _____ plants. But they are actually _____ called _____. Polyps live on top of the _____ and eat small _____. They die and become hard like _____. Dead polyps create coral reefs. Lots of _____ live around the reefs. There are _____, clownfish, lionfish, and eels. They all make the area beautiful.

10 Earth's Magnetic Field

地球的磁場

Write the meaning of the words and phrases in Chinese.

請寫出單字和片語的中文。

1. magnetic field
2. compass
3. point to
4. core
5. iron

6. magnet
7. pole
8. attract
9. metal
10. direct

Listen to the passage and fill the blanks.

聆聽段落內容並填寫空格。

R_10.mp3

Do you have a _____? Look at it. It always points to the _____. This is because of Earth's field. The Earth's core has a ball of _____. This ball _____ around and acts like a magnet. So, Earth has a magnetic field. Like all magnets, Earth has two _____. These are _____ and _____, and they attract _____. The poles _____ the metal needle of a compass. That's how compasses work.

Animals Can Use Electricity!

 Write the meaning of the words and phrases in Chinese.
請寫出單字和片語的中文。

1. electricity
2. electric eel
3. hunt
4. charge
5. shock

6. hunter
7. sense
8. hidden
9. faraway

 Listen to the passage and fill the blanks.
聆聽段落內容並填寫空格。

R_11.mp3

Humans make and use _____. But some _____ can too! They use electricity in many ways. Electric eels live in _____, and other fish hunt them. These eels can _____ their bodies with electricity. They _____ the hunters to _____ themselves. Animals can also find food with _____. Sharks can _____ electricity in other creatures. They can find hidden fish this way! They can even hunt _____ fish.

Can a Ball Fly Forever?

球可以永遠飛在空中嗎？

Write the meaning of the words and phrases in Chinese.

請寫出單字和片語的中文。

1. forever
2. law
3. motion
4. object
5. straight

6. speed
7. gravity
8. slow down
9. space
10. pull

Listen to the passage and fill the blanks. 🎧

聆聽段落內容並填寫空格。

R_12.mp3

Let's throw a ball in the air. Can it fly _____ ? Well, Isaac Newton's First _____ of _____ has the answer. A moving object moves in a _____ line with the same _____ . Only an _____ force can change this. On Earth, _____ pulls all objects down. So the ball _____ and falls down. Gravity is the outside _____ here. Now in space, there is no _____ . It might _____ forever there!

Write the meaning of the words and phrases in Chinese.

請寫出單字和片語的中文。

1. desert

2. mostly

3. sandy

4. cool down

5. heavy

6. rainfall

7. survive

8. cactus

9. store

10. spine

Listen to the passage and fill the blanks. 🎧

聆聽段落內容並填寫空格。

R_13.mp3

Deserts are mostly   areas with little   .
They are very hot and dry. But deserts can be very cold
too! In fact, the sand   quickly at
night. So, hot deserts become very   at night.
Sometimes they have a heavy   too. Some animals
and plants can   there. For example, cactuses
store   in their bodies. The spines
     help them keep the water.

螞蟻和他們的工作
Ants and Their Jobs

Write the meaning of the words and phrases in Chinese.

請寫出單字和片語的中文。

1. job
2. colony
3. millions of
4. worker
5. mound

6. soldier
7. defend
8. drone
9. male
10. mate

Listen to the passage and fill the blanks. 🎧

聆聽段落內容並填寫空格。

R_14.mp3

Ants live together in a _____ . A colony can have _____ of ants! The ants have different _____ . Most are worker ants. They _____ food and _____ the mound, or home. Some ants are _____ . They defend the colony. There are also _____ . These are male ants. They _____ with the queen and _____ shortly after. Finally, there is the queen ant. She _____ all the eggs.

The Secret of Fossils

Write the meaning of the words and phrases in Chinese.

請寫出單字和片語的中文。

1. secret
2. fossil
3. dinosaur
4. remains
5. original

6. shape
7. possible
8. sink
9. mud
10. disappear

Listen to the passage and fill the blanks. 🎧

聆聽段落內容並填寫空格。

R_15.mp3

You can see _____ bones in museums. Are they real bones? They are _____ . Fossils are the old _____ of animals and plants. They keep their _____ shapes. How is this possible? After an animal _____ , it may sink deep into mud. It _____ there for _____ of years. It will not _____ but become hard like rock. When we find a fossil, it gives us lots of _____ about the past.

Write the meaning of the words and phrases in Chinese.
請寫出單字和片語的中文。

1. underwater
2. vent
3. ocean floor
4. shoot out
5. poisonous

6. material
7. pressure
8. heat
9. feed
10. bacteria

Listen to the passage and fill the blanks. 🎧
聆聽段落內容並填寫空格。

R_16.mp3

The ocean floor has many holes. These are   .
They shoot out hot water and   material. This area
is very   , and the water   is strong.
Also, there is no   . But strange worms, fish, and
shrimp live here. They can   the heat and pressure.
What   them? Special   also live near
the vents. Some plants eat these bacteria. And some animals
                   the plants.

Caribou vs. Reindeer

Write the meaning of the words and phrases in Chinese.

請寫出單字和片語的中文。

1. caribou
2. reindeer
3. the Arctic
4. belong to
5. species

6. antler
7. wild
8. tame
9. fur
10. sled

Listen to the passage and fill the blanks. 🎧

聆聽段落內容並填寫空格。

R_17.mp3

Large deer live in the Arctic. These are caribou and
_____. They belong to the _____ species. Both
have large antlers. But there is one important _____.
Caribou are _____. Reindeer are _____. People
use _____ for their meat or fur. Reindeer can also
pull _____. With good care, reindeer _____
more and _____ better. They are usually _____
than caribou. However, _____ must survive in a
_____ environment.

Write the meaning of the words and phrases in Chinese.

請寫出單字和片語的中文。

1. muscle
2. move
3. surprisingly
4. skin
5. be attached to

6. stretch
7. shrink
8. skeleton

Listen to the passage and fill the blanks.

聆聽段落內容並填寫空格。

R_18.mp3

Do you run and play every day? Then you use your
_____ a lot. Muscles make your body _____. You need
_____ muscles for moving. Surprisingly,
the body has over 600 muscles! They are under the skin and
_____ bones. Muscles _____ and
_____. This moves the _____ in different ways.
When you want to _____, you just need to think about
it. Then the _____ makes your leg muscles work.

🐾 Write the meaning of the words and phrases in Chinese.
請寫出單字和片語的中文。

1. canyon
2. amazing
3. deep
4. cut into
5. ground

6. course
7. layer
8. take
9. million

🐴 Listen to the passage and fill the blanks. 🎧
聆聽段落內容並填寫空格。

R_19.mp3

The Grand _____ is an amazing place in the US. It is in Arizona. It is one of Earth's _____ canyons. Canyons are _____ areas under high _____. This one is about 2km _____ ! Long ago, the Colorado River _____ the ground. The river made its _____ through the area. This slowly formed the canyon and the rock _____ around it. It took over five _____ years!

Write the meaning of the words and phrases in Chinese.

請寫出單字和片語的中文。

1. atom

2. molecule

3. countless

4. basic

5. unit

6. matter

7. tiny

8. hydrogen

9. combine

10. molecule

Listen to the passage and fill the blanks. 🎧

聆聽段落內容並填寫空格。

R_20.mp3

Everything has countless _____ ! They are the basic _____ of matter. Atoms are tiny, but they have different sizes. For example, _____ atoms are bigger than _____ atoms. Atoms can _____ each other. This makes a _____ . That's a _____ unit. Hydrogen and oxygen atoms can combine to make _____ . A water _____ has two hydrogen atoms and one oxygen _____ . We call it H_2O.

Write the meaning of the words and phrases in Chinese.

請寫出單字和片語的中文。

1. warm-blooded
2. mammal
3. body temperature
4. stay
5. environment

6. sweat
7. cool down
8. stick out
9. tongue
10. shiver

Listen to the passage and fill the blanks. 🎧

聆聽段落內容並填寫空格。

R_21.mp3

Mammals, like you and me, are a kind of _____ . We are warm-blooded, so our _____ temperature stays the same. It's the same in a warm or cool _____ . Mammals keep their body _____ the same in different ways. We _____ when we are too warm. Sweat _____ our bodies. Dogs _____ their tongues to cool down. We shiver when we are too cool. That's because it _____ our bodies. Dogs _____ to warm up too. Warming up and cooling down is easy for _____ mammals like us!

Communicating with Lights

👩 **Write the meaning of the words and phrases in Chinese.**

請寫出單字和片語的中文。

1. communicate
2. distance
3. flash
4. message
5. code

6. develop
7. popular
8. pulse
9. pattern
10. sink

👧 **Listen to the passage and fill the blanks.** 🎧

聆聽段落內容並填寫空格。

R_22.mp3

How did people communicate   phones and radio?
Lights helped us   over long distances. Flashing
a light sent   as a code. Samuel Morse developed
a popular code in the 1840s. Morse code uses long and short
           . A pulse is a   of light or sound.
Each letter of the alphabet has its own pulse   .
For example, "S" is three   pulses. "O" is three
           pulses. Ships used   and Morse code
to communicate. Sinking ships would pulse SOS. That means
to send   right away!

Designs from Nature

 **Write the meaning of the words and phrases in Chinese.**

請寫出單字和片語的中文。

1. incredible
2. feature
3. survive
4. environment
5. Velcro

6. invention
7. spiky
8. seed
9. hook
10. stick

Listen to the passage and fill the blanks. 🎧

聆聽段落內容並填寫空格。

R_23.mp3

Plants and animals are _____. They have unique features that help them _____ in their environment. Sometimes scientists use _____ designs to make useful things. Did you know that Velcro is an _____ from nature? In 1941, George de Mestral _____ burrs in his dog's fur. Burrs are _____ seeds with little hooks at the end. These hooks _____ to clothes and hair. George got a great idea from the burr's _____. He created the first Velcro out of cotton. Velcro sticks together and _____ easily. You've probably used it on your _____ or bag before!

24 印度狐蝠
Indian Flying Foxes

Write the meaning of the words and phrases in Chinese.
請寫出單字和片語的中文。

1. village
2. hundreds of
3. hang
4. strange
5. leathery

6. bat
7. a bit
8. disease
9. pollinate
10. nectar

Listen to the passage and fill the blanks. 🎧
聆聽段落內容並填寫空格。

R_24.mp3

Mena and his father were in the forest outside their
_____ in India. They saw hundreds of foxes _____ in the trees.
These foxes had _____, leathery arms. "Father, I'm
_____," Mena said. His father smiled and _____,
"Those are Indian flying foxes, my son. They are actually a
kind of bat. They are a bit _____ because they often
carry diseases. But they eat only fruit, _____, and insects.
Flying foxes also help _____ flowers by drinking
nectar. So, they are an _____ part of the environment."

Write the meaning of the words and phrases in Chinese.
請寫出單字和片語的中文。

1. material
2. engineer
3. especially
4. absorb
5. wave

6. go through
7. fabric
8. cardboard
9. stop *A* from -ing
10. bounce off

Listen to the passage and fill the blanks. 🎧

聆聽段落內容並填寫空格。

R_25.mp3

I'm a materials _____ . I especially study _____ ,
like wood and metal. I check to see how well they absorb
_____ . Sound travels in waves. Sound waves can get
absorbed by a material or _____ it. Soft
materials, like fabric, sponge, or cardboard, _____
sounds well. Builders put these materials _____ walls
to stop sound from traveling. Hard materials, like
or _____ , don't absorb sound well. The sound waves
usually _____ off these materials. Builders also use these
hard materials to _____ sound from entering an area.

以後沒有蜜蜂了嗎？

No More Bees?

👧 **Write the meaning of the words and phrases in Chinese.**
請寫出單字和片語的中文。

1. disappear
2. colony
3. collapse
4. pesticide
5. millions of

6. keep *A* away
7. poisonous
8. contact
9. weaken
10. harm

🦓 **Listen to the passage and fill the blanks.** 🎧

聆聽段落內容並填寫空格。

R_26.mp3

Bees are disappearing. Their colonies are collapsing. Scientists think that _____ are killing millions of bees each year. Farmers use pesticides on food crops to _____ insects _____ . Pesticides are _____ , and bees are contacting them. They weaken the bees so diseases _____ them. Also, pesticides affect the _____ of the bees. This causes them to get lost while looking for _____ . When bees travel for nectar, they help _____ crops. Bees cannot _____ alone, and humans wouldn't have very much to eat without bees. We should change how we farm or bees might _____ .

爆炸性的事實！

Explosive Facts!

🐧 **Write the meaning of the words and phrases in Chinese.**
請寫出單字和片語的中文。

1. explosive
2. crust
3. underneath
4. mantle
5. be made up of

6. call *A B*
7. magma
8. surface
9. erupt
10. extinct volcano

🐴 **Listen to the passage and fill the blanks.** 🎧
聆聽段落內容並填寫空格。

R_27.mp3

We live on the Earth's _____, but it is really hot underneath. Under the crust is the _____. The mantle _____ hot, red rocks. We call it _____. This magma sometimes comes to the _____. Magma can erupt from volcanoes! We call it _____. Lava can only erupt from active volcanoes. There are over 1,900 active _____ on Earth! There are also volcanoes that are not _____. They won't erupt for a long time. The other volcanoes are extinct volcanoes, and they will never _____ again.

Write the meaning of the words and phrases in Chinese.
請寫出單字和片語的中文。

1. cave
2. wonder
3. mysterious
4. natural
5. hole

6. enough
7. form
8. erosion
9. acid
10. wear away

Listen to the passage and fill the blanks. 🎧

聆聽段落內容並填寫空格。

R_28.mp3

Caves are dark and ＿＿＿＿＿＿. They are large, natural ＿＿＿＿＿＿ leading into Earth's surface. They are big ＿＿＿＿＿＿ for people and animals to enter and live. How were these large ＿＿＿＿＿＿ made? Most were formed by ＿＿＿＿＿＿. Erosion happens when the ＿＿＿＿＿＿ in water wears away rock. It can take millions of years for rock to ＿＿＿＿＿＿. Son Doong in Vietnam is the ＿＿＿＿＿＿ cave in the world. It's over 2 million years old. It is much bigger than scientists first ＿＿＿＿＿＿. It's about 9 kilometers long!

✍ Write the meaning of the words and phrases in Chinese.
請寫出單字和片語的中文。

1. birth
2. living thing
3. life cycle
4. include
5. unique

6. hatch
7. caterpillar
8. protective
9. shell
10. pupa

🐴 Listen to the passage and fill the blanks. 🎧

聆聽段落內容並填寫空格。

R_29.mp3

All living things on Earth have a _____ .
This cycle always includes _____ and death. Each
living thing has a _____ cycle between being born
and dying. For example, butterflies start as an egg. Then,
the egg _____ and a larva is born. It eats and grows
into a _____ . But it's still in the larva _____ .
Next, it builds a hard _____ shell around itself. It's a
_____ . After 10 to 14 days, an adult butterfly hatches
from the _____ . The butterfly then _____ eggs
before it dies, and the cycle begins _____ !

Write the meaning of the words and phrases in Chinese.
請寫出單字和片語的中文。

1. electricity
2. generate
3. power plant
4. source
5. pollution

6. run out
7. improve
8. renewable
9. solar
10. wind power

Listen to the passage and fill the blanks. 🎧
聆聽段落內容並填寫空格。

R_30.mp3

We use _____ for our computers and _____.
That electricity is generated in power _____. Often,
power plants use and burn nonrenewable sources like coal, oil,
or gas for _____. That's because they're
_____ to get and use. But most non-renewable sources generate
air and water _____. Also, they will
_____ someday. These days, scientists are improving
_____ energy sources. Solar energy comes from the
_____, so it's renewable. Wind power and hydrogen
energy are also _____ energy sources. They produce
almost no _____ and will never run out.

Science 31 歡迎來到叢林 Welcome to the Jungle

Write the meaning of the words and phrases in Chinese.
請寫出單字和片語的中文。

1. jungle
2. breathe
3. oxygen
4. carbon dioxide
5. rainforest

6. equator
7. the middle of
8. wet
9. environment
10. billions of

Listen to the passage and fill the blanks.
聆聽段落內容並填寫空格。

R_31.mp3

We breathe in oxygen and _____ out carbon dioxide. Around 40% of Earth's oxygen comes from _____. You can find rainforests near the _____. The equator is a _____. It goes around the middle of the Earth. Rainforests have a _____ and _____ environment. Plants grow well there. In rainforests, billions of plants produce _____ and consume carbon dioxide. This helps _____ oxygen and carbon dioxide in _____. This balance is important for plant and _____ life on Earth. We can't breathe with too much or too little _____.

Coyotes in the Arctic

 Write the meaning of the words and phrases in Chinese.
請寫出單字和片語的中文。

1. coyote
2. adaptive
3. North America
4. compete
5. territory

6. extinction
7. population
8. expand
9. Alaska
10. harsh

 Listen to the passage and fill the blanks. 🎧
聆聽段落內容並填寫空格。

R_32.mp3

Coyotes are very _____ to their environment. In North America, wolves and coyotes _____ for food and territory. Wolves often killed people and farm animals. So, they were hunted to near _____. This caused the coyote _____ to grow and expand in the last 200 years. They even _____ into northern Canada and Alaska. The harsh, cold environment forced the coyotes to _____. Their _____ color slowly changed to white. It let them _____ better in the snow. Their fur also became thicker to _____ them from the harsh cold.

Science 33 Powerful Flash Floods

強大的山洪暴發

✎ Write the meaning of the words and phrases in Chinese.

請寫出單字和片語的中文。

1. flash flood
2. natural disaster
3. unexpectedly
4. rise
5. rainfall

6. heavy rain
7. raise
8. stream
9. property
10. deadly

🐗 Listen to the passage and fill the blanks. 🎧

聆聽段落內容並填寫空格。

R_33.mp3

Natural disasters can happen suddenly and _____ . Flash floods are one type of _____ . A flash flood is when _____ rise within six hours of rainfall. Heavy rains or a broken dam _____ the water level of rivers or streams. The rising water moves _____ and quickly over land. It causes _____ to property. And it can be _____ to people. In 2013, a _____ in Kedarnath, India killed around 5,000 people! Local weather warnings can help you _____ these disasters. They can also tell you when to get to _____ ground.

290

Write the meaning of the words and phrases in Chinese.
請寫出單字和片語的中文。

1. shape
2. useful
3. weapon
4. tool
5. serious

6. weakness
7. rust
8. decay
9. break apart
10. chemical

 **Listen to the passage and fill the blanks.** 🎧
聆聽段落內容並填寫空格。

R_34.mp3

Iron is a strong metal. People can _____ it into useful things such as _____ and tools. People have used it for thousands of years. But, iron has a serious _____. It can _____ and decay, or break apart. Water and air cause a chemical reaction with _____. This creates rust. Rust can make an iron tool _____. An iron tool outside in the rain will _____ in a few days. To protect iron from rust, you can _____ it with paint or oil.

Write the meaning of the words and phrases in Chinese.
請寫出單字和片語的中文。

1. endangered
2. polar bear
3. destroy
4. habitat
5. the Arctic

6. hidden
7. be good at
8. seal
9. whale
10. global warming

 Listen to the passage and fill the blanks. 🎧
聆聽段落內容並填寫空格。

R_35.mp3

Humans are changing the _____ . As our population grows and expands, we are destroying the _____ of several animals. Some animals fail to _____ to their changed habitats. Then, they become _____ . Polar bears are adapted to live in the Arctic. Their white fur keeps them warm and _____ . They are good at _____ seals and whales in Arctic waters. However, _____ is melting the Arctic ice. Polar bears' habitats are _____ and disappearing. They cannot _____ south of the Arctic. Soon, they may only live in zoos.

能量波

36 Waves of Energy

Write the meaning of the words and phrases in Chinese.

請寫出單字和片語的中文。

1. wave
2. travel
3. electromagnetic
4. vacuum
5. matter

6. outer space
7. radio wave
8. satellite
9. microwave
10. in minutes

Listen to the passage and fill the blanks. 🎧

聆聽段落內容並填寫空格。

R_36.mp3

How can sunlight _____ through space to Earth? It's because light is a type of _____ wave(EW). EWs are _____, and they can travel through a vacuum. A _____ is a place with no matter in it, like outer space. Radio _____ are another type of EW. The waves can travel from your phone to a _____ in space. The satellite can then _____ those waves to someone on the other side of the world! _____ are also electromagnetic. They travel very fast, and they can cook food _____!

Write the meaning of the words and phrases in Chinese.

請寫出單字和片語的中文。

1. journey	6. appear
2. a little	7. reflect
3. go through	8. little
4. phase	9. eventually
5. new moon	10. full moon

Listen to the passage and fill the blanks.

聆聽段落內容並填寫空格。

R_37.mp3

Every night, the _____ looks a little different. That's because each night it is at a different stage of its _____. The moon travels around the Earth in 29.53 days. Each month, the moon goes _____ 8 _____. The first phase is the _____ moon. New moons _____ very small because they _____ little of the sun's light. It eventually grows into a _____. It reflects the sun's light like a _____. Over the next phases, the moon appears smaller and smaller. Then, it _____ to a new moon.

食物鏈中的角色

Roles in the Food Chain

 Write the meaning of the words and phrases in Chinese.

請寫出單字和片語的中文。

1. food chain
2. be made up of
3. producer
4. consumer
5. decomposer

6. take a look at
7. plain
8. produce
9. ground
10. worm

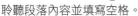 **Listen to the passage and fill the blanks.** 🎧

聆聽段落內容並填寫空格。

R_38.mp3

Plants and animals live in a _____. All habitats have a _____. Food chains are made up of _____, consumers, and decomposers. Let's take a look at an _____ in a habitat like the African plains. Plants and grass produce energy from the sun and the _____. These producers are then eaten by a _____, such as a zebra. The zebra uses the plant's energy to _____. When the zebra dies, it _____ to the ground. Decomposers, such as _____ and bacteria, turn the zebra's energy into the _____. Producers then use that energy to make food!

🐧 **Write the meaning of the words and phrases in Chinese.**
請寫出單字和片語的中文。

1. sphere

2. consist of

3. system

4. biosphere

5. include

6. geosphere

7. mineral

8. hydrosphere

9. atmosphere

10. surround

 Listen to the passage and fill the blanks. 🎧
聆聽段落內容並填寫空格。

R_39.mp3

The Earth consists of four _____ . We call them
_____ . The first system is the biosphere. It
_____ all living things on Earth. Next, the geosphere system is all of
the rocks and _____ on Earth. All of the water on Earth
is part of the _____ . Finally, the atmosphere is the
gases or air, and it _____ Earth. These 4 systems are
all _____ connected. For example, _____ from
the atmosphere causes _____ in the geosphere. All the
plants and animals of the _____ need water from the
hydrosphere.

Write the meaning of the words and phrases in Chinese.
請寫出單字和片語的中文。

1. twinkle

2. apparent magnitude

3. measure

4. brightness

5. distance

6. absolute magnitude

7. far away

Listen to the passage and fill the blanks. 🎧

聆聽段落內容並填寫空格。

R_40.mp3

Why do some stars in the sky look   than others?
The   magnitude of a star is how bright it looks to
us. We measure it with the brightness of the   and
its   from Earth. The sun appears really bright.
That's because it's very large and   to Earth.
However, the absolute magnitude is how   a star
really is. Many stars   in space are
bigger and brighter than the sun. But they appear less bright
than the sun. They have a   absolute magnitude
than their apparent magnitude.

41 The Extended Family

Write the meaning of the words and phrases in Chinese.
請寫出單字和片語的中文。

1. extended family
2. nuclear family
3. elder
4. grandparent
5. unmarried

6. adult
7. related
8. each other
9. work

Listen to the passage and fill the blanks. 🎧
聆聽段落內容並填寫空格。

R_41.mp3

Parents and their children _____ most families. This is a _____ family. But there are _____ types of families too. For example, Brady has a mother, a father, and an _____ sister. But his grandparents live with them too. Also, his _____ aunt lives with the family. This is an _____ family. In this _____ family, all the adults are _____ each other. And they all work together for the _____.

Write the meaning of the words and phrases in Chinese.
請寫出單字和片語的中文。

1. North America
2. globe
3. continent
4. cover
5. farthest

6. population
7. ocean
8. surround
9. the Pacific Ocean
10. lie

Listen to the passage and fill the blanks. 🎧
聆聽段落內容並填寫空格。

R_42.mp3

North America is a large _____ in the north part of the globe. Three countries _____ most of it. Canada is the farthest _____. It has the _____ area. Just below that is the United States. It has the largest _____. Below that is _____, and there are 20 more countries. Two oceans _____ the continent. The Pacific Ocean lies to the _____. The Atlantic Ocean lies to the _____.

299

43 Culture Is Changing

Write the meaning of the words and phrases in Chinese.
請寫出單字和片語的中文。

1. refer to

2. shared

3. lifestyle

4. language

5. differently

6. older

7. rock

8. hip-hop

9. popular

10. media

Listen to the passage and fill the blanks. 🎧
聆聽段落內容並填寫空格。

R_43.mp3

Culture refers to people's _____ ideas or lifestyles. This can be the foods, arts, and _____ of a country. But culture is always _____ . Why? First, people change it. They do things differently from _____ people. And they _____ a new culture. They may listen to different _____ . Rock and hip-hop became _____ this way. Also, media and technology can change _____ . TVs and smartphones _____ to do so today.

44 Disappearing Resources

✎ Write the meaning of the words and phrases in Chinese.
請寫出單字和片語的中文。

1. resource
2. nature
3. oil
4. coal
5. energy

6. wood
7. unfortunately
8. waste
9. natural
10. run out of

✎ Listen to the passage and fill the blanks. 🎧
聆聽段落內容並填寫空格。

R_44.mp3

We get many resources from _____. These include

_____ and _____ for energy. We also use

_____ for paper and wood. Unfortunately, we _____

many resources. Sometimes people waste _____.

Also, they build new _____ all the time. This wastes

land, trees, and other natural _____. Because of

this, our resources are _____ disappearing! We may

_____ them in the near

future.

Write the meaning of the words and phrases in Chinese.
請寫出單字和片語的中文。

1. citizen
2. member
3. community
4. responsibility
5. mean

6. take care of
7. vote
8. pay
9. tax
10. serve in the army

Listen to the passage and fill the blanks. 🎧

聆聽段落內容並填寫空格。

R_45.mp3

Are you a citizen? Yes, you are! You are a _____ of your country and community. Citizens have responsibilities to their _____. It means they must _____ their communities. Usually, adults _____ and _____ taxes. Some may serve in the _____. As a _____ citizen, you can _____ help in other ways. You can trash or help needy people. This way, you can be a good _____!

46 Celebrate St. Patrick's Day

Write the meaning of the words and phrases in Chinese.

請寫出單字和片語的中文。

1. celebrate
2. St. [saint]
3. holiday
4. honor
5. Ireland

6. spread
7. Christianity
8. Irish
9. parade
10. shamrock

Listen to the passage and fill the blanks. 🎧

聆聽段落內容並填寫空格。

R_46.mp3

St. Patrick's Day is a popular _____ . It honors Ireland's Saint Patrick on _____ 17. He spread Christianity throughout _____ . At first, only Irish people _____ it. Today, people all around the world do. On this day, people have many parties and _____ . And they _____ green and even _____ green food! Why green? Green is the _____ of a shamrock. It's a small green _____ plant. It is a _____ of the saint.

47 What are Canals?

Write the meaning of the words and phrases in Chinese.

請寫出單字和片語的中文。

1. canal
2. man-made
3. waterway
4. dig
5. channel

6. fill *A* with *B*
7. use
8. crop
9. connect
10. shortcut

Listen to the passage and fill the blanks. 🎧

聆聽段落內容並填寫空格。

R_47.mp3

Canals are man-made _____ . People _____ channels and _____ them with water. Canals have many uses. Small canals bring _____ to farms. This helps _____ grow well. Big canals _____ lakes and oceans. Look at the Panama Canal. It is 77km. It connects the _____ and Pacific Oceans. Ships use this as a _____ . Without it, they would have to _____ around South America. That's _____ 13,000 km!

48 Lincoln and the Civil War

Write the meaning of the words and phrases in Chinese.

請寫出單字和片語的中文。

1. the Civil War
2. president
3. fight over
4. slavery
5. slave

6. order
7. end
8. Southern
9. pass
10. unite

Listen to the passage and fill the blanks.

聆聽段落內容並填寫空格。

R_48.mp3

Abraham Lincoln became the 16th US _____ in 1861. That year, the _____ also began. America's North and South fought over _____. Black slaves were not _____ in the US. The North wanted to end this. The South didn't. In 1863, Lincoln _____ an end to Southern slavery. And the North finally _____ the war in 1865. After this, Lincoln _____ many laws. These ended slavery and _____ the country.

49 Benefits of Recycling

Write the meaning of the words and phrases in Chinese.

請寫出單字和片語的中文。

1. benefit

2. recycling

3. throw away

4. save

5. resource

6. cut down

7. reduce

8. pollution

9. recycle

10. pollute

Listen to the passage and fill the blanks. 🎧

聆聽段落內容並填寫空格。

R_49.mp3

Don't _____ your paper or plastic. You can use it _____ in new products. This is _____ , and it has many benefits. First, it _____ resources. People _____ trees for new paper. So recycling paper can save trees. Also, recycling _____ pollution. When you recycle plastic, it won't _____ water or land. Also, factories will make less new _____ . This also reduces _____ in the air!

Write the meaning of the words and phrases in Chinese.

請寫出單字和片語的中文。

1. urban

2. suburban

3. transportation

4. business

5. crowded

6. lively

7. mainly

8. peaceful

Listen to the passage and fill the blanks. 🎧

聆聽段落內容並填寫空格。

R_50.mp3

People live in _____ areas. Many people live in _____ areas. These are large cities with big buildings. They have good _____. There are many businesses and museums too. Streets are _____, but they are _____. People also live in _____ areas. These _____ are outside cities, but they are _____ to cities. They are _____ than urban areas. They mainly have houses, _____, and green areas. People here _____ a peaceful life.

51 Lines on Maps

🐧 **Write the meaning of the words and phrases in Chinese.**
請寫出單字和片語的中文。

1. map
2. longitude
3. latitude
4. measure
5. degree

6. prime meridian
7. equator
8. cross
9. exact
10. location

🦔 **Listen to the passage and fill the blanks.** 🎧

聆聽段落內容並填寫空格。

R_51.mp3

Maps show _____ on the _____. They use lines of longitude and lines of _____. Lines of longitude _____ from north to south. They _____ degrees east or west of the prime meridian. Lines of _____ run from east to west. They measure _____ north or south of the _____. Lines of longitude _____ lines of latitude. The points where they meet show exact _____.

52 The Washington Monument

Write the meaning of the words and phrases in Chinese.

請寫出單字和片語的中文。

1. monument
2. stone
3. be located in
4. capital
5. construction

6. elevator
7. whole

Listen to the passage and fill the blanks. 🎧

聆聽段落內容並填寫空格。

R_52.mp3

What is the world's _____ stone building? It's the Washington Monument! It _____ Washington, D.C. That's the US _____. This white tower is almost 170 meters tall. It _____ George Washington, the first US _____. Its construction _____ in 1848. However, _____ stopped several times because of the _____. It was finally finished in 1884. Today, the _____ takes people to the top. They can see the _____ city from there.

Write the meaning of the words and phrases in Chinese.
請寫出單字和片語的中文。

1. Industrial Revolution
2. steam engine
3. bring
4. factory
5. produce
6. goods
7. travel
8. railroad
9. steamship
10. long-distance

 Listen to the passage and fill the blanks.
聆聽段落內容並填寫空格。

R_53.mp3

The steam engine changed _____ forever. It brought the _____ in the 1700s. England was first to build _____. The factories quickly produced _____ like clothes and tools. This made goods _____. More people could buy them. People had new _____ in cities too. So many people moved to cities. This _____ new ways of _____. The railroad and steamship allowed _____ travel.

54 Multiple Cultures

Write the meaning of the words and phrases in Chinese.
請寫出單字和片語的中文。

1. multiple
2. multicultural
3. American
4. European
5. ancestor

6. language
7. religion
8. respect
9. peacefully

Listen to the passage and fill the blanks. 🎧

聆聽段落內容並填寫空格。

R_54.mp3

Every society has a _____ . But some have more
than one. These are _____ societies. America is an
example. Most Americans have _____ ancestors.
They brought their culture to _____ . Later, people
_____ all over the world. Some came
from South America. Others came from Africa and Asia. They
all _____ their cultures too. They have different foods,
_____ , and religions. But they must _____ each
other. That way, they can live together _____ .

Write the meaning of the words and phrases in Chinese.

請寫出單字和片語的中文。

1. civilization
2. human
3. system
4. farming
5. government

6. protect
7. share
8. custom

Listen to the passage and fill the blanks. 🎧

聆聽段落內容並填寫空格。

R_55.mp3

People living together is part of human _____.
There, a _____ starts. And different systems help
it. First, people have a system for _____. This was
usually through _____ in the past. They also have a
_____ system. This makes laws and _____ the
people. These people also create a _____ and share it.
They share a language, a _____, and customs. This is
how a civilization _____ people.

Write the meaning of the words and phrases in Chinese.

請寫出單字和片語的中文。

1. Native American
2. disease
3. war
4. hard
5. over time

6. reservation
7. native
8. tribe
9. include

Listen to the passage and fill the blanks. 🎧

聆聽段落內容並填寫空格。

R_56.mp3

Before Europeans came to _____, people lived there. These were _____. Europeans called them "Indians." Disease and _____ made their lives _____. Over time, their _____ grew smaller. Today, some of them live on _____. These are special areas for the native _____. Reservations have their own _____ and laws. The Native Americans want to _____ their own culture there. This includes their _____, stories, arts, and religions.

57 The Same Amount of Tax?

Write the meaning of the words and phrases in Chinese.
請寫出單字和片語的中文。

1. amount
2. provide
3. service
4. include
5. health care

6. education
7. half
8. unfair
9. collect

Listen to the passage and fill the blanks. 🎧
聆聽段落內容並填寫空格。

R_57.mp3

Governments ＿＿＿＿＿ many services for people. These include health care and ＿＿＿＿＿. And people must pay ＿＿＿＿＿ for these services. But there are many ways of ＿＿＿＿＿ taxes. First, everyone all can pay the same ＿＿＿＿＿. Let's say everyone pays $100 in taxes. For a person with $1,000, that's only ＿＿＿＿＿ percent. But a person with $200 pays ＿＿＿＿＿ of their money! Many people think this is ＿＿＿＿＿. So most countries have different ways to ＿＿＿＿＿ taxes.

Write the meaning of the words and phrases in Chinese.

請寫出單字和片語的中文。

1. globalization
2. get closer
3. through
4. company
5. trade

6. Russian
7. Canadian
8. product
9. foreign
10. taco

Listen to the passage and fill the blanks. 🎧

聆聽段落內容並填寫空格。

R_58.mp3

Nations are _____ every day. How?

Through globalization. Companies from different countries

always _____ .A Russian company provides

_____ . A Canadian company _____ wood.

And Chinese factories make _____ . They all trade

money, _____ , and resources. Also, many people often

_____ to foreign countries. They _____ foreign

TV programs or movies too. This spreads _____ .

Someone in Italy can watch a Hollywood movie and eat

_____ .

59 A Station for Immigrants

🐦 **Write the meaning of the words and phrases in Chinese.**
請寫出單字和片語的中文。

1. station
2. immigrant
3. European
4. better
5. life
6. arrive

7. immigration station

8. government officer

9. thousands of
10. settle

🫏 **Listen to the passage and fill the blanks.** 🎧

聆聽段落內容並填寫空格。

R_59.mp3

In the 1800s and 1900s, many Europeans came to _____ . They had _____ lives in their countries. They wanted a _____ life in America. Most arrived first on Ellis Island near New York. This _____ island was an immigration station. _____ worked there. The _____ was very busy. Ships arrived with thousands of _____ every day. And these people _____ all over the US.

60 Rights for Black Americans

😀 Write the meaning of the words and phrases in Chinese.

請寫出單字和片語的中文。

1. right
2. legal
3. allow
4. serve
5. customer

6. march
7. leader
8. movement
9. civil rights
10. win

🦔 Listen to the passage and fill the blanks. 🎧

聆聽段落內容並填寫空格。

R_60.mp3

In the 1960s, black people had few _____ rights
in America. Schools did not _____ black students.
_____ and restaurants did not _____ black
customers. It was especially _____ in the South. So
they _____ fight this. Lots of black
people _____ in the streets. Martin Luther King was
the _____ of this peaceful movement. This Civil Rights
_____ changed America a lot. Black Americans won
their _____.

317

61 Neighborhoods vs. Communities

Write the meaning of the words and phrases in Chinese.
請寫出單字和片語的中文。

1. neighborhood
2. community
3. confused
4. put up
5. difference

6. neighbor
7. physical
8. on the other hand
9. race
10. occupation

Listen to the passage and fill the blanks. 🎧

聆聽段落內容並填寫空格。

R_61.mp3

When the teacher was explaining something, I was
_____ . So I put up my hand. "What's the
_____ between a neighborhood and a community? I don't get
it." He answered, "A _____ is where you and your
neighbors live. It's a _____ place, and you can find it
on a _____ . My neighborhood is in South Chicago. On
the other hand, a _____ is a group of people, and they
have something in _____ such as race, occupation, or
_____ . In my neighborhood, for example, we have a
large Asian community and a community of _____ ."

Write the meaning of the words and phrases in Chinese.

請寫出單字和片語的中文。

1. African American
2. holiday
3. connect *A* to *B*
4. traditional
5. celebrate

6. identity
7. flag
8. prepare
9. feast
10. rhythm

Listen to the passage and fill the blanks.

聆聽段落內容並填寫空格。

R_62.mp3

Most African Americans _____ early on December 26. It's the first day of Kwanzaa. Kwanzaa is an African American _____ . It connects African Americans to their _____ African culture. They celebrate their African _____ . African families in America put up African _____ . And they _____ a large feast. They have the _____ together with family and friends. Then, they play traditional African _____ . Everyone dances to the _____ . January 1 is the last day of Kwanzaa. Time to open the Kwanzaa _____ !

319

Write the meaning of the words and phrases in Chinese.

請寫出單字和片語的中文。

1. good
2. service
3. physical
4. meal
5. cost

6. earn
7. provide
8. customer
9. skill
10. effort

Listen to the passage and fill the blanks. 🎧

聆聽段落內容並填寫空格。

R_63.mp3

What do you usually _____ with your money? Money can be used to buy _____ or services. Goods are _____ things, so you can see or touch them. A meal from a restaurant is a good. It takes money to make goods, so it _____ money to buy them. _____ are what people do to earn money. Servers in a restaurant _____ a service by bringing the _____ to customers. Their time, skill, and _____ cost money. Customers _____ for both goods and services at places like stores and restaurants.

Write the meaning of the words and phrases in Chinese.
請寫出單字和片語的中文。

1. soldier
2. take part in
3. Memorial Day
4. dedicated
5. fallen

6. Civil War
7. citizen
8. sacrifice
9. cemetery
10. grave

Listen to the passage and fill the blanks. 🎧
聆聽段落內容並填寫空格。

R_64.mp3

Soldiers keep their countries safe. Sometimes, they _____ in a war, and even give their lives to their countries. Memorial Day in America is a holiday dedicated to _____ soldiers. It was started in 1868 after the American _____. American citizens remember their soldiers' _____ on Memorial Day. They visit _____ and bring flowers. Many volunteers place American flags on soldiers' _____. Memorial Day is on the last Monday of May. Most workers and students have the _____. It is important not to forget the _____ sacrifice soldiers made.

Write the meaning of the words and phrases in Chinese.

請寫出單字和片語的中文。

1. Roman
2. politician
3. primary
4. primary source
5. past

6. journal
7. modern times
8. historian
9. appearance
10. ancient

Listen to the passage and fill the blanks. 🎧

聆聽段落內容並填寫空格。

R_65.mp3

Julius Caesar is in many   museums and books.
He lived over 2,000 years ago. He was a Roman   .
We know about his life from   sources. Primary
sources are   and pictures from the past. Caesar
kept a journal, and it survived until   .
Historians learned a lot about his life from his   .
We can also see Caesar's   on ancient Roman
coins. These primary sources help us   people
from the past. Without them, much of their past would be a
     .

Write the meaning of the words and phrases in Chinese.
請寫出單字和片語的中文。

1. interest
2. piggy bank
3. adult
4. regular
5. keep *A* safe

6. meanwhile
7. lend
8. borrower
9. on time
10. earn

 Listen to the passage and fill the blanks. 🎧
聆聽段落內容並填寫空格。

R_66.mp3

Where do you _____ your money? Most kids have a piggy bank or another _____ place to keep their money. Most adults use _____ banks. Banks keep peoples' money safe and pay _____ for it. Interest is the _____ of money. So, you can make money by saving it in a _____. Meanwhile, banks use _____, saved money. They _____ it to other people. The _____ must pay back the money on time and pay interest for it to the bank. In this way, interest lets both people and banks _____ some money.

67 Laws and Rules

Write the meaning of the words and phrases in Chinese.

請寫出單字和片語的中文。

1. law
2. rule
3. government
4. function
5. politician

6. against
7. steal
8. universal
9. local
10. resident

Listen to the passage and fill the blanks. 🎧

聆聽段落內容並填寫空格。

R_67.mp3

Parents and teachers make   to keep children safe.
The government also makes rules to keep   safe.
It's one of the many   of a government. Politicians
make   for citizens to follow. They can make
laws against killing and   , for example. Those are
                   laws. Every country has these laws. However,
                   often make   laws. These laws are
important to the   in that area. In Singapore, for
example, it's   the law to feed pigeons. But in
most other countries, you can!

Write the meaning of the words and phrases in Chinese.
請寫出單字和片語的中文。

1. settler
2. Native American
3. attack
4. capture
5. captain

6. chief
7. tribe
8. mercy
9. symbol
10. peace

Listen to the passage and fill the blanks. 🎧

聆聽段落內容並填寫空格。

R_68.mp3

Life was _____ in Jamestown, Virginia. In 1607,
English _____ built a town there. But, they couldn't
_____ or find enough food. The Native Americans often
_____ their town. One day, they _____ John
Smith, the _____ of the settlers. The _____ of
the tribe wanted to kill Smith. His daughter felt
_____ and saved Smith. Soon, Smith became friends with the
_____. Pocahontas showed the English the way to grow
and find food. She became a _____ of peace between
the two groups. Today, we can even see Pocahontas' story in a
Disney _____!

Write the meaning of the words and phrases in Chinese.

請寫出單字和片語的中文。

1. value
2. expensive
3. supply
4. demand
5. good

6. valuable
7. the amount of
8. everywhere

Listen to the passage and fill the blanks. 🎧

聆聽段落內容並填寫空格。

R_69.mp3

Why is gold more _____ than water? It's because of _____ and demand. If many people want to buy a _____, then there is high _____. High demand makes something more _____. Supply is the _____ a good in markets. Low supply of a good makes it more valuable. Many people want to buy gold or water, so both have high _____. Water is everywhere, but there isn't _____ gold in the world. So, _____ demand and _____ supply makes gold more expensive than water.

Write the meaning of the words and phrases in Chinese.

請寫出單字和片語的中文。

1. folktale
2. folklore
3. pass down
4. generation
5. preserve

6. continue
7. over time
8. lesson
9. honesty
10. kindness

Listen to the passage and fill the blanks. 🎧

聆聽段落內容並填寫空格。

R_70.mp3

Folklore is the stories and traditions of a   . They
are passed down from   to generation. This
helps   and continue the culture
           . Folktales are an important part of   .
Every culture has its own   of folktales. In Europe,
these stories often begin with, "Once upon a time..." Parents
teach their children   through these stories.
Folktales often teach children about honesty, kindness, or
           . Some famous   include *The Little
Red Hen* and *Cinderella*. What folktales have your parents
                to you ?

Write the meaning of the words and phrases in Chinese.
請寫出單字和片語的中文。

1. slavery   6. slave

2. common   7. own

3. colonial   8. property

4. plantation   9. return

5. owner   10. hut

Listen to the passage and fill the blanks. 🎧
聆聽段落內容並填寫空格。

R_71.mp3

Slavery was common in   America. In the 18th
century,   owners used African slaves for farm
work. These   lived on the plantation and were
owned like   . After working all day in the hot sun,
they returned to their   . The whole family lived
and slept on the   of their small huts.
     was often rice, beans, or other plants. Meat was usually
only for the plantation   . Slaves owned few
      and no money. They just had some
for sleeping and dishes for cooking.

Write the meaning of the words and phrases in Chinese.
請寫出單字和片語的中文。

1. gold rush   6. bring
2. rush   7. business
3. the State of   8. equipment
4. discover   9. miner
5. spread   10. businessman

Listen to the passage and fill the blanks.
聆聽段落內容並填寫空格。

R_72.mp3

John Marshal helped _____ the State of California.
In 1848, he discovered gold in California. The news
soon _____ around the world. Anyone could find
_____ gold there! At the time, only about 1,000
Americans lived in California. The _____ to find gold
brought over 300,000 people from around the world there.
Most could not find any gold. But many _____ made
a lot of money. They sold food, clothes, and equipment to the
_____. The miners and _____ needed roads,
churches, and schools. So the _____ built them.

73 An Entrepreneur in the Animation Industry

Write the meaning of the words and phrases in Chinese.

請寫出單字和片語的中文。

1. entrepreneur
2. industry
3. millions of
4. animated
5. fire

6. reject
7. successful
8. face
9. risk
10. failure

Listen to the passage and fill the blanks. 🎧

聆聽段落內容並填寫空格。

R_73.mp3

These days, millions of people enjoy _____ shows and movies. Walt Disney was the first to _____ one, and it became popular. He was an _____ with a great idea. He wanted to _____ his drawings and characters into a _____. TV shows at the time only had real actors in them. His idea was to make TV shows and movies with his animated _____. But, he was _____ and rejected over 300 times before becoming _____! Entrepreneurs like Disney _____ risks and failure. But they also have _____ for great success!

女性的投票權
74 Women's Right to Vote

✎ Write the meaning of the words and phrases in Chinese.
請寫出單字和片語的中文。

1. right

2. vote

3. legal

4. movement

5. equal

6. suffrage

7. main

8. goal

9. form

10. political

Listen to the passage and fill the blanks. 🎧
聆聽段落內容並填寫空格。

R_74.mp3

Just 100 years ago in America, women had few legal
_____. They couldn't _____, own homes, or
do most jobs. The women's rights _____ began in
the 1800s. They fought for _____ rights. The right to
vote, Women's _____, was their main goal. But, the
laws of the United States did not _____ them to vote.
They formed _____ groups to change the law. Susan
B. Anthony was an important _____ of these groups.
Because of their _____, the law was changed. Women
now have equal _____ rights.

75 Balance of Power

Write the meaning of the words and phrases in Chinese.
請寫出單字和片語的中文。

1. balance
2. branch
3. Congress
4. Congressman
5. president

6. leader
7. final
8. judge
9. remove
10. check

Listen to the passage and fill the blanks. 🎧
聆聽段落內容並填寫空格。

R_75.mp3

Three branches of the American government
_____ each other's power. The first branch is _____.
Congressmen can create new _____. The next branch
is the _____. He is the leader of the country. The final
branch is the _____. Judges can change or
_____ laws. Each branch can _____ the power of the other
branches. This makes sure that all three _____ follow
the law. They even have the power to _____ the
actions of other branches. For example, the President can
_____ new laws of Congress. Congress can even
_____ to remove judges or the President.

Write the meaning of the words and phrases in Chinese.

請寫出單字和片語的中文。

1. trail
2. southern
3. population
4. expand
5. pass

6. removal
7. act
8. territory
9. homeland
10. soldier

Listen to the passage and fill the blanks. 🎧

聆聽段落內容並填寫空格。

R_76.mp3

Before 1830, Native Americans lived free in the USA. But, the American _____ was growing quickly. They wanted to _____ into Native American lands. The government passed the Indian _____ Act. This law created the Indian _____ in Oklahoma. This territory was very _____ from the Native Americans' _____. Government soldiers _____ the Native Americans thousands of kilometers to their new home. There wasn't much food, and the _____ took months. Thousands of Native Americans became sick and died. That's why it's remembered as the _____ of Tears.

✎ Write the meaning of the words and phrases in Chinese.
請寫出單字和片語的中文。

1. choice
2. economics
3. opportunity cost
4. decide
5. valuable

6. measure
7. education
8. happiness
9. imagine
10. choose

🐴 Listen to the passage and fill the blanks. 🎧
聆聽段落內容並填寫空格。

R_77.mp3

In economics, opportunity cost is the _____ you lose
when you make a choice. Every _____ has a value
and a cost. Sometimes we have to _____ between two
valuable choices. But value and costs are not just _____
in money. For example, friendship, education, and happiness
all have _____. Imagine you should choose to play or
study. Both activities are _____. When you choose
to play, you are happy. But the _____
is knowledge. Choosing to study can allow you to gain
_____, but losing fun is the opportunity cost.

Write the meaning of the words and phrases in Chinese.
請寫出單字和片語的中文。

1. democracy
2. democratic
3. rule
4. citizen
5. direct

6. vote
7. decision
8. representative
9. election
10. equal

Listen to the passage and fill the blanks. 🎧
聆聽段落內容並填寫空格。

R_78.mp3

Democratic _____ are ruled by its citizens. There are two different kinds of _____. In a direct democracy, citizens meet and _____ for every decision of the government. Most countries are too large and their citizens are too busy for a _____ democracy. Instead, in a _____ democracy, citizens choose government leaders. Citizens vote for leaders in free and fair _____. It's important all citizens have the _____ right to vote in a representative democracy. These leaders _____ the citizens and make _____ for them. America, France, and India are _____ of representative democracies.

Write the meaning of the words and phrases in Chinese.

請寫出單字和片語的中文。

1. common
2. constitution
3. author
4. include
5. founder

6. a set of
7. imagine
8. society
9. believe
10. limited

Listen to the passage and fill the blanks.

聆聽段落內容並填寫空格。

R_79.mp3

The US _____ was written in 1787. Its authors included George Washington, Ben Franklin, and other early _____ of America. The Constitution is a set of _____ . It says how the American government _____ . The founders _____ a new kind of free society. At that time, some _____ in Europe had a powerful king and queen. Unlike them, the founders believed that governments should have _____ power. They _____ the Constitution to give _____ control of the government. A limited government and _____ citizens helped America grow and become powerful.

80 Human Rights for All

Write the meaning of the words and phrases in Chinese.
請寫出單字和片語的中文。

1. human right
2. the Bill of Rights
3. allow *A* to *B*
4. freely
5. safely

6. speech
7. arrest
8. opinion
9. protest
10. innocent

Listen to the passage and fill the blanks. 🎧

聆聽段落內容並填寫空格。

R_80.mp3

The Bill of Rights allows American citizens to live freely and safely. James Madison created it in 1789. The basic _____ from it are now common in _____ everywhere. One important right is freedom of _____. With this right, citizens cannot be _____ for giving their opinions. They can even _____ government decisions. Other human rights make laws _____ for citizens. For example, citizens are _____ until judges prove them _____ in modern democracies. Another basic right is _____ of religion. Citizens are free to choose and follow any _____.

Write the meaning of the words and phrases in Chinese.

請寫出單字和片語的中文。

1. percussion
2. instrument
3. shake
4. beat
5. drum

6. maracas
7. tambourine
8. rattle
9. rhythm
10. note

Listen to the passage and fill the blanks. 🎧

聆聽段落內容並填寫空格。

R_81.mp3

Hit or shake some instruments, and they make   .
These are percussion   . Some create a   .
Drums do this. Musicians hit   and make a beat.
But you   maracas and tambourines. They rattle
and make   . Other percussion instruments create
notes. Xylophones and   do this. There are
     sizes of bells and xylophone keys. They produce
different   . Together, the notes make   ,
like in songs.

Write the meaning of the words and phrases in Chinese.

請寫出單字和片語的中文。

1. hay
2. barn
3. fall asleep
4. ox
5. wake up

6. growl
7. wave
8. stick
9. chase ~ away
10. greedy

Listen to the passage and fill the blanks. 🎧

聆聽段落內容並填寫空格。

R_82.mp3

In a barn, a dog _____ on hay. Later, a
_____ ox came in. He wanted to eat the _____.
However, the dog woke up and _____ at the ox. The
_____ saw this. He waved a stick and _____ the
dog away. "You _____ dog!" he yelled. "You don't eat
hay. But the ox can _____ eat hay! Sleep
else!" The dog must not _____ hay from the ox.

Write the meaning of the words and phrases in Chinese.
請寫出單字和片語的中文。

1. statue
2. pharaoh
3. ancient
4. giant
5. stone

6. ruler
7. god
8. temple
9. tomb
10. afterlife

Listen to the passage and fill the blanks. 🎧
聆聽段落內容並填寫空格。

R_83.mp3

Ancient Egypt had many giant stone _____. Some were statues of _____. They were the _____ of ancient Egypt. Many thought the pharaohs were _____. So people made their statues for _____. The statues are in pharaohs' _____ too because Egyptians believed in an _____. They thought that pharaohs lived there _____. Ramses II is a famous pharaoh. The number of his statues is the _____! That's why many people _____ him.

平均數、中位數和眾數

Mean, Median, and Mode

 Write the meaning of the words and phrases in Chinese.
請寫出單字和片語的中文。

1. mean	6. say
2. median	7. add
3. mode	8. divide
4. a set of	9. sum
5. range	10. order

Listen to the passage and fill the blanks. 🎧

聆聽段落內容並填寫空格。

R_84.mp3

With a set of _____, you can study their _____.
Say you have five numbers: 2, 4, 10, 2, and 7. First, _____ these numbers. Then _____ the sum by 5. The answer 5 is the _____. Next, order the numbers from _____ to _____. The middle number, or 4, is the _____. Finally, there is the _____. That number appears the _____. Here, it is 2.

Write the meaning of the words and phrases in Chinese.
請寫出單字和片語的中文。

1. primary color

2. mix

3. form

4. purple

5. secondary color

6. complementary color

7. pair

8. bright

9. stand out

Listen to the passage and fill the blanks.
聆聽段落內容並填寫空格。

R_85.mp3

Colors come in _____ types. Primary colors are _____. These are red, blue, and _____. Now let's _____ different colors. Red and blue form purple. Red and yellow form orange. Blue and yellow _____ green. These are _____ colors. Last, there are _____ colors. These are _____ of one primary and one secondary color. These pairs make each other _____. So red letters on green paper will _____.

👤 **Write the meaning of the words and phrases in Chinese.**
請寫出單字和片語的中文。

1. tale
2. common
3. Chinese
4. wolf
5. act

6. trick
7. tasty
8. nut
9. climb

🦊 **Listen to the passage and fill the blanks.** 🎧
聆聽段落內容並填寫空格。

R_86.mp3

Some cultures have _____ stories. For example, *Lon Po Po* is a Chinese _____ . This story is like a _____ one, *Little Red Riding Hood*. In *Lon Po Po*, a wolf _____ three sisters. It acts like their _____ . But the girls know this and _____ the wolf. They talk about _____ nuts in a tree. When the wolf _____ the tree, the girls _____ it. The wolf falls and _____ .

Write the meaning of the words and phrases in Chinese.

請寫出單字和片語的中文。

1. jazz
2. unique
3. style
4. nowadays
5. mix

6. musician
7. written
8. player
9. complex
10. steady

Listen to the passage and fill the blanks.

聆聽段落內容並填寫空格。

R_87.mp3

Jazz is popular nowadays. It is a ＿＿＿ of various types of music. But it is ＿＿＿. Why? Most musicians play only ＿＿＿ music. Jazz players ＿＿＿ parts as they play. They often play ＿＿＿ notes. So, a song ＿＿＿ different each time. Also, jazz has complex ＿＿＿. These are not ＿＿＿. The beat may become ＿＿＿ or slower throughout the song. But it ＿＿＿ the song.

One Very Talented Man
非常有才華的人物

Write the meaning of the words and phrases in Chinese.
請寫出單字和片語的中文。

1. talented
2. be born
3. talent
4. painter
5. painting

6. smiling
7. supper
8. the Bible
9. inventor
10. designer

Listen to the passage and fill the blanks. 🎧

聆聽段落內容並填寫空格。

R_88.mp3

Leonardo da Vinci _____ in 1452
in Italy. He had many _____ . As a _____ ,
Leonardo painted two great _____ . The first is *Mona
Lisa*, a _____ woman. The other is *The Last Supper*,
from _____ . Leonardo was also a great
_____ and designer. He designed many
_____ and machines. You know what? He even designed an
_____ over 500 years ago!

👤 **Write the meaning of the words and phrases in Chinese.**
請寫出單字和片語的中文。

1. zero
2. mathematics
3. hundred
4. thousand
5. meaning

6. version
7. India
8. modern
9. spread
10. all over the world

🐴 **Listen to the passage and fill the blanks.** 🎧
聆聽段落內容並填寫空格。

R_89.mp3

Zero is important in _____. It means "no _____."
Also, it creates _____ amounts. Put one or more
zeros after a _____. This creates tens, hundreds, and
thousands. So who created _____? Some
people did. But their zeros had _____ shapes or
meanings. Today's _____ comes from India. It
appeared about 1,500 years ago! People there
_____ it for math. And this modern zero _____ all over the
world.

Write the meaning of the words and phrases in Chinese.

請寫出單字和片語的中文。

1. genius
2. electric
3. device
4. teenager
5. magazine

6. be interested in
7. image
8. continue

Listen to the passage and fill the blanks. 🎧

聆聽段落內容並填寫空格。

R_90.mp3

Philo Farnsworth _____ in Utah in 1906.

He was a _____ with electric devices. As a teenager,

he read many science _____. And he

_____ TV. At that time, TVs didn't send

_____ quickly, like today. So he designed a special

_____. This could show _____ images quickly.

He was still a _____ then! He _____ his work.

In 1929, he _____ the first electric television.

347

Write the meaning of the words and phrases in Chinese.
請寫出單字和片語的中文。

1. banjo
2. string
3. string instrument
4. pluck
5. though

6. look like
7. produce
8. unique
9. popular
10. traditional

Listen to the passage and fill the blanks. 🎧
聆聽段落內容並填寫空格。

R_91.mp3

Can you play the banjo? How about the _____? Both are string _____. Sounds are made by their strings. Thicker or longer _____ make lower sounds. Thinner or _____ strings make higher sounds. Banjos and guitars _____ different though. That's because banjos have a different _____ than guitars. The body of a banjo is round and looks like a _____. This produces a _____ sound. It is popular in American music. You can hear that sound in a song like "Oh! Suzanna."

你是 2D 還是 3D 的形狀？
Are You in 2D or 3D Shape?

👧 **Write the meaning of the words and phrases in Chinese.**
請寫出單字和片語的中文。

1. dimension
2. in other words
3. height
4. length
5. width

6. either *A* or *B*
7. add
8. cube
9. sphere

🐿 **Listen to the passage and fill the blanks.** 🎧
聆聽段落內容並填寫空格。

R_92.mp3

You and I have three dimensions (3D). In other words, we have _____, length, and width. But a picture or drawing of you only has two _____ (2D). It only has height and _____. The same is true for some _____, and they can be _____ 3D _____ 2D. Sometimes, you can take a 2D shape and add _____ to make a 3D shape. If you give a _____ width, it becomes a _____. A 2D _____ becomes a 3D sphere. What are some other 3D shapes?

Is That Number prime or Composite?

 ## Write the meaning of the words and phrases in Chinese.
請寫出單字和片語的中文。

1. prime number
2. composite number

3. count
4. whole number

5. distinguish
6. divide
7. remainder

 ## Listen to the passage and fill the blanks. 🎧

聆聽段落內容並填寫空格。

R_93.mp3

We can _____ whole numbers. Whole numbers _____ than 1 can either be prime or composite numbers. How do we _____ between prime numbers and composite numbers? It's easy! Prime numbers can only be divided without _____ by 1 or the prime number itself. Is 3 a _____? Yes, because 3 can only be _____ without remainder by 1 or 3. How about 4? Is it a _____ number? No, because 4 can also be divided by 2 _____ remainder. It is a _____ number. Is 5 a prime or composite number?

Write the meaning of the words and phrases in Chinese.

請寫出單字和片語的中文。

1. ancient

2. Greek

3. goddess

4. harvest

5. fall in love with

6. underworld

7. agree

8. return

Listen to the passage and fill the blanks.

聆聽段落內容並填寫空格。

R_94.mp3

The Ancient _____ had a story about how Demeter changed the _____. There was only one season before this story. Demeter was goddess of the _____. Long ago, the god Hades _____ love with Demeter's daughter, Persephone. But she didn't love him back. He took Persephone to the _____. Demeter was _____ so she didn't allow any plants to grow. Hades agreed to let Persephone _____ for six months every year. During those six months, Demeter was happy and everything _____. People call this season _____. People call the season when nothing grows _____.

A Joyful Day of the Dead

Write the meaning of the words and phrases in Chinese.
請寫出單字和片語的中文。

1. joyful
2. the dead
3. gather
4. ancestor
5. spirit

6. cemetery
7. celebration
8. altar
9. grave
10. skeleton

Listen to the passage and fill the blanks. 🎧
聆聽段落內容並填寫空格。

R_95.mp3

In Mexico, the Day of the _____ is an important _____. Families gather together to _____ their ancestors. On this day, they believe the _____ of the dead can join their families again. It may sound sad and a bit _____, but it's a joyful _____. Families make altars in their homes. Then, they put their _____' favorite food and drinks there. After that, they bring gifts to their ancestors' _____. Often, they wear ghost or _____ costumes. On the Day of the Dead, the _____ are full of celebration!

Write the meaning of the words and phrases in Chinese.
請寫出單字和片語的中文。

1. country music
2. genre
3. appear
4. folk music
5. Ireland

6. Scotland
7. European
8. lyrics
9. romance
10. struggle

Listen to the passage and fill the blanks. 🎧

聆聽段落內容並填寫空格。

R_96.mp3

Millions of Americans love country music. It's a popular

_____ of music. It first appeared around 100 years ago

with _____ folk music from Ireland and Scotland. And

then, it changed and _____ with other cultures when

Europeans moved into North America. Folk music usually

uses guitars and _____. Modern country music still uses

these _____. The songs tell stories about life outside

of big cities. The lyrics are about _____, struggles,

_____, and traditions. In America, country music

_____ to grow and change, and it is still _____

today!

Write the meaning of the words and phrases in Chinese.
請寫出單字和片語的中文。

1. impressive   6. collect

2. object   7. tool

3. sculpture   8. passionate

4. structure   9. artwork

5. garbage   10. eventually

 Listen to the passage and fill the blanks. 🎧
聆聽段落內容並填寫空格。

R_97.mp3

Simon Rodia created   art by finding

himself and using only them. In Watts, California, he created

       and structures from garbage. He

it because he didn't have much money. Rodia did all of this

work alone, and with   tools. He was

about his artwork. He spent 34 years working on it! His work

       covered an 800-meter-long area of Watts. He

made many tall   in this area. The tallest was

over 30 meters high! Today, the Watts Towers is a popular

museum.

98 Understanding Idioms

Write the meaning of the words and phrases in Chinese.

請寫出單字和片語的中文。

1. idiom
2. creative
3. express
4. language
5. grammar

6. use
7. bucket
8. literally
9. literal
10. punch

Listen to the passage and fill the blanks. 🎧

聆聽段落內容並填寫空格。

R_98.mp3

Idioms are creative and _____ ways to express language in a certain culture. You cannot understand idioms simply by knowing _____ or the words in the idiom. You can only understand them by their popular _____. What does it mean when someone kicked the _____? It usually doesn't mean _____ that a person really kicked a bucket. It means that someone died. Here's another _____: I hit the books! The literal _____ is that I punched the books. It really means that I studied. What do you think " _____ the beans" means? It means to _____ a secret!

99 Painting with Points
用點點作畫

Write the meaning of the words and phrases in Chinese.
請寫出單字和片語的中文。

1. painting
2. point
3. Pointillism
4. dot
5. image

6. closely
7. individual
8. blend
9. describe
10. performer

Listen to the passage and fill the blanks. 🎧
聆聽段落內容並填寫空格。

R_99.mp3

Pointillism is a _____ way to paint pictures. It uses _____ or points of color to create _____. If you look closely, you can see many _____ points. If you look from far away, it looks like a regular _____. That's because the points of color appear to _____ together. Georges Seurat was a French artist, and he created _____ in the 1800s. He made some _____ paintings, such as *The Circus*. It describes the circus _____ and people watching them. And, it is made up of _____ colored dots!

100 The Declaration of Independence

Write the meaning of the words and phrases in Chinese.

請寫出單字和片語的中文。

1. The Declaration of Independence

2. British

3. colony

4. colonist

5. respect

6. support

7. liberty

8. pursuit

9. state

10. independent

Listen to the passage and fill the blanks.

聆聽段落內容並填寫空格。

R_100.mp3

Long ago, America was a British _____. But the
American colonists were angry at the _____ government.
That's because they never _____ Americans. So on
July 4, 1776, Thomas Jefferson wrote The _____ of
Independence. Let's take a look at part of it. "All men are
equal and certain basic _____ support them. These are
life, liberty, and the _____ of happiness." Also, the
Declaration stated why Americans should be _____.
It said that Britain had no right to _____ Americans.
Following the Declaration of Independence, America started its
fight for _____.

Answer Key
解答

Answer Key 解答

Check True or False

1. 地球會繞著太陽轉動。T
2. 我們一整天都看到星星。F

Comprehension Checkup

A. 1. 實際上是什麼在移動？ⓑ
   ⓐ 太陽　　　ⓑ 地球　　　ⓒ 星星
  2. 地球繞著什麼運轉？ⓐ
   ⓐ 太陽　　　ⓑ 月亮　　　ⓒ 星星
  3. 當地球自轉時，會產生白天和黑夜。ⓒ
   ⓐ 空間　　　ⓑ 季節　　　ⓒ 白天和黑夜
  4. 我們在白天看不到星星。ⓑ
   ⓐ 日光　　　ⓑ 星星　　　ⓒ 天空

B. 地球會繞著太陽移動，並且也會自轉。

Wrap Up

①Earth ②sun ③spins ④orbit

地球以兩種方式移動。	
● 地球會繞著太陽轉動。	▸ 地球的軌道
● 地球會自己旋轉。	▸ 產生白天和黑夜

Check True or False

1. 震動會產生所有的聲音。T
2. 耳膜不會振動。F

Comprehension Checkup

A. 1. 震動是如何移動的？ⓒ
   ⓐ 僅移動一次ⓑ 緩慢移動　ⓒ 來回移動
  2. 震動會傳遞到耳朵的耳膜。ⓐ
   ⓐ 傳遞到　　ⓑ 撥動　　　ⓒ 識別

3. 什麼會識別聲音？ⓑ
  ⓐ 弦　　　　ⓑ 大腦　　　ⓒ 耳膜
4. 我們透過一樣的方式聽到音樂和人聲。
  ⓑ
  ⓐ 耳朵　　　ⓑ 人聲　　　ⓒ 資訊

B. 所有的聲音都是震動，而我們的大腦會識別聲音。vibrations

Wrap Up

1️⃣撥動吉他上的弦。
3️⃣聲波傳遞到我們的耳朵。
5️⃣大腦識別聲音。
2️⃣震動發生並產生聲波。
4️⃣聲波將資訊發送到大腦。

Check True or False

1. 物質會在溶液中分解。T
2. 鹽水很快就會變回水和鹽。F

Comprehension Checkup

A. 1. 下列何者為溶液的例子？ⓑ
   ⓐ 鹽的晶體 ⓑ 鹽水　　　ⓒ 鹽和胡椒粉
  2. 鹽的晶體會發生什麼現象？ⓒ
   ⓐ 會漂浮　　ⓑ 會下沉　　ⓒ 會溶解
  3. 鹽的晶體會讓水變鹹。ⓑ
   ⓐ 變甜　　　ⓑ 變鹹　　　ⓒ 變清澈
  4. 鹽水會像新的物質一樣維持不變。ⓐ
   ⓐ 維持不變　ⓑ 攪拌　　　ⓒ 分解

B. 溶液是一種物質的混合物，但會變成一種新的物質。mixture

Wrap Up

①Substance　②breaks　③solution　④water

製作一種新的物質		
方法	● 一種物質分解在另一種物質中	▸ 溶液
例子	● 鹽在水裡分解	▸ 鹽水

Unit 4 颶風　　p.22

Check True or False

1. 颶風來臨時，海岸十分安全。F
2. 科學家可以向人們發出颶風的警報。T

Comprehension Checkup

A. 1. 颶風從哪裡生成？ⓐ
   ⓐ 暖水上方　　　ⓑ 炎熱的陸地上方
   ⓒ 冷水上方
   2. 颶風**不會**造成何種影響？ⓒ
   ⓐ 洪災　　　ⓑ 龍捲風　　　ⓒ 空氣乾燥
   3. 科學家可以<u>預測</u>並追蹤颶風。ⓐ
   ⓐ 預測　　　ⓑ 摧毀　　　ⓒ 旋轉
   4. 人們可以為即將到來的颶風先<u>做好準備</u>。ⓑ
   ⓐ 形成　　　ⓑ 準備　　　ⓒ 移動

B. 颶風是強大的風暴，而且可能會十分<u>危險</u>。dangerous

Wrap Up

①oceans　②land　③flooding　④track

颶風	
形成	● 形成於海洋的暖水上方
移動	● 旋轉並移動到陸地上
結果	● 引發洪災和其他風暴
預防	● 預測和追蹤

Unit 5 青蛙的生命週期　　p.24

Check True or False

1. 青蛙是從水中的卵孵化而成的。T
2. 蝌蚪可以在水面上呼吸。F

Comprehension Checkup

A. 1. 嬰兒時期的青蛙稱做什麼？ⓐ
   ⓐ 蝌蚪　　　ⓑ 魚　　　ⓒ 生命週期
   2. 青蛙在小時候如何游泳？ⓑ
   ⓐ 用腳　　　ⓑ 用尾巴　　　ⓒ 用肺
   3. 青蛙長大後，尾巴會變得<u>更短</u>。ⓒ
   ⓐ 更快　　　ⓑ 更長　　　ⓒ 更短
   4. 青蛙會用肺在水面上<u>呼吸</u>。ⓑ
   ⓐ 游泳　　　ⓑ 呼吸　　　ⓒ 吃東西

B. 青蛙在歷經轉變後，便可以在<u>陸地上</u>和水中生活。land

Wrap Up

青蛙的生命週期

③為了呼吸而發育出肺。
④身體已經發育成熟。
②長出腿，尾巴也變更短。
①在水中從卵孵化成蝌蚪。

WORD REVIEW Unit 1 ~ 5　　p.26

A.

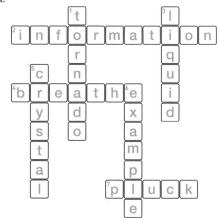

B. 1. ⓓ 耳膜：當接收到聲音時，耳朵內會震動的部位
   2. ⓒ 颶風：在海洋的暖水上方形成的強大風暴
   3. ⓐ 地球的軌道：地球環繞著太陽移動的路徑
   4. ⓑ 溶液：物質的混合物，通常是液體

C. 1. spins   2. recognizes
   3. float   4. track
   5. full-grown

D. 1. 我們只會<u>在晚上</u>看到星星。
      at night
   2. 弦會快速地<u>來回</u>移動。
      back and forth
   3. 在溶液當中，一種物質會在另一種物質中完全<u>分解</u>。 breaks down
   4. 颶風會快速旋轉，<u>並行進到陸地上</u>。
      travel to
   5. 但實際上太陽是<u>靜止不動的</u>，只有地球在移動。 stays still

Unit 6 舊式溫度計是如何運作的？ p.28

Check True or False

1. 舊式溫度計是由玻璃製成的。T
2. 熱度會讓管子內的空氣下降。F

Comprehension Checkup

A. 1. 家中的什麼物品會有溫度計？ⓐ
   ⓐ 冰箱   ⓑ 電視螢幕   ⓒ 玻璃窗
   2. 舊式溫度計裡面有什麼？ ⓒ
   ⓐ 熱度   ⓑ 玻璃   ⓒ 水銀
   3. 舊式溫度計的管子上會有<u>刻度</u>。 ⓒ
   ⓐ 螢幕   ⓑ 液體   ⓒ 刻度
   4. 熱的時候，舊式溫度計中的紅色液體會
      <u>升得更高</u>。 ⓑ
   ⓐ 下降   ⓑ 升得更高   ⓒ 變成藍色

B. 舊式溫度計用水銀測量<u>溫度</u>。 temperature

Wrap Up

① scales   ② glass   ③ mercury   ④ Heat

舊式溫度計

溫度顯示方法	● 玻璃管上的刻度
管子中的物質	● 水銀
溫度計的原理	● 熱度使水銀膨脹 ▸ 水銀上升

Unit 7 植物會自己製造食物 p.30

Check True or False

1. 植物通常透過葉子取得水分。F
2. 植物在光合作用後會釋放出氧氣。T

Comprehension Checkup

A. 1. 植物會吸入什麼氣體？ ⓑ
   ⓐ 氧氣   ⓑ 二氧化碳   ⓒ 水
   2. 植物會從哪裡取得水分？ⓐ
   ⓐ 地底下   ⓑ 空氣   ⓒ 糖分
   3. 植物利用<u>太陽光</u>作為光合作用的能量。
      ⓑ
   ⓐ 氣體   ⓑ 太陽光   ⓒ 植物的葉子
   4. 植物結合二氧化碳和水，並製造出<u>糖分</u>。 ⓒ
   ⓐ 水果   ⓑ 能量   ⓒ 糖分

B. 植物透過<u>光合作用</u>製造食物。
   photosynthesis

Wrap Up

① water   ② combine   ③ oxygen

光合作用

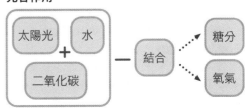

Unit 8 震動的板塊　　p.32

Check True or False

1. 大多數的地震會持續很長一段時間。F
2. 地球表面在移動的板塊上。T

Comprehension Checkup

A. 1. 板塊在哪裡？ ⓒ
　　ⓐ 在地表上　ⓑ 在海裡　　ⓒ 在地表下
2. 板塊通常會有什麼現象？ ⓑ
　　ⓐ 下沉　　　ⓑ 漂浮　　ⓒ 靜止不動
3. 板塊有時候會卡住。 ⓑ
　　ⓐ 變弱　　　ⓑ 卡住　　ⓒ 變短
4. 當板塊鬆動時會震動。 ⓐ
　　ⓐ 震動　　　ⓑ 摩擦　　ⓒ 創造

B. 當地球的板塊鬆動時，板塊會震動，並引發地震。earthquake

Wrap Up

是什麼引發地震？

② 板塊卡住了。

③ 板塊會以巨大的力量不斷地推擠，而突然間便鬆動了。

① 地球的板塊會移動並彼此摩擦。

④ 突如其來的變化震動了板塊。

Unit 9 植物還是動物？　　p.34

Check True or False

1. 珊瑚礁實際上是海洋植物。F
2. 魚類吃珊瑚蟲並製造出珊瑚礁。F

Comprehension Checkup

A. 1. 什麼動物生活在珊瑚礁上？ ⓐ
　　ⓐ 珊瑚蟲　ⓑ 獅子　　ⓒ 鰻魚
2. 珊瑚蟲會吃什麼？ ⓑ
　　ⓐ 石頭　　ⓑ 小生物　ⓒ 小丑魚
3. 珊瑚蟲死掉後，身體會變硬。 ⓒ
　　ⓐ 軟　　　ⓑ 大　　　ⓒ 硬
4. 珊瑚礁和許多的魚類讓海底世界變美麗。 ⓒ
　　ⓐ 星星　　ⓑ 珊瑚蟲　ⓒ 魚類

B. 死亡的珊瑚蟲會形成珊瑚礁，有非常多魚類生活在它們的周圍。coral reefs

Wrap Up

① animals　② on　③ hard　④ Dead

什麼是珊瑚礁？

① 牠們是〔動物／植物〕。

② 珊瑚蟲生活在珊瑚礁〔下方／上方〕。

③ 珊瑚蟲死掉後會變〔硬／軟〕。

④ 〔死亡的／小的〕珊瑚蟲會形成珊瑚礁。

Unit 10 地球的磁場　　p.36

Check True or False

1. 指南針可以吸引金屬。F
2. 地球的核心有著像磁鐵一樣的作用。T

Comprehension Checkup

A. 1. 指南針總是指向何方？ ⓒ
　　ⓐ 東方　　ⓑ 西方　　ⓒ 北方
2. 地球的核心裡面有什麼？ ⓐ
　　ⓐ 鐵球　　ⓑ 指南針　ⓒ 磁極
3. 所有的磁鐵都有兩個磁極，而且會吸引金屬。 ⓑ
　　ⓐ 核心　　ⓑ 磁極　　ⓒ 針
4. 地球的磁極會引導指南針的指針。 ⓒ
　　ⓐ 旋轉　　ⓑ 指向　　ⓒ 引導

B. 指南針用地球的磁場指示方向。magnetic

Wrap Up

①iron　②magnetic　③metal　④needles

為什麼指南針總是指向北方？

- 地球的核心有一顆鐵球。
- 它會旋轉並產生磁場。
- 地球的兩個磁極會吸引金屬。
- 兩極引導了指南針的金屬指針。

WORD REVIEW Unit 6 ~ 10　p.38

A.

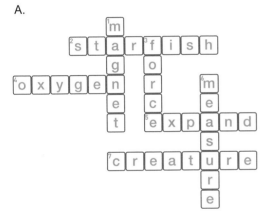

B. 1. ⓒ 地震：地球的表面震動時，引發的危險情況
2. ⓐ 水銀：舊式溫度計內的紅色液體
3. ⓓ 珊瑚蟲：生活在礁石上的動物，死後會形成新的礁石
4. ⓑ 光合作用：植物自己製造的食物過程

C. 1. thermometers　2. combines
3. plates　4. marine
5. core

D. 1. 天氣涼爽的時候，水銀就會下降。
went down
2. 依照順序，植物會為我們釋放出氧氣。
gives off
3. 有時會互相摩擦，然後就卡住了。

---

get stuck

4. 牠們死後會變得像石頭一樣堅硬。
like rocks
5. 指南針總是指向北方。 points to

Unit 11 動物會使用電力！　p.40

Check True or False

1. 只有人類會製造和使用電力。F
2. 鯊魚會製造電力來捕食遠處的魚。F

Comprehension Checkup

A. 1. 電鰻可以幫自己的身體充入什麼？ⓐ
ⓐ 電力　　ⓑ 水分　　ⓒ 食物
2. 鰻魚會用電力來做什麼？ ⓑ
ⓐ 建造家園　　ⓑ 電擊獵食者
ⓒ 尋找方向
3. 鯊魚可以感應其他生物的電流。ⓒ
ⓐ 充電　　ⓑ 狩獵　　ⓒ 感應
4. 運用電力，鯊魚可以找到躲藏的魚。ⓒ
ⓐ 捕捉到　　ⓑ 死掉的　　ⓒ 躲藏的

B. 有些動物利用電力來保持安全和尋找食物。electricity

Wrap Up

①charge　②sense　③shock　④hunt

有些動物會使用電力。

動物	電鰻	鯊魚
如何用電	幫身體充電	感應其他生物的電流
結果	電擊獵食者	狩獵魚類

Unit 12 球可以永遠飛在空中嗎？　p.42

Check True or False

1. 地球上沒有萬有引力。F
2. 球在外太空可能永遠不會降落。T

Comprehension Checkup

A. 1. 牛頓定律是關於什麼？ⓑ
　　ⓐ 力的定律　　　　ⓑ 運動定律
　　ⓒ 外太空的萬有引力
　2. 在沒有外力作用的情況下，移動的物體
　　中保持不變的是什麼？ⓒ
　　ⓐ 風　　　　ⓑ 顏色　　　ⓒ 速度
　3. 只有外部的力量才能改變移動中的物
　　體。ⓑ
　　ⓐ 移動的　　ⓑ 外部的　　ⓒ 緩慢的
　4. 地球的萬有引力會將所有物體拉下來。
　　ⓐ
　　ⓐ 萬有引力　ⓑ 外太空　　ⓒ 方向

B. 在地球上，空中的球一定會降落到地上。
　　fall (down)

Wrap Up

①force　②change　③gravity　④slow

運動定律

---

　3. 為了在沙漠生存，仙人掌會在體內儲存
　　水分。ⓒ
　　ⓐ 沙子　　　ⓑ 熱氣　　　ⓒ 水分
　4. 仙人掌的側面有刺。ⓐ
　　ⓐ 刺　　　　ⓑ 葉子　　　ⓒ 植物

B. 沙漠很少下雨，但有些動物和植物可以在
　　那裡生存。survive

Wrap Up

①little　②heavy　③store　④Spines

	白天	少雨、炎熱、乾燥
天氣	晚上	非常寒冷
	有時候	下大雨
植物	仙人掌	儲存水分 刺幫助它們儲存水分

> **Unit 14 螞蟻和牠們的工作**　　p.46

Check True or False

1. 一個蟻巢可以容納超過數百萬隻螞蟻。T
2. 雄蟻的壽命比蟻后長。F

Comprehension Checkup

A. 1. 集體生活的螞蟻叫做什麼？ⓑ
　　ⓐ 卵　　　　ⓑ 蟻巢　　　ⓒ 土丘
　2. 兵蟻的工作是什麼？ⓑ
　　ⓐ 收集食物　ⓑ 保衛蟻巢　ⓒ 和蟻后交配
　3. 雄蟻是雄性的螞蟻。ⓐ
　　ⓐ 雄性的　　ⓑ 幼小的　　ⓒ 工作的
　4. 蟻后會產下所有的卵。ⓑ
　　ⓐ 兵蟻　　　ⓑ 蟻后　　　ⓒ 雄蟻

B. 螞蟻有不同的工作，並一起住在蟻巢裡。
　　jobs

> **Unit 13 沙漠的天氣**　　p.44

Check True or False

1. 沙漠在晚上變得非常炎熱。F
2. 有些動物可以在沙漠中生存。T

Comprehension Checkup

A. 1. 大部分的沙漠有什麼？ⓐ
　　ⓐ 沙子　　　ⓑ 洪水　　　ⓒ 瀑布
　2. 沙漠的天氣通常是什麼樣子？ⓑ
　　ⓐ 寒冷又乾燥　　ⓑ 炎熱又乾燥
　　ⓒ 炎熱又潮濕

Wrap Up

①ⓐ ②ⓒ ③ⓑ ④ⓓ

我們的工作是什麼？

①蟻后 　　　　　　　ⓐ 產卵
②工蟻 　　　　　　　ⓑ 保衛
③兵蟻 　　　　　　　ⓒ 收集食物
④雄蟻 　　　　　　　ⓓ 交配

Unit 15 化石的祕密　　　p.48

Check True or False

1. 在某些博物館裡看得到化石。T
2. 化石會失去原本的形狀。F

Comprehension Checkup

A. 1. 什麼不會成為化石？ ⓑ
　　ⓐ 動物　　　ⓑ 石頭　　　ⓒ 植物
2. 動物死後會沉入哪裡？ⓐ
　　ⓐ 泥土裡　　ⓑ 樹木裡　　ⓒ 石頭裡
3. 化石可以維持動物原始的形狀。ⓒ
　　ⓐ 年　　　　ⓑ 數字　　　ⓒ 形狀
4. 遺骸會變得像石頭一樣堅硬。 ⓑ
　　ⓐ 柔軟　　　ⓑ 堅硬　　　ⓒ 沉重

B. 化石形成超過數百萬年，並提供我們資訊。information

Wrap Up

化石的形成
⑤人們發現化石。
③化石保留在那裡，不會消失。
④化石變得像石頭一樣堅硬。
②死去的動物沉入泥土深處。
①動物死去。

WORD REVIEW Unit 11 ~ 15　　p.50

A.

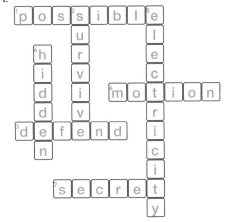

B. 1. ⓑ 沙漠：少雨的沙地
2. ⓒ 雄蟻：和蟻后交配的雄性螞蟻
3. ⓓ 化石：具動植物原始形狀的古老遺骸
4. ⓐ 萬有引力：地球上將所有物體往下拉的力量

C. 1. charge　　　2. speed
3. rainfall　　　4. colony
5. past

D. 1. 一個蟻巢可以容納數百萬隻螞蟻！
　　millions of
2. 因此球會變慢並落下來。 slows down
3. 事實上，沙子在晚上會快速冷卻。
　　cools down
4. 在側邊的刺幫助它們保留水分。
　　on the sides
5. 動物死後，可能會沉入泥土深處。
　　deep into

Unit 16 海底熱泉　p.52

Check True or False

1. 靠近海底熱泉的水壓很弱。F
2. 有些動物生活在熱泉附近。T

Comprehension Checkup

A. 1. 什麼是海底熱泉？ⓑ
　　ⓐ 魚類　　　ⓑ 孔洞　　　ⓒ 石頭
2. 熱泉會噴出什麼？ⓐ
　　ⓐ 熱水　　　ⓑ 陽光　　　ⓒ 蟲
3. 熱泉附近不會有陽光。ⓒ
　　ⓐ 空氣　　　ⓑ 熱度　　　ⓒ 陽光
4. 生活在熱泉附近的植物會吃特殊的<u>細菌</u>。ⓐ
　　ⓐ 細菌　　　ⓑ 蝦子　　　ⓒ 毒物

B. 海底<u>火山口</u>是奇特海洋動物的家。vents

Wrap Up

① pressure　② poisonous　③ worms
④ bacteria

海底熱泉	
環境	棲息生物
• 熱度	• 奇怪的蟲、魚、蝦
• 強烈的水壓	• 植物和特殊的細菌
• 有毒物質	

Unit 17 北美馴鹿和馴鹿　p.54

Check True or False

1. 北美馴鹿沒有很大的鹿角。F
2. 馴鹿可以拉雪橇。T

Comprehension Checkup

A. 1. 北美馴鹿和馴鹿的相同之處是什麼？ⓒ
　　ⓐ 體型　　　ⓑ 家　　　ⓒ 物種
2. 什麼動物是野生的？ⓐ
　　ⓐ 北美馴鹿　　ⓑ 馴鹿　　ⓒ 狗
3. 人們會得到馴鹿的肉或<u>毛皮</u>。ⓑ
　　ⓐ 雪橇　　　ⓑ 毛皮　　　ⓒ 照顧
4. 在這兩者之中，<u>馴鹿</u>過得比較好，體型也較大。ⓑ
　　ⓐ 北美馴鹿　　ⓑ 馴鹿　　ⓒ 人類

B. 馴鹿是<u>被馴化的</u>，而北美馴鹿則是生活在惡劣的環境中。tame

Wrap Up

① wild　② survive　③ tame　④ better

北美馴鹿	馴鹿
• 有很大的鹿角	• 有很大的鹿角
• 是野生的	• 是被馴化的
• 在惡劣的環境中存活下來	• 吃得更多，過得更好
	• 體型比北美馴鹿大

Unit 18 肌肉如何運作　p.56

Check True or False

1. 肌肉在皮膚底下。T
2. 肌肉讓骨頭伸展和收縮。F

Comprehension Checkup

A. 1. 肌肉附著在什麼上面？ⓐ
　　ⓐ 骨頭　　　ⓑ 頭髮　　　ⓒ 大腦
2. 肌肉如何移動？ⓐ
　　ⓐ 伸展和收縮　　　ⓑ 拉長和伸展
　　ⓒ 跑步和玩耍
3. 肌肉運動使骨骼移動。ⓑ
　　ⓐ 皮膚　　　ⓑ 骨骼　　　ⓒ 思考
4. 在跑步時，<u>大腦</u>讓肌肉運作。ⓒ
　　ⓐ 臉　　　ⓑ 腿　　　ⓒ 大腦

B. 肌肉幫助身體以不同的方式<u>移動</u>。move

Wrap Up

① b   ② d   ③ c   ④ a

我們應該怎麼做？

① 肌肉的功用是什麼？
② 肌肉位在哪裡？
③ 肌肉如何移動？
④ 是什麼讓肌肉運作？

ⓐ 思考之後，大腦就會讓肌肉運作
ⓑ 讓我們的身體運動
ⓒ 伸展和收縮
ⓓ 在皮膚下面

Unit 19 大峽谷   p.58

Check True or False

1. 大峽谷位在科羅拉多州。F
2. 大峽谷是在五百萬年前形成的。F

Comprehension Checkup

A. 1. 峽谷位在哪裡？ ⓑ
   ⓐ 河流中　　ⓑ 山底下　　ⓒ 地底下
   2. 大峽谷有多深？ ⓑ
   ⓐ 500 公尺　ⓑ 2 公里　　ⓒ 5 公里
   3. 科羅拉多河的路線經過這個區域。ⓒ
   ⓐ 地面　　　ⓑ 岩石　　　ⓒ 路線
   4. 這條河流在峽谷周圍形成了岩層。ⓐ
   ⓐ 岩層　　　ⓑ 大石頭　　ⓒ 海洋

B. 河流切入地面，並形成了大峽谷。ground

Wrap Up

① ground   ② river   ③ canyon   ④ layers

大峽谷	
地點	● 位於亞利桑那州
深度	● 有 2 公里深
生成過程	● 科羅拉多河切入地面 ● 河流經過這個區域 ● 形成了峽谷和岩層

Unit 20 原子和分子   p.60

Check True or False

1. 原子存在於所有物質中。T
2. 分子可以製造出更大的原子。F

Comprehension Checkup

A. 1. 物質的基本單位是什麼？ ⓑ
   ⓐ 分子　　　ⓑ 原子　　　ⓒ 氧氣
   2. 氫原子和氧原子何者較大？ ⓑ
   ⓐ 氫原子　　ⓑ 氧原子　　ⓒ 一樣大
   3. 原子相互結合，並形成分子。ⓒ
   ⓐ 尺寸　　　ⓑ 較小的單位　ⓒ 分子
   4. 一個水分子有兩個氫原子。ⓐ
   ⓐ 兩個　　　ⓑ 三個　　　ⓒ 無數個

B. 原子和分子是物質的單位，而分子包含了原子。units

Wrap Up

① unit   ② sizes   ③ combine   ④ molecule

物質的基本單位

微小的 ─ 原子 ─ 不同的大小

相互結合 → 分子

A.

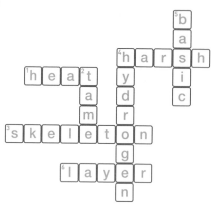

B. 1. ⓒ 峽谷：高山下的深處
　 2. ⓐ 海底熱泉：位於海底的孔洞，會噴出
　　　 熱水和有毒物質
　 3. ⓓ 分子：比較大的物質單位，其中包含
　　　 不同的原子
　 4. ⓑ 北美馴鹿：生活在北極的大型野生鹿

C. 1. pressure　　　　2. care
　 3. shrink　　　　　4. course
　 5. countless

D. 1. 有些植物會吃細菌，而有些動物會以這
　　　 些植物為食。 feed on
　 2. 北美馴鹿和馴鹿屬於同一個物種。
　　　 belong to
　 3. 肌肉在皮膚底下，並附著在骨頭上。
　　　 attached to
　 4. 在很久以前，科羅拉多河切入地面。
　　　 cut into
　 5. 氧原子比氫原子更大。 bigger than

Unit 21 恆溫動物　p.64

Read and Complete

1. 恆溫動物的體溫不會改變。 change
2. 人們透過流汗降溫。 sweat

Comprehension Checkup

A. 1. 下列何者不是哺乳動物的例子？ⓐ
　　 ⓐ 魚　　　　ⓑ 狗　　　　ⓒ 人類
　 2. 人類覺得冷的時候會做什麼？ⓐ
　　 ⓐ 發抖　　　ⓑ 睡覺　　　ⓒ 流汗
　 3. 狗在炎熱的環境下會怎麼做？ⓒ
　　 ⓐ 牠們會發抖。
　　 ⓑ 牠們會流汗。
　　 ⓒ 牠們會伸出舌頭。
　　 ⓓ 牠們會改變體溫。
　 4. 關於哺乳動物的敘述，何者錯誤？ⓓ
　　 ⓐ 牠們是恆溫動物。
　　 ⓑ 牠們是一種動物。
　　 ⓒ 牠們的體溫維持一致。
　　 ⓓ 牠們降溫和升溫的方式都一樣。

B. 哺乳動物的體溫維持 ① 一致，人們透過流
　 汗降溫，也會透過發抖 ② 升溫。
　 ① same　② warm

Wrap Up

① body　② cool　③ sweat　④ shiver

恆溫動物如何維持體溫？	
● 降溫	▶ 牠們會流汗。
● 升溫	▶ 牠們會發抖。

Unit 22 用燈光溝通　p.66

Read and Complete

1. 人們用燈光進行遠距離的溝通。 lights
2. 塞繆爾·摩斯開發了一種很受歡迎的脈衝
　 密碼。 code

Comprehension Checkup

A. 1. 摩斯密碼是什麼時候開發的？ⓒ
　　 ⓐ 最近　　ⓑ 幾年前　　ⓒ 一百多年前
　 2. 什麼是脈衝？ⓐ
　　 ⓐ 燈光的閃爍　　　ⓑ 有訊息的密碼
　　 ⓒ 字母的形式

3. 每個字母的密碼有何不同？（請選出2個答案）ⓐ, ⓓ
ⓐ 脈衝的長度　　ⓑ 燈光的種類
ⓒ 脈衝的強度　　ⓓ 脈衝的數量

4. 為什麼作者會提到沉沒的船隻？ⓒ
ⓐ 為了描述燈光的脈衝。
ⓑ 為了解釋摩斯如何開發出密碼。
ⓒ 為了提供使用摩斯密碼的實例。
ⓓ 為了強調某些字母。

B. 在很久以前，人們在遠 ② 距離的情況下會使用燈光 ① 溝通。摩斯密碼使用 ③ 閃爍的燈光，我們稱之為脈衝，我們可以透過脈衝傳遞訊息。
① communicate　② distances
③ flashing

Wrap Up

① long　② flash　③ alphabet　④ pulse

摩斯密碼	
用途	● 在遠距離的情況下溝通
方法	● 使用燈光的閃爍作為脈衝 ● 以長和短脈衝模式當作字母的代表

Unit 23 來自大自然的設計　p.68

Read and Complete

1. 自然的設計幫助植物和動物存活下來。survive

2. 芒刺有細小、尖刺的鉤子，所以它們會黏在衣服上。hooks

Comprehension Checkup

A. 1. 科學家如何利用自然的設計？ⓐ
ⓐ 創造有用的東西　　ⓑ 改變環境
ⓒ 用自然的東西製造商品

2. 喬治·梅斯特拉爾在哪裡找到芒刺？ⓒ
ⓐ 鞋子上　　ⓑ 衣服上　　ⓒ 狗毛上

---

3. 芒刺的什麼特色讓梅斯特拉爾有了想法？ⓒ
ⓐ 很容易將芒刺連接到塑膠上。
ⓑ 芒刺的尖刺種子長得快又容易生長。
ⓒ 芒刺的小鉤子可以很容易地與東西黏住或分開。
ⓓ 芒刺的種子裡面有非常多的尖刺鉤子。

4. 關於魔鬼氈的敘述，何者錯誤？ⓐ
ⓐ 它在狗毛裡面。
ⓑ 它是來自大自然的設計。
ⓒ 它可以輕易地黏住和分開。
ⓓ 它可用於鞋子和包包上。

B. 人們使用自然的 ① 設計來製作有用的東西。② 魔鬼氈就是源自於 ③ 芒刺的設計。
① designs　② Velcro　③ burr

Wrap Up

① spiky　② hair　③ stick　④ shoes

芒刺	魔鬼氈
● 有小鉤子的尖刺種子 ● 小鉤子會黏在衣服和頭髮上	● 來自芒刺的發明 ● 可以輕易地黏在一起和分開 ● 用於鞋子或包包

Unit 24 印度狐蝠　p.70

Read and Complete

1. 印度狐蝠生活在印度的森林裡。India

2. 這些狐蝠有奇怪的皮質雙臂。leathery

Comprehension Checkup

A. 1. 梅納是在哪裡發現印度狐蝠的？ⓐ
ⓐ 樹上　　ⓑ 村莊內　　ⓒ 靠近花朵處

2. 印度狐蝠是什麼種類的動物？ⓑ
ⓐ 狐狸　　ⓑ 蝙蝠　　ⓒ 昆蟲

3. 為什麼印度狐蝠很危險？ⓐ
ⓐ 他們可能帶有疾病。
ⓑ 他們吃有益的昆蟲。

ⓒ 牠們在村莊裡飛來飛去。

ⓓ 牠們有奇怪的皮質雙臂。

4. 關於印度狐蝠的敘述，何者錯誤？ ⓓ

ⓐ 牠們幫花朵授粉。

ⓑ 牠們吃水果和吸花蜜。

ⓒ 牠們是蝙蝠，但外觀像狐狸。

ⓓ 牠們會嚇人來取得食物。

B. 印度狐蝠在印度被發現，牠們可能是 ① 可怕的，因為牠們的身上或許帶有 ② 疾病，但是印度狐蝠透過為花朵 ③ 授粉來幫助環境。

① scary　② diseases　③ pollinating

Wrap Up

① leathery　② diseases　③ pollinate

④ environment

印度狐蝠

身體特徵	有奇怪的皮質雙臂
風險	帶有疾病
優點	幫花朵授粉 ▸ 對環境有益

Unit 25 聲音的傳播　p.72

Read and Complete

1. 柔軟的材料能阻止聲音傳播。stop/block

2. 硬質的材料不能充分吸收聲音。Hard

Comprehension Checkup

A. 1. 哪一種材料吸收聲音的效果很好？ ⓒ

ⓐ 木頭　　ⓑ 玻璃　　ⓒ 海綿

2. 聲音是如何傳播的？ⓐ

ⓐ 透過聲波　ⓑ 在材料中　ⓒ 透過彈跳

3. 建築工人如何使牆壁隔音？ ⓑ

ⓐ 用柔軟的材料建造牆壁。

ⓑ 將柔軟的材料放進牆壁裡。

ⓒ 建造更厚和更高的牆壁。

ⓓ 用布料或紙板覆蓋牆壁。

4. 關於聲波的敘述，何者錯誤？ ⓒ

ⓐ 聲波會在硬質材料中反彈。

ⓑ 聲波可以被織物吸收。

ⓒ 聲波可以穿透柔軟的材料。

ⓓ 有時聲波的傳播會被阻擋。

B. 聲音是以 ① 波的形式傳播。柔軟的材料可以充分 ② 吸收聲音。另一方面，聲波會在硬質材料中 ③ 反彈。

① waves　② absorb　③ bounce

Wrap Up

① soft　② hard　③ absorb　④ bounce

聲音的傳播

區分	種類	聲音的移動
● 柔軟的材料	▸ 織物、海綿、木板	▸ 充分吸收聲音
● 硬質的材料	▸ 木頭、金屬、玻璃	▸ 聲波會在這些材料中反彈

WORD REVIEW Unit 21 ~ 25　p.74

A.

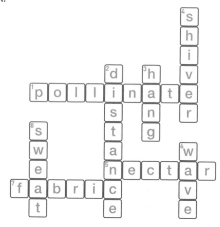

B. 1. ⓓ 吸收：接收聲音，不讓聲音反彈

2. ⓒ 芒刺：末端帶有小鉤子的尖刺種子

3. ⓐ 脈衝：燈光或聲音的閃爍

4. ⓑ 恆溫的：體溫維持溫暖不變

C. 1. environment   2. Sinking
   3. survive   4. diseases
   5. materials

D. 1. 狗會伸出舌頭來降溫。 cool down
   2. 芒刺的鉤子很容易就會黏在衣服和頭髮上。 stick to
   3. 梅納在森林裡看到數百隻的狐蝠掛在樹上。 hundreds of
   4. 聲波能夠被材料吸收或穿透過去。 go through
   5. 建築工人會將這些材料放在牆壁內，以阻止聲音傳播。 stop, from

Unit 26 以後沒有蜜蜂了嗎？ p.76

Read and Complete

1. 蜜蜂群正在消失。 colonies
2. 殺蟲劑殺死數百萬隻蜜蜂。 killing

Comprehension Checkup

A. 1. 農夫用什麼來保護農作物？ ⓒ
   ⓐ 蜂群   ⓑ 昆蟲   ⓒ 殺蟲劑
  2. 什麼會傷害蜜蜂？ ⓒ
   ⓐ 農作物   ⓑ 花蜜   ⓒ 疾病
  3. 殺蟲劑會對蜜蜂造成什麼影響？ ⓒ
   ⓐ 移除蜜蜂的食用作物。
   ⓑ 使蜜蜂不吃東西。
   ⓒ 使蜜蜂變弱和生病。
   ⓓ 造成蜜蜂接觸到危險的農作物。
  4. 從段落中可以推斷出什麼？ ⓑ
   ⓐ 人類需要多養一些蜜蜂。
   ⓑ 蜜蜂在生產農作物上扮演重要的角色。
   ⓒ 蜜蜂從人類那邊偷許多花蜜。
   ⓓ 人類別無選擇，只好使殺蟲劑。

B. 殺蟲劑是 ①有毒的，而且會使蜜蜂生病。殺蟲劑會 ②影響蜜蜂的大腦，所以蜜蜂會很難去尋找 ③花蜜。人類必須要改變耕作的方式。
  ①poisonous ②affect ③nectar

Wrap Up

①poisonous ②contact ③brains
④nectar

消失的蜜蜂

農夫使用有毒的殺蟲劑。
▶ 蜜蜂會接觸到殺蟲劑，因而生病。
▶ 殺蟲劑影響了蜜蜂的大腦。
▶ 蜜蜂很難找到花蜜，因而無法生存。

Unit 27 爆炸性的事實！ p.78

Read and Complete

1. 地球的地殼下面非常炎熱。 crust
2. 岩漿會浮出水面，我們將它稱為熔岩。 lava

Comprehension Checkup

A. 1. 地球表面的下方叫做什麼？ ⓑ
   ⓐ 地殼   ⓑ 地函   ⓒ 火山
  2. 岩漿是由什麼組成？ ⓒ
   ⓐ 熔岩   ⓑ 地殼   ⓒ 熾熱的岩石
  3. 火山噴發時會發生什麼事？ ⓑ
   ⓐ 變成死火山。
   ⓑ 熔岩噴發至地表。
   ⓒ 地函會冷卻。
   ⓓ 地球的表面會分成兩塊。
  4. 關於火山的敘述，何者錯誤？ ⓓ
   ⓐ 活火山產生熔岩。
   ⓑ 死火山無法再度噴發。
   ⓒ 某些火山很長一段時間內都不會噴發。
   ⓓ 超過 1,900 座火山在不久後會變死火山。

B. 當在地殼下的岩漿噴出時，①火山就會噴發。我們稱地表上的岩漿為 ②熔岩，它只能從 ③活火山噴發。
  ①Volcanoes ②lava ③active

Wrap Up

① lava ② extinct ③ again ④ active

火山		
活火山 岩漿噴發後變 成熔岩	死火山 永遠不會再 噴發	很長一段時間 都不會活躍的 火山

Unit 28 奇蹟的洞穴！　　p.80

Read and Complete

1. 洞穴是通向地球表面的大型孔洞。holes
2. 洞穴是由侵蝕作用所形成的。erosion

Comprehension Checkup

A. 1. 是什麼導致侵蝕作用？ⓐ
　　ⓐ 水中的酸性物質　ⓑ 水中的岩石
　　ⓒ 洞穴中的動物
2. 世界上最大的洞穴有多長？ⓑ
　　ⓐ 約 2 公里長　　　ⓑ 約 9 公里長
　　ⓒ 約 10 公里長
3. 為什麼作者會提到人類和動物？ⓑ
　　ⓐ 解釋洞穴是如何形成的。
　　ⓑ 強調某些洞穴有多大。
　　ⓒ 提供一個著名洞穴的例子。
　　ⓓ 抱怨某些洞穴被摧毀。
4. 關於山水洞的敘述，何者錯誤？ⓓ
　　ⓐ 位於越南。
　　ⓑ 超過 200 萬年的歷史。
　　ⓒ 是世界上最大的洞穴。
　　ⓓ 比科學家一開始想的還要古老。

B. 洞穴是地球 ①表面上的大型孔洞，因為侵
蝕作用而產生這些洞穴，水中的 ②酸性物
質在數百萬年間 ③磨損岩石。
①surface　②Acid　③wears

Wrap Up

① large ② holes ③ acid ④ Erosion

洞穴	
定義	通向地球表面的大型天然孔洞
如何形成	水中的酸性物質會磨損岩石 ▶ 侵蝕作用需要經過數百萬年 的時間
最大的洞穴	位於越南的山水洞

Unit 29 從出生到死亡　　p.82

Read and Complete

1. 蝴蝶從卵開始牠的生命週期。egg
2. 毛毛蟲建立了一個保護殼，並變成一個
蛹。shell

Comprehension Checkup

A. 1. 蝴蝶的卵在下一階段會變成什麼？ⓑ
　　ⓐ 蛹　　　　ⓑ 幼蟲　　　ⓒ 成蝶
2. 什麼會從保護殼當中孵化出來？ⓒ
　　ⓐ 卵　　　　ⓑ 毛毛蟲　　ⓒ 成蝶
3. 蝴蝶的生命週期是如何再次開始的？ⓒ
　　ⓐ 蝴蝶會盡可能地進食。
　　ⓑ 蝴蝶會教孩子如何取得食物。
　　ⓒ 蝴蝶在死亡之前會產卵。
　　ⓓ 蝴蝶在死後會重新變成毛毛蟲。
4. 關於蝴蝶的生命週期，何者錯誤？ⓓ
　　ⓐ 蛹有堅固的保護殼。
　　ⓑ 毛毛蟲處於幼蟲階段。
　　ⓒ 蝴蝶從出生開始，並以死亡結束。
　　ⓓ 毛毛蟲的外觀幾乎和成年的蝴蝶一樣。

B. 生命週期是從 ①出生開始，並以 ②死亡結
束。不同的生物從出生到死亡之間，都有
③獨特的生命週期。
①birth　②death/dying　③unique

Wrap Up

①larva ②adult

蝴蝶的生命週期

卵 → 幼蟲（毛毛蟲） → 蛹 → 成年的蝴蝶

Unit 30 能源的來源　　p.84

Read and Complete

1. 發電廠產生<u>電力</u>。electricity
2. 風力發電是<u>可再生的</u>能源。renewable

Comprehension Checkup

A. 1. 下列何者為非再生資源的例子？ ⓑ
   ⓐ 太陽　　ⓑ 煤炭　　ⓒ 風
   2. 哪一種能源不會產生汙染？ ⓒ
   ⓐ 石油　　ⓑ 天然氣　　ⓒ 氫
   3. 為什麼發電廠經常使用非再生能源？ⓐ
   ⓐ 因為很容易使用。
   ⓑ 因為很快就會耗盡。
   ⓒ 因為會造成空氣污染。
   ⓓ 因為會造成水汙染。
   4. 關於可再生能源的敘述，何者錯誤？ ⓑ
   ⓐ 可再生能源不會耗盡。
   ⓑ 可再生能源是由發電廠製造的。
   ⓒ 可再生能源可以產生電力。
   ⓓ 可再生能源不會產生汙染。

B. 煤炭、石油和天然氣是 ①<u>非再生</u>資源，它們很容易使用，但是會產生 ②<u>汙染</u>。可再生能源來自太陽、風和 ③<u>氫</u>現在正在改進中。
   ①non-renewable　②pollution
   ③hydrogen

Wrap Up

①pollution ②use ③solar ④never

	非再生資源	可再生資源
例子	• 煤炭、石油和天然氣	• 太陽能、氫能和風力
汙染	• 產生空氣和水汙染	• 不會產生汙染
特性	• 很容易取得和使用 • 有天會耗盡	• 永遠不會耗盡

WORD REVIEW Unit 26 ~ 30　　p.86

A.

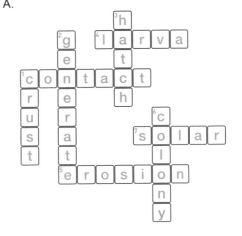

B. 1. ⓒ 洞穴：通向地球表面的大型天然孔洞
   2. ⓑ 熔岩：岩漿噴出地表後所變成的東西
   3. ⓐ 殺蟲劑：農夫使用在農作物上來趕走蟲的東西
   4. ⓓ 蛹：蝴蝶在幼蟲和成蟲之間的階段

C. 1. erupt　　　2. erode
   3. life cycle　4. non-renewable
   5. pollution

D. 1. 殺蟲劑會導致蜜蜂在尋找花蜜時<u>迷路</u>。
   get lost

2. 地函是由熾熱的紅色岩石所組成的。
   is made up of
3. 當水中的酸性物質磨損岩石時，就會發生侵蝕。 wears away
4. 在 10 到 14 天後，成蝶就會從殼中孵化出來。 hatches from
5. 可再生能源永遠不會耗盡。 run out

Unit 31 歡迎來到叢林
p.88

Read and Complete

1. 熱帶雨林產生大量的氧氣。oxygen
2. 赤道環繞地球的中間。equator

Comprehension Checkup

A. 1. 大部分的雨林位於哪裡？ⓑ
   ⓐ 赤道下方　ⓑ 赤道附近　ⓒ 赤道中間
   2. 植物會消耗什麼？ⓐ
   ⓐ 二氧化碳　　　　　ⓑ 氧氣
   ⓒ 氧氣和二氧化碳
   3. 為什麼氧氣和二氧化碳的平衡很重要？ⓓ
   ⓐ 植物不能在氧氣過多的情況下生長。
   ⓑ 人們無法混和氧氣和二氧化碳。
   ⓒ 人們不能在二氧化碳太少的情況下生長。
   ⓓ 如果平衡失調，人們就不能呼吸。
   4. 關於熱帶雨林的敘述，何者錯誤？ⓒ
   ⓐ 有很多植物。
   ⓑ 在溫暖又潮濕的環境。
   ⓒ 製造地球上 40％的氧氣。
   ⓓ 對地球上的生命很重要。

B. ①熱帶雨林位於赤道的附近，幫助維持空氣中二氧化碳和氧氣的 ②平衡，這個平衡對 ③地球上的生命很重要。
   ①Rainforests　②balance　③Earth

Wrap Up

①pollution　②use　③solar　④never

熱帶雨林	
地點	在赤道附近
氣候	溫暖又潮濕的環境使植物生長良好。
環境作用	幫助維持氧氣和二氧化碳的平衡。

Unit 32 北極的郊狼
p.90

Read and Complete

1. 隨著狼的消失，郊狼的總數開始增加。
   population
2. 郊狼被迫要適應寒冷的環境。 adapt

Comprehension Checkup

A. 1. 狼和郊狼為了什麼而競爭？ⓐ
   ⓐ 生活的區域　　　　ⓑ 有雪的地方
   ⓒ 一起生活的人
   2. 郊狼擴展到哪裡？ⓐ
   ⓐ 阿拉斯加　ⓑ 歐洲　　　ⓒ 北美洲
   3. 為什麼人們要獵殺狼群？ⓑ
   ⓐ 狼群殺死了郊狼。
   ⓑ 狼群殺死了農場的動物。
   ⓒ 狼群從人類那裡取得食物。
   ⓓ 人們想要取得狼群的皮毛。
   4. 郊狼如何適應嚴峻的環境？（請選出 2 個答案）ⓐ, ⓓ
   ⓐ 皮毛會變得更厚以保持溫暖。
   ⓑ 為了找到食物而開始攻擊農場。
   ⓒ 北上擴展自己的領地。
   ⓓ 皮毛會變成不同的顏色。

B. 郊狼和狼相互競爭，但人們獵殺 ①狼群，因此郊狼的總數快速增加，甚至 ②擴展到阿拉斯加。郊狼能夠 ③適應新環境。
   ①wolves　②expanded　③adapt

Wrap Up

③郊狼的總數擴展到加拿大北部和阿拉斯加。
①狼和郊狼會競爭食物和領地。
④郊狼適應了寒冷的環境。
②狼被獵殺到瀕臨絕種的程度。

Unit 33 強大的山洪暴發　p.92

Read and Complete

1. 山洪暴發是一種自然災害。disaster
2. 山洪暴發時，水位會突然上升。rise

Comprehension Checkup

A. 1. 什麼是山洪暴發的徵兆？ ⓑ
　　ⓐ 任何降雨　ⓑ 高水平面　ⓒ 財產損失
　 2. 什麼可能有助於人們避免自然災害？ ⓒ
　　ⓐ 關閉水壩　ⓑ 製造長流　ⓒ 看天氣預報
　 3. 關於山洪暴發的敘述，何者錯誤？ ⓒ
　　ⓐ 山洪暴發會損害人們的財產。
　　ⓑ 損壞的水壩或暴雨可能會造成洪災。
　　ⓒ 我們可以事先預防山洪暴發。
　　ⓓ 當山洪暴發時，人們應該要待在更高的
　　　　地方。
　 4. 為什麼作者提到凱達爾納特洪災？ ⓒ
　　ⓐ 為了解釋經常發生山洪的地方。
　　ⓑ 為了提供一個致命的山洪暴發的例子。
　　ⓒ 為了強調天氣警報的重要性。
　　ⓓ 為了提出一個最突然的山洪暴發案例。

B. 像是①山洪暴發的自然災害可能會致命。
　 在山洪暴發的期間，②水平面會無預警
　 地上升。洪災發生時，人們應該要看天氣
　 ③警報。
　 ① flash　② water　③ warnings

Wrap Up

① levels　② six　③ dam　④ damage

山洪暴發	
發生條件	● 水平面在六小時的降雨內上升
造成水平面上升	● 暴雨或損壞的水壩
結果	● 造成財產損失 ● 也可能會讓人致命

Unit 34 水和鐵　p.94

Read and Complete

1. 人們用鐵製造了許多有用的東西。iron
2. 鐵製工具生鏽或腐朽時，可能會失去作
　 用。rust

Comprehension Checkup

A. 1. 鐵的缺點是什麼？ⓐ
　　ⓐ 生鏽　　ⓑ 融化　　ⓒ 彎曲
　 2. 什麼物質之間的化學反應導致生鏽現
　　　象？ⓒ
　　ⓐ 油和鐵　ⓑ 水和空氣　ⓒ 水和鐵
　 3. 怎麼做可以防止鐵腐朽？ⓐ
　　ⓐ 把油塗在鐵上面
　　ⓑ 把鐵放在雨中
　　ⓒ 把鐵放在箱子裡
　　ⓓ 把硬紙板蓋在鐵上面
　 4. 下列何者不是鐵的特徵？ⓑ
　　ⓐ 鐵是堅固的金屬。
　　ⓑ 鐵一碰到雨之後馬上就會生鏽。
　　ⓒ 鐵是製作武器的好材料。
　　ⓓ 鐵可以被塑造成有用的工具。

B. 鐵是一種堅固的金屬，而人們會將它 ①塑
　 造成武器和工具。水和 ②空氣會造成鐵生
　 鏽。為了 ③防止鐵腐朽，可以用油漆或油
　 覆蓋在鐵的表面上。
　 ① shape　② air　③ protect

Wrap Up

① reaction ② water ③ rust ④ cover

鐵有個嚴重的缺點。

原因	水和空氣所產生的化學反應
結果	可能會生鏽、腐朽或斷裂
保護方法	可以用油漆或油包覆在表面上

Unit 35 瀕臨絕種的北極熊 p.96

Read and Complete

1. 人類正在破壞動物的<u>棲息地</u>。 habitats
2. 北極熊是其中一種<u>瀕臨絕種</u>的動物。
   endangered

Comprehension Checkup

A. 1. 是什麼導致北極冰層融化？ ⓑ
   ⓐ 建造動物園　　ⓑ 全球暖化
   ⓒ 瀕臨絕種的海豹

   2. 北極熊的棲息地正在發生什麼事？ⓐ
   ⓐ 正在減少　　ⓑ 正在變冷
   ⓒ 海豹和鯨魚快要死亡

   3. 下列何者不是北極熊適應於北極地區的例子？ⓒ
   ⓐ 可以待在冰水裡。
   ⓑ 獵殺海豹和鯨魚。
   ⓒ 可能會往南邊移動。
   ⓓ 白色的皮毛幫助他們躲藏。

   4. 從段落中可以推斷出什麼？ⓐ
   ⓐ 人類是全球暖化的主要因素。
   ⓑ 人類會獵捕北極熊來養在動物園裡。
   ⓒ 北極以南的地區太狹小，無法讓北極熊在那裡生存。
   ⓓ 許多人到北極地區看北極熊。

B. 動物的棲息地因為 ①<u>人類</u>而正在改變。北極熊住在北極地區，但是全球暖化 ②<u>融化</u>北極冰層，北極熊的棲息地正在縮小和 ③<u>消失（／破壞）</u>。

① humans ② melting
③ disappearing (/destroying)

Wrap Up

① environment ② animals ③ warming
④ habitats

原因	• 人類改變環境 • 我們正在摧毀動物的棲息地
結果	• 全球暖化融化北極冰層 • 北極熊的棲息地正在消失

WORD REVIEW Unit 31 ~ 35 p.98

A.

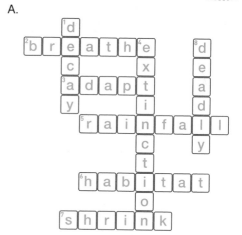

B. 1. ⓓ 瀕臨絕種的：動物無法適應被改變的棲息地時，他們的後果
   2. ⓐ 赤道：環繞地球中間的一條假想線
   3. ⓒ 鐵：一種堅固的金屬
   4. ⓑ 自然災害：洪災和地震等現象

C. 1. consume　　2. competed
   3. avoid　　4. useless
   5. Global warming

D. 1. 熱帶雨林讓氧氣和二氧化碳保持<u>平衡</u>。
      in balance
   2. 嚴峻的環境<u>迫使</u>郊狼去適應。 forced, to

3. 山洪暴發對財產造成損失。 cause, to
4. 鐵可能會生鏽、腐蝕或斷裂。
   break apart
5. 北極熊擅長在北極水域捕獵海豹和鯨
   魚。 are good at

Unit 36 能量波 p.100

Read and Complete

1. 真空是一個沒有任何物質的地方。 vacuum
2. 電磁波在太空中傳導。 travel

Comprehension Checkup

A. 1. 下列何者為真空的例子？ ⓑ
   ⓐ 衛星　　ⓑ 外太空　　ⓒ 電磁波
   2. 下列何者為電磁波的一種？ ⓒ
   ⓐ 聲音　　ⓑ 電力　　ⓒ 陽光
   3. 人們如何使用微波？ ⓑ
   ⓐ 用微波找到方向。
   ⓑ 用微波烹飪食物。
   ⓒ 用微波照亮黑暗。
   ⓓ 用微波四處移動。
   4. 衛星對無線電波有什麼作用？ ⓓ
   ⓐ 衛星幫助無線電波迅速傳播。
   ⓑ 衛星讓無線電波更強大。
   ⓒ 衛星收集了世界上許多的無線電波。
   ⓓ 衛星接收和發送來自手機的無線電波。

B. 陽光、①無線電波和②微波等電磁波可以
   在③真空中傳導。人們將這些電磁波用於
   許多事情，例如：講電話和烹飪食物。
   ①radio　②microwaves　③vacuum

Wrap Up

①electromagnetic　②energy　③vacuum
④microwaves

電磁波	
特性	● 一種能量波 ● 可以在真空中傳導
種類	● 陽光、無線電波和微波

Unit 37 月亮的週期 p.102

Read and Complete

1. 月亮繞著地球轉動。 Earth
2. 月亮的週期有 8 個階段。 journey

Read and Complete

A. 1. 月亮繞地球一周需要花多少時間？ ⓑ
   ⓐ 8 天　　ⓑ 29.53 天　　ⓒ 8 個月
   2. 是什麼使月亮看起來更大或更小？ ⓐ
   ⓐ 反射的太陽光　　ⓑ 行進的速度
   ⓒ 離地球的距離
   3. 為什麼月亮每天晚上看起來都有點不一
   樣？ ⓒ
   ⓐ 因為月亮會規律地出現和消失。
   ⓑ 因為月亮有時候無法反射太陽光。
   ⓒ 因為月亮行進時會呈現不同的階段。
   ⓓ 因為每天晚上的天氣都不一樣。
   4. 關於月亮的敘述，何者錯誤？ ⓑ
   ⓐ 人們將第一個階段稱為新月。
   ⓑ 新月會變更小，最後成為滿月。
   ⓒ 滿月像圓圈一樣反射太陽光。
   ⓓ 新月沒有反射許多太陽光。

B. 月亮在行進時會經歷 8 個①階段。在每一
   個階段，月亮會②反射更多或更少的太陽
   光，這使得月亮看起來更大或③更小。
   ①phases　②reflects　③smaller

Wrap Up

①travels　②new　③light　④circle

月球繞行地球	
新月	較小，反射很少太陽光
滿月	像圓圈一樣反射太陽光

Unit 38 食物鏈中的角色　　p.104

Read and Complete

1. 生產者、消費者和<u>分解者</u>共同生活在一個棲息地。decomposers
2. 消費者會吃<u>生產者</u>。producers

Comprehension Checkup

A. 1. 植物如何獲得能量？ ⓒ
　　ⓐ 從消費者　　　　ⓑ 從動物
　　ⓒ 從太陽和土壤
　2. 下列何者為分解者的一種？ ⓑ
　　ⓐ 草　　　　ⓑ 蟲子　　　ⓒ 斑馬
　3. 分解者會做什麼？ ⓓ
　　ⓐ 吃生產者。
　　ⓑ 獵殺消費者，例如斑馬。
　　ⓒ 從植物身上生產能量。
　　ⓓ 將能量回歸給土地。
　4. 關於食物鏈的敘述，何者錯誤？ ⓒ
　　ⓐ 食物鏈存在於棲息地。
　　ⓑ 生產者會被消費者吃掉。
　　ⓒ 消費者最重要。
　　ⓓ 分解者會分解消費者。

B. 每個 ①<u>棲息地</u>都有食物鏈，食物鏈是由生產者、消費者和分解者所組成的。②<u>消費者</u>從生產者身上獲得能量，然後分解者會將這些能量回歸 ③<u>土地</u>。
　① habitat　② Consumers　③ soil/ ground

Wrap Up

① ⓑ　② ⓒ　③ ⓐ
① 生產者從太陽和土地中生產出能量。
② 消費者會吃生產者。
③ 分解者將消費者的能量轉移到土壤中。

Unit 39 四個重要的圈層　　p.106

Read and Complete

1. 地球有四個稱為<u>圈層</u>的系統。spheres
2. 四個系統是緊密<u>連結的</u>。 connected

Comprehension Checkup

A. 1. 人類在哪一個系統當中？ ⓐ
　　ⓐ 生物圈　　ⓑ 水圈　　　ⓒ 大氣圈
　2. 什麼是岩石圈的一部分？ ⓑ
　　ⓐ 雨　　　　ⓑ 礦物　　　ⓒ 植物
　3. 大氣圈會如何影響岩石圈？ ⓓ
　　ⓐ 動物會吃植物。
　　ⓑ 暴雨導致洪災。
　　ⓒ 植物需要水分才能成長。
　　ⓓ 風慢慢導致岩石和土壤的侵蝕。
　4. 下列何者是生物圈和大氣圈之間連結的例子？ ⓐ
　　ⓐ 人們汙染空氣。
　　ⓑ 人們吃其他的動物。
　　ⓒ 人們生活在土地上。
　　ⓓ 人們挖掘有價值的礦物。

B. 地球的四大系統包括 ①<u>生物圈／水圈</u>、大氣圈、岩石圈和 ②<u>水圈／生物圈</u>，這些圈層都 ③<u>緊密地</u>連結。
　① biosphere/ hydrosphere
　② hydrosphere/ biosphere　③ closely

Wrap Up

① living　② minerals　③ water　④ Earth

地球的系統			
生物圈	岩石圈	水圈	大氣圈
所有的生物	岩石和礦物	水	包圍著地球的氣體或空氣

Unit 40 一閃一閃亮晶晶　　p.108

Read and Complete

1. 視星等告訴我們恆星看起來有多亮。
   apparent
2. 絕對星等指的是一顆恆星真正的亮度。
   absolute

Comprehension Checkup

A. 1. 人們不會用什麼來衡量視星等？ ⓑ
   ⓐ 恆星的亮度　　　ⓑ 附近恆星的數量
   ⓒ 恆星與地球的距離
2. 人們用什麼來衡量絕對星等？ⓐ
   ⓐ 恆星本身的亮度　ⓑ 恆星與地球的距離
   ⓒ 恆星與太陽的距離
3. 為什麼太陽看起來真的很亮？ ⓒ
   ⓐ 因為太陽離地球很遠。
   ⓑ 因為太陽是宇宙中最亮的恆星。
   ⓒ 因為太陽非常大，而且離地球很近。
   ⓓ 因為太陽附近沒有任何恆星。
4. 為什麼有些大又亮的星星在我們眼中沒有那麼亮？ ⓐ
   ⓐ 因為它們離地球很遠。
   ⓑ 因為它們經常互相覆蓋。
   ⓒ 因為它們的溫度太高了。
   ⓓ 因為它們離太陽太近。

B. 視星等指的是恆星從 ①地球上看起來的亮度，絕對星等指的是恆星 ②實際的亮度。
   ① Earth　② really

Wrap Up

① absolute　② brightness　③ distance
④ really

視星等	絕對星等
• 恆星從地球上看起來的亮度	• 恆星真正的亮度
▸ 恆星的亮度	
▸ 從地球到恆星的距離	

WORD REVIEW Unit 36 ~ 40　　p.110

A.

B. 1. ⓒ 分解者：食物鏈中的一部分，會分解消費者
2. ⓑ 新月：月亮週期的第一個階段
3. ⓓ 土壤：地球表面的物質，植物會生長在上面
4. ⓐ 真空：沒有任何物質的地方

C. 1. satellite　　　2. reflects
3. surrounds　　　4. includes
5. measure

D. 1. 微波的傳導速度很快，並且可以在幾分鐘內烹飪食物。 in minutes
2. 每個月，月亮會經歷 8 個階段。
   goes through
3. 我們來看一下棲息地的例子，例如非洲平原。 take a look at
4. 地球由四個系統組成，我們將它稱為圈層。 consists of
5. 在宇宙中許多遙遠的恆星比太陽更大、更亮。 far away

Check True or False

1. 核心家庭比大家庭更大。F
2. 大家庭中可以包括祖父母。T

Comprehension Checkup

A. 1. 哪一種家庭只有包含父母和小孩？ⓐ
　　ⓐ 核心家庭　　ⓑ 大家庭　　ⓒ 大型家庭
　　2. 布雷迪的家中有幾個成員？ⓒ
　　ⓐ 4　　　　ⓑ 6　　　　ⓒ 7
　　3. 布雷迪的姑姑也和大家住在一起。ⓑ
　　ⓐ 兄弟　　　ⓑ 姑姑　　　ⓒ 叔叔
　　4. 在大家庭中，所有成年人會為了家庭共
　　　同努力。ⓐ
　　ⓐ 所有成年人ⓑ 祖父母　　ⓒ 只有母親

B. 大家庭包含與父母有親緣關係的成年人。
　　extended

Wrap Up

①nuclear　②grandparents　③extended

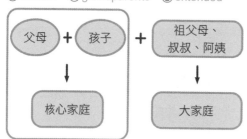

父母 ＋ 孩子 ＋ 祖父母、叔叔、阿姨
↓　　　　　　　↓
核心家庭　　　大家庭

Check True or False

1. 墨西哥佔北美洲最大的區域。F
2. 太平洋位於北美洲的西邊。T

Comprehension Checkup

A. 1. 哪一個國家在北美洲的最北方？ⓐ
　　ⓐ 加拿大　　ⓑ 墨西哥　　ⓒ 美國
　　2. 哪一個北美洲國家的人口最多？ⓒ
　　ⓐ 加拿大　　ⓑ 墨西哥　　ⓒ 美國
　　3. 北美洲總共有 23 個國家。ⓒ
　　ⓐ 3 個　　　ⓑ 20 個　　　ⓒ 23 個
　　4. 大西洋位在北美洲的東邊。ⓐ
　　ⓐ 東邊　　　ⓑ 北邊　　　ⓒ 西邊

B. 北美洲是位在北半球的一個大陸。
　　continent

Wrap Up

①the United States　②Pacific/ Atlantic
③Atlantic/ Pacific

北美洲

國家	周圍海洋
● 加拿大 ● 美國 ● 墨西哥和其他國家	● 太平洋 ● 大西洋

Check True or False

1. 文化包含一個國家的食物。T
2. 年輕人不喜歡改變年長者的方式。F

Comprehension Checkup

A. 1. 什麼是人們共同的觀念或生活方式？ⓐ
　　ⓐ 文化　　　ⓑ 音樂　　　ⓒ 媒體
　　2. 什麼是年輕人的特徵？ⓒ
　　ⓐ 不會改變　　　　ⓑ 變得受歡迎
　　ⓒ 做事很不同
　　3. 年輕人會聽不同的音樂，像是搖滾樂和
　　　嘻哈樂。ⓐ
　　ⓐ 嘻哈樂　　ⓑ 古典樂　　ⓒ 鄉村歌曲
　　4. 像是智慧型手機的科技可以改變人們的
　　　生活方式。ⓒ
　　ⓐ 藝術　　　ⓑ 食物　　　ⓒ 智慧型手機

B. 年輕人、媒體和科技總是在<u>改變</u>文化。
   change

Wrap Up

①shared ②language ③changes
④media

文化	
意義	• 人們共同的觀念或生活方式
包含	• 食物、藝術和語言
特性	• 總是在改變
改變的原因	• 年輕人 • 媒體和科技

Unit 44 消失的資源　　p.118

Check True or False

1. 人們有時候會使用過多資源。T
2. 我們有足夠的自然資源供未來使用。F

Comprehension Checkup

A. 1. 人們從何處取得能源？ⓐ
   ⓐ 大自然　　ⓑ 紙張　　ⓒ 建築物
   2. 紙張是用什麼製成的？ⓑ
   ⓐ 煤炭　　ⓑ 樹木　　ⓒ 石油
   3. 新的建築物會<u>浪費</u>土地和其他資源。ⓒ
   ⓐ 得到　　ⓑ 建造　　ⓒ 浪費
   4. 在未來，我們可能會<u>用盡</u>所有資源。ⓒ
   ⓐ 重複使用　　ⓑ 丟棄　　ⓒ 用盡

B. 人們浪費許多天然<u>資源</u>，所以它們正在消
   失。resources

Wrap Up

①energy ②paper ③waste ④run

消失的資源	
從大自然取得的資源	• 以石油和煤炭當作能源 • 使用樹木當作紙張和木材
問題	• 人們浪費資源
結果	• 我們可能會用盡所有資源

Unit 45 做個好公民！　　p.120

Check True or False

1. 公民是社區的一份子。T
2. 你可以清理附近的垃圾。T

Comprehension Checkup

A. 1. 公民對他們的社區需要負有什麼？ⓒ
   ⓐ 成員　　ⓑ 金錢　　ⓒ 責任
   2. 下列何者**不是**公民要照顧社區的事情？
   ⓒ
   ⓐ 投票　　ⓑ 繳稅　　ⓒ 違規
   3. 有些公民會為了國家到<u>軍隊</u>服役。ⓐ
   ⓐ 軍隊　　ⓑ 監獄　　ⓒ 公司
   4. 身為一個年輕的公民，你可以幫助<u>貧窮</u>
   <u>的</u>人。ⓑ
   ⓐ 有錢的　　ⓑ 貧窮的　　ⓒ 乾淨的

B. 公民對社區負有責任，並且要照顧他們的
   <u>社區</u>。communities

Wrap Up

①vote ②taxes ③changes ④media
公民負有責任。

成年人應該	年輕的公民可以
• 投票 • 繳稅 • 在軍隊服役	• 清理垃圾 • 幫助需要幫助的人

A.

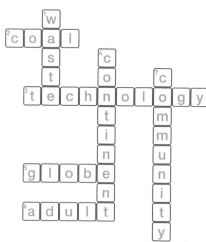

B. 1. ⓒ 文化:人們共同的觀念或生活方式
   2. ⓐ 核心家庭:只有父母和孩子的家庭類型
   3. ⓓ 公民:國家或社區的一份子
   4. ⓑ 北美洲:位於北半球的大陸,包含加拿大、美國和墨西哥

C. 1. grandparents   2. oceans
   3. popular   4. nature
   5. vote

D. 1. 在大家庭中,所有成年人彼此都是有親緣關係的。 each other
   2. 太平洋位於西邊。 lies to
   3. 他們做事與年長者不同。
      differently from
   4. 在不久的將來,我們可能會用盡所有資源。 run out of
   5. 這代表公民必須照顧他們的社區。
      take care of

Check True or False

1. 聖派翠克在美國傳教。F
2. 人們在聖派翠克節當天會遊行。T

Comprehension Checkup

A. 1. 聖派翠克節是為了什麼? ⓑ
      ⓐ 節慶   ⓑ 紀念一位聖人   ⓒ 環境
   2. 聖派翠克傳播什麼遍布整個愛爾蘭?ⓐ
      ⓐ 基督教   ⓑ 遊行   ⓒ 節日
   3. 人們通常在聖派翠克節穿成綠色的。 ⓐ
      ⓐ 綠色的   ⓑ 紅色的   ⓒ 白色的
   4. 酢漿草是聖派翠克節的一種象徵。 ⓒ
      ⓐ 國家   ⓑ 食物   ⓒ 象徵

B. 人們會以綠色的衣服和食物來慶祝聖派翠克節。 green

Wrap Up

① holiday ② honor ③ parades ④ plant

聖派翠克節	
日期	● 3 月 17 日
意義	● 愛爾蘭的節日 ● 為了紀念聖派翠克
活動	● 舉辦聚會和遊行慶祝 ● 穿綠色的衣服和吃綠色的食物
象徵	● 酢漿草,一種小株的綠色愛爾蘭植物

Check True or False

1. 人們必須為運河挖掘渠道。T
2. 人們可以利用小型的運河來耕作。T

Comprehension Checkup

A. 1. 運河可以如何幫助農夫？ ⓒ
　 ⓐ 蓋農場　　ⓑ 清理土壤　ⓒ 提供水源
　 2. 巴拿馬運河有多長？ ⓑ
　 ⓐ 107 公里　　　　ⓑ 77 公里
　 ⓒ 13,000 公里
　 3. 巴拿馬運河連接兩個海洋。 ⓐ
　 ⓐ 海洋　　ⓑ 大陸　　ⓒ 船隻
　 4. 沒有巴拿馬運河，船隻就必須繞過南美洲。 ⓒ
　 ⓐ 印度洋　　ⓑ 北美洲　ⓒ 南美洲

B. 運河是有許多用途的人造水道／渠道。
　 waterways/ channels

Wrap Up

①waterways　②channels　③farms
④lakes

運河	
意義	● 人造的水道
製作方法	● 挖掘渠道，並用水填滿
用途	● 為農場供水 ● 連接湖泊和海洋
例子	● 巴拿馬運河

Unit 48 林肯和南北戰爭　　p.128

Check True or False

1. 亞伯拉罕・林肯是美國第 6 任總統。F
2. 北方和南方在南北戰爭中交戰。T

Comprehension Checkup

A. 1. 亞伯拉罕・林肯什麼時候成為總統？ ⓐ
　 ⓐ 1861 年　ⓑ 1863 年　ⓒ 1865 年
　 2. 哪一方想要終止奴隸制度？ ⓐ
　 ⓐ 北方　　ⓑ 南方　　ⓒ 雙方

3. 在戰爭期間，林肯下令結束南方的奴隸制度。 ⓑ
　 ⓐ 北方的　　ⓑ 南方的　　ⓒ 民間的
4. 北方贏得戰爭，也終止了美國的奴隸制度。 ⓒ
　 ⓐ 聯合　　ⓑ 通過　　ⓒ 贏得

B. 亞伯拉罕・林肯終止奴隸制度，並統一美國。 slavery

Wrap Up

④北方贏了戰爭。
②南北戰爭開始。
①亞伯拉罕・林肯成為美國第 16 任總統。
⑤林肯通過多項法律，並終止奴隸制度。
③林肯下令終止南方的奴隸制度。

Unit 49 回收的好處　　p.130

Check True or False

1. 你可以回收並節省資源。T
2. 回收塑膠將會汙染空氣。F

Comprehension Checkup

A. 1. 下列何者是回收？ ⓑ
　 ⓐ 砍伐樹木　　　ⓑ 再次使用材料
　 ⓒ 製造塑膠
　 2. 要如何來拯救樹木？ⓐ
　 ⓐ 回收紙張　　　ⓑ 製造更少的塑膠
　 ⓒ 丟棄垃圾
　 3. 回收不會汙染水或土地。 ⓒ
　 ⓐ 拯救　　ⓑ 清除　　ⓒ 汙染
　 4. 如果工廠製造較少的新塑膠，在空氣中也會製造較少的煙霧。 ⓑ
　 ⓐ 資源　　ⓑ 煙霧　　ⓒ 森林

B. 回收可以節省資源，並減少汙染。 reduce

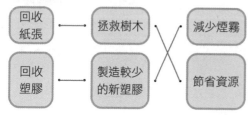
Wrap Up

回收的好處

```
回收紙張  ──→  拯救樹木  ──╮  ╭──  減少煙霧
                        ╳
回收塑膠  ──→  製造較少     ╰──  節省資源
              的新塑膠
```

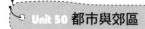
Check True or False

1. 都市區域沒有高聳的建築物。F
2. 郊區離城市很近。T

Comprehension Checkup

A. 1. 下列何者為都市區域？ ⓑ
   ⓐ 小城鎮　　　　ⓑ 大城市
   ⓒ 有森林的區域
   2. 下列何者在都市區域並不常見？ ⓒ
   ⓐ 運輸良好　ⓑ 公司　　ⓒ 許多住宅
   3. 郊區比都市區域更小。 ⓐ
   ⓐ 更小　　　ⓑ 更大　　ⓒ 一樣大
   4. 郊區主要有住宅、學校和綠地。 ⓑ
   ⓐ 高聳建築　ⓑ 綠地　　ⓒ 博物館

B. 人們會居住在都市區域或郊區，而兩個地方的生活方式也不一樣。 suburban

Wrap Up

Urban - ①, ②, ④
Suburban - ③, ⑤, ⑥
① 有高聳建築的大城市
② 擁擠又熱鬧
③ 住宅和綠地
④ 公司和博物館
⑤ 在都市區域外
⑥ 更小和更平靜

A.

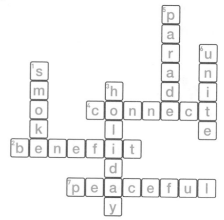

B. 1. ⓒ 回收：在新的產品中再次使用紙張或塑膠
   2. ⓓ 都市區域：有高聳建築和良好運輸的大城市
   3. ⓐ 運河：人造的水道
   4. ⓑ 南北戰爭：美國北方和南方之間為了奴隸制度的戰爭

C. 1. spread　　　　2. dig
   3. president　　　4. pollute
   5. crowded

D. 1. 在那一天，大家會穿綠色的衣服，甚至還會吃綠色的食物！ wear green
   2. 船隻將巴拿馬運河作為捷徑。 as a shortcut
   3. 林肯下令終止南方的奴隸制度。 an end to
   4. 人們為了取得新的紙張而砍伐樹木。 cut down
   5. 郊區比都市區域更小。 smaller than

Unit 51 地圖上的線條　　p.136

Check True or False

1. 地圖上有四種線條。F
2. 緯線測量赤道以北或以南的度數。T

Comprehension Checkup

A. 1. 地球上的線條顯示出什麼？ⓐ
　　ⓐ 位置　　　ⓑ 時間　　　ⓒ 空間
　2. 經線是從北到什麼方向？ⓒ
　　ⓐ 東　　　　ⓑ 西　　　　ⓒ 南
　3. 經線測量本初子午線以東或以西的度數。ⓑ
　　ⓐ 位置　　ⓑ 本初子午線ⓒ 赤道
　4. 經線與緯線會交叉。ⓒ
　　ⓐ 錯過　　ⓑ 延伸　　　ⓒ 交叉

B. 經線與緯線顯示地圖上確切的位置。
　locations

Wrap Up

①longitude　②latitude　③equator
④locations

經線	緯線
• 從北向南延伸 • 測量本初子午線以東或以西的度數	• 從東向西延伸 • 測量赤道以北或以南的度數

它們會彼此交叉 ▶ 顯示確切的位置

Unit 52 華盛頓的紀念碑　　p.138

Check True or False

1. 紀念碑是由石材製成的。T
2. 紀念碑沒有電梯。F

Comprehension Checkup

A. 1. 華盛頓紀念碑在哪裡？ⓒ
　　ⓐ 紐約　　　ⓑ 華盛頓州　ⓒ 美國首都

2. 這座紀念碑是為了紀念誰？ⓐ
　ⓐ 第一位美國總統　　ⓑ 南北戰爭的英雄
　ⓒ 紀念碑的設計師
3. 南北戰爭導致紀念碑的建設工程數次中斷。ⓑ
　ⓐ 開始　　　ⓑ 中斷　　　ⓒ 座落於
4. 這座紀念碑歷經 36 年才完工。ⓒ
　ⓐ 48個月　　ⓑ 24年　　　ⓒ 36年

B. 華盛頓紀念碑是世界上最高的石製建築。
　tallest

Wrap Up

①stone　②honor　③president

華盛頓紀念碑	
特別之處	世界上最高的石製建築 （將近 170 公尺高）
建築物緣由	為了紀念喬治・華盛頓，即美國第一任總統
建造期間	從 1848 年到 1884 年

Unit 53 工業革命　　p.140

Check True or False

1. 工業革命開始於 1700 年代。T
2. 革命帶來了蒸汽機。F

Comprehension Checkup

A. 1. 英國是第一個建立什麼的國家？ⓑ
　　ⓐ 城市　　　ⓑ 工廠　　　ⓒ 工具
　2. 蒸汽機讓商品變得如何？ⓒ
　　ⓐ 變得更稀少　　　ⓑ 變得更糟糕
　　ⓒ 變得更便宜
　3. 更多人為了新工作而搬到城市。ⓐ
　　ⓐ 城市　　　ⓑ 農場　　　ⓒ 英國
　4. 出現鐵路和蒸汽船等新旅行方式。ⓑ
　　ⓐ 長距離　　ⓑ 鐵路　　　ⓒ 新工作

B. 蒸汽機的誕生引起了工業革命。 steam

Wrap Up

①發明蒸汽機。
④在城市有新的工作機會。
⑤鐵路和蒸汽機載運人們到城市。
③工廠快速生產出許多商品。
②英國建造了工廠。

Unit 54 多元文化　　p.142

Check True or False

1. 有些美國人來自南美洲。T
2. 美國有不同的食物和宗教。T

Comprehension Checkup

A. 1. 最早期的美國人來自哪裡？ⓐ
　　ⓐ 歐洲　　　ⓑ 亞洲　　　ⓒ 非洲
　　2. 美國有多少文化？ⓒ
　　ⓐ 零個　　　ⓑ 一個　　　ⓒ 許多個
　　3. 不同的人都將他們的文化帶到美國。ⓑ
　　ⓐ 社會　　　ⓑ 文化　　　ⓒ 祖先
　　4. 來自不同文化的人們必須互相尊重。ⓒ
　　ⓐ 帶來　　　ⓑ 知道　　　ⓒ 尊重

B. 一個多元文化的社會有許多不同的文化。
　　multicultural

Wrap Up

①culture　②respect　③Americans
④Africa

多元文化的社會	
特性	● 有超過一種以上的文化。 ● 人們必須互相尊重。
例子	● 最早期的美國人有歐洲人的祖先。 ● 來自南美洲、非洲和亞洲的人帶來他們的文化。

Unit 55 什麼是文明？　　p.144

Check True or False

1. 農業在過去不是一種食物的系統。F
2. 人們在文明中共享語言。T

Comprehension Checkup

A. 1. 人們共同生活的地方是什麼的開始？ⓐ
　　ⓐ 文明　　　ⓑ 大自然　　　ⓒ 過去
　　2. 什麼在過去是食物的系統？ⓒ
　　ⓐ 法律　　　ⓑ 文化　　　ⓒ 農業
　　3. 政府的系統為人民制定法律。ⓑ
　　ⓐ 習俗　　　ⓑ 政府　　　ⓒ 語言
　　4. 人們創造文化，並共享語言、宗教和習俗。ⓐ
　　ⓐ 習俗　　　ⓑ 系統　　　ⓒ 人民

B. 一個文明有不同的系統使人民團結。
　　systems

Wrap Up

①farming　②government　③culture
④customs

文明的系統	
● 食物的系統	▶ 過去的農業
● 政府的系統	▶ 制定法律、保護人民
● 文化	▶ 語言、宗教和習俗

A.

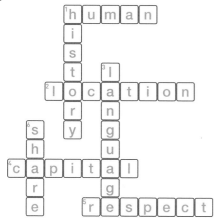

B. 1. ⓒ 多元文化的：有超過一種以上的文化
2. ⓐ 經線：在地球儀上從北向南延伸的線
3. ⓓ 政府：社會中制定法律和保護人民的系統
4. ⓑ 蒸汽機：引發工業革命的東西

C. 1. exact   2. construction
3. goods   4. ancestors
5. farming

D. 1. 華盛頓紀念碑位於華盛頓特區。
   is located
2. 現今，電梯可以將人們帶至最高處。
   to the top
3. 鐵路和蒸汽船讓人們可以長途旅行。
   long-distance travel
4. 人們來自世界各地。 came from
5. 人們搬到城市，這也創造了新的旅行方式。 moved to

Unit 56 **美國原住民的土地** p.148

Check True or False

1. 歐洲人將美洲原住民稱為「印第安人」。T
2. 保留地不會保護美洲原住民的文化。F

Comprehension Checkup

A. 1. 最早住在美國的是誰？ ⓒ
   ⓐ 歐洲人   ⓑ 英國人   ⓒ 美洲原住民
2. 是什麼使美洲原住民的生活更艱難？ ⓑ
   ⓐ 宗教   ⓑ 疾病和戰爭 ⓒ 小的汙染
3. 保留地有他們自己的政府和法律。 ⓑ
   ⓐ 疾病   ⓑ 政府   ⓒ 艱難的生活
4. 美洲原住民想要保護他們的文化。 ⓐ
   ⓐ 文化   ⓑ 戰爭   ⓒ 時間

B. 在美國，有些原住民部落在保留地生活。
   reservations

Wrap Up

① disease   ② reservations   ③ government
④ culture

美洲原住民的保留地	
人口減少的原因	● 疾病和戰爭
居住地	● 保留地
原住民法律	● 他們自己的政府和法律
他們想要什麼	● 保護他們的文化

Unit 57 **一樣的稅金？** p.150

Check True or False

1. 稅金會支付在教育上。T
2. 如果每個人都繳納相同的稅金，是件公平的事。F

Comprehension Checkup

A. 1. 人們為了什麼而繳稅？ ⓒ
   ⓐ 企業   ⓑ 宗教   ⓒ 政府服務
2. 大家對於繳納相同金額的稅金有什麼想法？ⓐ
   ⓐ 不公平   ⓑ 公平   ⓒ 沒有意見
3. 在例子當中，有一千美元的人只需要繳百分之十。 ⓑ
   ⓐ 百分之五   ⓑ 百分之十   ⓒ 百分之二十

4. 大多數的國家都有<u>不同的</u>徵稅方式。 ⓑ
ⓐ 相同的 　ⓑ 不同的 　ⓒ 沒有其他的

B. 人們必須繳納<u>稅金</u>，但每個人都繳相同的金額是不公平的。 taxes

Wrap Up

① government 　② education 　③ ways
④ amount

繳稅	
● 稅金的去向	▶ 政府
● 稅金的用途	▶ 健康照護和教育
● 繳稅的方式	▶ 每個人都是一樣的金額 ▶ 不同的方式

Unit 58 全球化 　　p.152

Check True or False

1. 來自不同國家的公司不會進行貿易。F
2. 全球化將文化傳播到世界各地。T

Comprehension Checkup

A. 1. 是什麼讓國家之間變得更緊密？ ⓐ
　ⓐ 全球化 　ⓑ 木材和石油 ⓒ 俄羅斯公司
2. 不同國家之間有什麼貿易往來？ ⓒ
　ⓐ 法律 　　ⓑ 工廠 　　ⓒ 金錢和資源
3. 許多人會出國旅行，並傳播<u>文化</u>。 ⓑ
　ⓐ 宗教 　　ⓑ 文化 　　ⓒ 國家
4. 人們可以享受來自其他<u>國家</u>的食物和電影。 ⓐ
　ⓐ 國家 　　ⓑ 外國人 　ⓒ 電視節目

B. 透過全球化，來自不同國家的人們變得<u>更加緊密</u>。 closer

Wrap Up

① trade 　② travel 　③ watch 　④ spread

全球化	
● 貿易	▶ 金錢、商品和資源
● 到國外旅行 ● 收看外國的電視節目和電影	▶ 傳播文化

Unit 59 移民站 　　p.154

Check True or False

1. 埃利斯島不在美國。F
2. 政府雇員在島上工作。T

Comprehension Checkup

A. 1. 許多移民想在美國得到什麼？ ⓑ
　ⓐ 艱困的生活 　　ⓑ 更好的生活
　ⓒ 一座島嶼
2. 埃利斯島位在哪裡？ⓐ
　ⓐ 紐約附近 　ⓑ 歐洲 　　ⓒ 美國各地
3. 船隻載著許多<u>移民</u>來到島上。 ⓒ
　ⓐ 金錢 　　ⓑ 政府雇員 ⓒ 移民
4. 這些人離開島嶼，到美國各地<u>定居</u>。 ⓐ
　ⓐ 定居 　　ⓑ 幫助 　　ⓒ 來自

B. 許多移民來到埃利斯島，並在美國展開新的<u>生活</u>。 lives

Wrap Up

① immigration 　② European 　③ wanted
④ settled

埃利斯島	
位置	● 在紐約附近
當時的角色	● 一個移民站
抵達的人們	● 歐洲人
移民的原因	● 他們想要更好的生活
抵達後的生活	● 人們在美國各地定居

Unit 60 美國黑人的權利　p.156

Check True or False

1. 許多美國黑人在 1960 年代無法去上學。T
2. 在南方的美國黑人擁有更多權利。F

Comprehension Checkup

A. 1. 民權運動在何時開始？ ⓑ
　　ⓐ 1940 年代　ⓑ 1960 年代　ⓒ 1980 年代
　2. 美國黑人如何對抗不好的對待？ ⓒ
　　ⓐ 離開美國　ⓑ 搬到南方　ⓒ 上街遊行
　3. 馬丁‧路德‧金恩是<u>和平</u>運動的領導
　　人。ⓒ
　　ⓐ 不公平的　ⓑ 較佳的　　ⓒ 和平的
　4. 民權運動結束後，美國黑人爭取到更多
　　的<u>權</u>利。ⓑ
　　ⓐ 金錢　　　ⓑ 權利　　　ⓒ 領導者

B. 這場民<u>權</u>運動幫助了許多在美國的黑人。
　Rights

Wrap Up

①legal　②schools　③marched　④won

民權運動

背景	執行內容
● 黑人在美國只有幾項合法權利 ● 沒有願意接納他們的學校 ● 沒有願意接納他們的商店和餐廳	● 黑人上街遊行 ● 美國黑人改變了美國，並爭取到他們的權利

WORD REVIEW Unit 56 ~ 60　p.158

A.

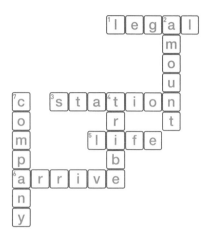

B. 1. ⓑ 稅金：人們為了政府服務所繳納的錢
　2. ⓐ 美洲原住民：在歐洲人來到美國之前
　　就已經在那裡生活的人
　3. ⓒ 移民：到另一個國家居住的人們
　4. ⓓ 民權運動：美國黑人在 1960 年代發
　　起爭取權利的運動

C. 1. Disease　　　　2. unfair
　3. foreign　　　　4. settled
　5. marched

D. 1. <u>隨著時間過去</u>，他們的總數越來越少。
　　Over time
　2. 對於只有 200 美元的人來說，100 美元
　　等於他們身上<u>一半的錢</u>！ half of
　3. 國家之間<u>變得</u>一天比一天<u>更緊密</u>。
　　getting closer
　4. 船隻每天都載著<u>幾千名的</u>移民。
　　thousands of
　5. 馬丁‧路德‧金恩是這場和平運動<u>的領
　　導者</u>。 the leader of

Read and Complete

1. 老師在解釋<u>鄰里</u>和社群。neighborhood
2. 社群中的人們有<u>共同的</u>事物。 common

Comprehension Checkup

A. 1. 老師的鄰里在哪裡？ⓒ
　　ⓐ 亞洲　　　ⓑ 社群　　　ⓒ 南芝加哥
2. 下列何者**不是**社群？ⓐ
ⓐ 紐約的一個區域
ⓑ 在洛杉磯的一群韓國人
ⓒ 在紐約的一群律師
3. 什麼是鄰里？ⓑ
ⓐ 地圖上的某個城市或城鎮。
ⓑ 人們生活的地方。
ⓒ 對相同種族的人很特別的地方。
ⓓ 在職業上共同的事物。
4. 為什麼老師會提到志工社群？ⓓ
ⓐ 舉出鄰里的例子
ⓑ 在地圖上指出他的鄰里
ⓒ 表示他對於志工有興趣
ⓓ 比較鄰里和社群

B. 鄰里是指 ①<u>鄰居</u>住的地方，可以在 ②<u>地圖</u>上找到。③<u>社群</u>是指一群人，他們有共同的事物，例如：職業或興趣。
　①neighbors　②map　③community

Wrap Up

①physical　②live　③people　④race

鄰里	社群
● 實際的地方 ● 鄰居住的地方	● 一群有共同事物的人 ● 種族、職業、興趣

Read and Complete

1. 非裔美國人的家庭會與他們的朋友舉辦盛大的<u>宴會</u>。feast
2. 人們隨著非洲鼓的<u>節奏</u>起舞。rhythm

Comprehension Checkup

A. 1. 誰會慶祝寬扎節？ⓒ
ⓐ 非洲人　　　　　ⓑ 在非洲的美國人
ⓒ 非裔美國人
2. 他們什麼時候會打開禮物？ⓑ
ⓐ 在寬扎節結束後
ⓑ 在寬扎節的最後一天
ⓒ 在寬扎節的第一天
3. 為什麼寬扎節對非裔美國人有意義？ⓓ
ⓐ 寬扎節讓他們可以回到非洲。
ⓑ 寬扎節展現了非洲音樂的力量。
ⓒ 寬扎節向美國人介紹非洲文化。
ⓓ 寬扎節連結他們傳統的非洲文化。
4. 下列關於寬扎節的敘述，何者錯誤？ⓑ
ⓐ 人們會掛非洲的旗幟。
ⓑ 人們會慶祝三或四天的時間。
ⓒ 人們會為彼此準備禮物。
ⓓ 人們會在宴會上飲食和跳舞。

B. 寬扎節是非裔 ①<u>美國人</u>的重要節日。寬扎節讓他們可以享受自己的 ②<u>傳統</u>文化，他們會為自己的非裔 ③<u>身份</u>慶祝。
　①Americans　②traditional　③identity

Wrap Up

①African　②celebrate　③identity　④feast

期間、意義	從 12 月 26 日到 1 月 1 日 非裔美國人的節日
紀念	非裔美國人慶祝他們的傳統文化
緣由	他們以自己的非洲人的身分為傲
會做的事	他們會一起享用盛宴

Read and Complete

1. 人們用金錢購買商品和服務。goods
2. 在餐廳的顧客會為服務付費。Customers

Comprehension Checkup

A. 1. 下列何者為商品的例子？ⓑ
　　ⓐ 演唱會　　ⓑ 漢堡　　ⓒ 搭乘公車
2. 下列何者為服務的例子？ⓒ
　　ⓐ 書　　　　ⓑ 手機　　ⓒ 鋼琴課程
3. 關於商品的敘述，何者正確？ⓒ
　　ⓐ 我們看不到也摸不到商品。
　　ⓑ 人們可以成為商品，像是顧客。
　　ⓒ 製造商品需要錢。
　　ⓓ 商品對你而言是時間和技能。
4. 為什麼顧客需要支付服務的費用？ⓐ
　　ⓐ 努力提供服務需要花錢。
　　ⓑ 服務是製造食物的行為。
　　ⓒ 服務對顧客而言是免費的。
　　ⓓ 服務是提供給顧客的。

B. 顧客使用 ①錢來購買商品和服務。商品是②物質的物品，服務是人們為了 ③賺錢而做的事情。
　①money　②physical　③earn

Wrap Up

①money　②goods　③services　④time

顧客為…花錢	
商品	服務
● 物質的東西	● 人們的行動
● 可以看得到也摸得到	● 時間、技能和努力

Read and Complete

1. 有些軍人為了保護國家而犧牲。protect
2. 有時軍人要上戰場打仗。war

Comprehension Checkup

A. 1. 陣亡將士紀念日要紀念的是誰？ⓒ
　　ⓐ 辛苦的工人　　ⓑ 勇敢的公民
　　ⓒ 殉職的軍人
2. 陣亡將士紀念日是在什麼時候開始的？ⓐ
　　ⓐ 美國南北戰爭之後
　　ⓑ 五月的最後一個星期一之後
　　ⓒ 在許多志工休假之後
3. 為什麼陣亡將士紀念日很重要？ⓒ
　　ⓐ 因為它維持美國的安全。
　　ⓑ 因為它給志工更多工作。
　　ⓒ 因為它讓人們記住軍人的犧牲。
　　ⓓ 因為它是美國其中一個重大的節日。
4. 美國公民在陣亡將士紀念日不會做什麼？ⓑ
　　ⓐ 他們會緬懷殉職的軍人。
　　ⓑ 他們會經歷戰爭。
　　ⓒ 他們會在墳墓上放上國旗。
　　ⓓ 他們會帶鮮花到墓地。

B. 陣亡將士紀念日是一個專門紀念殉職軍人的節日。美國公民 ①緬懷軍人為保護他們的國家所做的犧牲。他們會帶 ②鮮花和國旗到軍人的 ③墳墓上。
　①remember　②flowers
　③graves/ cemeteries

Wrap Up

①Monday　②remember　③sacrifice
④cemeteries

陣亡將士紀念日	
日期	● 五月的最後一個星期一
意義	● 為了緬懷殉職軍人的節日
會做的事	● 緬懷軍人的犧牲 ● 去基地時帶上鮮花和國旗

Read and Complete

1. 凱撒大帝是羅馬政治家。politician
2. 歷史學家研究第一手資料以了解凱撒的生平。primary

Comprehension Checkup

A. 1. 凱撒留下了哪一個第一手資料？ⓐ
　　ⓐ 日記　　ⓑ 博物館　　ⓒ 歷史學家
2. 我們如何知道凱撒長什麼樣子？ⓐ
　　ⓐ 從硬幣上　　　　ⓑ 從信件上
　　ⓒ 從書本上
3. 下列何者不是第一手資料？ⓒ
　　ⓐ 硬幣　　　　　　ⓑ 信件
　　ⓒ 博物館　　　　　ⓓ 日記
4. 為什麼第一手資料很重要？ⓓ
　　ⓐ 已經存在超過兩千年。
　　ⓑ 使過去變得神秘。
　　ⓒ 使歷史學家研究羅馬。
　　ⓓ 幫助我們了解歷史人物。

B. ①歷史學家利用第一手資料來了解過去。
我們從羅馬硬幣得知了凱撒 ②看起來的樣子，而他的 ③日記告訴我們他的生活。
①Historians　②looked　③journal

Wrap Up

①past　②understand　③journal
④Historians

第一手資料	
種類	過去的信件和圖片
意義	幫助我們了解過去的人們
例子	凱撒的日記： 歷史學家得知很多有關他生平的資訊

A.

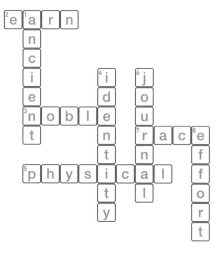

B. 1. ⓑ 社群：一群有共同事物的人
2. ⓒ 商品：看得到或摸得到的實體物品
3. ⓐ 鄰里：你和鄰居居住的地方
4. ⓓ 第一手資料：過去的信件和圖片

C. 1. prepare　　　2. provide
3. dedicated　　　4. sacrifice
5. mystery

D. 1. 老師在解釋的時候，我一頭霧水，於是舉起手發問。 put up
2. 寬扎節連結了非裔美國人與傳統非洲文化。 connects, to
3. 在我的鄰里，舉例來説，我們有一個大的亞裔社群。 for example
4. 顧客在商店和餐廳等地方支付商品和服務兩者的費用。 pay for
5. 有時，他們要參與戰爭。 take part in

Unit 66 金錢與利息　　p.172

Read and Complete

1. 人們將錢存在銀行裡。money
2. 銀行為客戶的錢支付利息。interest

Comprehension Checkup

A. 1. 人們不會把錢存在哪裡？ ⓒ
   ⓐ 安全的地方　　　ⓑ 小豬撲滿
   ⓒ 正規的地方
2. 什麼是金錢的成本？ ⓑ
   ⓐ 安全　　　ⓑ 利息　　　ⓒ 借款人
3. 你要如何利用銀行賺錢？ ⓐ
   ⓐ 銀行保存你的錢，並支付利息。
   ⓑ 你可以安全地存錢，但沒有利息。
   ⓒ 你可以借錢給銀行，並收利息。
   ⓓ 你可以透過介紹銀行給朋友來獲得利
   　息。
4. 銀行會如何賺錢？ⓐ
   ⓐ 借款人會支付利息給銀行。
   ⓑ 銀行連結放款人和借款人。
   ⓒ 銀行保存客戶的存款。
   ⓓ 客戶為了存錢，會付利息給銀行。

B. 人們把錢 ①存到銀行裡，銀行會支付利
   息。銀行用客戶的存款 ②借給其他人，借
   款人應該要 ③支付本金加上一些利息。
   ①keep/ save　②lend　③pay

Wrap Up

①keep　②get　③lend　④pay

誰	做什麼事	關於利息
顧客	把錢安全地存在銀行裡	獲得利息
銀行	將顧客的錢借給其他人	借款人支付本金和利息

Unit 67 法律與規則　　p.174

Read and Complete

1. 法律有助於維持公民的安全。 citizens
2. 政府制定普遍的和當地的法律。universal

Comprehension Checkup

A. 1. 下列何者為普遍法律禁止的事情？ ⓒ
   ⓐ 抽菸　　ⓑ 養鴿子　　ⓒ 偷竊
2. 下列何者為當地的法律禁止的事情？ ⓑ
   ⓐ 遵守規則　ⓑ 餵鴿子　ⓒ 殺人
3. 關於法律的敘述，何者錯誤？ ⓒ
   ⓐ 政客制定法律。
   ⓑ 公民應該遵守法律。
   ⓒ 當地的法律在各地都是一樣的。
   ⓓ 禁止殺人的法律為普遍法律。
4. 關於段落中提到的政客，可以推斷出什
   麼？ ⓓ
   ⓐ 政客不必遵守法律。
   ⓑ 政客只能制定當地的法律。
   ⓒ 政客必須居住在特定的區域。
   ⓓ 政客為政府和公民工作。

B. 政府的政客制定 ①法律以維持公民的安
   全，②普遍的法律無論到哪裡都必須遵
   守，但是 ③當地的法律只有在特定的地方
   才適用。
   ①laws　②Universal　③local

Wrap Up

①safe　②universal　③country　④area

制定法律	
目標	• 為了維持公民的安全
種類	• 普遍法律：每個國家都適用 • 當地法律：僅適用於該區域的居民

Read and Complete

1. 英國的殖民者在詹姆士敦建立了一個小鎮。
   settlers
2. 寶嘉康蒂是部落酋長的女兒。 chief

Comprehension Checkup

A. 1. 英國的殖民者遇到了什麼困難？ⓐ
   ⓐ 種植食物 　ⓑ 建造城鎮 　ⓒ 尋找朋友
   2. 誰試圖殺約翰・史密斯？ⓒ
   ⓐ 殖民者 　　ⓑ 寶嘉康蒂 　ⓒ 部落的酋長
   3. 關於美洲原住民的敘述，何者錯誤？ⓒ
   ⓐ 他們組成了部落。
   ⓑ 他們經常攻擊殖民者。
   ⓒ 他們想要和殖民者做朋友。
   ⓓ 他們抓住了英國殖民者的上尉。
   4. 寶嘉康蒂如何幫助英國殖民者？
   （請選出 2 個答案）ⓐ, ⓑ
   ⓐ 她救了殖民者的上尉。
   ⓑ 她教殖民者如何尋找食物。
   ⓒ 她抓住了部落的酋長。
   ⓓ 她為殖民者在維吉尼亞州建立城鎮。

B. 約翰・史密斯上尉是一個在維吉尼亞州的
   英國 ①殖民者，而寶嘉康蒂 ②救了他的性
   命，並且幫助殖民者，她也幫忙帶來了美
   洲 ③原住民和殖民者之間的和平。
   ① settler ② saved ③ Native

Wrap Up

③ 寶嘉康蒂幫助一位英國男子。
② 美洲原住民攻擊英國殖民者。
① 英國殖民者在維吉尼亞州的詹姆士敦建立一
　個城鎮。
④ 寶嘉康蒂成為和平的象徵。

Read and Complete

1. 有些人想買某種商品，這就是需求。
   demand
2. 黃金之所以有價值／昂貴，是因為世界上
   沒有很多黃金。 valuable/ expensive

Comprehension Checkup

A. 1. 什麼是指商品在市場上的數量？ⓒ
   ⓐ 價值 　　　ⓑ 需求 　　　ⓒ 供應
   2. 什麼事情會讓某些東西更有價值？ⓑ
   ⓐ 需求量低 　ⓑ 供應量低 　ⓒ 供應量高
   3. 商品的需求量高意味著什麼？ⓓ
   ⓐ 那個商品很容易買到。
   ⓑ 沒有人想要那個商品。
   ⓒ 有些人想要那個商品。
   ⓓ 很多人想要那個商品。
   4. 關於黃金的敘述，何者錯誤？ⓑ
   ⓐ 供應量很低。
   ⓑ 沒有很人想要。
   ⓒ 需求量很高。
   ⓓ 比水更有價值。

B. 黃金比水更貴是因為 ①供應量低，兩種商
   品都有很 ②高的需求量，但是黃金不容易
   取得，所以更 ③有價值／昂貴。
   ① supply ② high ③ expensive/ valuable

Wrap Up

① demand ② supply ③ valuable ④ gold
商品的價值

需求量高
：許多人想要買 ＋ 供應量低 → 昂貴、有價值，如：黃金

Read and Complete

1. 民俗是一種文化的傳統。Folklore
2. 民間故事包含給孩童的教訓。lessons

Comprehension Checkup

A. 1. 是誰經常講民間故事給孩子聽？ⓐ
   ⓐ 父母　　　ⓑ 老師　　　ⓒ 演講者
   2. 民間故事通常會教孩子什麼教訓？ⓒ
   ⓐ 如何賺錢　　　ⓑ 如何變得更聰明
   ⓒ 如何好好表現
   3. 關於民俗的敘述，何者錯誤？ⓑ
   ⓐ 保存傳統。
   ⓑ 大部分來自歐洲。
   ⓒ 是文化中重要的一部份。
   ⓓ 會一代傳承一代。
   4. 段落提到的民間故事，可以推斷出什麼？
   ⓒ
   ⓐ 民間故事有一套的格式。
   ⓑ 歐洲人特別喜歡民間故事。
   ⓒ 每個文化都有自己著名的民間故事。
   ⓓ 《灰姑娘》是世界上最知名的民間故事。

B. 民俗幫助 ①保存／延續文化的傳統。父母
   會用 ②民間故事 來教導孩子關於誠實和
   勇敢的教訓，這將一種文化傳給了下一個
   ③世代。
   ①preserve/ continue　②folklore
   ③generation

Wrap Up

①traditions　②culture　③folklore
④bravery

民俗	民間故事
• 文化的傳統 • 一個世代傳承給下個世代 • 保存和延續文化	• 民俗中很重要的部分 • 教導孩子關於誠實、善良或勇敢的教訓

A.

B. 1. ⓑ 需求：購買商品或服務的需要
   2. ⓓ 民俗：文化的故事和傳統
   3. ⓐ 利息：金錢的成本／銀行為你的存款所提供的東西
   4. ⓒ 供應：商品在市場上的數量

C. 1. regular　　2. earn
   3. functions　　4. residents
   5. peace

D. 1. 借款人必須準時還錢，並向銀行支付借款的利息。 pay back
   2. 寶嘉康蒂向英國人展示了種植和尋找食物的方法。 showed, the way
   3. 需求量高和供應量低使得黃金比水更昂貴。 more, than
   4. 在歐洲，民間故事通常以「很久很久以前……」開頭。 begin with
   5. 你的父母傳承了哪些民間故事給你呢？
   passed down

Unit 71 美國的奴隸制度
p.184

Read and Complete

1. 殖民時期的美國有很多奴隸。slaves
2. 這些奴隸大多來自非洲。Africa

Comprehension Checkup

A. 1. 奴隸大多在哪裡工作？ⓐ
　ⓐ 農園　　　　　　ⓑ 園主的小屋
　ⓒ 非洲的農場
2. 奴隸工作會獲得什麼報酬？ⓐ
　ⓐ 什麼都沒有　　　ⓑ 少許的財產
　ⓒ 少量的金錢
3. 關於奴隸生活條件敘述，何者錯誤？ⓓ
　ⓐ 他們沒有足夠的基本用品。
　ⓑ 他們沒辦法吃到品質好的食物。
　ⓒ 他們睡在簡陋小屋的地板上。
　ⓓ 他們從來不被允許擁有家庭。
4. 關於農園園主的敘述，何者正確？ⓐ
　ⓐ 他們虐待奴隸。
　ⓑ 他們為了吃肉而飼養農場動物。
　ⓒ 他們白天和奴隸一起工作。
　ⓓ 他們會付錢來支持奴隸。

B. 許多奴隸生活在18世紀①殖民時期的美國，他們被當作②財產，所以園主並不會付薪水給他們，而他們會在園主的③農園生活和工作。
　① Colonial　② property　③ plantations

Wrap Up

① common　② owned　③ huts
④ possessions

美國的奴隸制度

身分狀態	生活
● 在 18 世紀殖民時期的美國十分普遍 ● 被當作財產來擁有	● 工作一整天 ● 住在簡陋的小屋 ● 吃米飯和豆類 ● 少許的財產

Unit 72 加州的掏金熱
p.186

Read and Complete

1. 約翰‧馬歇爾是第一個在加州發現黃金的人。gold
2. 成千上萬的人湧入加州尋找黃金。California

Comprehension Checkup

A. 1. 在淘金熱之前，有多少人住在加州？ⓐ
　ⓐ 約 1,000 人　　　ⓑ 1,848 人
　ⓒ 約 30 萬人
2. 在淘金熱期間，誰賺了很多錢？ⓑ
　ⓐ 教師　　ⓑ 商人　　ⓒ 政府
3. 為什麼許多人對約翰‧馬歇爾的消息有興趣？ⓐ
　ⓐ 因為這讓大家做起了發財夢。
　ⓑ 因為他在找淘金的人。
　ⓒ 因為這有助於大家成為礦工。
　ⓓ 因為這宣傳了加州的新工作。
4. 關於淘金熱的敘述，何者錯誤？ⓒ
　ⓐ 許多人沒有找到黃金。
　ⓑ 掏金熱幫助建設加州。
　ⓒ 政府雇用礦工去尋找黃金。
　ⓓ 來自世界各地的人都前往加州。

B. 約翰‧馬歇爾於 1848 年在加州①發現／找到了黃金，世界各地的人都到這裡尋找黃金。在淘金熱期間，②商人販賣食物和衣服而賺了很多③錢。
　① discovered/ found　② businesses
　③ money

Wrap Up

③ 許多公司賺了很多錢。
① 約翰‧馬歇爾在加州發現黃金。
④ 政府建造道路、教堂和學校。
② 淘金熱湧入了超過 30 萬人。

Read and Complete

1. 華特・迪士尼是一位有偉大想法的<u>企業家</u>。entrepreneur
2. 人們依舊很喜歡華特・迪士尼的<u>動畫電影</u>。 animated

Comprehension Checkup

A. 1. 華特・迪士尼是第一個創造出什麼的人？ ⓒ
   ⓐ 電影　　ⓑ 電視節目　ⓒ 動畫節目
   2. 在華特・迪士尼的想法提出前，人們在電視節目上都看什麼？ ⓑ
   ⓐ 配音演員　　　ⓑ 只有真人演員
   ⓒ 動畫畫作
   3. 關於像華特・迪士尼這樣的企業家，何者正確？ ⓒ
   ⓐ 他們從來沒有面臨風險或失敗。
   ⓑ 他們有時候會抄襲舊的想法。
   ⓒ 他們有成功的機會。
   ⓓ 他們討厭看電視節目和電影。
   4. 關於文中提到的華特・迪士尼，可以推斷出什麼？ ⓑ
   ⓐ 他想要成為電視節目的演員。
   ⓑ 他對於描繪角色很有興趣。
   ⓒ 他厭倦看電視節目。
   ⓓ 他富有到可以實現夢想。

B. 華特・迪士尼是一位知名的企業家，他新的 ①<u>想法</u>就是想用動畫 ②<u>畫作</u>來製作電視節目和電影。在面臨 ③<u>風險</u>和失敗後，最終獲得成功。
   ①idea　②drawings　③risks

Wrap Up

①face　②create　③fired　④drawings

企業家	華特・迪士尼
• 有偉大想法的人 • 面臨風險和失敗 • 第一個創造某些事物	• 動畫的電視節目和電影 • 被解雇和被拒絕 • 把畫作變成一門生意

Read and Complete

1. 直到大約一百年前，美國的女性還不能<u>投票</u>。vote
2. 女性努力去改變<u>法律</u>。law

Comprehension Checkup

A. 1. 1800 年代女權運動的目的是什麼？ⓐ
   ⓐ 擁有平等的權利　ⓑ 和男性對抗
   ⓒ 改變總統
   2. 女性的選舉權代表什麼？ⓐ
   ⓐ 投票的權利　　　ⓑ 擁有房產的努力
   ⓒ 擁有工作的權利
   3. 女性做了什麼以改變法律？ ⓑ
   ⓐ 辭去工作。
   ⓑ 組成政治團體。
   ⓒ 為女性投票。
   ⓓ 請求男性的幫助。
   4. 關於女權運動的敘述，何者錯誤？ ⓒ
   ⓐ 幫助改變不公平的法律。
   ⓑ 給予女性平等的合法權利。
   ⓒ 主要目標是為了爭取擁有財產的權利。
   ⓓ 蘇珊・安東尼是女權團體的重要領導人。

B. 在 1800 年代，女權 ①<u>運動</u>展開，目的是為了要爭取平等的 ②<u>投票權</u>。女性組成政治團體來 ③<u>改變法律</u>。由於有她們的努力，女性現在擁有平等的合法權利。
   ①movement　②vote　③change

Wrap Up

①legal　②vote　③political　④equal

女權運動

100 年前的美國	• 女性只有少許的合法權利
女性想要什麼	• 選舉權：投票的權利
女性做了什麼	• 組成政治團體並改變法律 • 現在擁有平等的合法權利

Read and Complete

1. 美國政府由三個部門所組成的。 branches
2. 三個部門的權力是平衡的。 power

Comprehension Checkup

A. 1. 國會議員的工作是？ⓐ
　　ⓐ 制定新法律　　ⓑ 廢除法律
　　ⓒ 領導國家

2. 國會如何確保法官遵守法律？ⓐ
　　ⓐ 投票罷免法官　　ⓑ 拒絕法官的法律
　　ⓒ 要求總統罷免法官

3. 關於總統的敘述，何者正確？ⓑ
　　ⓐ 總統有權破壞新的法律。
　　ⓑ 總統有權否決新的法律。
　　ⓒ 總統的主要工作是找出法律的問題。
　　ⓓ 總統透過罷免法官以檢查他們的權力。

4. 為什麼三個部門會檢查彼此的權力？ⓑ
　　ⓐ 他們試著不要互相影響。
　　ⓑ 他們必須確保所有部門都遵守法律。
　　ⓒ 他們想要盡可能地擁有最大的權力。
　　ⓓ 他們必須討論新的法律。

B. 美國政府有三個部門：①總統、國會和法官，他們相互 ②檢查和 ③制衡彼此的權力。
　①President　②check　③balance
　（②和③不分順序）

Wrap Up

①Congress　②the President　③Judges

美國政府

國會	總統	法官
• 制定新的法律 • 可以投票罷免法官和總統	• 國家的領導者 • 可以否決新的法律	• 可以修改或廢除法律

A.

B. 1. ⓒ 企業家：成立或經營企業賺錢的人
　 2. ⓑ 淘金熱：世界各地的人到加州尋找黃金的時期
　 3. ⓓ 總統：國家的領導人
　 4. ⓐ 奴隸：被當作財產擁有的人

C. 1. Colonial　　　2. Businessmen
　 3. opportunities　4. political
　 5. Congressmen

D. 1. 非洲奴隸住在農園裡。 lived on
　 2. 華特・迪士尼想把他的畫作和角色變成一門生意。 turn, into
　 3. 女性在 1800 年代爭取平等的權利。 fought for
　 4. 美國的法律不允許她們投票。 allow, to
　 5. 檢查和制衡可以確保三個部門全都遵守法律。 make sure

Read and Complete

1. 《印第安人遷移法案》將美洲原住民從他們的家園驅離。Removal
2. 美洲原住民被迫行走數千公里到達他們的新家。marched

Comprehension Checkup

A. 1. 美洲原住民搬遷到哪裡？ⓐ
   ⓐ 奧克拉荷馬州　　ⓑ 美國南方
   ⓒ 美國的領土
   2. 誰引導美洲原住民去他們的新家？ⓑ
   ⓐ 印第安人　　ⓑ 政府軍人
   ⓒ 政府領導人
   3. 政府為什麼通過《印第安人遷移法案》？
   ⓑ
   ⓐ 因為美洲原住民經常攻擊他們。
   ⓑ 因為他們想要奪取美洲原住民的土地。
   ⓒ 因為他們想要和美洲原住民一起生活。
   ⓓ 因為他們試著使美洲原住民的生活過得更好。
   4. 關於眼淚之路的敘述，何者錯誤？ⓓ
   ⓐ 在路上很難找到充足的食物。
   ⓑ 路途長達數千公里。
   ⓒ 許多美洲原住民因此生病和過世。
   ⓓ 美洲原住民花好幾年才到達新家。

B. 在 1830 年，《印第安人遷移法案》迫使美洲 ①原住民必須搬移到新的領土。他們被迫行走了數千公里，有許多人在路上生病和 ②過世，所以我們將它稱為「③眼淚之路」。
   ① Native　② died　③ Tears

Wrap Up

③ 美洲原住民被迫搬遷到新家。
② 政府通過《印第安人遷移法案》。
① 許多美洲原住民在路途中生病和過世。
④ 美國的人口快速增加。

Read and Complete

1. 選擇通常會有機會成本。opportunity
2. 機會成本發生在兩種選擇都有價值的時候。value

Comprehension Checkup

A. 1. 機會成本的概念是來自哪裡？ⓑ
   ⓐ 科學　　ⓑ 經濟學　　ⓒ 數學
   2. 我們可以如何衡量機會成本？ⓒ
   ⓐ 用時間衡量　　ⓑ 用金錢衡量
   ⓒ 用失去的價值衡量
   3. 下列何者是不學習的機會成本？ⓓ
   ⓐ 失去樂趣　　ⓑ 失去時間
   ⓒ 變得快樂　　ⓓ 獲得知識
   4. 下列哪一個選項沒有機會成本？ⓒ
   ⓐ 睡覺或吃飯。
   ⓑ 學習或見朋友。
   ⓒ 減少壓力或增加壓力。
   ⓓ 找工作或上大學。

B. 機會 ①成本可能發生在我們必須在兩個 ③有價值的活動之間做 ②選擇時，我們做選擇所失去的價值就是機會成本。
   ① cost　② choice　③ valuable

Wrap Up

① choice　② decide　③ values　④ measured

機會成本	
意義	在選擇時失去的價值
發生情況	在兩個有價值的選擇之間做決定的時候
特性	有些價值和成本不能用金錢來衡量

Read and Complete

1. 公民在民主國家擁有權力。Citizens
2. 在選舉中，公民可以投票選出他們的領導人。vote

Comprehension Checkup

A. 1. 在直接民主中，公民如何有權力去管政府的決定？ⓐ
　　ⓐ 透過集會和投票　　ⓑ 透過做出其他決定
　　ⓒ 透過選擇政府領導人
　　2. 在代議民主中，領導人會為公民做什麼？ⓑ
　　ⓐ 控制公民的權利　　ⓑ 為公民做決定
　　ⓒ 集結公民去投票
　　3. 為什麼有些國家是代議民主？ⓑ
　　ⓐ 大部分的政府不信任公民。
　　ⓑ 大部分國家的公民太過忙碌。
　　ⓒ 公民討厭做重要的決定。
　　ⓓ 好的領導人可能比公民更聰明。
　　4. 為什麼作者提到美國、法國和印度？ⓒ
　　ⓐ 為了反對直接民主
　　ⓑ 為了解釋選舉應該要公平的原因
　　ⓒ 為了提供代議民主的例子
　　ⓓ 為了比較直接民主和代議民主

B. 在 ①直接民主中，公民會集會並投票表決政府的決定。在另一方面，公民則是在 ③代議民主中會 ②投票選出領導人。
　 ① direct　② vote　③ representative

Wrap Up

① meet　② decision　③ choose　④ elections

直接民主	● 公民會集會並投票表決政府的每一項決定
代議民主	● 公民選擇政府領導人 ● 公民在自由和公平的選舉中投票選出領導人

Read and Complete

1. 美國早期的開國元勛撰寫了美國憲法。Constitution
2. 開國元勛希望能建立擁有自由公民的社會。citizens

Comprehension Checkup

A. 1. 美國憲法說明了什麼？ⓐ
　　ⓐ 政府的運作方式
　　ⓑ 早期的開國元勛如何建立政府
　　ⓒ 如何控制國王和女王的權力
　　2. 對於開國元勛來說，建立一個社會最重要的是什麼？ⓑ
　　ⓐ 法律　　　　　　　ⓑ 公民的自由
　　ⓒ 強力的政府
　　3. 關於美國政府的敘述，何者正確？ⓐ
　　ⓐ 擁有有限的權力。
　　ⓑ 由來自歐洲的公民領導。
　　ⓒ 被國王和女王控制。
　　ⓓ 權力被早期的開國元勛所掌控。
　　4. 美國憲法如何幫助美國成長？ⓒ
　　ⓐ 透過使公民擁有很少的權力
　　ⓑ 透過廢除政府體系
　　ⓒ 透過賦予公民自由和權力。
　　ⓓ 透過設計強大的政府體系。

B. 在 1787 年，美國早期的 ①開國元勛撰寫美國憲法。他們 ②設計憲法是為了賦予公民更多 ③權力。
　 ① founders　② designed　③ power

Wrap Up

① laws　② society　③ control　④ limited

美國憲法	
意義	● 說明美國政府如何運作的一套法律
制定理由	● 為了擁有自由的新社會
制定方向	● 讓公民能夠控制政府 ● 有限的政府和自由的公民

Read and Complete

1. 《權利法案》保護美國公民的基本權利。
   rights
2. 人權在民主國家中是很重要的。
   democracies

Comprehension Checkup

A. 1. 《權利法案》的目的是什麼？ⓒ
   ⓐ 制定法律　　　　ⓑ 不被逮捕
   ⓒ 自由和安全地生活
   2. 詹姆斯・麥迪遜的成就是什麼？ⓐ
   ⓐ 制定《權利法案》
   ⓑ 制定宗教的法律
   ⓒ 制定如何證明一個人有罪的過程
   3. 什麼是言論自由？（請選出 2 個答案）
   ⓒ, ⓓ
   ⓐ 公民可以從事新聞工作。
   ⓑ 公民可以自由信奉任何宗教。
   ⓒ 公民可以自由表達意見。
   ⓓ 公民可以抗議政府的決定。
   4. 下列何者為忽視人權的例子？ⓒ
   ⓐ 經常改變宗教信仰
   ⓑ 集結在一起以表達異議
   ⓒ 在某人被證明有罪前就逮捕他
   ⓓ 在沒有任何人的同意就搬到新居住地。

B. 《①權利法案》保護美國公民的權力，像
   是②言論自由和 ③宗教自由等人權是非常
   重要的。
   ① Rights　② Speech　③ religion
   （② 和 ③ 不分順序）

Wrap Up

① created　② safely　③ fair　④ freedom

《權利法案》

制定時間	詹姆斯・麥迪遜在 1789 年創造出來
制定原因	讓美國公民能夠自由和安全地生活
主要內容	言論自由、對公民公平的法律、宗教自由

A.

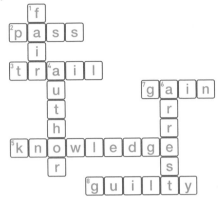

B. 1. ⓑ 選舉：一種讓公民選出政府領導人的
   公平方式
   2. ⓓ 無罪的：沒有罪的
   3. ⓐ 機會成本：做出選擇時所失去的價值
   4. ⓒ 憲法：一套法律

C. 1. marched　　　2. measured
   3. represent　　4. imagined
   5. protest

D. 1. 美國人想擴展到美洲原住民的土地。
   expand into
   2. 有時我們必須在兩個有價值的選擇之間
   做決定。 have to
   3. 公民在自由和公平的選舉中投票選出領
   導人。 vote for
   4. 他們設計憲法是為了讓公民能夠控制政
   府。 give, control
   5. 公民可以自由去選擇和信奉任何宗教。
   are free to

Check True or False

1. 有些打擊樂器會產生節奏。T
2. 沙鈴可以產生不同的音符。F

Comprehension Checkup

A. 1. 音樂家如何在鼓上產生聲音？ⓒ
　　ⓐ 搖動鼓　　ⓑ 讓鼓發出聲響　　ⓒ 打擊鼓
　　2. 鈴鼓是如何產生節奏的？ⓒ
　　ⓐ 鳴響　　ⓑ 產生音符　　ⓒ 發出聲響
　　3. 木琴和鈴鐺可以產生不同的音符。ⓑ
　　ⓐ 鼓　　ⓑ 鈴鐺　　ⓒ 節拍
　　4. 木琴琴鍵有不同的大小。ⓐ
　　ⓐ 大小　　ⓑ 音樂家　　ⓒ 旋律

B. 透過打擊或搖動打擊樂器，就可以產生聲音。 percussion

Wrap Up

① shake　② rhythm　③ drums　④ notes

打擊樂器		
發聲方法	音樂元素 1	音樂元素 2
● 打擊或搖動	● 節拍或節奏 ▸ 鼓、沙鈴、鈴鼓	● 音符 ▸ 木琴和鈴鐺

Check True or False

1. 狗只能吃乾草。F
2. 農夫對那隻狗很生氣。T

Comprehension Checkup

A. 1. 誰在穀倉裡睡著了？ⓒ
　　ⓐ 公牛　　ⓑ 農夫　　ⓒ 狗
　　2. 誰想要吃乾草？ⓐ
　　ⓐ 公牛　　ⓑ 狗　　ⓒ 馬
　　3. 狗對公牛咆哮。ⓑ
　　ⓐ 叫喊　　ⓑ 咆哮　　ⓒ 微笑

4. 農夫用棍子把狗趕走了。ⓑ
　　ⓐ 乾草　　ⓑ 棍子　　ⓒ 食物

B. 貪心的狗沒辦法從飢餓的公牛那邊把乾草帶走。 greedy

Wrap Up

④ 狗醒了過來，對著公牛吠叫。
① 有隻狗在乾草上睡覺。
③ 公牛想要吃乾草。
⑤ 農夫把狗趕走。
② 飢餓的公牛進來了。

Check True or False

1. 埃及有許多法老的雕像。T
2. 埃及人不相信來世。F

Comprehension Checkup

A. 1. 在古埃及，法老是誰？ⓐ
　　ⓐ 統治者　　ⓑ 藝術家　　ⓒ 軍人
　　2. 許多人認為法老是什麼？ⓒ
　　ⓐ 雕像　　ⓑ 廟宇　　ⓒ 神
　　3. 法老的雕像放在廟宇和墳墓裡。ⓑ
　　ⓐ 來世　　ⓑ 墳墓　　ⓒ 山上
　　4. 拉美西斯二世是一位擁有最多雕像的知名法老。ⓐ
　　ⓐ 雕像　　ⓑ 人們　　ⓒ 數字

B. 古埃及人為了法老的來世製作了雕像。 pharaohs

Wrap Up

① rulers　② gods　③ tombs　④ afterlife

法老的雕像	
誰是法老？	法老石雕像的位置
● 古埃及的統治者 ● 人們認為他們是神。	● 廟宇和法老的墳墓 ● 埃及人相信有來世。

Check True or False

1. 你可以用三種方式來研究數字的範圍。T
2. 中位數是最大的數字。F

Comprehension Checkup

A. 1. 要如何從 5 個數字中找出平均數？ ⓑ
　　ⓐ 將數字相加　　　ⓑ 將總和除以 5
　　ⓒ 找出中間的數字
　　2. 在例子的中位數是多少？ ⓑ
　　ⓐ 2　　　　　ⓑ 4　　　　ⓒ 10
　　3. 眾數出現最多次。 ⓒ
　　ⓐ 總和　　　ⓑ 中位數　　ⓒ 眾數
　　4. 例子當中的眾數是 2。 ⓐ
　　ⓐ 2　　　　　ⓑ 4　　　　ⓒ 7

B. 在一組數字的範圍中，我們可以找到平均
　數、中位數和眾數。 range

Wrap Up

① sum　② middle　③ most

研究數字的範圍		
平均數	中位數	眾數
將所有數字相加，並將總和除以數字的數量	找出順序中間的數字	找到出現最多次的數字

Check True or False

1. 綠色加黃色會變成橘色。F
2. 原色會產生二次色。T

Comprehension Checkup

A. 1. 下列何者為原色？ ⓑ
　　ⓐ 綠色　　　ⓑ 紅色　　　ⓒ 橘色
　　2. 下列何者不是二次色？ ⓐ
　　ⓐ 藍色　　　ⓑ 橘色　　　ⓒ 紫色

3. 互補色會讓兩種顏色都變得更鮮明。 ⓒ
　ⓐ 原始的　　　ⓑ 二次的　　　ⓒ 互補的
4. 紅色和綠色放在一起會更鮮明。 ⓒ
　ⓐ 黃色　　　ⓑ 藍色　　　ⓒ 綠色

B. 這三種類型的顏色可以相互混合，或搭配
　成組合。 mix

Wrap Up

① complementary　② blue　③ primary
④ green

原色	二次色	互補色
● 紅色、黃色、藍色	● 混合兩種原色 ▶ 紫色、橘色、綠色	● 一個原色和一個二次色的組合

A.

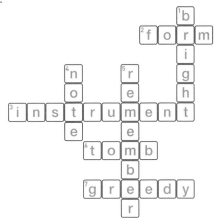

B. 1. ⓒ 眾數：一組數字中出現最多次的數字
　2. ⓑ 法老：古埃及的統治者
　3. ⓓ 原色：三種基本色分別是紅色、藍色
　　和黃色
　4. ⓐ 打擊樂器：用敲擊或搖動來發出聲音
　　的樂器

C. 1. beat   2. growled
   3. giant   4. divide
   5. pairs

D. 1. 有不同尺寸的鈴鐺和木琴琴鍵。
      There are
   2. 在一間穀倉裡，有隻狗在乾草上睡著
      了。 fall asleep
   3. 他的雕像數量是最多的！這就是很多人
      記得他的原因。 That's why
   4. 將這些數字從最低排列到最高。
      to highest
   5. 紅色的字在綠色的紙上會非常顯眼。
      stand out

Unit 86 《狼婆婆》的故事   p.220

Check True or False

1. 有些文化有著一樣的故事。T
2. 《狼婆婆》和美國的故事很類似。F

Comprehension Checkup

A. 1. 大野狼去拜訪誰？ⓑ
      ⓐ 牠的奶奶 ⓑ 三姊妹 ⓒ 親近的朋友
   2. 大野狼假裝是誰？ⓒ
      ⓐ 媽媽 ⓑ 女孩 ⓒ 奶奶
   3. 這些女孩談論到樹上有好吃的堅果。 ⓐ
      ⓐ 堅果 ⓑ 蘋果 ⓒ 小鳥
   4. 大野狼爬到樹上後，這些女孩就去搖晃
      那棵樹。ⓑ
      ⓐ 欺騙 ⓑ 搖晃 ⓒ 砍倒

B. 《狼婆婆》是中國的故事，但是和歐洲的
   故事很相似。 European

Wrap Up

①China ②grandmother ③trick ④dies

《狼婆婆》	
國家	中國
相似的故事	《小紅帽》
登場角色	大野狼：假裝是奶奶
	三姊妹：她們欺騙大野狼，而大野狼也死了

Unit 87 爵士樂：一種獨特的音樂風格   p.222

Check True or False

1. 爵士音樂家只演奏寫好的音樂。F
2. 爵士歌曲有很簡單穩定的節拍。F

Comprehension Checkup

A. 1. 爵士樂是由什麼組成的？ⓐ
      ⓐ 各種類型的音樂 ⓑ 新的音樂
      ⓒ 簡單的節拍
   2. 爵士樂手在演奏時會做什麼？ⓑ
      ⓐ 寫歌 ⓑ 改變音符 ⓒ 犯錯
   3. 爵士歌曲可能每次聽起來都不一樣。ⓒ
      ⓐ 簡單的 ⓑ 穩定的 ⓒ 不一樣
   4. 爵士樂的節拍在歌曲中可能會變快或變
      慢。ⓑ
      ⓐ 樂手 ⓑ 節拍 ⓒ 樂器

B. 與大多數的音樂不同，爵士樂手會用獨特
   的方式改變歌曲的內容。 change

Wrap Up

①notes ②different ③complex ④beat

爵士樂是獨特的。	
● 爵士樂手會改變內容和演奏不同的音符。	● 爵士樂的節拍很複雜
▶ 一首歌每次聽起來都不一樣。	▶ 節拍會變快或變慢

Unit 88 非常有才華的人物　p.224

Check True or False

1. 達文西出生於法國。F
2. 達文西沒有畫過女人。F

Comprehension Checkup

A.
1. 《蒙娜麗莎》是關於什麼的畫作？ⓐ
   ⓐ 一個微笑的女子　ⓑ 一個有才華的人
   ⓒ 一台機器
2. 《最後的晚餐》是出自哪裡？ⓑ
   ⓐ 一項設計
   ⓑ 一則《聖經》的故事
   ⓒ 一棟建築物
3. 達文西設計了建築物和機器。ⓒ
   ⓐ 畫作　　ⓑ 發明家　　ⓒ 機器
4. 達文西在五百多年前就設計出一架飛機。ⓑ
   ⓐ 義大利　　ⓑ 飛機　　ⓒ 晚餐

B. 達文西是一位有才華的畫家、設計師和發明家。 inventor

Wrap Up

①painter　②inventor　③airplane

李奧納多・達文西	
身為畫家	身為設計師和發明家
• 《蒙娜麗莎》 • 《最後的晚餐》	• 設計了許多建築物和機器 • 設計了飛機

Unit 89 誰創造了零？　p.226

Check True or False

1. 古代的零有不同的形狀。T
2. 現代的零第一次出現在一百五十年前。F

Comprehension Checkup

A.
1. 零在數學裡表示什麼？ⓑ
   ⓐ 版本　　ⓑ 沒有數量　　ⓒ 沒有限制
2. 一百需要幾個零？ⓐ
   ⓐ 2 個　　　ⓑ 3 個　　　ⓒ 4 個
3. 古代人創造了不同形式的零。ⓑ
   ⓐ 現代的　　ⓑ 古代的　　ⓒ 印度的
4. 印度人為了數學開發出零。ⓒ
   ⓐ 發現　　ⓑ 移除　　ⓒ 開發

B. 現代的零第一次出現在印度，並傳播到世界各地。 spread

Wrap Up

①no　②new　③created　④math

零	
零的意義	零的創造與進化
• 表示「沒有數量」。 • 創造出新的數量。	• 由古代人創造出來的 • 印度人為了數學而開發出零▶現在的版本

Unit 90 男孩與電視　p.228

Check True or False

1. 費羅・法恩斯沃斯出生於 1929 年。F
2. 他在青少年時期設計出一個裝置。T

Comprehension Checkup

A.
1. 費羅・法恩斯沃斯是哪方面的天才？ⓑ
   ⓐ 電視節目　ⓑ 電子裝置　ⓒ 照相
2. 費羅・法恩斯沃斯在青少年時期會閱讀什麼？ⓑ
   ⓐ 報紙　　　ⓑ 科學雜誌　ⓒ 漫畫書
3. 在當時，電視不能快速地發送圖像。ⓐ
   ⓐ 電視　　　ⓑ 電力　　　ⓒ 科學
4. 費羅・法恩斯沃斯設計的裝置可以快速顯示電子圖像。ⓒ
   ⓐ 照片　　　ⓑ 有趣的　　ⓒ 電子

B. 費羅・法恩斯沃斯製作出第一台電子電視。 television

Wrap Up

① genius ② show ③ quickly ④ electric

費羅・法恩斯沃斯：電子裝置的天才

青少年時期	1929 年
● 對電視很感興趣 ● 設計一個可以快速顯示電子影像的裝置	● 開發出世界上第一台電子電視

WORD REVIEW Unit 86 ~ 90　p.230

A.

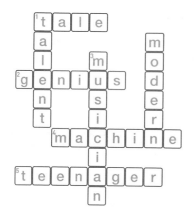

B. 1. ⓑ 零：本身沒有數量，也能創造新數量的數字
2. ⓒ 發明家：第一個做出實用物品的人
3. ⓓ 《聖經》：基督徒收錄神聖故事的書
4. ⓐ 爵士樂：一種有複雜節拍的音樂類型，樂手在演奏時會改變音符

C. 1. trick
2. unique
3. designed
4. meanings
5. electric

D. 1. 有一隻大野狼去拜訪三姊妹，牠假裝成她們的奶奶。 acts like
2. 節拍可能會變快或變慢，但是與歌曲搭配得很好。 goes well
3. 李奧納多・達文西於 1452 年出生在義大利。 was born
4. 現代的零傳播到世界各地。
all over the world
5. 費羅・法恩斯沃斯對電視有興趣。
interested in

Unit 91 所有美國的聲音　p.232

Read and Complete

1. 班卓琴和吉他是弦樂器。 string
2. 班卓琴的音色在美國傳統音樂中很受歡迎。 music

Comprehension Checkup

A. 1. 哪一種弦會發出更高亢的聲音？ ⓑ
ⓐ 長的弦　　ⓑ 短的弦　　ⓒ 粗的弦
2. 是什麼導致班卓琴和吉他之間有不同的音色？ ⓐ
ⓐ 琴身形狀　ⓑ 演奏方式　ⓒ 受歡迎程度
3. 關於班卓琴的敘述，何者正確？ ⓒ
ⓐ 看起來很像吉他。
ⓑ 音色聽起來像鼓。
ⓒ 美國人很喜歡班卓琴獨特的音色。
ⓓ 班卓琴較細的琴弦會發出更低的音色。
4. 為什麼作者會提到《哦，蘇珊娜》？ ⓓ
ⓐ 為了比較班卓琴和吉他
ⓑ 為了解釋美國音樂的歷史
ⓒ 為了展現班卓琴的精采演奏
ⓓ 為了提供用班卓琴演奏的音樂

B. 吉他和班卓琴都是弦 ①樂器，它們的外觀不同，所以它們也會 ②產生／製造不同的聲音，而班卓琴在傳統的美國音樂中很 ③受歡迎。
① instruments　② produce/ make
③ popular

Wrap Up

① strings　② low　③ unique　④ traditional

班卓琴

發聲方式	● 透過撥動琴弦
音域	● 細和短的琴弦：高亢的音色 ● 粗和長的琴弦：低沉的音色
特別之處	● 產生獨特的音色 ● 在傳統的美國音樂中很受歡迎

Unit 92　你是 2D 還是 3D 的形狀　p.234

Read and Complete

1. 3D 形狀具有<u>高度</u>、長度和寬度。height
2. 形狀可以是二維或三維。dimensions

Comprehension Checkup

A. 1. 下列何者是 2D 的形狀？ ⓒ
　　ⓐ 立方體　　ⓑ 球體　　ⓒ 正方形
　2. 要如何把 2D 的形狀變成 3D 的形狀？ⓑ
　　ⓐ 加上長度　ⓑ 加上寬度　ⓒ 加上高度
　3. 為什麼作者會提到「你的照片」？ ⓑ
　　ⓐ 為了解釋 3D 的意思
　　ⓑ 為了提供兩個維度的例子
　　ⓒ 為了描述如何製作 3D 的形狀
　　ⓓ 為了證明 2D 的形狀比 3D 的形狀更自然
　4. 關於 2D 和 3D 的敘述，何者錯誤？ ⓓ
　　ⓐ 某些物品的圖畫有兩個維度。
　　ⓑ 如果把圓形加上寬度，它就會變成球體。
　　ⓒ 兩個維度的形狀有高度和長度。
　　ⓓ 如果去掉正方形的寬度，它就會變成立方體。

B. 二維的 ①<u>形狀</u>有高度和 ②<u>長度</u>，如果我們將一個 2D 的形狀加上 ③<u>寬度</u>，就會變成三維的形狀。
　① Shapes　② length　③ width

Wrap Up

① length　② square　③ width　④ sphere

| 二維 | — | 高度、長度 | — | 正方形、圓形 |
| 三維 | — | 高度、長度、寬度 | — | 立方體、球體 |

Unit 93　這個數字是質數還是合數　p.236

Read and Complete

1. 我們可以<u>計算</u>整數。 cunt
2. 整數如果不是<u>質數</u>，就是合數。prime

Comprehension Checkup

A. 1. 下列何者為質數？ ⓑ
　　ⓐ 0　　　ⓑ 7　　　ⓒ 8
　2. 下列何者為合數？ ⓒ
　　ⓐ 3　　　ⓑ 5　　　ⓒ 6
　3. 質數可以被什麼整除？ ⓓ
　　ⓐ 被任何數字整除。
　　ⓑ 被任何質數整除。
　　ⓒ 被任何合數整除。
　　ⓓ 被質數本身整除。
　4. 關於合數的敘述，何者錯誤？ ⓒ
　　ⓐ 合數是整數。
　　ⓑ 合數包含 9。
　　ⓒ 合數只能被 1 整除。
　　ⓓ 合數可以被兩個以上的數字整除。

B. 質數和 ①<u>合</u>數是 ②<u>整</u>數。質數只能被兩種數字 ③<u>除</u>、沒有餘數，而合數可以被兩個以上的數字除、沒有餘數。
　① composite　② whole　③ divided

Wrap Up

① Whole ② itself ③ numbers ④ more

整數	
質數	**合數**
只能被 1 或質數本身的數字除	可以被兩個以上的數字除、沒有餘數

Unit 94 關於季節的故事　　p.238

Read and Complete

1. 黑帝斯愛上了狄蜜特的<u>女兒</u>珀耳塞福涅。
   daughter

2. 狄蜜特很<u>生氣</u>，因為黑帝斯帶走了珀耳塞福涅。upset

Comprehension Checkup

A. 1. 這個希臘故事主要的內容是什麼？ⓑ
   ⓐ 母親和女兒　ⓑ 季節　　ⓒ 冥界

   2. 黑帝斯把珀耳塞福涅帶到哪裡？ⓒ
   ⓐ 希臘　　ⓑ 狄蜜特身邊　ⓒ 冥界

   3. 關於狄蜜特的敘述，何者錯誤？ⓐ
   ⓐ 她愛上了黑帝斯。
   ⓑ 她是豐饒女神。
   ⓒ 她阻止植物生長。
   ⓓ 女兒回來時她很高興。

   4. 為什麼植物只在夏天生長？ⓒ
   ⓐ 狄蜜特在夏天的時候很不高興。
   ⓑ 黑帝斯只讓植物生長六個月。
   ⓒ 狄蜜特在珀耳塞福涅回來的期間讓植物生長。
   ⓓ 珀耳塞福涅在夏天期間待在冥界。

B. 黑帝斯把珀耳塞福涅帶到冥界，生氣的狄蜜特不讓任何植物①<u>生長</u>，這個季節就是②<u>冬天</u>。黑帝斯讓珀耳塞福涅每年有六個月的時間可以回到人間，在這時，狄蜜特會讓各個生物生長，這個季節就是③<u>夏天</u>。
   ① grow ② winter ③ summer

Wrap Up

⑤ 狄蜜特很高興，所以各個植物在那六個月中生長。
① 黑帝斯愛上了珀耳塞福涅。
③ 狄蜜特很生氣，所以不讓任何植物生長。
② 黑帝斯把珀耳塞福涅帶到冥界。
④ 黑帝斯同意讓珀耳塞福涅每年有六個月可以回到人間。

Unit 95 歡樂的亡靈節　　p.240

Read and Complete

1. 亡靈節是在<u>墨西哥</u>的節日。Mexico
2. 家人聚在一起來紀念他們的<u>祖先</u>。
   ancestors

Comprehension Checkup

A. 1. 有些家庭會在哪裡設立祭壇？ⓑ
   ⓐ 在墳墓上　ⓑ 在家裡　　ⓒ 在墓地裡

   2. 在亡靈節當天，什麼會再次與家人相聚？ⓒ
   ⓐ 老人　　　　　ⓑ 可怕的鬼魂
   ⓒ 逝者的靈魂

   3. 關於亡靈節的敘述，何者錯誤？ⓐ
   ⓐ 亡靈節對墨西哥家庭是悲傷的日子。
   ⓑ 人們通常會穿上特別的服裝。
   ⓒ 人們會帶禮物到祖先的墓地。
   ⓓ 給祖先的食物和飲料會放在祭壇上。

   4. 從段落中可以推斷出什麼？ⓑ
   ⓐ 墨西哥人討厭感到悲傷。
   ⓑ 墨西哥人相信死後的人生。
   ⓒ 鬼魂的象徵在墨西哥很受歡迎。
   ⓓ 在墨西哥的墳墓比在其他國家的墳墓更大。

B. 在墨西哥，許多家庭會慶祝①<u>亡靈節</u>，這是一個重要的②<u>節日</u>，因為家人會③<u>聚集</u>在一起，歡樂地紀念他們的祖先。
   ① Dead ② holiday ③ gather

Wrap Up

①spirits　②joyful　③altars　④costumes

亡靈節

意義	家人聚在一起並紀念祖先。
特別之處	逝者的靈魂再次團聚。 ▶ 歡樂的慶祝活動
會做的事	設立祭壇、帶禮物到墳墓、穿上特別的服裝

WORD REVIEW Unit 91 ~ 95　p.242

A.

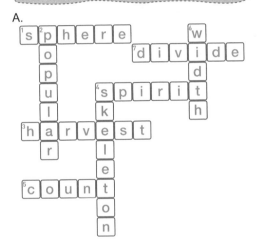

B. 1. ⓓ 合數：可以兩個以上的數字整除的數字
   2. ⓒ 質數：只能被 1 或自己整除的數字
   3. ⓐ 弦樂器：弦振動時，會發出聲音的樂器
   4. ⓑ 三維：高度、長度和寬度

C. 1. add　　　　2. underworld
   3. agreed　　　4. gather
   5. altars

D. 1. 班卓琴的琴身是圓的，<u>看起來像</u>鼓。
   looks like

2. 對於某些形狀也是如此，它們<u>不是</u> 3D <u>就是</u> 2D。 either, or
3. 我們如何分辨質數<u>和</u>合數<u>之間</u>的不同？ between, and
4. 冥王黑帝斯<u>愛上了</u>狄蜜特的女兒珀耳塞福涅。 fell in love with
5. 在亡靈節當天，墓地裡<u>充滿</u>慶祝的氛圍！ are full of

Unit 96 鄉村音樂仍然活躍著　p.244

Read and Complete

1. 鄉村音樂是一種流行的音樂<u>類型</u>。 genre
2. 現代鄉村音樂仍然在成長和<u>改變</u>。
   changing

Comprehension Checkup

A. 1. 鄉村音樂最早出現在哪裡？ⓐ
   ⓐ 愛爾蘭　　　　ⓑ 北美洲
   ⓒ 美國的大城市
   2. 民俗音樂通常不會使用哪種樂器？ⓑ
   ⓐ 班卓琴　　ⓑ 小提琴　　ⓒ 吉他
   3. 鄉村音樂並不是關於什麼？ⓐ
   ⓐ 失去的非洲
   ⓑ 驕傲和傳統
   ⓒ 浪漫和奮鬥
   ⓓ 大城市外的生活
   4. 關於鄉村音樂的敘述，何者正確？ⓑ
   ⓐ 代表來自愛爾蘭的民俗音樂。
   ⓑ 在北美洲仍然很受歡迎。
   ⓒ 幾乎和傳統民俗音樂一樣。
   ⓓ 無法吸引新的世代。

B. ①<u>鄉村</u>音樂在 ②<u>北美洲</u>很受歡迎，鄉村音樂隨著時間在成長和 ③<u>改變</u>。
   ①Country　②North　③changed

Wrap Up

① folk　② banjos　③ life　④ traditions

鄉村音樂	
起源	● 來自愛爾蘭和蘇格蘭的傳統民俗音樂
主要樂器	● 吉他、班卓琴
談論的主題	● 大城市外的生活 ● 浪漫、努力、驕傲和傳統

Wrap Up

① collect　② alone　③ simple　④ outdoor

華茲塔	
材料	收集並使用垃圾
建造方法	獨自工作，使用簡單的工具
建造時間	34 年
完成品	華茲塔：受歡迎的戶外博物館

Unit 97 奇妙的華茲塔　p.246

Read and Complete

1. 西蒙・盧地亞用垃圾建造出華茲塔。
   garbage
2. 現在，人們將他的作品當作戶外博物館來欣賞。museum

Comprehension Checkup

A. 1. 盧地亞如何取得物品來創造藝術品？ⓐ
   ⓐ 自己收集　　　ⓑ 向鄰居購買
   ⓒ 向博物館租借
   2. 盧地亞在作品上花了多少時間？ⓒ
   ⓐ 800 天　　ⓑ 30 個月　　ⓒ 34 年
   3. 盧地亞是如何工作的？
   （請選出 2 個答案）ⓑ, ⓒ
   ⓐ 他工作非常慢。　ⓑ 他只使用垃圾。
   ⓒ 他獨自工作。　　ⓓ 他花了錢買物品。
   4. 關於盧地亞在華茲的藝術品，何者錯誤？ⓓ
   ⓐ 現在還是很受歡迎。
   ⓑ 在華茲有很多建築物。
   ⓒ 最高的塔超過 30 公尺。
   ⓓ 涵蓋 800 公尺長區域的博物館。

B. 西蒙・盧地亞利用垃圾和簡單的 ①工具建造出高塔，也就是位於加州的華茲 ②塔，他花了 34 ③年才完成這些作品。
   ①tools　②Towers　③years

Unit 98 認識慣用語　p.248

Read and Complete

1. 慣用語在某種文化中可以普遍被理解。
   Idioms
2. 「不要打翻豆子」的意思是「不要洩漏祕密」。secret

Comprehension Checkup

A. 1. 「他踢到水桶」是什麼意思？ⓐ
   ⓐ 他過世了。　　　　ⓑ 他很生氣。
   ⓒ 他踢到垃圾桶。
   2. 在讀書時，哪一個慣用語可以表達這個情況？ⓒ
   ⓐ 我打翻豆子。（洩漏祕密）
   ⓑ 我在拳擊書本。
   ⓒ 我在打書本。（念書）
   3. 關於慣用語的敘述，何者錯誤？ⓓ
   ⓐ 慣用語不能按照字面上的意思使用。
   ⓑ 慣用語很有創意，也很流行。
   ⓒ 慣用語在語言中很常見。
   ⓓ 慣用語通常會使用錯誤的文法。
   4. 如果想確保朋友保守祕密，可以使用哪一個慣用語？ⓐ
   ⓐ 不要打翻豆子。（不要洩漏祕密）
   ⓑ 不要踢水桶。（不要死）
   ⓒ 希望你打翻豆子。
   ⓓ 我想要你去踢那個桶子。

B. 慣用語是 ①有創意又常見的表達方式，慣用語和 ②字面的意義不同，可以透過流行的 ③用法來理解慣用語。
①creative　②literal　③use

Wrap Up

①creative　②culture　③use　④meaning

慣用語	
特色	● 在某種文化中有創意的和普遍的語言表達方式 ● 可以透過流行的用法來理解 ● 並非字面的意義
例子	● 踢水桶（過世）、打書（念書）、打翻豆子（洩漏祕密）

Unit 99　用點點作畫　p.250

Read and Complete

1. 在點描法中，彩色的點可以創作出圖像。
   Points/ Dots
2. 許多單獨的點似乎混合在一起。 blend

Comprehension Checkup

A. 1. 藝術家在點描法中會使用什麼？ⓐ
　ⓐ 彩色的點　　　ⓑ 混合的圖像
　ⓒ 有創意的照片
　2. 畫作《馬戲團》是關於什麼？ⓒ
　ⓐ 無數個彩色的點　ⓑ 音樂演奏
　ⓒ 馬戲團的表演者
　3. 點描法很有創意的特色是什麼？ ⓑ
　ⓐ 藝術家可以用一種顏色來表現任何事物。
　ⓑ 根據距離，畫作看起來會有所不同。
　ⓒ 點描法的畫作應該要靠近觀賞。
　ⓓ 彩色的點在顛倒時看起來會不一樣。
　4. 關於喬治・秀拉的敘述，何者錯誤？ⓒ
　ⓐ 他是法國人。
　ⓑ 他是點描法的第一位藝術家。
　ⓒ 他在畫作當中只會使用一種顏色。
　ⓓ 他其中一幅知名的畫作是《馬戲團》。

B. 喬治・秀拉在 1800 年代創造了 ①點描法，藝術家可以用 ②彩色的點表現任何事物。《馬戲團》是使用點描法作畫的作品當中，其中一幅最知名的 ③畫作。
①Pointillism　②color　③paintings

Wrap Up

①dots　②closely　③individual　④far away

點描法	
使用方法	● 彩色的點
效果	● 近看 ▸ 許多單獨的點 ● 遠看 ▸ 普通的畫作
代表畫作	● 喬治・秀拉 ▸ 創造點描法

Unit 100　獨立宣言　p.252

Read and Complete

1. 英國使美洲成為其殖民地。 colony
2. 美國人想要從英國獨立。 independence

Comprehension Checkup

A. 1. 在《獨立宣言》中不包含什麼？ⓐ
　ⓐ 抗議的權利　　　ⓑ 自由的權利
　ⓒ 快樂的權利
　2. 美國人透過《獨立宣言》讓英國人了解到什麼？ⓐ
　ⓐ 所有人都應該擁有的權利
　ⓑ 美國人的優點
　ⓒ 美國人統治英國的權利
　3. 為什麼殖民地居民對英國政府很憤怒？ⓐ
　ⓐ 他們不尊重美國人。
　ⓑ 他們逮捕了湯馬斯・傑佛遜。
　ⓒ 他們持續擴張殖民地。
　ⓓ 他們不會講美式英語。

4. 在發表《獨立宣言》之後，發生了什麼事？ ⓓ
ⓐ 美洲建立了一個新的國家。
ⓑ 英國摧毀了美國。
ⓒ 美洲成為英國最大的殖民地。
ⓓ 美國人開始向英國抗議。

B. 在 1776 年，美洲 ① 殖民地居民宣布從英國獨立，根據他們的宣言，人人生而 ② 平等，並享有基本的權利。此外，他們再也不想要英國人 ③ 統治美洲了。
① colonists ② equal ③ govern

WrapUp

① Britain ② equal ③ liberty ④ pursuit

獨立宣言

日期	• 起草於 1776 年 7 月 4 日
目的	• 宣布美洲從英國獨立
內容	• 人人生而平等 • 所有人都有基本的權利，例如生命權、自由權，和追求幸福的權利

B. 1. ⓐ 鄉村音樂：使用吉他和班卓琴的流行音樂類型
2. ⓑ 俚語：在某種文化中，有創意又常見的表達語言的方式
3. ⓓ 獨立的：不被其他人統治
4. ⓒ 點描法：用彩色點點繪圖的創意方式

C. 1. outside   2. passionate
3. grammar   4. countless
5. govern

D. 1. 在美國，鄉村音樂持續在成長和變化。
continues to
2. 西蒙・盧地亞花了 34 年的時間進行他的藝術品。 working on
3. 那是因為這些彩色的點似乎混合在一起。
appear to
4. 喬治・秀拉創作了一些著名的畫作，像是《馬戲團》。 such as
5. 基本的權利包括生命權、自由權和追求幸福的權利。 the pursuit of

WORD REVIEW Unit 96 ~ 100 p.254

A.

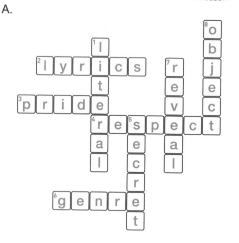

不管什麼時候開始都不晚！

我的第一本英文課本

初學、再學都適用！
第一本專為華人設計，同時學會「字母、發音、句型、文法、聽力、會話」，自學、教學都好用！

作者 / 彭彥哲
定價 / 399元

附 MP3

我的第一本英文文法

讓多益寫作測驗滿分的英文達人Joseph Chen為你規劃最完整好學的英文文法學習書！
架構完整好學＋清楚講解＋系統性分析＝扎實文法實力，讓你不再似懂非懂！

作者 / Joseph Chen
定價 / 380元

附 MP3

學自然發音不用背

針對非英語系國家設計，最棒的發音書！
不管是以前從未學過、自己要教小孩、老師要教學生，怎麼用都行！

作者 / DORINA（楊淑如）
定價 / 299元

附 MP3 + QR 碼 + DVD

重學、自學都好用的英文學習書

我的第一本自然發音記單字

針對非英語系國家設計，最棒的單字記憶法！
「記憶口訣」×「RAP音韻」×「情境圖像」×「故事聯想」，66堂發音課，2000單字開口一唸就記住！

作者 / Dorina（楊淑如）、陳啟欣
定價 / 399元

附 MP3 + QR 碼

我的第一本中高齡旅遊英語

【大字版型×雙書設計】

第一線空姐、英文老師聯手打造，4大部分、9大主題、25個場景，只要基礎的50個句型，大小事都可以自己搞定！

作者 / 裴鎮英、姜旼正
定價 / 449元

附隨身會話手冊 + MP3 + QR 碼

實境式照單全收！圖解單字不用背

單字與圖像照片全收錄！
「型」與「義」同時對照再也不說錯！全場景1500張實境圖解，讓生活中的人事時地物成為你的英文老師！

作者：簡孜宸（Monica Tzuchen Chien）
定價：399元

附 MP3

學習不中斷、英語家庭化 營造最佳英語學習環境!

我的第一本親子英文

外銷中國、韓國、泰國,亞洲最暢銷的親子英文學習書!行政院新聞局中小學優良課外讀物推薦掛保證!在家就能學英文,輕鬆、快樂、又能增進親子關係~!

作者 / 李宗玥、蔡佳妤、
　　　Michael Riley
定價 / 399元

附 MP3 + QR 碼

我的第一本親子英文單字書

「情境式全圖解」提升學習興趣、看圖就懂,自然就記住!「主題式分類」串聯日常生活主題,創造英文學習環境!收錄教育部頒布常用 2000 字、44 個主題,內容豐富又多元!

作者 / 李宗玥
定價 / 399元

附 MP3

我的第一本經典故事親子英文

史上第一本涵蓋中外經典故事!
啟發孩子天生的英文學習天賦、點燃孩子學習英文的專注力、培養孩子自學英文的最佳工具書!

作者 / 李宗玥、高旭銚
定價 / 399元

附 MP3 + QR 碼

台灣廣廈 國際出版集團
Taiwan Mansion International Group

國家圖書館出版品預行編目（CIP）資料

美國家庭的100堂閱讀課：學英文同時學知識，在家最有效的親子互動，立
即提升英文閱讀力！/ TinyFolds 著；蔡宜庭譯. -- 新北市：國際學村出版社，
2022.07
　面；　公分
ISBN 978-986-454-222-2(平裝)
1.CST：英語 2.CST：讀本

805.18　　　　　　　　　　　　　　　　　　　111005981

國際學村

美國家庭的100堂閱讀課
學英文同時學知識，在家最有效的親子互動，立即提升英文閱讀力！

作　　　者／TinyFolds
譯　　　者／蔡宜庭

編輯中心編輯長／伍峻宏
編輯／陳怡樺
封面設計／林珈仔・內頁排版／菩薩蠻數位文化有限公司
製版・印刷・裝訂／東豪・弼聖・紘億・秉成

行企研發中心總監／陳冠蒨
媒體公關組／陳柔彣
綜合業務組／何欣穎

線上學習中心總監／陳冠蒨
產品企製組／黃雅鈴

發　行　人／江媛珍
法律顧問／第一國際法律事務所 余淑杏律師・北辰著作權事務所 蕭雄淋律師
出　　　版／國際學村
發　　　行／台灣廣廈有聲圖書有限公司
　　　　　　地址：新北市235中和區中山路二段359巷7號2樓
　　　　　　電話：（886）2-2225-5777・傳真：（886）2-2225-8052

代理印務・全球總經銷／知遠文化事業有限公司
　　　　　　地址：新北市222深坑區北深路三段155巷25號5樓
　　　　　　電話：（886）2-2664-8800・傳真：（886）2-2664-8801
郵政劃撥／劃撥帳號：18836722
　　　　　　劃撥戶名：知遠文化事業有限公司（※單次購書金額未達1000元，請另付70元郵資。）

■出版日期：2022年08月
ISBN：978-986-454-222-2

Original Title: 미국교과서핵심 리딩 100 1 & 2
American Textbook Core Topics 100 Vol. 1 & 2 by TinyFolds
Copyright © 2021 Gilbutschool
All rights reserved.
Original Korean edition published by Gilbutschool, 2021, Seoul, Korea
Traditional Chinese Translation Copyright © 2022 by Taiwan Mansion Publishing Co., Ltd.
This Traditional Chinese edition published by arranged with Gilbutschool through MJ Agency.